Hauling ASHE

L.B. DUNBAR

www.lbdunbar.com

L.B. Dunbar

ROMANCE. FOR SEXY SILVER FOX LOVERS.

HAULING ASHE
Copyright © 2022 Laura Dunbar
L.B. Dunbar Writes, Ltd.
https://www.lbdunbar.com/

ISBN: 978-1-956337-06-8

Cover Design: Outlined With Love
Editor: Melissa Shank
Editor: Evident Ink
Proofread: Gemma Brocato
Proofread: Karen Fischer

Other Books by L.B. Dunbar

<u>Road Trips & Romance</u>
Hauling Ashe
Merging Wright
Rhode Trip

<u>Lakeside Cottage</u>
Living at 40
Loving at 40
Learning at 40
Letting Go at 40

<u>The Silver Foxes of Blue Ridge</u>
Silver Brewer
Silver Player
Silver Mayor
Silver Biker

<u>Silver Fox Former Rock Stars</u>
After Care
Midlife Crisis
Restored Dreams
Second Chance
Wine&Dine

<u>Collision novellas</u>
Collide
Caught

<u>Smartypants Romance (an imprint of Penny Reid)</u>
Love in Due Time
Love in Deed
Love in a Pickle

<u>The World of True North (an imprint of Sarina Bowen)</u>
Cowboy
Studfinder

L.B. Dunbar

4

DEDICATION

From Walt Whitman, "Song of the Open Road"

Afoot and light-hearted I take to the open road,
Healthy, free, the world before me,
The long brown path before me leading where I choose.

Henceforth I ask not good-fortune, I myself am good-fortune,
Henceforth I whimper no more, postpone no more, need nothing,
Done with indoor complaints, libraries, querulous criticisms,
Strong and content I travel the open road.

5

1

PRE-TRIP

Playlist: "Unwritten" - Natasha Bedingfield

[Mae]

I'd been looking for a sign.

After stepping off the electric train affectionally known as the 'L' in downtown Chicago, I'd breathed in the fumes of the city on a warm summer day. The robotic voice of the conductor stated that the doors were closing and mixed with the chaotic sounds of people moving on the platform toward the stairs. The noise around me was different from my small hometown with its quiet afternoons of whispered breezes and chirping birds. I'd ridden the train in this dynamic city with my sister before, but never alone. And today's adventure had to be done on my own.

I'd stepped forward with the flow of people pressing toward the staircase like sugar grains filtering through a funnel and descended to the street below as the overhead train continued its loop through this city like a steel serpent, weaving in a perpetual circle around brick and mortar.

I have always loved the magnetism of this metropolis, but it wasn't home for me. My older sister Jane lived here, and it was a pit stop on the journey I was about to embark on.

My spirit trip awaited me. I was in search of renewing my soul and perhaps my heart, as mine had been shattered by Adam. My seventeen-year marriage was over. We'd been distant for some time and divorced for three years. After his first affair, I stayed with him. He made promises. He made plans. Now, I had a plan of my own. Eight states. Fourteen days. The open road. I'd hit the highlights as I went, where I pleased, when I pleased.

This was the starting point and that's why I was looking for a sign. An actual brown and white metal rectangle that signifies the beginning of something special. It marks the start of Route 66, the iconic highway from Chicago to Los Angeles. Using the GPS on my phone, I had worked my way to the corner of Wabash and Adams and then headed east on Adams toward Michigan Avenue. A coffee shop on the corner had distracted me and I reminded myself I was in no rush. Ahead of me were two weeks with no timetables and wide-open highway. The Mother Road was my destination and I wanted to plant my feet at the beginning.

When I entered the coffeeshop, I'd decided on the unusual. Instead of black coffee with limited cream and sugar, I ordered something that sounded fancy and fun.

"I'll take a mochaccino." Mocha-*ccino* had rolled off my tongue in a sassy, saucy way and I sashayed my hips a bit as I ordered. I wanted to be flirty. I wanted to be fun. I wanted to remember who I was before marriage and kids and commitments. I didn't begrudge those things in my life, but I was ready for…adventure. I hadn't really ever been anywhere, and I wanted to say I'd been somewhere. If I hadn't been in a coffeeshop on a street corner in Chicago, I might have broken out in song like Belle in Disney's *Beauty and the Beast*. Somehow, I didn't think the other patrons would appreciate me swinging out my arms and spinning in a circle in the cramped space singing off key about a great wide somewhere.

Once I'd exited the café, I popped the lid off my to-go cup and took a sip. The liquid was too hot to fully enjoy the chocolate-flavored zing I anticipated, so I took a short slurp and let the sweetness rush past my tongue in hopes of not burning it. Struggling to snap the lid back in place, I crossed the street obeying the crosswalk signal. The people around me acted like cattle herded over cement and I had laughed at the image since I'd been in this town when the famous painted cow statues had been placed in various locations as decoration. A tourist mission at the time was to find all the cows.

Today's mission felt almost as daunting. Tons of signs on steel poles lined the sidewalks and as I hit the walkway opposite the coffee shop, I noticed the Art Institute on the other side of Michigan Avenue. I paused and spun in that circle like some animated peasant girl, trying to find my bearings. I pulled my phone from my oversized bag and struggled one handed to open the app where I had saved the coordinates while I stepped forward, looking at the device in my palm.

"Umph."

I slam into something hard but pliable before me. In fear of spilling my coffee, I was desperately trying not to bump into anyone on the packed city sidewalk. But the hot liquid washes over the front of me and something else. Or rather, down the impeccably tailored suit jacket stretched over the back of *someone* else.

"What the fu—" The remainder of the expletive spoken in a harsh, deep masculine tenor drones out like an echo at the end of its stream. Steel gray eyes lock on mine. For a moment I forget where I am, who I am, and what I'd been doing. Taking a moment to assess the damage, I notice the lid has popped off my cup resulting in hot liquid spilling over my wrist, splattering my once-white blouse, and dripping down my bare legs beneath the hem of my cut-off jean shorts. My sandaled feet are coated in mochaccino, and I step back from the person I've collided with.

But my foot slips off the raised sidewalk and I struggle once more with the uncovered cup in my hand. Attempting to balance the semi-full container, I'm off kilter with one foot down in the street and the other on the raised sidewalk.

"Easy there, sunshine." Long fingers catch my upper arm and yank me forward. The endearment throws me off balance even more and additional chocolate-flavored drink spurts from the cup like a sputtering fountain, sprinkling the front of his suit jacket.

"I'm so sorry." Not only is my skin hot, but I'm a hot mess, and of course, my savior and victim is a hot man. He looks like he stepped off a poster advertising professional business attire for men. His frame is a good half-foot taller than mine, with solid shoulders and long arms. His hair distracts me next as it's more salt than pepper. His cheekbones are clean-shaven cliffs but given a few days, I imagine the scruff on that firm jaw will match the coloring of the hair on his head. The potential ruggedness of ink and chrome facial hair in combination with that sharp jacket screams *sexy silver fox suit porn*. However, a sliver of leather and beads at his wrist hints there might be a rebel underneath that silk and gabardine material.

9

L.B. Dunbar

"Whatcha got in that cup?" His voice drips with insinuation. The playfulness of calling me sunshine dissipates a bit.

Sharp, silvery eyes ensnare mine and heat rushes across my cheeks because I'm caught staring. Forcing my gaze away from those eyes, I look at my cup. "Uh...nothing, anymore." He doesn't smile at my joke. "I wasn't drinking," I defend next, although I feel a little drunk just looking at him.

I'm always stupid around good-looking people, especially handsome men. I'd like to say I'm out of practice—with men, flirting and otherwise. However, I can hold my own with the best of flirty people. I'm the one with teasing comments at work or subtle remarks under my breath in public, but today I'm off my witty comebacks game.

Releasing my arm, he shakes out his, flicking droplets of coffee off the expensive-looking coat in a summer khaki color. He tips his head, attempting to glance over his shoulder, and spins in a circle like a dog chasing his tail. The sight of such a handsome man twirling around causes me to giggle like a schoolgirl. Then again, the rhythmic squeak could be the sudden anxiety rippling up my center.

I just spilled coffee on a hot man.

He abruptly stops twirling and his gaze falls to my lips. The corner of his mouth hints at a potential grin. "What's so funny?" His warm voice washes over me like the drink still soaking my thin shirt. His cadence is lyrical, like a classic rock star or maybe someone in a blues band.

Shaking my head, I apologize a second time. "Let me get your suit cleaned for you." Suddenly, I have visions of him stripping out of that suit right here on the street and my breath hitches at the possibility. *The lazy removal, slowly shrugging the jacket down his arms. The pop of buttons on his dress shirt. The quiet snick of his suit pants zipper.* Another part of me strums to life and I clench my thighs. *What is happening to me?* Is this a hot flash? I thought I wasn't due for them for another ten years.

Deciding I need his phone number, and that I can figure out the logistics of getting him out of his suit...I mean, getting his suit *from him* later, I realize I've dropped my phone and I begin my own tailspin, scanning the cement at my feet.

"My phone." Spotting the device in the street, I step down off the curb, and my ankle twists, throbbing as a result of my earlier slip. I wince as I bend at the waist, pitching forward at the last second to retrieve my phone. With my backside in the air, aimed at my coffee-spill victim, I pick up the device at the same time he grips my hips and tugs me back up onto the sidewalk. A taxi driver wails on his horn as the yellow vehicle zips past us.

"Sunshine, you're a real hazard to yourself." The rough sound near my ear sends shivers down my spine.

I spin to face him, forcing his hands to release me, and my face heats once more at the flirtatious endearment and sensual voice. We stand closer than two people who don't know one another should. I definitely do not look like sunshine. I'm a forty-three-year-old brunette with hints of gray; a mother of two with a belly scarred like a taxi ran over my midsection; and an exhausted business owner who has bags under her eyes packed with sorrow and stress.

"I was looking for a sign," I say to him for some reason, as if that explains knocking into him, spilling coffee, dropping my phone, and fumbling—*twice*—into the street.

He tilts his head, assessing me, perhaps wondering once more if I'd been day-drinking instead of savoring syrupy chocolate mixed with coffee.

He takes a cautious step backward. "Maybe you need some…help." His tone mocks me a bit, deepening in concern for my mental stability.

Holding my phone in my hand, I swipe the screen against my hip to wipe off the street dirt. "Let me get your number."

His chiseled face shutters to stillness. "Now you're hitting on me?" Incredulity fills his voice. His brows arch and the corner of his pale red lips twitch. The grin is more forced than flirtatious. He thinks I'm a nut.

"I wasn't… I mean, I'm not… I never… I just want to have your suit cleaned." Well, that pretty much covers it all. In my line of work, a pleasant attitude helps sales. The customer is always right, so I've learned how to master words and a wink to soothe someone who is disgruntled. Of course, a little banter never hurt anyone and some of my best customers enjoy the repartee. The innocent jesting might even be

11

the reason they return to my garden center. But in the case of this encounter, I'm surprisingly flustered.

"It's a thousand-dollar suit. A mere dry-cleaning won't salvage this mess." He glances down at the arm of his jacket and at the once-white shirt he wore, now looking like freckles dot the material. The underscore to his statement resonates louder than the hint of his concern I was hitting on him. He's not joking about the cost and his expression tightens even more. Disgust and disappointment etch his fine cheekbones.

"Made of gold-laden thread?" I joke, hoping to lighten the moment, but in return those silver eyes pinch. His gaze becomes colder, matching the metallic posts holding up a variety of signs along this street.

"Something like that." His voice is suddenly devoid of all emotion, monotone and dry, which is everything opposite my clothing still soaked with coffee. Absentmindedly, I reach for the middle of my peasant blouse and squeeze the material, which looks like I've tried to tea-stain fabric at home. Warm liquid seeps over my fist like I've wrung out a sponge. His eyes follow the motion, and narrow when his gaze reaches my chest. I look like I've entered a wet T-shirt contest.

Without another word, he reaches into his suit coat and pulls out his own phone. My breath hitches for some reason, momentarily thinking he'll ask me for my number. Instead, he stabs the device with a forceful finger and lifts it to his ear. His eyes peer upward, locking on mine once more before he abruptly turns and walks away.

"Hope your day gets better," I holler after him, taking a mental snapshot of him walking away. He shoots me a one-handed wave over his shoulder, then closes his fingers leaving only the one in the middle upright.

Well.

My gaze falls to his backside. The slightly lifted jacket in his single arm salute gives me a clear view of firm globes in form-fitting suit pants. Those thousand dollars were well spent to accentuate him there. However, a man with a fine ass does not make him a fine man. It normally just makes him an ass.

Too bad. He was nice to look at.

Hauling Ashe

On that note, I glance around me, taking in the rush of the 'L' down the block, racing over Wabash Avenue. Brakes screech and horns honk as all types of vehicles come to a stop at the red light down the street ahead of me. I scan the tall buildings shadowing the walkway and then I see it.

A brown and white sign marked with the iconic emblem for Route 66.

Underneath the landmark rectangle is another sign with one word. BEGIN.

2

Playlist: "Julia" - The Beatles

[Tucker]

What is happening today?

I'm definitely having an out-of-body experience. One minute, I'm standing on the sidewalk, checking an email notification on my phone and the next minute, someone slams into me. Something warm and liquid coats the back of my suit jacket and when I spin to bitch out my fellow pedestrian, I'm slammed a second time by incredible eyes.

Blue as a summer lake, the cool color caught mine like a fish reeled in on a hook. *Foolish fish.*

Yet there I'd stood on the cramped sidewalk during rush hour, shell-shocked by the woman's innocent look. What was it about her that had me tongue-tied, but calling her sunshine? Where did that even come from? Flirting with a woman was second nature. A soft smile. A teasing wink. Nothing too suggestive. I understood women; they'd been my business for decades. Over the years, I never gave into offers aimed to tempt me. Room keys in my pocket. Phone numbers on a cocktail napkin. Suggestive comments on social media. *Never.*

Then she'd mentioned looking for a sign, sounding like a nut, before the trigger of all triggers, she asked me for my phone number.

It wasn't nine in the morning yet and today had already been a shitty day.

As I stand in my office, ripping off my coffee-stained dress shirt, buttons fly across the room like my agitation, pinging all over the place. The shirt is ruined anyway as is my brand-new suit. I'd already tossed the jacket on the couch. The coffee-speckled shirt goes next, and I stalk for the closet outside my private bathroom where I keep a collection of secondary shirts. Tugging on the fresh-pressed material, I continue to chide myself about earlier.

I had just stood there, ready to sandwich that ray of sunshine between the building and my body. Her blue eyes struck me first, sunny-sky bright and eager. The way she looked at me—all apologetic and anxious—as she should be. She'd ruined a thousand-dollar suit.

Which she offered to have dry-cleaned, I weakly remind myself.

When she had stepped into the street and narrowly missed being run over by a taxi, I nearly had a heart attack.

More coffee splatters. More ruin to my clothing.

Then she asks me for my number, and like a hit-and-run, I fled the scene. She'd tipped me in the wrong direction of an already downhill day. I didn't need her knowing who I was, where I worked, or what I did for a living. I don't trust women, although my business for years was to support them, motivate them, empower them. However, I no longer believe in the intentions of most women and that was my wife's fault.

Reaching for my phone, I call my daughter.

"Hey Dad." Julia greets me before I can say hello. I love this girl, now a beautiful woman of twenty-four, paving her own path through life.

"Jellybean, I have a problem." I hate to distress her. She has more important things on her mind right now than my transportation. "The car company cancelled."

"Dad, you cannot miss this." Julia doesn't whine often, but this is important to her *and to me.*

"I promise I'll be there." I don't feel half as confident as the reassurance I'm trying to give her. I don't know how things got so messed up. The car service confirmed only days ago that I would be transported from Chicago to Los Angeles in a timely manner. Once there, I would meet Julia and we would travel north to Napa together. The road trip would give us some father-daughter time before her big day.

"I can't believe this happened," Julia continues, and I squeeze my forehead, agreeing with her. By nine o'clock this morning, this day had officially been a shitshow.

"I know, Jellybean." Julia is my only daughter, but she isn't spoiled. If anything, she's the least spoiled person I've ever known, which is surprising considering how her mother was revered like royalty. Julia is quiet and kind, and everything opposite of Rochelle.

15

L.B. Dunbar

When my daughter decided to head to California for college, her mother and I were stunned. Secretly, I was pleased she'd chosen the place I'd once run off to. A place I recall with fond memories and deep regrets. Even more surprising was when Julia eventually decided to become a baker despite earning her business degree. Her mother had always hoped Julia would follow in her footsteps. Those were some steep six-inch stilettoes to fill, though, and I'd been proud of our daughter for forging her own way, even if it meant baking cupcakes over two thousand miles away.

"Can you hire another service?" Her voice is tender with empathy. The best solution is to head to O'Hare International Airport, hop on a plane and be in L.A. in a matter of hours. But I don't fly. Julia knows my reasons.

"I'll figure something out." Pressing my forehead harder, I realize I hadn't seen my assistant Daniel outside my office. "I'll be there if I have to start walking tonight." I chuckle at the notion, because I'd never make a cross-country trek on foot, but I'd do what I could to get to Julia. I'd do anything for my daughter, except fly.

"You know, Daddy, you could have ridden with Jude."

Ah, my son. He was also not an option, and I didn't want to discuss that right now.

"Jellybean, give me some time and I'll get back to you on my plans, okay? If I have to leave tomorrow, I will." My work is my life, but I'll figure something out. I'll find someone else to drive me.

"Okay Dad. Can you message me when you're on the road?" Her soft plea expresses her unspoken concern. Julia's had to grow up a lot over the past three years. Not like my daughter isn't a mature, responsible adult, but the reality of her mother's life had been an eye-opener. The need exists to constantly reassure Julia I'll always be here for her, as I always have.

"Of course, baby girl. Love you." It feels important to remind her in the moment. She's the only person I use the phrase with.

"Love you, too, Dad." And that response right there reminds me no matter what it takes I need to get to a Napa Valley winery for my daughter's wedding.

+ + +

"Where the fuck is Daniel?" I blurt, bursting into Jane Fox's office. As our top account executive, I swear this woman runs this office in more ways than one. She isn't Human Resources. Hell, she isn't even responsible for my assistant's whereabouts, and yet Jane seems to know everything about everyone here. She was one of the few women who handled Rochelle, and that was a real feat, taking a strong constitution.

"Mr. Ashford," she stands to address me. "He called in sick today."

"I can't fucking believe this," I bark.

"What happened?" Jane's concerned voice does nothing to settle my agitation.

"The car service Daniel booked for California cancelled. They don't have another driver for such a trip on such short notice and I'm royally fucked."

"What?" Jane shrieks. She's been working for Impact—a media marketing company I own with my business partner, Machlan Wright—for roughly eight years. As much as I know about Jane, there is just as much I don't. Her employment credentials were my only interest when we hired her. She reports to Mach more than to me.

"They sent me an email this morning."

Jane bends for the computer on her desk, rapidly typing on the keyboard. "We discussed you taking the train," she reminds me. She is one of the few who empathizes when I say I don't fly.

"I'm not taking some cramped, smelly train, sharing a food car with strangers, and sleeping on a thin, lumpy mattress for three nights." I huff, sounding petulant. "And to top off this crazy morning, some lunatic ran into me and spilled coffee all over a new suit. The piece is completely ruined."

Slowly, Jane stands from her bent position where she was frantically hitting the keys on her laptop. She stares at me, blue eyes behind yellow framed glasses narrowing a bit.

"Spilled coffee," she whispers, and I wonder why she's looking at me like she is. The corner of Jane's mouth curls upward, taking its time to break into a grin that hints I shouldn't trust what she says next. Her eyes dart to something in her office and I twist only enough to notice someone else is in the room. I turn back to Jane, realizing too late that I've interrupted her meeting, but just as quickly my head swivels in the direction of a woman sitting before Jane's desk, hands clutching the armrest of a chair, glaring up at me.

"No," I groan.

"Yes." The woman from the sidewalk, dangerous with a cup of coffee, leers at me. The scowl she wears suggests I'm gum under her shoe.

Yeah, well, she ruined my suit. "Did you follow me?"

Her head flinches back. "I was here first." Her tight grip on the armrest confirms her position. She was in Jane's office before me.

Jane clears her throat. "Tucker Ashford, this is my sister Mae Fox-Holland. She's visiting today before she..." Her voice trails off, or maybe that's the unease inside me that dulls the sound of Jane speaking. I stare at the woman sitting before Jane's desk.

How is *she* sitting in Jane's office? She's in the late summer of her life as am I, but she's pure sunshine as I called her upon first meeting her. Unfortunately, I'm in a rainy-day kind of mood.

"Just Mae Fox," the woman mutters at the introduction before turning away from my gaze. She glares at Jane. *Her sister?* How did I not know Jane has siblings?

"My sister happens to be driving to California. She could take you across the country."

"What?" Mae and I both say at the same time.

"No." My rebuttal is definitive. *Absolutely not.* I need someone responsible to drive me to the west coast. This morning's encounter with Mae floats through my head. How she slipped into the street after we collided. How she purposely stepped into it for her phone, narrowly missing a taxi. Add in her bumping into me, and she can't be trusted to walk down a sidewalk with coffee in her hand, let alone drive two-thousand miles.

"She's already planned a trip and I don't want her to travel alone. She'd be the perfect traveling companion." The tension in Jane's voice is aimed at her sister as they stare at one another, having a silent conversation as only sisters can.

"I need to be in Napa Valley by Wednesday." That's seven days away from today.

"Well, I'm going to Los Angeles, and I'm not scheduled to arrive until two weeks from Sunday." Mae's voice drips saccharine-sweet and full of sarcasm. She doesn't want to drive me anymore than I want to ride with her.

"I'm sure Mae could speed up her trip to accommodate you," Jane says to me first before sheepishly glancing at her sister. "You said you weren't on a timetable. You can always drive Mr. Ashford to California and do your trip in reverse."

Mae shakes her head just the slightest bit, silently telling her sister *no way*.

"Could you even make it to Los Angeles by next Wednesday?" What the hell am I asking? Am I even entertaining this thought?

"No," Mae snaps at her sister, still clutching the armrest of the chair as if clinging to a lifeline. Her answer should settle it. I cannot possibly take a ride from this woman.

"You could if you left tomorrow," Jane suggests to her sister.

"What?" Mae and I again say in unison. I watch as Mae's shoulders fall, her eyes fixed on Jane. This isn't a good idea. This isn't the plan. I do not want to sit in the car for one, two—I count in my head—six days with this woman. *Six!*

"Drive yourself," Mae offers, her voice full of vinegar. Her head tips as she scans up my body from leather shoe-tips to the top of my head. I'd done the same thing to her on the street, taking in her casual appearance. She was a petite thing but there was something solid behind her small stature. She has iridescent blue eyes that cut me like sharp glass as she glares at me in *my* workplace. Her hair is slightly lighter than the dark head of her sister and based on what she is wearing—strappy flat sandals, cut-off jean shorts, and a once-white blouse now covered by a cardigan—she's heavy on casual attire. Then again, it is summer and warm in the city.

19

L.B. Dunbar

Our ages are roughly within a decade of each other. Nearing fifty has hit me hard and while I am still a year away from the daunting age, I am also close enough to that finish line that I'm struggling with the final sprint. I no longer have direction. Sure, I have the marketing firm with my best friend and brother from another mother, which is a story in and of itself. I also have Julia and then there's Jude, but I don't have the fulfillment I expected to have as I near half-time in the game of life.

"No," I snap at Mae again as if that explains why I won't drive myself. I don't have the time or the patience for a six-day car trip, thus wanting a driver.

I work. Someone else drives.

Without excusing myself, I step out of Jane's office and head to my own to search other services for availability while cursing my assistant's absence. Within twenty minutes, I'm further frustrated as no other transportation company has an open driver on such short notice.

I return to Jane's office.

She watches me, as does her sister, and something unsettling fills the quiet between all of us. The silence isn't something unsaid. It is the truth that I'm struggling to accept.

Riding with Mae Fox might be the only option to get me to the church on time for my daughter's wedding.

3

Playlist: "You Don't Own Me" – Leslie Gore

[Mae]

My sister and I had been having the same conversation we'd already had yesterday, and the day before, and a month ago, when we were so rudely interrupted by this man.

"I can't believe you're really doing this," my older sister said.

"I know, right? It's one of the craziest ideas I've ever had." Marry my college sweetheart. *Not unheard of.* Open my own business under his family's corporate umbrella. *Risky but worth it.* Finally find the nerve to dump Adam's ass. *Long overdue.* But this stunt—traveling the iconic Route 66 on my own—is simply…insane.

However, I'd been living under the auspice of sanity for too long. I'd done what was expected of me. I married young and had children immediately. Owning my own business wasn't something I ever planned to do, but I did it well. I also needed a break. Adam said I was self-centered for taking this trip during the summer when our eldest was home from college and our second was ready to leave the nest in the fall. Both our boys were self-sufficient, though, and worked for me at Mae's Flowers, a play on the *Mayflower* ship. My thriving garden center and flower shop was co-owned with my business partner, Pam Vincentia, and I trusted her to keep my boys busy during their summer employment. They wouldn't be in the way of Adam's newest conquest. Perhaps my trip was selfish, but it was also time. I'd given up two decades for everyone else. And I was ready to take back me. *Whoever that might be.*

I was in need of a long overdue life assessment. A restart to my engine. Like the travelers on that iconic seagoing vessel, I considered myself a voyager, setting sail across the country on a maiden trip even if I wasn't a fair, young maiden.

"I don't like you doing this alone, though." The eldest Fox sister is a worrier by nature. Fear has kept her single for all her forty-five years.

L.B. Dunbar

Fear and drive. She's been determined to work in an industry that's fast paced, everchanging, and productive. Her job has been the entirety of her life. My work and family have been the extent of mine.

"I'm only going alone because I couldn't convince you to go with me."

"You know I can't leave."

Actually, I don't really know if that is true. Jane wants to be a partner at Impact one day, and she likes to think she's indispensable. Perhaps she is, but my sister could use a major life-break herself. She works long hours and buries herself in projects. Sometimes I wonder if her dedication to work has to do with her potentially unhealthy obsession with Mach, the other owner of Impact. She needs to get out of this office and seriously get laid. However, I can't concern myself with her. *See? Selfish.* I only want to think about me and this trip.

Then, *boom*, a deep masculine interruption happens, and Jane militantly stands as if the mayor or someone important had entered her office. A ripple of confusion rushes over my spine at the sharp attack of his voice until I hear the words *lunatic* and *spilled coffee* in the same sentence.

I'm still wearing my coffee-stained shirt but placed a cardigan I had in my bag over it. I didn't have time to return to Jane's condo for a clothing change. A paper napkin in the public restroom at the coffee shop was the best I could do to clean off the sticky liquid that coated my bare legs and covered my sandals. I smell of day-old coffee and melted chocolate.

Spinning in the chair I sit in before Jane's desk, I immediately note three things about *the* Mr. Ashford Jane has mentioned over the years.

One, I don't know why she's speaking so formally to him like he's some eighty-year-old fogy instead

of a man with fine lines of fifty around his eyes.

Two, he's no longer wearing the coffee-stained shirt or the soiled jacket, returning me briefly to those wayward thoughts of him sexily striping out of the aforementioned ruined suit.

Which leads to number three, where I recognize him instantly and he notices me—*the lunatic.*

"No," he groans.

"Yes," I mock, straightening my back before peering at my sister who introduces us, sort of.

Oh, and number four, I do not appreciate his demeaning tone with Jane. Where is her gumption? What has happened to my feisty, take-no-shit older sister? She's the bossy one. The mother hen one. The I'm-in-charge one. *What is this?*

If I didn't know better, I'd say Mr. Ashford holds Jane's heart. Her eyes reflect admiration, perhaps respect for him, but his business partner is the man Jane pines for. Her love-hate relationship with Mr. Wright— Machlan Wright—is a dynamic I don't understand. Underneath all her complaints about long hours and working on days off, she has a serious crush and desperate desire to get laid by someone she's deemed Volde-*Mach.*

Then I notice Jane leering at me. A tight grin forms on her thin lips. The animated Grinch in *How the Grinch Stole Christmas* has nothing on the face my sister wears and I recognize that look. I fear that look. That look suggests a plan has just formed in her small, caged heart and that plan somehow involves me.

No, Jane. *Don't you do it.* I shake my head before she speaks. Then, she announces my travel plans for California and suggests I give Mr. *Ass*ford a ride. I nearly fall out of the office chair.

He's headed to California, too? Why isn't he flying? This is Chicago, a hub for air travel.

However, I already have a hint of his haughty airs. Not on a plane. Not on a train. He won't drive a car. I want to tell him where to shove his soiled suit and just how far.

When he rejects Jane's offer of my services, I bite my tongue. *Yeah, right back at ya'.* I am not driving this ass—despite the firmness of it in his one-thousand-dollar suit pants—across the country. He can find his own car and drive it off a cliff for all I care. I hope the gear stick gets shoved up his— Thank goodness our timing doesn't match up.

But then Jane opens her mouth again. "I'm sure Mae could speed up her trip to accommodate you. You said you weren't on a timetable.

You can always drive Mr. Ashford to California and do your trip in reverse."

Jane and I glare at one another. *How is his problem suddenly mine?* Even more so, this is the exact thing I'm avoiding in this trip. I do not want, nor need, nor desire a traveling companion, especially one as arrogant as this guy. I'm doing things my way on the highway.

Not to mention, Jane has had a difficult time understanding the purpose of this trip. Despite the blessed divorce. Despite happy motherhood. Despite my business success. I'm in search of myself. *Who am I?* Where am I going in the future? Going in reverse defeats the purpose. I'm moving forward in life. My carefully constructed, otherwise known as creatively unplanned, trip is from Chicago to L.A., not L.A. and back.

When suit-man asks if I can make it to California by Wednesday, I'm only too pleased to respond in a firm negative. We couldn't possibly make it that far that fast. And he can't possibly be considering Jane's suggestion.

I glance over at Mr. Ash*hole* and notice him looking back at me. He's leveling me with a glare that could bury me. Disgust fills his expression. His strong nose wrinkles like he smells a stench. However, I'm a fan of dirt. Flowers are my business. And I've perfected the I-dislike-you-too stare, compliments of my ex-husband. I break away from looking at this man, wondering just what my sister is thinking.

Eventually, the ultimate idea arrives, and I tell him to drive himself, again gnashing my teeth at the desire to tell him a few other choice things he can do.

His sharp "no" doesn't surprise me, but what does is when he leaves the office in a manner similar to how he left me on the sidewalk this morning. Without a word, he spins on his heels and retreats from Jane's office.

"What the hell were you thinking?" I snap at my sister as soon as we are alone again.

Jane lowers herself to her desk chair as if the weight of this conversation presses on her. "I don't want you alone."

"I *want* to be alone. That's the point. Do something for myself. Be free to be me." I pat my chest, exasperated that my sister doesn't understand and upset that she'd suggest I take on her boss as a rider. "I am not hauling his fine ass across the country."

Jane tilts her head, and a grin pokes at the corner of her mouth. "Fine ass?"

"Just ass. I am not driving that ass anywhere." On those words, I suddenly sense said ass's return. He hovers just inside Jane's door and the three of us remain in tense silence.

I cross my arms and fall back into the chair across from Jane's desk. The position reminds me I'm uncomfortably damp from the coffee that ruined my shirt and seeped into my bra underneath. The cardigan is also absorbing some of the mess and the entire moment feels like a bad omen.

"I'll meet you tomorrow morning at six." The directive hangs in the air before he spins once again on his expensive leather loafers and exits Jane's office.

"He cannot be serious," I turn on my sister. Her shoulders fall in relief.

"Please, just do this for me," Jane folds her hands and lifts them under her chin, pleading with me like she did when we were kids and she wanted something done, by me or our younger sister Lindee.

"Why, Jane? Why?" Why him? Why this? How is this…this… insufferable man suddenly riding in my car with me all the way to California?

She softly shrugs. "He needs you."

My brows pinch. The shift in her voice makes my skin pebble. She isn't making any sense.

"And you might need him." *Because she doesn't want me on the road alone.*

Shaking my head, I disagree with her.

There is no way I will ever need Tucker Ashford.

4

ILLINOIS – DAY 1

Playlist: "Sweet Home Chicago" written by Robert Johnson (1936)

[Mae]

If my sister hadn't told me the exorbitant price Tucker Ashford was willing to pay a car service to haul his ass across the country—which would be paid to me instead—I wouldn't be parked before Lou Mitchell's at six on Friday morning. The infamous diner is noted as a traditional starting point ritual. Before hitting the Mother Road, travelers stopped here to fuel up on their world-famous coffee. Upon visiting, every woman is given a box of Milk Duds. According to the internet, Greeks are known for their hospitality and when entering their home, women and children are offered something sweet as a warm welcome. I'm nearly giddy with the possibility.

That body-ripple excitement comes to a crash when I see Tucker Ashford in another business suit, tugging a rolling suitcase behind him and wearing an over-the-shoulder computer bag. *A man purse. Why am I not surprised?* What I am surprised about is that he showed. I was hoping he wouldn't. Which isn't exactly true, but it's what I'm telling myself. When my sister bamboozled me into giving this insufferable man a two-thousand miles ride across the country, cutting into my spirit trip, I drew the line at picking him up at his condominium like a damn chauffeur.

"If he's so desperate for a ride, he can meet me at Lou's."

Jane wasn't happy with my ultimatum, but neither was I. My trip was scheduled for two full weeks of cross-country bliss including cheesy pitstops and cheeky locations. I wanted to see everything. Realistically, two weeks didn't allow me to visit every single highlight along the way. I'd spend more time pausing than driving and I wanted the drive time. One thing I knew about myself was that driving long distances often led to reflection. Of course, on the last long-distance trip I'd taken, it became abundantly clear it was time to leave my husband. There was also the fact he was in the shower with his lover in our home when I returned, but I'm not allowing thoughts of Adam on this trip. Adam is ceasing to exist for me as anything other than the sperm donor for my sons.

"Good morning," I call out, sounding more cheerful than I feel at seeing Mr. Hot Suit Pants. We'll be in the car for long stretches of time, and I can't imagine a business suit is the most comfortable attire to ride in, but then again, what do I know about fashion? My professional wear is jeans and T-shirts. If I could wear pajamas to work, I would, but my industry involves dirt, sweat, and weather conditions, therefore I dress accordingly.

Mr. *Ass*ford grunts in response to my greeting. Gone is the momentarily flirtatious silver fox from the sidewalk yesterday morning. *Fine.* I open the door to the restaurant for him.

"What is this?" he asks, noting my hand on the door handle.

"It's called opening a door. Anyone who is a gentleman might recognize it." I don't need a man to open doors for me, but the traditionalism of gentlemanly behavior would be welcome. In my early years, this action was called manners. But, he's the one lugging baggage and I have free hands, so I opened the door for him.

"I mean, why are you going inside?"

"*We* are going inside for breakfast," I state. "It's the most important meal of the day." Plus, I love pancakes and I'd read the ones here are delicious.

Tucker, as my sister had reminded me was his first name, tilts his head as he glares back at me. "I don't think I can trust you around a cup of coffee."

If he were anyone else, I'd be expecting a slight smile to follow his sarcasm, but from what I've learned of him, he's dead serious. Jane told me *Mr. Ashford* is the strictest of professionals. And I wonder for the millionth time how my sister talked me into this situation.

Swallowing back the chuckle in my throat, I shrug. "Suit yourself." My eyes roam his attire, which might be another thousand-dollar suit for all I know. The dark navy color of this one highlights his eyes, hinting at a touch of blue within the steely gray irises. His more salt than pepper facial hair is apparent today as a thin sheen of bristle speckles his jaw. Those edgy cheekbones are male model-worthy, and I wonder for half a second if he was a model. Jane informed me he has expensive taste and fashion sense, but she wouldn't give me more information. She hesitated when I asked what his deal was. Why did he talk to her the way he did? Why did she address him as she did?

"It's a sign of respect. He's my boss."

"He's only a man." A good looking one at that, but he's arrogant. "And he's our age."

Jane only shook her head, dismissing me as the country bumpkin she thinks I am. I hate to remind my sister that I *own* my business while she's working *for* someone, so I don't mention it. What Jane does is important in its own right, and most of all, what Jane does she does because it's her life. No two Fox sisters have traveled the same path.

While Tucker decides to remain on the sidewalk, I enter the restaurant and take a deep breath.

Step One.

I wanted to return to the BEGIN sign this morning and then travel to the diner, taking my time to mentally absorb the fact I'm really doing this. I'm really going to drive across the country from one coast to another. Okay, Lake Michigan isn't considered a coast of the United States, but it should be. The third coast should be a thing. However, I took my pictures yesterday by the sign and as my trip is being condensed to a week's journey, I'm forging onward.

The hostess leads me to a booth, and I slip onto the bench seat, perusing the menu after ordering a black coffee with cream and sugar. No mochaccino here. As I scan the breakfast selections, a body flops into the seat across from me. I don't look up.

"Look, I'm sorry how things went down yesterday. I know this isn't the best of solutions, but I have a business to run. I have calls to make and reports to read, and we need to get on the road. I need to be in California by Wednesday."

Refusing to visually acknowledge him, I continue to stare at the menu when I respond. "I don't think we can make it before Friday."

"My daughter's rehearsal dinner is Friday. I need to be in L.A. by Wednesday."

My head pops up, and I stare at him, ignoring his dictating tone but suddenly understanding *his* rush to reach California. "Friday gives us wiggle room."

"I don't want wiggle room." On anyone else, that statement might sound silly. On him, it's ridiculous and I can't help the chuckle that finally escapes at his expense. He's so uptight compared to the smiling man of yesterday. The one with sparkling silver eyes and firm hands on my hips.

"Again, suit yourself." I glance back at the menu, but the stiff plastic is pressed down to the table, followed by the sharp thud of his palm.

"I'm not joking around with you."

"I'm not anything with you. You need the ride, not me." Slipping the menu free of his flattened hand, I lift it to cover my face and block out the view of him.

Who does he think he is? A fucking rock star or something?

He exhales. "Fine. Breakfast. Only coffee and to-go."

I lower the menu enough to see that silver-sheened hair on him and I'm grateful the waitress returns to take my order before I smack him over the head with the flimsy plastic sheet.

"What can I get you?" she asks, all Midwestern sweet.

"Coffee. To-go," *Mr. Ashford* barks.

"Pancakes and bacon. For here." My eyes narrow at him while the waitress takes my menu and steps away. The tension between myself and the ass I'm hauling across the country is thicker than the chocolate syrup in a mochaccino, and if I had some, I'd pour it over my breakfast companion. He needs some sweetening.

"We need to establish a few things," he states, and I narrow my eyes even more at him. His eyes avoid mine. "I have work to conduct during the day, but I could share in some driving time in the evenings if that gets us there faster."

No way in hell is he driving my car.

"We need to discuss sleeping arrangements."

"I am not sleeping with you," I blurt. The waitress happens to return with our coffees as I make my announcement and she snorts. Our eyes meet for a brief second and her nod says, *you tell him, girl*. I thank her for the hot drink while Tucker doesn't acknowledge her presence. Instead, those metallic eyes of his watch me. His nose wrinkles as it did yesterday when he saw me the *second* time. As if he smelled something stinky.

"Of course not," he huffs.

Same, pal. While I haven't had sex in I don't know how long, and the last thing I'll be doing is shacking up with this guy along the road, his adamant tone is a teeny bit hurtful. His harshness stings, pinpricking at my insecurities. Adam didn't want to sleep with me either and I was his wife. Tucker's disgruntled words along with the wrinkle of his nose make me feel like day-old trash. I might be forty-three, but I'm not old, and while I'm no beauty queen, I'm not a Cabbage Patch kid. Maybe he's used to pretty and peachy, and that's on him. I'm homegrown, sunburnt, and proud of both characteristics.

"I simply meant we'll need to rest along the way."

I nod. I've actually mapped out a few places where I'd consider stopping. The truth is, I wanted the road to take me where it will, and I don't have confirmed hotel reservations anywhere. I figured I'd stop when I wanted and keep driving when I could.

Suddenly, I'm excited again about the journey.

"Let me show you the map." I reach for my oversized tote and pull out an extensive binder I've made, highlighting the route per state, marking locations where I want to stop, and places I want to see. Laying the three-ring binder flat, I flip to the first page and point to our current location.

"We're starting here because it's—"

His cell phone rings, and he doesn't hesitate to answer it at the table. This is rude and something Adam would often do on official date nights when we were trying to 'repair our marriage'. I don't know what he could possibly talk to his assistant about at seven in the evening or what customer was so important he'd take a call at nine at night, but Adam did

Hauling Ashe

it. He allowed business to interrupt everything. Dinner. Vacations. Private times.

Without glancing down at my booklet, Tucker slips from the booth and begins talking while walking to the diner's exit. Once he's outside, I watch him pace back and forth along the sidewalk. While my ex-husband was everything opposite Hot Suit Man, this type of behavior is synonymous…married to his phone more than his wife. Then again, Jane assured me Tucker isn't married. *Widower*, she said without providing additional details.

My breakfast arrives hot and fast, and I tap on the window in hopes of catching Tucker's attention. He doesn't look up, and I take a deep breath. The inhale causes the scent of fresh pancakes, sweet syrup, and crisp bacon to invade my olfactory senses and my mouth waters.

Who needs sexy silver fox suit porn when you can have pancakes instead?

Not this girl. No siree, not me.

31

5

Playlist: "Life is a Highway" – Tom Cochrane

[Tucker]

"Is this a joke?" I blurt once Mae finally exits the restaurant and approaches a vehicle. I'd gotten a call from Jude and the argument inflated my irritation with this driving situation.

"No, it's Louie," she scoffs, her voice full of delight, and I glance at her hand on the driver's door handle.

"It's a fucking Toyota Prius," I clip.

A bright blue, four-door sedan that screams dad-mobile, and while I'm a dad, I wouldn't be caught dead driving one of these cars.

"So?" Her hand leaves the handle and fists land on her hips, hitching one to the side as she gives me her best death glare. I'll give it to her that she tries to stab me with those bright blue flares but she's just too...cute...to pull off an evil look. "You need a car with a V8 engine to prove your manhood? One that guzzles gas like a sorority sister drinking vodka and Gatorade?" She pauses as if she expects an answer. Bitter mockery rings in her voice and I'm wondering if she's projecting on me an experience with someone else.

She adds, "It's ecofriendly and fuel efficient."

"Nope," I snap. *I'm not riding in that thing.*

"Yep." She shrugs again, turning for the driver's door and I swear I never want to see that shoulder hitch again. We haven't even lasted half an hour, nor have we hit the road and I already want to run her over. She's so...*her.* "You should be thankful I didn't go with a VW campervan."

The mention of the iconic road trip van reminds me of days long gone. When some new friends and I used something similar to cart around equipment and hit local bars until— I pause. I don't want to think about those days. *Not* recalling those days is best.

I don't respond to Mae's comment about the campervan as she pops the trunk on the sedan. Several suitcases of her own rest inside, plus a reusable grocery bag. *Ecofriendly.* When she removes it, I set my carry-on beside her luggage. My suit has already been shipped to the wedding location. I had another one custom made, as my only daughter gets married only once. It's an important moment I'll want to commemorate.

Closing the trunk, Mae returns to the driver's side, and I circle the back of the car, opening the right-side rear passenger door.

"What are you doing?" Mae questions. Ignoring her, I slip into the backseat with my laptop bag. Mae leans into the front seat, glaring at me in that way she does—like a blue sky on a clear day—over the headrest. I ignore the unsettling ripple running through my body as she leers at me.

"I have work to do," I remind her.

"This isn't *Driving Miss Daisy*," she snaps.

"Of course not," I remark, and her voice echoes mine, mocking me under her breath. "Just get in and drive," I demand. It's going to be a long couple of days, especially since even when she's beaming those flaming blues at me, my heart beats in a rhythm I don't recognize. She huffs, tossing herself into the driver's seat and places the reusable bag she removed from the trunk next to her in the passenger seat. Reaching over her shoulder, she locks her seat belt in place and starts the ignition.

"Buckle up, buttercup," she mutters. "Or should I say, keep your hands and feet inside the vehicle at all times, Mr. Ashford. I'd hate to dismember you."

The hint of her desire to maim me isn't missed and I fight the curve of my lips. She's snarky and quick. Now, if only she'll be speedy on this highway.

A few minutes after we pull into the never-ending city traffic, Mae speaks. "So, I have a playlist made for the journey, but I'm open to requests." Her voice lifts, sounding like a radio announcer or a nightclub disc jockey. "I also have a selection of audiobooks but those might be a bit inappropriate." From my vantage point to the rearview mirror, I see her wrinkle her nose as a soft laugh crosses her lips.

I'll assume inappropriate is synonymous with dirty, raunchy perhaps, even porn-worthy, and I'm a little taken aback. Not offended, just surprised. Could I listen to something of that nature with a stranger? Most likely not. I'm not being some dick-headed prude, but I'm more afraid my dick will have a mind of its own.

My gaze remains on Mae in the rearview mirror. She's pretty in a natural way. Her chestnut-colored hair is a bit wild, loose and long. Her skin is sun-kissed, making her eyes sparkle and her teeth brighter when she smiles. And Mae is smiling...to herself. I called her Sunshine yesterday. She was a singular ray of it, planted on that sidewalk for some reason.

What is she thinking up there?

I don't know why I care and decide I don't. Pulling my laptop out of my bag, I open it and connect the portable Wi-Fi I'll need to use for internet service on this trip. I already anticipate inconsistency, but as long as I can be online for a little while, I can always reconnect when we take pit stops. I'd been warned by Jane about occasional pauses in our travels. I still can't believe I've accepted this option.

"So, where should we begin?" Mae asks, interrupting the first email I'm trying to read.

"I thought you had this mapped out." Her hands rest at a perfect ten and two on the steering wheel while her phone dictates travel status for the highway exiting Chicago.

"I do. I simply meant where should we begin in our life stories?" Glancing over her shoulder, she clicks on her blinker and properly changes lanes.

"Our life stories?" I echo, my mouth falling open.

"Yeah. Since we're stuck together for the next few days, we should probably get to know one another. I'm Mae. I run a garden center in northern Michigan. Now, your turn." Her tone teases but I'm not taking the bait.

"We don't need to talk. In fact, let's not." My eyes lower to the laptop screen and the car jolts to an abrupt stop. My head pops upward again and I notice bright red taillights on the car before us.

"Sorry about that. Traffic." Friday morning is gridlock, and I blame the growing number of cars on our delay. She didn't need breakfast. "Anyway, we might as well be friends."

"We don't need to be friends," I mutter.

"Everybody could use another friend."

"Not me," I state, turning my attention out the side window a second. I've only had one true friend, and that's Machlan, which is surprising considering how our friendship began.

"Is this a *When Harry Met Sally* moment?" she asks, tipping upward in her seat to peer at me better through the rearview mirror.

"A what?"

"You know, the movie *When Harry Met Sally*? They drove from Chicago to New York City, and Billy Crystal's character told Meg Ryan men and women could never be friends because the sex part always gets in the way."

"I am not thinking about sex with you," I retort.

Her lips twist a bit as her shoulders fall and she settles back into her driving position. "I didn't say you were thinking about sex with me. I'm simply asking, if you are suggesting you can't be friends with me because of the sex thing? A male-female thing. Whether attracted to me or not, you're thinking about sex because I'm a woman."

"I don't know what you're talking about. As for a male-female thing, I'll be keeping my male thing away from your female thing, so we don't need to discuss this. We can add it to the rules."

"What rules?" she pauses before answering her own question. "Rules of the Road 101. No sex between passenger and driver?"

I choke on air, then cough to clear my throat. There is no way she's propositioning me; however, it's happened before and often. Rochelle and I would be at a conference. Women would profess their admiration of me, my dedication to my wife, and then hint I should ditch the devotion.

I'm in room 403 if you'd like to discuss vagina power a little deeper, harder, faster.

I'll be in the bar if you want to share a drink and show me how to Liven Up Thursdays.

Does she really appreciate all you do for her?

L.B. Dunbar

I shake my head, ridding it of thoughts of Rochelle and her made up terms for spicing up marriages. Taking a sip of my coffee, I try to loosen my clogged throat.

"That's okay," Mae proudly states. "I don't fake orgasms anyway."

Coffee sprays forward, splattering over my laptop screen, the back of the seat before me, and my fresh-pressed shirt.

"Excuse me?"

"You know, in the movie, Sally fakes that orgasm in a diner to prove a point. Women can fake them. Men don't recognize them. I don't do that anymore. My orgasms are all real and all mine."

Good God. *Stop the car*, I want to yell. *Let me off this ride.*

Instead, I choke again, struggling with the laughter tickling the back of my esophagus. Just who is this woman and where has she come from?

"I think I'm okay with you keeping your orgasms and your friendship to yourself." Peering at Mae's face once more in the rearview mirror, her brows pinch and I realize I might have said too much, gone a little too far. I should apologize. She's right. We have days together in this car, if this thing can be called a car, but we don't need to talk. We don't need to get personal or physical. Definitely not getting physical, even if that wounded look in her eyes sends a strange sensation to my sternum.

Quickly, I glance down at my laptop, realizing for the second day in a row, I'm wearing coffee because of this woman. And while hot coffee seeping into my shirt has me thinking of warm places, wet and dripping on a woman, I shut that thought down and focus on the emails awaiting my attention.

+ + +

"Mach, I already told you no deal."

Currently, Impact has a publisher hounding us for a biography about Rochelle. They want us to immortalize the grassroots girl-turned-woman-empowerment motivator, but then we'd need to uncover the disturbing truth. Rochelle had never been grassroots and despite the pretty face, six-inch stilettos, and winning smile, an unpleasant woman resided within that picture-perfect form. I would know firsthand about the unattractive creature she'd become because I was married to her for almost twenty-four years.

Mae has detoured us off the highway at an exit promoting the original Route 66. I didn't question the shift, but as we hit a two-lane highway with zero cars on the road around us, her window goes down and the papers surrounding me begin to fly.

"Mae," I holler over the sudden noise of air whooshing into the vehicle and the flapping of papers.

"Who's Mae?" Mach asks.

"My driver."

"You have a driver named Mae?" Mach snorts. "Tell me she's an eighty-year-old grandma who can barely see over the steering wheel." My eyes flit to Mae as I try to capture the papers now disorganized and spilling over the back seat. I'll need to re-shuffle everything once I'm off the phone. Mae rolls her window back up a little bit and I hold my gaze on the side of her face, noting once again the chestnut coloring of her hair as the strands whip around her cheeks in the breeze from the open window. Her fingers delicately brush long locks off her face, exposing the side of her neck. Her index finger twirls the wayward hairs around it for a brief second before slipping free and the tendrils dance around her cheek once again.

"She's not," I say, my voice cracking as I answer Mach. He knows about my predicament. The transportation service cancelled. When I told him Jane's suggestion of her sister, Mach laughed as I had.

Is she hot? If I'd had coffee in my mouth yesterday when he'd asked, I'd have sputtered and choked around the liquid as I did a bit ago. Hot isn't the right word, but there is something warm about her. Maybe it was that tan skin giving off proof that she enjoyed sunrays and summer days. Maybe it was that soft brown hair floating around her face. Maybe it was those blue eyes, which give me a quick glance over her shoulder.

Sunshine.

"Better?" she asks.

Am I better? In the years since Rochelle's passing, the question has been asked by many. Was I better off without her? The thought was terrible to consider after her death and how it happened. The question was honest, though.

"So. Mae?" Mach hums in my ear, taunting me with the name and drawing my attention back to him.

"She's Jane's sister."

Mach laughs harder. Had he already forgotten her name? Had I mentioned it yesterday?

"You didn't?" He chuckles harder, implying he can't believe I hired Jane's sister.

"I had no other choice." I really didn't. Flying wasn't an option. The train wasn't either. Mae seemed to be the answer when I was still struggling with the question. *Why?* "She owes me a suit. The least she could do was drive me to California."

The trade wasn't exactly even.

"Well, this certainly sounds interesting." Mach snickers and I purse my lips as if he can see me.

"Not interesting," I state, catching Mae's eyes in the rearview mirror again. *Dammit.* Why does she need to look at me like that? Then she narrows those azure beams and returns her sight to the road where she should be concentrating.

Suddenly, music fills the interior of the car. Rapid drumbeats and an electric guitar count off the beginning of "Life is a Highway." *Is she kidding me?* Not joking in the least, Mae begins to sing with all the wrong lyrics.

Mach chuckles again through the phone. "She sounds like heaven."

"She's from hell."

My clearly inexperienced singer belts out line after line of mumbled words, as she doesn't know the song until the chorus hits. Then at the top of her lungs, she's on point and shaking her head, tapping without rhythm on the steering wheel. She's killing this song and I cringe.

"I gotta go," I mutter to Mach, disconnecting us before addressing Mae over the riotous song. "Dogs are crying on the side of the road."

"What?" she yells over the music, cupping her ear.

"You can't sing," I tell her, a little too harshly. "Turn that down." Suddenly, I sound like my father and a memory I keep locked in the recesses of my mind stumbles forward.

"What is that noise?" Jonathon Ashford would yell at me as my fingers flew over the piano keys.

"It's not noise, Jonathon. He's a prodigy." My mother defended my love of music. I didn't know what prodigy meant when I was young, but I played on those eighty-eight keys like a master. Like the ebony and ivory were part of my fingers. Their sound was part of my soul. The 'noise,' as my father called it, was heaven. Blissful, aural nirvana, drowning out all the silences of our home, or at times, the screaming matches between my parents.

After another rendition of the chorus returns, Mae belts at the top of her lungs before turning down the music.

"Maybe you need noise canceling headphones," she suggests.

I actually have a pair as I'd assumed I might need them to concentrate on the trip. However, I'm not pulling them out simply because she recommended them.

"Just wait until I put on the dirty romance novels," she warns. Her body shimmies in her seat and a cute-evil grin curls the side of her mouth. Her shoulders wiggle and her upper body squirms while she continues to mutter the wrong words to the song.

She wouldn't dare switch to a naughty romance book. She said no fake orgasms, and the last thing I need to witness is a real one as she gets off to the sound of some deep tenor reading words like pussy and cock to her.

The thought causes stirrings in my own pants, and I wonder what this reaction is to her. *Don't even go there.* Shaking my head, I disagree with the lyrics of the song.

This woman will not get in my blood.

She will not make me a no-longer lonely man.

I will not fall in love with her.

This highway *is* a dead end.

L.B. Dunbar

6

Playlist: "Soul Man" - Sam and Dave
"Think" - Aretha Franklin

[Mae]

If life was a highway, somewhere along the way I'd gotten a flat tire.

I didn't know who I was anymore or what direction I was going. I remained stranded on the side of the proverbial road, looking at the other drivers as they passed me by in their shiny Audis and practical Hondas. I stood speechless, wondering if anyone would stop and help me, or if I'd be on my own, as I always have been, to fix things myself.

I wanted to ride that highway...or at least, take a journey to rediscover myself.

Who am I? Who do I want to be? Where have I been?

The physical answer is I haven't been anywhere. Born and raised in Missouri. Planted and currently living in Michigan. I've been a mother, a wife, and a business owner but I am still lost.

This trip was about me searching for a deeper answer. A truer version of myself. Because somewhere over the years, I'd become someone I didn't recognize. I don't have much to complain about so being unhappy sounds unreasonable. I have beautiful grown children— something many women dream of having grace their lives. I own my own profitable business—in an economy where jobs are rare and coveted. The main unhappiness in my life ebbed and flowed around a volatile marriage—one that had more ups and downs than a rollercoaster. Traveling around curves, mood swings happened like the sudden drop of a cart, or my anxiety increased like a slow, steady climb to the top of the rails. The unpredictability of marriage might be something romance-lovers crave, but I don't hunger for it. I thirst from *the lack* of romance. My life should feel better without Adam. Yet despite being an independent, confident, *hear me roar*, kind of woman, I don't feel that way. I am still missing something. I recognize the hole, but I don't know how to fill it.

Love seems like an obvious answer.

Dating in the new age as an older woman leaves me numb. Beautiful men make me stupid, and most of them aren't attracted to me anyway. Case in point, my backseat passenger. I resent his good looks, and the image of his life as perfect. Then again, why wouldn't it be? Willing women throwing themselves at a handsome man? *Yeah, it must suck to be a good-looking guy.* I have no sympathy.

For some reason, my sister's warning returns to me. *"I don't think it's safe for a woman of your age to drive across the country."*

A woman of my age? What did that even mean? Was I incapable, uneducated, disillusioned? I was forty-three, not six feet under. Forty was the new twenty. I could do whatever I pleased, when I pleased, how I pleased and be proud. *Snap-snap-snap.* However, my worried sister had planted a seed of doubt in my head. Should I really drive across the country alone? Would it be smart? Would it be safe? What if I did get that dreaded flat tire? Then again, that's what AAA is for.

"I'll be fine. This is just what I need," I'd argued back.

"I'm not saying you can't. I'm just saying I'd feel better if you weren't alone."

Her wish came true. I am not alone. A stupidly good-looking man sits behind me, staring at his laptop as the country air whirls inside the car and the scenic view of slowly growing crops whizzes past him. He isn't on a journey of discovery. He knows very well who he is, and I bet women do throw themselves at him all the time. He doesn't have trouble being friends with those women. Friendship doesn't get in the way because sex is all he thinks about with *them*. *They* have sex with him.

I heard what he said to his partner on the phone.

Jane's sister. She owes me a suit. Not interesting. She's from hell.

Well, he's no picnic and strangely, I feel even more alone with him in the car than if I'd been by myself.

As we pass through Joliet, Illinois, where an infamous prison is located, an iconic blues song fills the car. Made popular by the characters Jake and Elwood Blues in *The Blues Brothers*, a classic 1980 film, the song feels appropriate. I've been sprung from a cage around my heart and it's time to be free. I will no longer be a passenger in my own life. The steering wheel is in my hand.

"Why aren't we on the highway?" my riding companion asks as we travel a portion of Route 66 covered by the modern path of I-55, which overlaps and interweaves with the original highway. In 1985, the original Route 66 was decommissioned to allow for the faster-paced interstate expressways instituted to connect city to city from Chicago to Los Angeles. Unfortunately, small towns paid the price. Quaint locations turned into abandoned vestiges of days gone by and I wanted those forgotten hints, those mysteries of the past. It was difficult to explain why, and I definitely did not think someone like Tucker Ashford could understand.

"We're headed for the Gemini Giant." One of three gentle giant structures, nicknamed Muffler Men, exist across Illinois, and I was in search of each one. The first was located in Wilmington in front of a diner, and I was almost giddy once again with the prospect of seeing something authentically antiquated from the old highway.

Tucker huffs at my explanation but doesn't ask for more information.

"Are you a blues fan?" he asks instead. Curiosity rings through his voice along with a touch of surprise. For once, he isn't snapping at me. My window remains at half-mast after his earlier outburst and the car warms with the rising heat of a Midwestern summer day. Outside the major city, the land is flat. I've turned down the music, after he insulted my singing, but he no longer seems bothered by my playlist.

"Not really." I don't know much about the sound attributed to Chicago. I recognize drums, horns, and throaty voices, but nothing more, and I briefly consider asking my passenger if he's a fan, but I don't. After his earlier comments about my singing, I decided against speaking to my traveling companion. I don't know a single lyric to this song other than the title but something about the sound makes me want to dance and I never dance in front of others.

Tucker returns to his phone and I'm starting to think I'm the one who needs noise canceling headphones. I'd consider purchasing a pair at the next major service station, if I didn't think they were dangerous to wear as I drove. Besides, I don't anticipate a gas station with a convenience store anytime soon and I'll need to keep that in mind as I travel.

In the silence that continues between Tucker and me, Aretha Franklin belts out "Think," emphasizing her warning to a man about his decisions, clarifying their need for one another, and asking him to consider her feelings. For a moment, my thoughts drift to Adam and my upset that he called me selfish with regard to this trip. I'd never known a more selfish person and the audacity of him accusing me— *Nope*. Not going there. Adam was not allowed head space on this journey.

Following the GPS, I weave toward a small town and almost miss the green giant I'd been seeking. Slowing, I pull into the parking lot of the diner where patrons are urged to take photos with the fiberglass man. Parking the car, I hop out while Tucker ducks his head, staring out the side window after me. The astronaut, reminiscent of space age dreams in the 1970s, is dressed in a Kelly-green outfit, with what looks more like a welder's hood on his head than an astronaut's helmet. He holds a silver rocket in his hand. For a moment, I breathe him in. He's nostalgic although I can't decide why. Turning around, I do my best to take a selfie, which I have not mastered. My arms are too short, my face always too close to the camera and the angle can't really capture both me and the large statue.

"Well?" Tucker questions when I return to the car.

Assuming the single word question wonders what I thought, I tell him the truth. "I thought he'd be bigger." Noting once more the rocket held in the statue's hand, I snicker to myself, my mind resorting to the twelve-year old boy inside me. "And that's what she said."

I snort, laughing at my own joke because the tension between me and the man in my backseat is getting to me. Going into this trip on my own, I accepted I wasn't going to share things I encountered. I'd been prepared for the singular experience. I'd been prepared to think my own thoughts and see what I sought, and then enjoy them—or not—on my own. Expressing my disappointment to a man clearly disinterested in our journey was equally disappointing and for a half second, I consider turning around and returning him to Chicago. We'd only gone a little over an hour and a half. I'd still have time to spend the weekend with my sister and Tucker could find another ride to California. I could start my quest on Sunday as initially planned.

Instead, I sigh.

"Would you like something?" The restaurant behind me is your classic drive-in, an original fast-food counter, and I envision a chocolate milkshake made with ice cream.

"I'm good." Tucker's disgruntled tone pisses me off. He's missing out, but I decide I'll pass as well. Pancakes and bacon from this morning have left my belly full, and I don't need the stomachache milk products give me as I age. The sad fact is I can't handle things like cheese and ice cream like I did when I was younger. There are a lot of things I don't handle as I had when I was in my twenties and thirties, and one of those things is pouty men.

Tucker's indignant silence unnerves me, and I start the ignition, reversing out of the parking lot and returning to a strip of Route 66 running parallel to the interstate. Eventually, I pull into another small town and park in a public lot.

Welcome to Pontiac.

"Now what?" Tucker mutters.

"This is one of the more famous Route 66 museums along the way. I'm not stopping at every one of them, but I've picked a few and this one wins in Illinois. You can stay in the car if you wish." The statement reminds me of bickering boys and their whining while I ran errands. When my sons were little, leaving them in the car was never an option. As teens, they could just sit and stew. As my passenger wants to be an adolescent, he can do the same.

"How long will you be?" he asks, reminding me once more of my grown boys.

"Not more than an hour."

"An hour?" he huffs.

"Consider it my lunch break."

"It's hardly ten." He continues to mumble while I'm exiting the car. After crossing the road, I enter an old fire station, which houses the museum. Wandering the aisles between display cases, I scan the memorabilia of the most iconic main street through the States—metal road signs, rusty tin cans of oil and gas, preserved menus, black and white photographs, toys and knick-knacks. The numerous mementos are too much to absorb and knowing an impatient man awaits me in the car, I don't take the time I might have to read every notice and explanation.

Instead, I imagine families with a mom, a dad, and two kids riding along these classic roads to their vacation destinations. Life has veered from that picture-perfect image, not only since the decommissioning of Route 66 but also since the opening of it. With the rise in divorces, women in the workforce, the extended longevity of life, and the expense of children, the world has shifted in what it considers the 'normal' family.

As a female divorcée, I'm marked as a single mother and am breaking that antiquated norm. I was also raised by one. I'm a working mother as well, and...*gasp*...own a successful business. None of these things are as unheard of today as they'd been fifty, sixty, seventy years ago, and it's incredible to consider it's only been just over fifty years since these changes in the familial structure occurred.

My mind continues to wander, imagining a young couple on their honeymoon, traveling along the highway as they start their new life together. Hopes and dreams fill their heads and their hearts. How long ago that had been for Adam and me. How young and disillusioned I was when I was in that newly married state. How I had loved my husband at first. My disappointment in him shouldn't still weigh heavy on me and perhaps it's a reflex, one in which I continue to blame myself for him straying in our marriage.

Why wasn't I ever enough for him? Why hadn't he loved me like I had loved him?

"What are you staring at?" The gruff male voice behind me startles me, and while my hand comes to my chest, I don't spin to face him. Instead, I catch his reflection in the glass enclosure housing history and preserving a time long past.

Why do we encapsulate memories?

"Just taking it all in. There's so much to look at."

45

L.B. Dunbar

He huffs. "Looks like a bunch of junk."

I twist at his assessment at the same time he leans forward, narrowing his eyes to better see something within the case. He stands close enough that his arm brushes mine and I inhale, catching the scent of him, spicy and wild, which surprises me. Amid the musty fragrance of the museum, my senses wreak havoc, and my imagination pulls me off to the side of a road, one lined with large, lush evergreens. In my head, my young honeymoon couple scrambles into the backseat, eager to touch one another, desperate with their mouths on each other, before clothing is lowered and body parts connected, rocking that parked car under perpetually green trees.

Tucker turns his head in my direction while this montage plays out in my mind. His face is close as he leans beside me. His eyes meet mine and all my thoughts merge into him and me in the same position. His suit pants lowered. My shorts removed. Our centers connecting.

I lick my lips, wondering what it would taste like to kiss him and just as quickly wondering where the thought comes from as I don't even like this man. Sure, he's attractive and I bet his rocket is bigger than the one the Gemini Giant was holding, but our mouths will not meet.

Two roads diverged... Our paths and body parts shall not connect.

Still, Tucker's gaze holds mine as he slowly stands taller. "Why do you like all this stuff?"

I shrug, unable to find an appropriate explanation let alone coherent thoughts with him staring at my mouth like he is.

"I'm coming to hate that shrug," he mutters under his breath, and he wrinkles his nose as I've witnessed him do several times. Is the musty smell too much for him? *Or do I smell bad?* His nearness is too much for me, and my reaction is something I don't understand. Forcing myself, I take a step to the right and wander down the remainder of the aisle. As I pass case after case, I decide I don't want to see the artifacts as much as I want to experience what I can of the open road.

Tucker stays behind me, keeping his distance and his hands in his pants pockets. While we've driven, he removed his suit jacket and rolled his sleeves to his elbows. He must be warm, and I wish he would relax. Shadowing me, he makes me nervous.

As we near a display case for the Arizona portion of the trip, Tucker pauses, and I turn back in his direction. My gaze tries to follow his, but I have no idea what he's looking at on the shelves behind glass.

"Is there something about Arizona you're excited to see?" I ask.

"Nope," he says, popping the -*p* as he does. Nodding at him, I glance back toward the case, scanning the exhibit once more in wonder. There's something in the display case about Winslow, Arizona which sounds familiar, but I don't understand why. I've never been there.

"We can go," I state, disappointed in yet another thing on my travels. My irritation isn't really with the trip, though, as much as my companion.

We return to the car, continuing our silence, and I pull up the GPS to recalibrate our location for directions leading south down the highway.

Near a town named Lexington, a roadside sign reads Memory Lane. The path is a strip of the original route.

"Think I can actually drive down that road?" I don't know why I'm asking Tucker, as if he'd know. However, I don't want to destroy anything intended to be a historical landmark. My curiosity is piqued, though. If closing my eyes and driving the strip were an option to feel the ambience of a time gone by, I would. Instead, I want my eyes wide open. No more shutting out what I can't accept as reality in my life. I'd closed my eyes too many times in the past.

"How should I know?" Tucker states snidely from the back seat, and I ignore him as I have from the last stop to this one. Slowly, I pull forward and drive down a small strip of original road, heavy with foliage on either side of the cracked cement path.

"How did people drive those big-as-boat cars down this thing?" I ask aloud, not really wanting an answer, just expressing my thoughts. The section of road isn't long, isn't wide, and isn't much, but something swells inside me. All those travelers. All those sightseers. All those hopers and dreamers. Did they make it to their destination? Did they find what they were looking for? Would I?

"Well, that was—"

"Have you never taken a road trip?" I interject over his comment, worried he'll ruin the moment.

47

L.B. Dunbar

"I have. I just—"

"Let me guess, you've always traveled by some cozy SUV, complete with A/C and high-tech stereo, plush leather seats, Bluetooth, and maybe a mini-bar," I mock.

"Actually, the road trip I once took involved something similar to that VW campervan you mentioned earlier."

My mouth falls open. "Where'd *you* go road trippin'?" I absolutely cannot imagine him in a beat-up van, but suddenly an image of him in jeans, a tight T-shirt, and flip-flops fills my head. He could pull off beach casual as much as he rocks the business suit.

Tucker squints, turning his head to peer out the side window. "California."

My heart hammers in my chest. "Have you already traveled Route 66?" *Why hadn't he mentioned it?*

"No. I went more direct. Straight out I-80 west through Iowa, Nebraska, Colorado, Utah, Nevada to L.A."

"Wow," I whisper, tugging on the steering wheel to pull myself upward and glance at him through the rearview mirror. "That must have been some trip." That direction is the way I've considered doubling back to Chicago. Then again, I haven't planned my return trip.

"It was." Softly, he smiles. Just the corner of his mouth crooks upward. His eyes squint again in the bright sunlight as he focuses out the window, lost in his own memories.

"Why?"

He turns back to me. "Why what?"

"Why did you take that trip?"

He softly huffs and I wish I could look at him better while we speak instead of the seats separating us, with him behind me. My attention needs to remain on the road before me.

"Just young and hopeful back then."

This surprises me. "What did you hope for?"

"Things that don't matter anymore."

This again surprises me, and I risk another peek through the rearview mirror. His head lowers. His forehead furrows. Then he reaches for his phone and the conversation is closed, just like him.

7

Playlist: "The Piano Man" - Billy Joel

[Tucker]

I'm losing my mind in this car. The fresh scent of Mae mingles with the warm air traveling through the car and I can't breathe. Her scent along with the continued attempts to talk to me, stifle me. *She's too much.*

We continue down the road again in silence and as much as I try to concentrate on the emails before me, I can't. My thoughts continue to wander to her question. *Why? What did I hope for?*

Sometimes it's difficult to recall the dreams I once held dear. The hopes I had of making it big, being someone in my own right. In my life, the path to success flipped. Instead of obtaining the accolades I desired, Rochelle received them. I wasn't a jealous man, but I'd been envious of the empire she'd built with my assistance. The following she had, all by looking pretty, exposing our home life, and giving away our secrets, empowered women to take control of who they wanted to be. I supported Rochelle in those ideals. I am not a chauvinist, but I am a realist. I'd given up my dreams and took the sideline while she achieved hers.

The irony in her accomplishments was that she never set out to be as famous as she was. Her initial intention had been a simple blog. She wanted to vent her grievances and connect with other women. She spoke about motherhood and loneliness. She talked about friendships and lost connections. She mentioned our immediate family and intimate rituals in a manner that weren't quite reality but sounded picture-perfect. She created a model image, not too far off from the cartoon replicas I'd seen in that museum we'd stopped at of perky-breasted, skirt-wearing mothers and suit-clad fathers from the 1950s.

The exterior of those images has changed but the ideal has not. A woman is more than a mother now; she is a superpower, a warrior, an innovator, and I'd support all these things, as long as someone is genuine. Rochelle had not been. She was moody, easily agitated, and spoiled

L.B. Dunbar

beyond reason. I faulted myself in many ways. In supporting her pursuit of all things, I'd become someone I never wanted to be.

Glancing out the window at the late morning sky, I quietly allow myself to mourn the person I had once wanted to be for a few seconds, and then return that dream to where it belongs, deeply suppressed within me.

Eventually, Mae pulls into another small town and we near a second Muffler Man, as she called the giant male statues. This one holds an oversized hot dog in his hands.

"He was originally located in Cicero at Bunyon's Hot Dog but was moved here." Her tour guide voice gives nothing away. I expected her to be more excited with every stop we've made but her quiet demeanor reminds me of Rochelle. *Is Mae not appreciating this trip?* This path was her plan. I'm certainly ready to come out of my skin with the slower paced by-way. I don't understand why we aren't hitting eighty miles per hour on the freeway and crossing this state off our list.

However, Mae parallel parks and exits the car, walking toward the fiberglass structure. She turns her back to it, posing as people do for selfies. Yet, she's struggling with the phone in her hand and lining up her stature with the taller one behind her. Rochelle had been a pro at selfies. Then again, she'd had a permanent camera man—me. As her right hand, I followed beside her everywhere she went, documenting so much of her day, her conferences, her life.

Frustrated by watching Mae's struggle, I forcefully open my door and step onto the sidewalk.

"Here. Let me take it." If I don't help her, we might be here all day as she tries for the right angle. Then again, she isn't exactly posing. She isn't fluffing her hair or positioning it over her shoulder in a certain way. She isn't standing sideways, bending a knee, placing a hand on her hip, and tilting her head. She's just...Mae.

Reaching for the phone, I tap camera mode and focus in on her and the hot dog holding man behind her.

"Think that wiener is big enough?" I ask, recalling her joke about the previous statue and his rocket.

Mae turns to glance at the structure, and I snap a picture of her. When she turns back to me, her face explodes in a smile and my finger presses on the red button again. *Click.*

"Did you just make a joke?" Her grin illuminates her face, highlighting her white teeth and sparking those blue eyes like miniature flames on a gas stove. *Click.*

"Nope," I mock, staring back at her and taking another picture of her, zooming in on the wide curve of her lips. *Click.* Mae isn't classically glamorous but she's perfectly pretty and that smile is…stunning. As in, I'm suddenly stunned in place by the force of it, and my finger presses the camera button once more. *Click.*

"Did you get a good shot?" she asks, slowly approaching me. Glancing at the phone in my hand, I scan the images, pausing on the last one.

"Yeah, I think I got something." For half a second, I almost ask her to text me the image. Instead, I do it myself, opening the message app and sending all the pictures to my phone.

"What are you doing?" She softly laughs, reaching out for the device.

"Just adding my number in your contacts. You should probably have it in case…"

"In case?" she questions.

In case something happens. I swallow the phrase, recalling how Rochelle sent a final text to me. I shake the memory.

"Just in case we get separated." My voice drops as I fight the confusing swell of emotion filling my throat. I don't want to be separated from Mae, which is a strange thought considering I don't know her. We aren't exactly getting along on this trip and it's all my fault. I'm keeping her at a distance for a reason.

I glance down at her phone once more and my mouth curls the slightest bit.

"Is that a smile?" she teasingly questions, and I look up at her, realizing she isn't looking at the image on her phone but at my face. "Don't you be smiling, pretty boy," she coyishly jests and the expression on her face is brighter than the sunshine overhead.

51

"Don't hit on me," I state more harshly than necessary.

Instantly, her beam of sunny rays collapses to a storm cloud. "I wasn't hitting on you."

Maybe she wasn't. Maybe it was just an innocent statement, but I need Mae to keep her distance. She needs to hold back because I don't need a woman in my life. I already had one who took over everything, and the last thing I need is a road trip fling with my driver. My tempting driver who looks at me one moment like a shining star and then clouds to the feisty woman standing before me now.

Better. This is better. Her irritation will maintain a barrier between us.

Mae's mouth falls open like she's about to speak but then her lips slam shut. She looks away from me, but I turn away from her as well because I cannot think about those lips. When we stopped at the museum, Mae stood too close to me. My shoulder brushed her arm as I leaned forward, and my concentration fell to her reflection in the case instead of the contents in the display. Briefly, I'd wondered how she'd react if I had pressed her up against the exhibit and kissed her senseless, ridding us of the tension swirling around us. Then I remembered that keeping that tension intact was important. I didn't need to cross some imaginary double line, swerving into the wrong lane, and come head-to-head with Mae. I already knew she was more than I could handle.

She takes her phone from my hand, glances down at the pictures I've taken, and creases her brows.

What's wrong with the photos? I almost ask, but don't. I already know I captured her face and that ridiculous statue with the giant wiener behind her.

"Not impressed with his sausage?" I mock and Mae's brow relaxes. She glances up at me, all innocent eyes like she gave me on the sidewalk when we collided only yesterday.

"Are you trying to be funny? Cracking a joke?" Her tone isn't harsh, but her cadence hints this is a serious question.

"I can be funny." I shrug as she's often done to me. Although, her shrug suggests she's keeping something from me, and I don't like it. Then again, I don't need all her secrets because I won't be sharing mine.

"I can be flirty. Doesn't mean I'm hitting on you."

"I—" I'm not certain how to respond. I've acted in the same way countless times. A wink. A smile. The gestures never meant anything. The motions weren't a promise to anyone. I'd been faithful to Rochelle.

"And as long as we're passing out 'don'ts,' and adding to our Rules of the Road 101, don't fall in love with me."

My brows pinch so hard, I'm certain I've made a permanent crease. "Of course not," I stammer.

"Good," she says, nodding once before brushing past me, dropping into the driver's seat and slamming her door.

Slowly, I saunter back to the passenger side and lift the handle, only briefly wondering if Mae would rather leave me here in this small town. Somehow, I wouldn't blame her. I'd left myself behind a long time ago. Strangely, I might end up missing her if she ditched me.

+ + +

When Mae nears a giant covered wagon minus the cloth and featuring a huge Abraham Lincoln statue in the driver's seat holding a book, I'm ready to lose it. The silence between us for the fifteen-minute ride has been heavier than the rest of the trip. Thankfully, Mae must read the tension coming off me because she continues onward.

"Your tour will continue for another forty minutes before we stop in Springfield for lunch." Mae's announcement, in a voice similar to that of a bus driver, pulls forth all kinds of memories. A van filled with the guys. A list of our destinations. Our excitement. Our failure.

My thoughts rush back to the museum where Mae had stopped, and where I'd refused to exit the car at first. Trying to recall how to hotwire a car, I fought the urge. It wasn't like I hadn't done it once or twice in my past. I was never stealing, I justified. Just borrowing the car for a little bit to see some band—a local gig I wanted to catch, a sound I wanted to hear.

If I only heard the music, I could replicate it.

In my head, I see the item that caught my attention in the museum— a rusty harmonica on the shelf. Playing harmonica is a dying skill, a lost

53

talent, and one I haven't used in so long I don't know if I could remember how to properly blow out and breathe in as one should with such an instrument. My fingers twitch, curling around an imaginary four-inch sound machine. I only had a 10-hole diatonic harmonica when I was young. It was a beginner's windpipe, but I could play that piece wicked well.

When I first returned to Chicago, I'd hit that harmonica like a nicotine addict unable to quit cigarettes. Hiding out in the farthest corner of my grandfather's backyard or in the dark alley behind Rochelle and mine's first apartment, I'd inhale the sound I would eventually give up. One day the piece I'd prized my entire life as a gift from my grandfather had disappeared, and I took the disappearance for the sign it was. I was never going back to who I wanted to be. My limited career and short stint of independence was over.

My soul feels that heartbreak once again.

To make matters worse, the car fills with "The Piano Man" by Billy Joel and Mae begins her version of singing.

"Turn that crap off," I snap, more harshly than I've spoken to Mae so far as echoes of my past rip through me. Mae huffs and clicks to the next song in her dreaded road trip playlist and loneliness hits me almost as hard as her finger jabbing the sound system for the next selection. I need out of this car, away from the intoxicating scent of my driver, her off-key sound, and the memories racing through my head.

8

Playlist: "When He Sees Me" (from *Waitress the Musical*) - Sara
Barielles

[Mae]

Don't fall in love with me. What a perfectly ridiculous thing to say to
him. His response was just as preposterous. I wouldn't expect Tucker
Ashford to love me even on a good day and he seems like he is having a
perpetually bad one.

"What is this?" Tucker asks when we pull up ninety silent minutes
later before a white brick building. The name should give the place away:
Cozy Dog Drive-in.

"Does that sign say 'home of the original hot dog on a stick'?" he
asks next, and I hear the curious displeasure in his voice.

"It sure does," I reply, opening my door and stretching my legs.
Although we've been stop and go, my knees are cramping, and I could
use a good walk. Not to mention my shoulders are tight after our last
altercation. One minute he's smiling that off-kilter smile and taking
pictures for me, and the next he's making a joke that dies like a punchline
you have to explain to someone.

I don't understand this man.

The pictures he took of me were not how I saw myself. He must
have played with some filter I don't know how to work on the
smartphone camera because I don't look like myself. I'm smiling and my
eyes are bright. They made me look...good.

Then he had to ask me not to hit on him. I could understand if I took
things too far. If I was throwing myself at him, begging him to take me
on the uncomfortable bench seat of Louie, but I hadn't suggested
anything of the sort. Speaking of bad moods, one minute I want to
request a backseat rendezvous, and the next, I want to stuff him in the
trunk and pretend I'm not carting a body back there. He is
so...frustrating.

He also isn't pleased with my lunchtime selection, but a deep-fried hot dog is on the menu and this place is classic Route 66. Admittedly, I don't know how my stomach will handle a hot dog, let alone one batter dipped, but I'm willing to try one for the experience. That's what this trip is about. Seeing places I haven't seen. Trying things I haven't tried. Partaking in activities I wouldn't normally partake in.

Surprisingly, there is comfort—albeit unsettling—to having Tucker with me. He doesn't talk much, and he calmed down about the music selection after the "Piano Man" outburst. His sharp command to cut the song left me puzzled, but obviously he isn't a Billy Joel fan. Maybe the lyrics hold a bad memory for him, but I can't imagine Mr. Picture Perfect having had bad moments in his life. Except maybe his wife's death.

Immediately, I realize my assessment isn't fair. I'm the first to admit you can't read what's underneath the skin of another human being. I'd been fooled too often by Adam.

Tucker follows me into the iconic-looking counter service diner. Of note, he held the door for me. Maybe he is a gentleman after all. Peering at him over my shoulder as I head for the counter, I decide against it. He's too hard-edged. His face too handsome.

He squints at the overhead menu. This is not his kind of eatery, and he looks out of place in his dark slacks and starched dress shirt. With his hands in his pockets, he continues to peruse the menu while I scan his profile.

Slowly, he turns to face me, and I should look away. He's already caught me glancing at him too many times through the rearview mirror. He's told me not to hit on him. His expression screams not to even consider flirting with him, and yet…underneath all that pretty skin with fine lines near his eyes is just a man. A man who hates a song and was staring at something in that display back in the museum.

I wonder if it was the rusty harmonica that held his attention. I have no idea how that could connect to anything other than the strong presence of the wind instrument in Billy Joel's famous song about people in a bar who are lonely and sad.

"What are you having?" Tucker asks me, interrupting my thoughts.

"The Cozy Dog, of course, with fries and a cola."

Tucker nods and we step forward until it's our turn. The teenage boy behind the counter who asks for our orders reminds me of my son, Owen. They share similar features—floppy dark hair and bright blue eyes.

"The lady will have a Cozy Dog, fries, and a drink. I'll have the same." I'm snapped from thoughts of my second son as Tucker orders for us. Reaching into my oversized bag, I scramble through the contents seeking my wallet when a hand comes to my lower back and gently nudges me to the side.

"What the—?" I stop when Tucker hands over his credit card. "What are you doing?"

Silvery eyes meet mine and the hint of a smile curls the corner of his mouth when he says, "I'm buying lunch."

"You don't have to do that." I'm ready to burst into a lecture about how I can pay for my own damn lunch and have every intention of us taking care of our own meals and lodgings along the way. I hadn't figured out the gas situation but assumed with the money I was intended to receive for hauling Mr. Ashford to California I could splurge on the gas charges. Obviously, I'd been planning to pay for everything all on my own anyway.

"I know," he replies to my comment and then faces the young cashier to retrieve his credit card.

"Well, thank you." I should sound more appreciative. His gesture is the first decent thing he's done on this trip next to holding the door for me, but there's still an edge to my voice. He confounds me.

After we're given a number to claim our food when it's ready, we take a seat. I notice a T-shirt pinned near the menu featuring two caricature hot dogs cuddling like a couple. It's cute. I'd considered grabbing souvenirs from every place I went but that would financially add up, and I was holding out for something special. Something truly unique to mark my passage through each state. I'd know it when I saw what I wanted.

Then again, I should grab something for my boys and the T-shirt reminds me again of Owen. He loves graphic tees.

L.B. Dunbar

"I noticed you staring at that kid," Tucker says. "Got a cougar thing happening?"

The inappropriateness of his question shouldn't shock me, but my mouth gapes. "He reminds me of my son."

The surprise on Tucker's face is almost priceless and I wish I'd had my camera ready to capture the moment.

"You have a son?"

"I have two."

Tucker's eyes roam my upper body as that's all that's visible above the table where we sit across from one another. "And you had them when you were ten?"

Now who's flirting with whom? However, he doesn't mean anything by his comment. "You're sweet, but I'm forty-three and had my first boy when I was twenty-three."

Tucker's brow arches as he stares back at me. He must know Jane is in her mid-forties and I'm close behind her. He's simply teasing me and a hint of the man on the sidewalk returns.

"My oldest is Wyatt. He's twenty and he'll be a junior in college in the fall. I fool myself into thinking he's there to study, but he's there on a hockey scholarship and just changed his major to communications. He's probably going to follow in his father's footsteps and work for Eden Landscaping when he graduates."

Adam's parents originally owned a farm supply shop which he shifted into commercial landscaping. Then a boom in second-home owners in our small lake town and do-it-yourself gardeners led me to turn a little section of garden plants into a thriving business.

If I had my way, Wyatt would have gone into environmental studies. He could have grown the landscaping business by learning more innovative pathways along the lines of sustainable design and green spaces. However, Adam didn't have to work too hard in his studies at our alma mater because he always intended to work for his father's business. Sadly, Wyatt seems to be following Adam's direction.

Tucker's face shifts, hardening a bit. "Jane told me you were divorced."

"I am." Skipping those details, I continue describing my sons. "The boy at the counter looks like my second son, Owen. He's eighteen and your typical second child. He keeps to himself and he's quieter than his brother. He's not much of an attention seeker but a sneaky troublemaker in his own right. He has a huge heart, though. If these were historical times, he might feel he doesn't matter as much as his older brother, being the second son. He's ignored a bit by Adam because he's into art more than athletics."

Sadly, Owen doesn't receive the attention he deserves from his father. Our creative child has a vision that could also profit Eden Landscaping or Mae's Flowers, but I'd be equally happy for him to forge his own path. While Owen is the lover and Wyatt is a protector, neither boy showed much interest in my spirit trip. I don't want to find fault with their lacking enthusiasm, as they are males and teenagers, and both those traits can make them selfish, but a pinch of disappointment pierced me by their absent support of my decision to take this trip.

"Owen will be a college freshman this fall. I'm hoping he'll major in art."

Tucker tilts his head, ready to question the comment but our order number is called out and he slips from his seat to retrieve the tray with our food. When he returns, he eyes the batter-dipped hot dog.

"Ketchup?" I ask.

"No self-respecting Chicagoan puts ketchup on a hot dog," he mocks, and I laugh, since I've heard this statement before from Jane. Only, the batter-covered hot dog isn't on a bun.

"It's a hot dog on a stick. I think you'll be forgiven." I wink at him, unable to stop myself. I hate to suppress what feels natural to me. I'm in a business where I interact with people daily, and there's no reason to be standoffish. It's not in my nature to be, but warning bells go off around Tucker and I almost apologize for teasing him.

He squirts a heavy dose of ketchup in the corner of the wax paper covering his plastic basket and I quietly laugh as he takes his first hesitant bite. When he hums next, the sound goes straight between my legs, and I imagine that hearty purr in response to him being touched some place private and sacred.

L.B. Dunbar

"I haven't had food like this in I don't know how long." He slowly chews as he savors the flavor of greasy batter wrapped around processed sausage. "This reminds me of my grandfather."

"How?" I softly smile, hoping he might open up a bit and prove he's human.

"He loved niche-y hot dog places and we'd stop in one when I was with him as a kid. *Don't tell your grandmother*, he'd warn but she always knew what we did." Slowly, his face morphs from pleasant childhood memories to his typical stern expression.

"You were close with your grandfather?" I question.

"I was. He was the cornerstone of our family." There's so much more in that statement but he doesn't expand so I let it slide. I could mention my own Granddad and how he was the glue of our family, especially after our father abandoned us, but I don't.

"You mentioned a daughter, but do you have any other children?" I say instead.

His brows pinch again before he begins. "Jude, my son, is twenty-seven, and we typically don't see eye to eye." He pauses as he swirls his hot dog on a stick in the ketchup once again and his sudden quiet tells me there's a story behind their battles. "My daughter Julia is twenty-four. She's the one getting married, thus the need for a ride to California."

At the mention of his daughter, Tucker's entire face lights up. The gleam in those silvery-blue eyes is evidence Julia is everything to him.

"Yeah, about that. Why didn't you just fly?" I chuckle as I ask. Jane hadn't told me anything other than Tucker was averse to flying. Maybe he has a fear of heights but the edginess coming off Tucker doesn't give the vibe he fears anything.

"I just don't."

If I thought mentioning granddads was an abrupt end to a conversation, the mention of flying slammed the door shut on speaking. Tucker clams up and the remainder of our meal is silent. Instead of savoring my greasy meat on a stick, I choke down the rest of my hot dog, willing away the prickle in my eyes. We had been one wiener on a skewer away from my passenger opening up to me, acting cordial even, but now, we are three bites back with no dessert in sight.

9

Playlist: "St. Louis Blues" - Louis Armstrong

[Tucker]

I am such a dick.

I'd cut off conversation again, when I was actually learning something about Mae. Although she'd proposed we share our life stories, suggesting we be friends, I'd dismissed the possibility. But after hours in the car with my off-key singer and curious sightseer, I am sensing there is more to Mae than I'd given her credit for and there is more I want to know about her.

When she mentioned her sons, she sounded sad; however, I hadn't wanted to discuss Jude myself. The relationship with my oldest child is complicated and complex. He pulled away from me because of the lies he felt he'd been told, and he'd had a right to an extent. He hadn't known the truth as a child. There wasn't a need to expose him to it. Jude was an Ashford in more ways than one and he was also mine in all the ways that mattered.

I want to scream and rant and kick something because this trip is not only taking a painful amount of time, but it is as if I am traveling in reverse. We haven't even left the state of Illinois and I'd already had two vivid memories of my grandfather—harmonicas and hot dogs. Collectively, a strange combination. Separately, they are powerful reminders of a relationship I once held dear and then dreaded.

Marshall Ashford's father had been a powerhouse in the department store industry. His once catalogue-based company was equivalent to internet shopping before the internet was even a thought. Grandfather turned his father's mail-order business into physical stores, separating departments by themes, specifically fashion and home furnishings. Ashford's provided babywear to formal attire, and kitchenware to bedroom sets. Coming to an Ashford's was an event, especially in an era when people dressed more formally for shopping excursions. We were a

L.B. Dunbar

dynasty until the internet was born and a specific monopoly began selling quality items for less with direct delivery to a shopper's front porch. Online purchasing was the death of my great grandfather's dream.

"I'm guessing the world's largest ketchup bottle is out, as you're a self-respecting Chicagoan," Mae says interrupting my thoughts. My laptop is open once more, but this day feels like a bust. I haven't gotten a thing done other than my morning phone call to Mach and a few emails answered. Every time I'm back in a groove, Mae stops on this road trip from hell and my concentration is for shit.

"That would be a firm pass," I mumble.

With the window still cracked, the fresh scent of her wafts through this fucking Prius along with some ripe country air. We should be to St. Louis in ninety minutes and the location brings on another wave of memories. I've traveled throughout most of the United States. Rochelle's success took us to the four corners of this country and on some very exciting family vacations. However, I couldn't remember the last time I'd been in St. Louis. The first time, I was in a certain bar near the river.

Slowly, I smile to myself recalling the blues sound and the night some unknown band allowed an even more unknown kid—harmonica in hand—to grace the stage with them.

You got talent, kid.

I'd heard it so many times before and I had enough cocky confidence to believe what I'd been told. Despite what my father thought. Despite what my grandfather said. I was going to make it and make it big.

My smile falters recalling the failure. Squinting out the window, I watch the scenery shift as we near the border of Illinois. Eventually, Mae detours once more and I read the sign for Old Chain of Rocks Bridge.

"Where are we going?" I ask, like a petulant child. At this rate, I'll be lucky to make California by a Wednesday in the next month.

"We're going to walk to Missouri." She must be kidding me, but the giddy sound of her voice tells me she's not exactly joking. She's rolled with the punches I've dealt today, and I give her credit for not dumping my ass a few times along the way. "Last stop before St. Louis," she states when she stops the car in a parking lot.

62

"Seriously, what are we doing here?"

"Seriously. We are walking to Missouri." Mae exits the car and stretches her arms over her head, then twists at the waist. She can't possibly be sore. We haven't sat in this car long enough in my opinion. However, I don't miss a peek of her lower back, all smooth skin with a distinct dip of her spine disappearing into her shorts. She has nice legs, I'll give her that. I've had to fight the pull that drew my attention to them on the numerous stops we've made. I also notice her backside—well-rounded globes filling out her jean shorts—as she bends forward to touch her toes, and that's my cue to get out of Louie. Popping open my door, I step out and narrow my eyes in the direction of a bridge that curves over the Mississippi River. People on bike and foot make the trek up the bridge.

"You can't be serious," I state a little louder.

"You can stay in the car," she says, as she did back at the museum. That was only this morning and yet it feels like days ago.

"Mae, this is ridiculous. We can't keep stopping every hour. I need to get to California."

"And I *need* to walk to Missouri." She nods in the direction of the bridge and the land on the other side of the river. "Do you have something more appropriate to walk in?"

I've removed my suit coat and rolled up my shirt sleeves, but my hard-soled, Italian leather shoes will not be the most comfortable to cross a bridge in. I have workout clothes in my bag, and I'll need to hit the gym hard once we stop at tonight's hotel. The tension in me has built to volcanic proportions.

"I'm good," I say, refusing to give in to another one of Mae's whims.

She eyes me up and down and I wonder what she sees. Her expression is evidence of what she *thinks* of me. She wants to pitch me into that river and watch me drown.

"Suit yourself," she mutters, as she did this morning. Then she shrugs and I hate that motion more than anything. The sign of indifference suggests she really doesn't care about me or my opinion, and for some reason, the possibility pisses me off.

"Mae, come on. We need to keep moving."

"We are. Over the bridge." Mae moves two fingers in midair in a walking motion. She isn't dressed in athletic attire herself, but the determination in her eyes says everything. She's crossing that bridge with or without me.

"Mae," I groan.

"Look, I'll let you pick the stops in Missouri."

This is not a consolation, but an idea sparks. I'll skip the entire state, driving straight on for the next one.

"But we aren't driving straight through."

"Fuck," I moan as she's clearly read my mind.

Mae slowly smiles while she stares at me. Then she huffs and finally she chuckles, shaking her head. I don't know what she's thinking but whatever it is, I've made her laugh, and the sound is doing strange things to me. My skin prickles. My heart beats faster. My fingers twitch. I've never wanted to run my fingers over piano keys as much as I do at this moment, hoping to chase Mae's laugh and match it to sharps and flats for a song.

Mae steps forward, interrupting the hum lingering in my head, and I spin on my hard-soled shoes, following her. Like a dog being taunted by a bone on a pull string, I'm starting to sense I might follow Mae anywhere, if she'll keep laughing.

+ + +

We take our time, especially as her flat shoes and my dressy ones are not conducive to power walking. The distance is a mile over and another one back, and we saunter among the other walkers and the bike riders. Mae stays quiet as we begin the ascent up the bridge. A placard by the entrance explained how the bridge was part of the original route. Due to necessary renovations, the historic landmark no longer allows motorized vehicles, only foot-powered ones.

"I grew up in Missouri," Mae says as we take our first step over the mighty Mississippi River dividing Illinois from her home state. "In a little town called River City in the southeast corner of the state. My mother still lives there."

"Next you're going to tell me we need to detour to see Mommy and Daddy." I exhale and slip my hands into my pockets. I do not have the patience for additional stops.

Mae gazes forward and narrows her eyes. "My dad left when I was a child, leaving our mother to raise us."

Shit. "I'm sorry, Mae. That was…insensitive." I can be an asshole, and this proves it once again. Mae shrugs in that manner I despise.

"It was a long time ago. Had Granddad as my father figure, but he's gone now, too." The sorrowful depth to her voice tells me she misses him.

"I'm sorry," I say again, because what else can I say? Her sad tone hints she was close to this paternal figure, and I'm reminded once more of my grandfather. I shouldn't ask. I don't want to ask, reminding myself I don't want to know more about Mae. I don't want to cross the personal line, but I can't fight the next question. "Besides Jane, how many brothers and sisters do you have?"

"We have an older brother, Garrett. Then comes Jane, me, and my younger sister Lindee."

I'm the only legitimate Ashford heir, but I don't mention it. The pressure was unbearable when I was young.

"Are you close with your mom?"

Mae sighs and squints into the distance. "My mother believes I should have stayed married to my ex." Mae pauses, and I admit it's not what I expected her to say.

"Why?" There were a hundred reasons why I thought my parents should have divorced when I was a child. First and foremost should have been their lack of desire to have a child—*me*.

"Adam had not only one affair but two, but it's the fact *he* stayed. He never left me, so she believes I shouldn't have left him. She thought I should have remained married to him despite learning about the second one. I disagreed." Bitterness rings through Mae's words, and I hear the hurt at her mother's lack of support. For my part, I want to pummel the man. *Who cheats on Mae?* She's been good-natured enough with my

65

assholeness, plus she's pretty, and those eyes… Plus, any man should be proud to have Mae smile at him like she does.

The thought presses on my sternum. Mae has smiled at me a few times today, and I've shot her down at every curve of those lips.

"Why did you stay with him after the first one?" I ask, not wanting to be intrusive but truly curious. My own mother stayed after repeated infidelity from my father, but I knew her reasoning. *Money.*

Mae shrugs again and I step before her, placing my hands on her shoulders to stop us from walking. "Don't shrug this off. You shouldn't have had to take one affair, let alone two."

Mae looks up at me with those sky-blue eyes and my knees feel like the liquid rippling below this bridge.

"He made me promises and I was foolish enough to believe him." Mae turns her head, but I grip her chin and force her to look back at me. "Fool me once, right? Shame on him. But fool me twice?" She shakes her head, and whispers, "Shame on me."

"Shame on him again. He was the fool, Mae, and he shouldn't have given you false promises. He should have kept his vow to love and honor you as his wife."

Her eyes fill with tears, and she rapidly blinks, swallowing hard as well. "That might be the nicest thing anyone has ever said to me." Her voice is small and her lids lower. A tear leaks out but she's quick to swipe it away.

"I'm sorry that happened to you, sunshine." I should tell her about Rochelle. I should admit the awful truth that's been locked inside me for years, but I don't. I stare at Mae with my fingers wrapped over her shoulders and my hand at her chin, desperate to pull her toward me and enfold her in my arms. The pain in her eyes mirrors the ache in my chest, but I don't do anything to soothe her.

Instead, she speaks around a strangled giggle. "You called me sunshine." Slowly, she grins again. Her eyes are brighter than ever with tears inside them and my heart thumps faster.

"Well, you are a ray among many," I say and Mae scoffs.

"Now, who's flirting with who?"

Ready to defend myself, Mae's arched brow suggests she's joking, and she pulls free from my hands, which kept her an arm's length away.

"Let's keep walking," she says, brushing past me while I'm frozen in place a moment, missing the feel of her under my palms and watching her step a few paces away from me.

No man in his right mind would let her walk away from him. No man should have ever cheated on her, hurt her, or made her feel unworthy. Those expressive eyes say it all.

Disappointment. Distrust. Disbelief in herself.

I see it because I recognize it.

It's how I've felt about myself.

+ + +

When we finally cross the bridge for automobiles leading to Missouri, Mae bypasses downtown St. Louis and pulls into a small motel just outside the city.

"What is this?" I ask for what I feel is the millionth time today.

"It's tonight's accommodations," Mae announces as I skeptically eye the brick houses that are no bigger than a king-sized bed.

"You're kidding, right?"

"Nope," she says with the straightest face before chuckling.

"I am not staying here," I warn her, tipping my head to glance out the window again.

"Suit yourself. I don't think that backseat will be comfortable, but you do you."

I glare back at her. "Take me to the Hilton downtown."

"I'm not a freaking chauffeur and I am not dropping you off someplace else."

"You don't have to drop me off. *We* can both get rooms there."

"*We* are not getting rooms there. I'm staying here." Mae opens her door and steps out and I follow on the opposite side of the car.

"Mae, take me to a decent hotel."

She scans the small buildings and stops her gaze on the sign which clearly states 'motel' on it. "I am not driving you to a hotel and then driving back here."

"Exactly. We'll both stay there."

"No," she adamantly states but I'm already cutting her off.

"Yes." A heavy pause falls between us. "Is this about money? I'll pay for your room."

Her mouth drops open at my suggestion, but before she utters a word, she turns on her heels and heads for the front office, another low building detached from the rest of them. She has to be kidding me, but this doesn't feel like a joke, and I stalk after her, entering the small office after a sharp yank on the front door.

"We'll need two rooms, please," I hear Mae state and the statement crushes my ire a second. *Of course*, we need two rooms. However, my head is arguing with other parts of my body. The part of my body that has no say in being Mae's roommate.

I am not sleeping in the same room as her.

Based on the size of these buildings, I can't imagine more than one bed fits in them anyway which leads to the argument...I am not sleeping in the same *bed* as Mae.

The thought of *not* doing it, has the thought of doing it springing to the forefront of my mind, and my eyes drop to Mae's backside again. Her legs are short but toned and the backs of her knees beg for me to bend her there, bring her down to the floor and take her from behind.

The image almost knocks me back through the front door and I stagger a second. The subtle sway causes Mae to turn her head in my direction, glancing over her shoulder at me, and another wave of images mixes with the first. Mae looking at me as she is, her hair draping over one shoulder, her chin aimed over the other. Her head on a pillow as I fuck her senseless from behind.

Jesus. I swipe a hand down my face as if it will erase the vision and calm the raging hard-on I'm suddenly sporting in my suit pants. I need to get away from this woman because I know the reason I want to fuck her. I want to drill some sense into her. We should not be staying in this dinky motel where I can't be convinced the sheets are clean. There isn't even turn down service or a coffee bar in the rooms.

My hotel snobbery is showing, and another memory comes to mind of three guys piling into one room, not too dissimilar from a place like this. We were high on music, women, and something not legal at the time. Laughter filters through my head. Lawson Colt and his rich Southern voice. Denton Chance and his soft Georgia twang.

Fuck.

Scrubbing two hands down my face, I reach out for a key Mae hands me. An old-fashioned metal key on a rhombus shaped, plastic fob with the motel name and room number stamped on it. Mae will be in number one; I'm in number four. Instantly, I don't like the distance between rooms but acknowledge the separation is for the best. Tugging the key from her hand, I turn for the office exit and cross the small lot toward Mae's car. I didn't offer my credit card, but I'll come back later. I need to get away from Mae and the memories this godforsaken road trip keeps bringing forward.

"Did you want to grab some dinner?" Mae asks, her voice sweet and quiet as she comes up behind me.

"No," I toss over my shoulder, waiting for the click of her trunk to allow me to open the hatch. Hastily, I reach for my bag. I should help her with hers and I grumble, "Which one of these do you want?"

"I can get my own bags," she says in that huffy voice she has when she's been offended by me. *Suit yourself,* I want to snap, mimicking her, but instead, I snag one suitcase and tug it forward. Dropping the bag to the ground on its wheels, I pull up the handle and Mae takes it from me. She doesn't argue whether this is the case she wants or not. I close the trunk lid with a slam and notice Mae is already stepping away from me. I should offer to eat with her. I should explain why I don't want dinner with her.

But mostly, I should get away from her before I follow her into her room and beg her to let me fuck her.

"Will you still go out for dinner?" The idea of her eating alone shouldn't upset me.

L.B. Dunbar

Mae sighs, pausing several feet away, keeping her back to me. "You know, I'm not feeling so great after the dog on a stick." She gazes over her shoulder again, making me think things I shouldn't. Envisioning images I shouldn't. "So, I think I'll call it a night. I'm tired."

The time isn't *that* late. The sun hasn't even set yet but we're well past the dinner hour.

"Okay. See you in the morning." I shouldn't be holding my breath, anxiously waiting on her response. She'll still be here in the morning, right?

"See you in the morning," she mutters before continuing to her room, and the statement has no business doing what it's doing to me.

Which is offering a hint of reassurance she isn't ready to dump me. Yet.

10

Playlist: "St. Louis Song" - Erin Bode

[Mae]

After a check-in call with my boys, who hardly had more than a few words to say, my ex-husband took the phone and had plenty of remarks about my absence. Taking excessive deep breaths, I hang up on him and call my business partner, Pam, to check in.

Pam had worked at Mae's Flowers as a second job but eventually became a good friend and my full-time manager. Once she married the love of her life, a writer of dark, scary stories, she had bought into the business. Her partnership has been invaluable in more ways than one. She's one of the few people I trust in my life.

When Adam and I divorced there was no way to amicably share the business with him. Mae's Flowers was under the umbrella of Eden Landscaping, originally owned and operated by my in-laws. The easiest way to claim the business I'd built from the dirt up was to buy out Adam's portion of the joint ownership. Loyalty toward my in-laws had me biting my tongue about Adam and his shenanigans with business funds. I couldn't afford to buy Adam out without loans or a deficit to the existing company, so Pam and a silent investor offered to buy in.

Next, I call Jane.

"How goes the road?" she teases after greeting me.

"I don't know how you work for him."

"Mr. Ashford?"

"Call him fucking Tucker. That's his name."

"Actually, at the office he goes by Ashe with an e from Volde-*Mach*." How had I not known this nickname for Tucker? And why isn't my sister calling him such a name? Then, I chuckle at another one of her labels for Mach.

"Anyway..." she drones.

"He's so hot and cold." Do I admit to my sister that one minute he's flirty and the next he's like a frozen pizza?

"He's had a lot go on in his life." Jane defends Tucker's behavior.

"Haven't we all? And just what does that mean?"

"I don't think I should be the one to tell you. Just give him time. He'll open up."

Sure, he will and then he'll slam the door in my face as he has with each hint into who he is.

"How is the trip?" Jane asks when I remain silent.

"Horrible." We've bypassed so many places I wanted to stop and explore, not to mention my spirit trip to reflect on all things isn't quite how I envisioned it going. Horrible might be too strong a word, but I am frustrated. "I just don't understand him. Sure, he's nice to look at, but how can he be so aloof underneath that pretty skin?"

"Oh, are we back to talking about Tucker?" Jane teases. "Careful Mae."

"What's there to be careful about?"

"Don't go falling in love with him."

I scoff. "Of course not." I sound exactly like him. Love is the furthest thing from my mind. "I'd like to throttle him instead."

"What was that? Thrust with him?" Jane laughs and the sister I recognize comes through the line. Not that passive creature saying *yes sir,* and calling Tucker *Mr. Ashford,* but the lighthearted woman underneath her power suits.

I laugh as well and recall Tucker's reaction when I told him about Adam. I stayed married because I was afraid to leave, at first. I was afraid Adam and his family would take from me all I'd built. Mae's Flowers had my name on it. The garden center had my heart and sweat in it. I didn't want to lose my business even if I lost my husband.

And Adam wasn't only a liar and a cheat, but also a thief; however, I didn't share that part with Tucker. It was hard enough admitting my husband had not one but two public affairs. In a small town, news travels, but somehow, I hadn't gotten the broadcast. I'd had my suspicions of the first infidelity but never had proof. When the second one occurred, Adam wasn't half as circumspect. The red in our financials proved his doings.

My then-manager Pam was the one to catch the discrepancies. She wasn't an accountant by trade and even second guessed herself at first, but she did the bookkeeping, and the bottom line was that Adam had stolen money from the company to pay for his extra-marital activities.

When Tucker told me I deserved better than Adam, the comment almost brought me to my knees, and on those knees, I'd have begged him to kiss me. For a minute, I thought he might meet my mouth with his, or at least pull me into a tight embrace, holding me against his firm chest. I would have settled for a hug. However, he didn't do anything but keep me at arm's length and give me sweet reassurance.

My eyes track toward the window where I have a view of Tucker's room. Narrowing my gaze, I notice a car parked before number four and Tucker steps out the door. He leans toward the dark car I can't distinguish and then hops into the backseat. *What is it with him and the backseat?* As the car circles through the small parking lot, I step back from the window but watch as the driver pulls onto the street.

Is he going to dinner after all? Is he going out on the town? Is he leaving the motel to stay someplace else? Is he finding another ride to take him to California?

"Jane." I choke on my sister's name. "I think he just ditched me."

"What? He wouldn't do that. He just checked in with Mach." Surprisingly, she calls Mr. Wright Mach behind his back but doesn't do the same with Tucker. On that note, how does Jane know Tucker checked in and what is she doing with Mach this late at night?

"Are you still at work?"

"I just had a few things I wanted to finish up."

"Jane," I groan. My sister works too hard.

"He didn't leave you," Jane says. The wording hits me hard in the chest. There are psychology case studies on little girls and their daddy-abandonment issues. I don't have those concerns regarding my father, but some might argue I do have anxiety for another reason. While Adam hadn't physically left me, he'd left our marriage long before it was officially over. I didn't like to think of my life that way, but the truth was there. I'd been sleeping with my husband, but he wasn't really mine. He

73

was the selfish one, doing what he wanted, when he wanted. He stole my heart and my hard-earned money.

"How do you know?" I ask, my weak voice cracking. Would Tucker leave the motel for a nicer place to sleep? Would he leave me here to continue on my own? Isn't that what I'd wanted all along? I wanted to be alone. But did I really?

"I just know," Jane says, interrupting my stream of unspoken questions.

Ideally, taking the trip I'm on would be more exciting if I could share the experience. If I had that husband to match his wife with our two children on a road trip to see the country. But I don't have that husband. And I don't have two children interested in sharing this adventure with me.

Why were all the men in my life so selfish?

Instantly, I regret the thought concerning my boys. They are children. Teenagers. Neither matters. They have their own lives to live as they should, and I have mine. That was the point of this trip. I was taking *me* back.

Exhaustion hits in a heavy wave. "I'm going to take a bath and head to bed." I should probably eat something healthy like a salad to clear my belly, but the idea of getting back in the car and searching for a restaurant doesn't sound appealing.

"You okay?" The apprehension in Jane's voice reminds me she's the worrier of my sisters. She's the second mother filled with concern for her chicks.

"I'll be fine," I tell her. I always am. Somehow.

+ + +

To my surprise, I find Tucker outside my motel room bright and early. He's wearing aviator glasses and leaning against my car. Dressed in jeans and a T-shirt, he looks like a rock star and it's not the first time my breath catches at his appearance. The hitch also comes with the shocking relief he's here. I went to bed thinking he'd honestly disappeared, and I wouldn't see him again. I'd slept horribly.

"Good morning," he says, tipping the sunglasses to the top of his head as he stands straighter. A leather string sticks out near the collar of his shirt, and I wonder what he wears around his neck, hidden behind the cotton tee. He holds a to-go cup in each hand. "Mochaccino?"

Softly, I laugh. "Where did you find one of those around here?" He tips his head and I notice a coffee shop across the busy street.

"I had to tell them how to make it, so I have no idea if it will be any good." He offers the cup and I take it.

"How did you know I drank mochaccino?" I typically don't, but he wouldn't know that either. He wrinkles his nose in that way he does.

"You smelled like mocha when we met."

I laugh again. *Hardly an official meeting.* I'm doubly surprised he recognized the scent.

"Shall we?" He tips his head toward the car at his side.

"You're the navigator today," I state, reminding him he can pick our stops in Missouri but there must be stops.

"I don't know anything about this highway or your plans."

"No plans. That's the joy in this trip. As far as the highway, it's stop when you see something of interest." Tucker stares at me, and slowly, the corner of his mouth curls as it does, one side hiking slightly higher than the other. Those silver eyes narrow on me.

"I'll let you know when to stop then," he says. *Did his voice just drop?* The tenor sounds deeper than normal, and I dismiss the gravelly timbre sending shivers up the inside of my thighs and landing on a spot that has no business throbbing.

Tucker pops the driver's side door handle and holds the door open for me. He settles our bags in the trunk, and I wait for him to round the car, expecting him to climb in the back as he did yesterday. When he opens the front passenger door and slips in beside me, I stare at him.

"It's Saturday," he says, looking back at me.

It certainly is and Saturday looks so good on him. My eyes roam his attire once more and my mouth waters, but it's not in anticipation of the chocolaty drink in my cup. That thigh-hugging denim. The tight fit of his tee. Even the bead and leather strip around his wrist. He puts sexy in a Saturday.

Pulling my gaze from him, I start the ignition and we re-route for the iconic highway. I'd double back for the famous Gateway Arch, but I've been to St. Louis two other times for hockey tournaments for Wyatt, and both times the gate to the west was closed. While a third time might be the charm, I don't want to tempt fate. Besides, the hour is early, and I doubt the historic place is open. There's also a museum of transportation in the city, but this is a road trip and I'm letting the road be my education.

11

MISSOURI – DAY 2

Playlist: "The Thrill Is Gone" – B.B. King

[Tucker]

"You seemed surprised to see me this morning," I eventually say as we barrel down I-44, which covers portions of the original route.

We've been quiet as we sip our drinks and adjust to sitting next to one another. Music fills the car once again and the smokey blues matches our pace. Although it's Saturday and I typically put in a couple hours of work even on the weekends, today I let business slide. Besides, my early morning wake-up call from Jude put me in a funk.

"You cannot miss Julia's day," my son chided me.

"I'm not missing it. I'm on my way."

"This is ridiculous, Dad. You need to get over your flying phobia."

Oh, to be twenty-seven, fearless and carefree. Also, to be the insensitive bastard my son has turned into. For too long, I took the blame for, and brunt of, his attitude. He'd been lied to his entire life. He struggled with the truth, but I'd done what I did to give him the spoiled life he's had, and I was over his ungratefulness.

"You left last night."

My neck swivels so I look over at Mae. Today she wears a loose flowing shirt in thin material and another pair of jean shorts. Flat strappy sandals cover her feet, and a low ponytail binds her chestnut-colored hair. She looks young for her age, and I marvel again that she has children who are in college. I didn't miss the hesitancy in her voice and the roll of her throat before I open up to her.

"I didn't leave. I went out." There's a difference, but Mae's face pinches as her fingers clench around the steering wheel. Rubbing a hand down my jean-covered thigh, I wonder for a second if I should share where I went.

L.B. Dunbar

"There's a place I'm familiar with in the city that's down near the river. We were so close I decided to Uber there." Once I'd learned that Strings was still open, I had to see the old place. It's exposed brick interior with low ceilings and fluorescent colored stage lights was exactly the same and yet entirely different than the place had been over twenty-five years ago. Time seemed to have stood still and it felt like only yesterday instead of half a lifetime.

"Was it fun?" Mae's voice is still quiet and I'm wondering what she's really trying to ask me.

"Yeah, I had a good time." Suddenly, I feel guilty for not asking Mae to join me. She said yesterday she wasn't familiar with blues music, but that doesn't mean she didn't like the sound, as her playlist holds several songs. I just wasn't certain she'd like the place. I wasn't certain I could enter Strings myself, but I had to see it. Like so many awakening memories, the old blues bar called to me.

Mae remains silent, and I decide to offer a little more. "I…There's a guy I once knew who used to play there. A band actually. Blues music is the forte of Strings, the place where I went, and I just wanted to see it again."

Mae softly smiles but it isn't reaching her eyes. The blue iris isn't flashing like those neon lights last night.

"Why?" I ask, puzzled by her quiet and the weak curve of her lips.

"It's nothing. Just curious." Did she really think I left her? I wouldn't do that.

"Did you think something else happened last night?" I don't know why I can't let it go but something is on her mind, and I want to know what it is. Mae shrugs and I swear to God I want to demand she pull over. "Tell me."

Mae turns her head for a second at my sharp command. Her fingers tighten on the wheel once more before her sight returns to the road.

"I thought maybe…" She exhales. "It doesn't matter what I thought. Your business is your business."

"Mae, come on. Tell me."

"I thought you went out to sleep with someone." Her eyes close for half a second and I'm grateful my coffee cup balances in my hand on my thigh or I'd be wearing coffee as I have two days in a row around this woman.

"Sunshine." I softly chuckle. "I did not go out looking to get laid." Would I have liked to fuck someone? Absolutely. But I have a strong sense that *that* someone is sitting next to me being all cute in her jealousy and anxiety over me sleeping with someone random.

Mae shifts in her seat. "Like I said, it's not my business." Her quiet tone sends a small current of regret over my chest. I should have invited her to come out with me. I should tell her the rest of the story. How amazing it was to hear live blues music. How energized I feel after the sound seeped under my skin, like a small, hidden cavern inside me has some light shining into it for the first time in a long time. Without thought, I reach over for Mae, brushing back hair that's come loose from her ponytail and scooping the fine strands behind her ear.

"I wouldn't leave you, Mae."

She nods as she swallows hard and my fingers coast along the exposed column of her neck. Her skin is so soft and the tempting fragrance of her floats around me, invading my nose as we sit beside one another. The tips of my fingers drift to her shoulder before slowly pulling away from her. I miss her skin instantly but as much as I want to linger, placing my hand around her nape and keeping it there, Mae seems sensitive this morning.

"What did you do last night?" I ask.

"I made some phone calls. Then took a bath and went to bed." The thought of Mae naked and wet is like a jolt of caffeine, hyperextending a part of my body that's desperate for attention. I've just had my first touch of her soft skin and now I imagine the rest of her, water lapping over her tan flesh, parts of her whiter than the rest. Her nipples are a rosy pink in my head and her pussy matches that tender color. Leaning forward, I shift my hard-on as best I can while sitting so close to Mae.

"Did you talk to Jane?" She answered Mach's phone when I called last night. They were both still at the office. Mach will be attending Julia's wedding, but he's flying out next Friday morning. I should have braved my fear and flown with him. He promised to get me drunk and assist me on and off the plane, but I didn't want to tempt fate.

"I did." She acts as if that simple sentence covers everything. What did they talk about? Did they discuss the trip? Did Mae mention me?

"Are you close to your sister?" I didn't have siblings in a traditional sense growing up, so the dynamic of them always intrigues me.

"Jane and my relationship has ebbed and flowed because we're pretty opposite. As we've grown older, we've grown closer. Unfortunately, Jane and our other sister, Lindee, butt heads. They're too similar in personality. Plus, Jane likes to play mother hen and that annoys Lindee."

"You mentioned a brother."

"Garrett? He's the golden child. As the only son and oldest Fox sibling, he can do no wrong in Mom's eyes. She's blind to the fact he basically left home and never looked back. He only visits once a year." Mae huffs. "He has a condo in California actually, but he permanently resides in Georgia now."

"That's a big shift," I say, chuckling at the extreme of one coast compared to another.

"He fell in love." Mae's smile grows more genuine. She's happy for her brother and that smile suggests love is the answer to everything life altering.

"It happens," I jest but my voice falls flat. Had I loved Rochelle? In some ways, I had. We'd grown together then shattered apart. I hadn't so much as fallen out of love with her as I'd felt betrayed by her. When I think of what Mae told me about her husband, I realize she might understand the duplicity I felt. I don't know how Mae could have taken her husband back after an affair, but I realize that pretty words spoken as promises can send mixed messages. Rochelle was only allowed to fool me once.

We continue on as the moody blues tunes fill the car before Mae skips a song.

"Does that say Meramec Caverns?" I point at the sign painted on the roof of a barn. Mae doesn't respond but her smile grows. "We should stop."

"What?" she laughs.

"We should see the caves."

"They're kind of commercial." She side-eyes me and I recall her saying she grew up in Missouri.

"Have you been?"

"No. But if you've seen one cave you've seen them all, right?" Her voice hesitates.

Slowly, I smile. "You said I could pick where we visit in Missouri and I want to stop at the caves. What are you afraid of?"

"Bats. Small spaces. The dark. Your typical top three."

"Bats?" I laugh. "They won't hurt you."

Mae shivers beside me. "When I was a kid, I was opening a barn door when a bat fell from the hinge and landed on my arm." Mae extends her arm, keeping one hand on the steering wheel. Her forearm is upright, and I want to trace my finger down her skin again. "The thing flipped back and forth."

Mae releases the wheel and slaps her other hand upside down and then palm side down to imitate the action of the bat.

"Sunshine," I snap as the car veers left. "Hands on the wheel at all times."

My errant driver laughs, clutching ten and two on the steering wheel once more, but she gives a full body shiver in her seat at the recall of her bat experience. I can't help myself and I reach for those wayward hairs again, tickling my fingertips along her neck.

"Bats only go for here," I state, running my fingers over her flesh, feeling her pulse near her throat. Legendary vampires would want a bite of her and so do I.

Mae laughs and tucks her chin to her shoulder, pinning my tickling fingers against her skin.

"No caves," she says, her voice lighter than it had been earlier.

"Yes caves."

"Oh, look a giant red rocking chair," she announces at the roadside advertisement for it.

"After the caves," I say, wiggling a brow at my driver and placing my hand on her wrist as if I'll tug her arm to make us exit.

"Fine," she grumbles but a smile still fills her voice.

L.B. Dunbar

12

Playlist: "Cars" – Gary Numan

[Mae]

The caves were pretty cool and chilly, and I wasn't prepared in my thin shirt and shorts. Being with Tucker as he soaked in the hollowed spaces and dangling stalactites was like seeing a new person. He was different today, like an unfolded map, revealing more and more land as it opened.

Our stop also felt like a date, especially when he'd place his arm around me and tuck me into his side or rub his hands up and down my bare arms to warm me up. I tried to shake off the idea several times, but the thought just wouldn't pass. We were two people sharing an experience, exploring caves, and learning their history, and it was the very definition of a date, especially when he touched me. He even took a few selfies of us together.

Adam and I hadn't gone to typical places when we dated although we'd had our share of movies and dinners. Being from a small town surrounded by natural beauty, many of our dates included outdoor activities like snowmobile riding and downhill skiing in the winter and boating or hiking in the summer.

Of course, summer was our busiest season and with marriage, children, and a business, dates fell further and further down the list of things to do. Taking two weeks off during the summer had been no small feat this year, but Pam had insisted I needed time away.

"You deserve this time. Explore. Seek. Renew." She sounded like a New Age pamphlet for spiritual revival, but Pam also understood I needed to get away and no time would be the perfect time. I couldn't keep waiting for the right moment. *"Just go."*

My best friend also knew I'd always wanted to take this great American road trip, and what a trip today's adventure was turning out to be. We took the cave tour but skipped all the extra stuff. However, I didn't want to pass up the gift shop. Once again, I couldn't decide on a souvenir and eventually walked out without making a purchase.

Traveling onward, we reach the giant red rocking chair within minutes of leaving the caverns. Pulling up before the Fanning Route 66 Outpost, I recount the history of this chair as we stand before it like I'm some expert tour guide.

"It originally was listed in the Guinness Book of Records as the tallest rocking chair. However, another one was built someplace else and took the title. For the longest time, this chair held the record as the second largest." I softly chuckle. "But I don't know why you'd brag about being in second place."

"That's cynical of you," Tucker says, and his comment startles me.

I'm not being cynical; I'm being honest. I'd been put in second place to Adam's interests. Business. Women. Second place was not worth bragging about.

"This chair needed to rock in order to stay on the record books but the owner or welder or someone, I forget who, was afraid the thing might tip over and crush visitors." I point to the braces that bind the chair in place. "Now, it's stationary and it's been painted red, giving this old icon a new boast as the red rocking chair on the route." I sound like a brochure.

Thinking of the new life breathed into this popular roadside attraction, a concept hits me. Some things are forgotten along the way. Other things are restored. This trip was my restoration tour.

"Restoration tour?" Tucker scoffs.

I hadn't realized I'd said that part out loud and I squint up at the rocker. "I just think sometimes you need a reboot, a new purpose."

Tucker glances up at the red structure. "And you got all that out of a giant rocking chair?"

"I got all that from what I want next in my life." A reset. I don't need to turn back the clock. My children are the number one reason I wouldn't go backward. The idea of erasing them isn't something I'd ever consider. But it's my time, and I need to start the timer over.

Tucker turns his head, staring at me for a moment like I've grown a second one, and once again, I decide he can't possibly understand. He's standing there all rock star handsome without a hair out of place and those silvery eyes, and I can't imagine he knows anything about reinventing himself. Starting over again. Rebuilding his life.

"Maybe you should let me drive a bit?" He holds out his hand for the keys, but I shake my head. "Come on, Mae. I promise not to run us off the road."

"You'll probably just keep us only on the road," I snark, letting go of my deep thoughts about change.

I'm holding the key fob in my hand, not having bothered with my bag as we only stopped for a quick photo. Tucker wiggles his fingers and I reach forward as if I'm going to give him the key and then retract. Tucker is fast, though, and he snatches my wrist. We wrestle a second like my boys do before I lift my arm and drop the keys down my shirt. The drop was all luck, and my breasts catch the fob on the edge of my bra where the suddenly achy globes are pressed together. Tucker freezes, glaring at my shirt which looks like I've grown a third boob because of the small bulge.

"You did not just do that," he says, tone flat. Shock fills his face before the corner of his mouth curves in that way it does, drawing one side higher than the other. "If you think I'm afraid to go fishing in there, you're sadly mistaken, sunshine."

I can't breathe. I can't even tease him, dare him. Words are caught in my throat as his eyes hold mine before they lower for the awkward spot where a key fob is stuck in my bra.

If I thought Tucker would just dip his hand through the wide expanse of my collar and tug out the keys, I am mistaken. Instead, he drops the wrist he's been holding and steps even closer to me. One hand lands on my hip, while the other goes for the hem of my loose shirt. Long fingers and a warm palm connect with the skin at my waist, and I suck in air. I'm not smooth and flat on my belly, and suddenly, I want this rocking chair to fall over and crush me as the builder once feared. Tucker cannot touch me where I'm lumpy and worn from the road trip of having children.

However, he ignores my sharp intake of breath and skims his hand higher underneath my shirt. My breathing accelerates, forcing my chest to rise and fall quicker. Any second, I'm going to be embarrassingly exposed to anyone close by and yet, I don't care. I want him to rip this shirt from me and cover each breast in turn with those large hands of his. I want him kneading each heavy swell and pinching my nipples...hard.

He continues to travel straight up the middle of my body and we both watch as his hand disappears under the loose material. Only his hand separates us from being chest to chest. His fingers hook over the center of my bra, and he gently tugs at the material, causing me to lean forward, almost knocking into him. With a kick of his fingers, the fob flicks upward and pops out of the wide collar, nearly clocking me in the chin. Tucker catches the key with the hand that had been on my hip, but that first hand...his fingers still hold my bra. One long finger skims upward along the edge of silky fabric, tracing back and forth, then left to right over the hint of cleavage exposed above the cups.

Tucker leans forward, bringing the side of his face against mine and his mouth near my ear.

"Mae." His voice is strained. "Don't tease me."

With that he releases his hold on my bra, drags his hand down my middle to my waist and steps back. He holds the fob up like it's a victory trophy and then tucks the key into his pocket. Stepping to the side, he waves out a hand for me to lead us to the car and a few seconds pass before my shaky knees can bend to walk me forward.

+ + +

We remain quiet after the key-fob-bra-incident and Tucker drives us along the iconic road until we reach Devil's Elbow Bridge, another bridge with a sharp turn in the middle but one that allows cars along the classic route. After crossing it, we weave along until we come to Munger Moss Motel, a mom-and-pop motel still open and operating to serve weary travelers. Being midday, we aren't ready to stop for the night, but I ask Tucker to pull into the parking lot anyway. A few classic cars sit in the lot, and to my surprise, Tucker is eager to walk around them.

"Now this is the kind of ride we should have for a road trip." His smile is wide as he inspects a car I only recognize as an Oldsmobile

L.B. Dunbar

because it bears the name. The vehicle is long and wide, mean and classy in cheery red with black interior. Tucker's admiration brightens his face and for the first time he seems on board with our travels. "This is a car for cruising in."

Unfortunately for me, all I can think about is that extra spacious backseat and what I want this man to do to me against the long leather bench. My heart still races from his fingers on my skin. A phantom sensation of his touch lingers against the swell of my cleavage, and my nipples remain hard. Thankfully, my blouse is loose enough not to give away the peaks protruding against the silk of my bra, but my breasts ache.

I haven't been touched by anyone else in a long time. While I've gone on dates, nothing progressed further than an occasional awkward goodnight kiss. Living in a small community, most men my age are married or simply not someone I'd be interested in long term. I tell myself it doesn't matter that I don't date often. I'm busy with Mae's Flowers, but some nights are lonely, and my battery-operated boyfriend doesn't offer the cuddle I expect after a good orgasm.

When we finally head back to the car—Tucker got caught up in a conversation with a classic car enthusiast—I hold out my hand for the key. "You've insulted Louie with your lust for that beauty." I nod at the car that Tucker learned was a 1966 Oldsmobile 442. He'd circled the machine twice, nearly drooling on the sleek exterior, before breaking away to investigate a second beast of an automobile.

He slips his hands into his jean pockets, one of which holds the fob for the Prius. "Right, and you're the one who named your car." He glances at the bright blue, modern vehicle. The sedan isn't actually mine, but I did name the thing, thinking it made more sense if I pretended to talk to Louie then talk to myself as I knew I'd eventually do on a road trip alone.

Again, I wiggle my fingers.

"Springfield is the next major city. Let me drive and I'll take you to lunch." He almost looks nervous as he asks. At the mention of food, my stomach rumbles. After skipping dinner last night, I am hungry. We have snacks, but you can only eat so many cherry-flavored Nibblers before you get a stomachache.

"You don't need to pay for my meals," I remind him. He bought lunch yesterday and coffee this morning. Despite being a pain-in-the-ass passenger, he isn't along to cover my expenses, which reminds me I didn't get a receipt from the motel last night.

"I know," he says as he did yesterday, and we hold eyes in a staring match.

"Okay," I acquiesce, and his forehead relaxes. His eyes brighten.

"I promise, you'll love it." His excitement is catchy.

Once we settle back in the car, and Tucker starts the ignition, I glance back at the neon sign for the motel.

"Traveling by day you're missing the bright lights of these places," he reminds me. We've already passed another historic landmark motel with quaint, stone cottages named Wagon Wheel Motel. I really wanted to stay a night there but onward we must travel so my companion gets to California on time.

I sigh. "I know, but I'm not good at night driving, and I didn't want to drive alone in the dark anyway." The plan was to be by myself and as a single female I didn't think night driving on unlit roads was a safe idea. Day driving only was a concession I had to make in my trip plans. Streetlamps don't exist along this older highway, not to mention, we aren't exactly passing through populated areas. We've seen vintage gas stations and an old post office, both turned into tourist stops, but nothing that would be open in the later hours.

"You wouldn't stay in a place like this, would you?" I comment. Tucker ducks his head beside me to gain a better view of the sign. He's close to me again, leaning over me and I get a whiff of him. Sharp. Wild. Expensive

"When we first went on tour, these were the only places the budget allowed for, and I swore I'd never stay in a place like this again once I could afford not to." He pulls away from me and I twist to face him.

His choice of words is curious. "What tour?"

Tucker looks straight ahead, over the steering wheel and out the windshield, as his brows pinch. "Did I say tour?"

L.B. Dunbar

"You did. Who was on tour?" And why did he have a budget?

Tucker glances at the gear shift and puts the car in reverse.

"I didn't mean tour," he says, gazing over his shoulder, avoiding his slip-up as the car moves backward. "I just meant when I'd been on the road."

"What road? When you traveled to California the first time?"

Tucker nods as he shifts to drive and checks the main road before pulling onto it. "Yeah, that's what I meant."

Only, he's not convincing, and I wonder what I'm missing.

13

Playlist: "Let the Good Times Roll" – The Cars

[Tucker]

Shit. I hadn't meant to hint I'd been on any kind of tour. I could have covered the slip by saying it had to do with Rochelle's conference schedule, but we haven't talked about my wife, and I don't want to discuss her. Mae hasn't even implied she knows who I was with Rochelle or my life before her.

Over a quarter of a century has passed, and while the guys thought we'd made it big then, we really hadn't. Still, every once in a while, our most famous song hits the radio. I almost always turn it off.

I'm not ready for Mae to know more about me. I'm not certain I'll ever be able to share everything there is to share. There's just so much baggage, and it isn't pretty luggage with designer names and rolling wheels, but the kind that's duct taped with faded stickers and a broken handle.

Despite the moment of weakness where my hands roamed under her shirt, Mae and I have had a great morning. The caves were cool. The ride over the bridge was kind of special, and the stop at the old motel with classic cars had been interesting.

The last thing I want to do is explain to Mae who I once was, because I'm not him anymore. I haven't been him for twenty-plus years.

Springfield is the next major city, and the place is another reminder of where I've been and how far I've come. The area has some great diners and coffee shops, and there's one place I think Mae might enjoy.

As we've driven along the route, I've noticed some of the rundown places along our path and imagine, as I suspect Mae has, that these locations were once spots for travelers to stop over night or fill their tanks with gas.

"It's kind of sad," Mae says as we pass yet another building that looks like it once was someplace special sometime in the past. Now the

L.B. Dunbar

structure is unidentifiable as to what it used to look like. It's simply an abandoned shell with lost history.

"I live in a small town, and small towns really lost out when people started to bypass them because of the interstate," Mae offers, keeping her eyes toward the window.

What affected those mom-and-pop places, like the one we stopped at with the classic cars, were high-rise hotels built more specifically for railway travelers. Then, hotel conglomerates courted traveler bliss, specializing in resort-type visits. Chain motels took over, along with franchise opportunities, and gone were the simple locations offering a warm bed and a night's rest. I fondly recall a few places the band slept when I was on the road with Lawson and Denton. We were three men trying to make the most of a dollar and sell our sound.

That was another lifetime, and I hadn't meant to hint at it.

Mae chatters as we drive into the large city, explaining the history of Route 66 up to this point. She's telling me how Springfield is considered the birthplace of Route 66, and this is a crossroads of some sort. I'm actually content to drive and give her this portion of our travels to explore. Her head whips around, glancing behind us at places we pass, or she reads signs as we near them, offering tidbits here and there. She's a roving tour guide and an encyclopedia of information. She's done her research and disappointment rings out once in a while when her internet searching seems to lead to a dead end.

"So where are we going again?" she asks once the route merges with the major interstate around this larger city.

"You'll see." My voice lifts at the potential surprise and my heart patters. I hope she likes this place. I discovered it about ten years ago when Rochelle was on a conference tour. We'd bussed through ten Midwestern cities that summer and I had escaped to this place for a much-needed hour alone.

When we pull up before the coffee shop that specializes in classic rock music, Mae smiles.

"Coffee?" she says, twisting to look at me.

"Lunch." I press open the driver's side door. Mae's quick to open hers and I should have asked her to wait for me. I could have gotten her door for her. I hate that she accused me of not being a gentleman. I'm all for women's equality and the right to open their own damn doors, but I still want to do it for Mae. Quickly, I stop her from reaching for the coffee shop entrance and tug the door open for her. I don't miss the hint of a smile as she steps inside, and we're enveloped in classic rock music. The philosophy here is that not all coffeehouses are quiet, and this one prides itself on noise.

At the counter, we order sandwiches and take a seat allowing the atmosphere to surround us.

"This place is so cool," Mae says taking in the replica memorabilia and pictures of classic rockers. "You asked me about blues music. Are you a music enthusiast?"

"Something like that," I say. "You have quite an eclectic playlist. I thought you might like this place."

"Music is a universal language. Everyone understands it."

My hands freeze as I reach for my sandwich, and I lower them back to my lap. I consider what she's said and feel those words deep in my soul.

"You mentioned how some things fade away while others are preserved or given new life. Music is the same way. An old song can be revived by a new band's rendition. Other songs just remain classic in their original state. There are fads but music never fades. When you hear a song, it conjures a memory or when you hear one for the first time, it builds a new one. Popular music shifts and changes over time, just like notes on sheet music and yet it's something every person can read. Maybe they don't know how to play an instrument or sing a tune." I arch a brow at Mae, and she chuckles. "But we love a good beat. Music evokes emotion, and our bodies respond."

I pat my chest over my heart in an iambic beat for emphasis. *Thump-thump. Thump-thump.* "It's how people know how to dance."

"Spoken like a true music lover." Mae gives me a broad smile. "But I don't dance." She glances around the coffee shop once more.

"What do you mean you don't dance? Everybody dances." The argument is weak coming from me. I can't remember the last time I did. Perhaps dancing is the wrong word. Our bodies react to rhythm. We sway. We tap. We nod in tandem to a beat we appreciate. Music feeds our souls.

And I wonder how I've ignored the hunger in mine for so long.

Looking around the space myself, noting the posters of famous rockers and bands, I acknowledge there was a time I wanted to be among them. Dreams die, though. Some things are preserved. Some repurposed. And others just disappear with time.

Mae's been watching me, and I weakly smile at her before lifting my sandwich and taking a bite. We listen as we eat and Mae nods at songs she recognizes, grinning between bites of her sandwich. She knows nothing about music history, and still gets most lyrics wrong, but her enthusiasm for a song or a burst of memory when one plays brightens her face. Those blue eyes gleam. That smile sparkles.

I should tell her.

"You mentioned you live in a small town. I feel guilty but I don't even know where you're from exactly," I say.

"Elk Lake City. It's a small town on Lake Michigan in Michigan."

"How did you end up there from Missouri?"

"Marriage," she says as if that explains everything. "What about you?"

"What about me?" Mae already knows I live in Chicago.

"Marriage. You mentioned your kids, but what about your wife?" Her voice lowers, hinting that she knows I'm a widower.

"What did Jane tell you?" My tone is defensive. Mae's sister has been around long enough to know a few things but not the full story. The office once indulged in speculation, but Mach was always the first to shut that shit down.

Mae is equally quick to defend her sister. "Jane didn't tell me anything. All I know about you is you own Impact with Volde-*Mach*. She mentioned you were a widower and *you* told me you have two children. You live in Chicago. That's it."

"Isn't that enough?" I question, knowing full well it's not.

"Because we can't be friends," Mae states, with a huff and a weak grin.

Are we friends? I don't even know what that would mean, but we're definitely something. I've touched her breast. I've wanted to kiss her. I want something from this woman, I just don't know what.

"I'm an ass. I get it," I chuckle.

"Yeah, well, that and you have a nice one."

"What?" My face heats although I'm not prone to blushing.

"And that wasn't hitting on you. It's just an observation."

Has Mae been checking me out? I've warned her not to hit on me but is she actually attracted to what she sees?

"Volde-*Mach*?" I change the subject, fighting the warmth in my face.

"Machlan Wright."

Ah. "Jane doesn't like him?"

"Oh, she likes him alright." Mae's eyes widen as the words slip out and she covers her mouth with her hand. Mumbling between her fingers, she says, "You did not hear that."

"Hear what?"

Mae watches me, wondering if I'm kidding or playing along. Jane wants to be partner one day, but our firm isn't there yet. She would definitely be a candidate, if we offered the position, but an affair between Jane and Machlan couldn't happen. We don't forbid office romances, but we don't encourage them either. Mach and I are the exceptions. No fraternizing with employees is our personal policy. *None.* Ever.

When we finally finish our lunches, I take a phone call from Mach before we re-enter the car. Mae has already told me the next leg is ninety minutes or so on the road. For many portions of our drive, the original route has been covered by interstate highway, but Mae has us pull off where we can.

The next section veers through small town after small town, and Mae is quiet. With the windows down and the music up, her bare feet rest on the dashboard. If this had been my car, I might have told her to take her toes down, but I like Mae's enthusiasm and her free spirit. She doesn't give a shit about some things. She definitely isn't all over my money.

L.B. Dunbar

We fought only briefly about lunch and while I was on the phone with Mach, she learned I'd covered our rooms at the motel last night.

"The hotel issued me a refund. Do you know anything about this?"

I simply shook my head.

As we travel, Mae eventually talks more about her small town and mentions again her business, telling me how she grew it from the dirt up, as she puts it. She doesn't mention her ex-husband, but she does talk a bit about her boys. They sound loyal to their mother, if a bit aloof, being teenagers.

"Sounds like you have a good relationship with them. I was close with my mother, too." Some might say I was a mama's boy, but I didn't mind. I loved Hestia Ashford with everything I had. She was in my corner against my father and his disapproval of my love of music. He wanted me to be a sports man.

"Are your parents still around?" she asks.

"They died in a plane crash."

Mae's head turns so fast, I'm worried she might have hurt herself. She stares at me, but I keep my eyes forward, focusing on the road. My hand swipes over the leather braided band on my wrist before reaching for the metal on the leather strap around my neck.

"Tucker, I'm so sorry."

I don't want to discuss my parents' tragic death or the reasons they were on that plane in the first place. They were coming to see me. A million scenarios have run through my head at what they might have wanted to discuss with me. I'll never know now what kind of conversation they intended to have, but I have a strong suspicion.

Instead, I turn my head briefly toward Mae. "You know, that might be the first time you've said my name."

"It was?" She pauses. "I guess in my head I've called you tons of names." She weakly huffs and I smile. I can only imagine.

"You can call me Ashe if you wish. My friends do."

I don't have to look at her to see the smile breaking out on her face. It's lighting up the entire car and heating my skin. It's also setting flame to my heart, and I might like the burn.

94

14

Playlist: "Route 66" – Chuck Berry

[Mae]

Ashe.

Ash with an "e," he explained, but I am still basking in the glow of him calling me his friend. Or at least lumping me in with his friends and allowing me to call him Ashe. While the name seems fitting, I've grown accustomed to thinking of him as Tucker. Maybe calling him the more formal name will make me stand out from his favorite people.

He deflected the bomb he dropped about his parents, but I let the announcement slide and return to random yacking about our route so far. I'm honored he took me to the classic rock-themed coffee house and paid for another lunch. Along with covering the expense of last night's motel, he also paid for our visit to the caves.

Today has been a much better day than yesterday, and as I thought earlier, Saturday looks good on him. He's slightly more relaxed and looks damn sexy driving Louie, even if he isn't a fan of the Prius. His long arms stretch for the steering wheel, letting his wrist do the driving at times, dangling over the upper curve. Once again, I check out the leather braid and beads around one wrist, wondering if they mean anything other than that he likes ornamentation.

Mid-afternoon, we pass another historic landmark—the Route 66 Drive-In in Carthage, Missouri.

"Ever been to a drive-in?" I ask, imagining him too busy feeling up a date in the backseat to watch a flick on the screen.

Tucker scoffs. "Can't say that I have."

My head turns in his direction. "You're kidding?"

"Nope." He pops the -*p* in his signature way.

"We must visit one," I remark. Being the middle of the day, this location is not possible, but maybe somewhere else along our travels. We

95

could find one near our next nighttime stop. Of course, that sounds like a date, but I'm only offering him the experience.

We drive through the small town and turn the corner as the GPS guides us. As we near another nostalgic looking motel, I squeal in delight. "We must stop."

The squat white building looks like an old trailer diner and in pictures I've seen the lights around this structure illuminate bright green at night. For some reason, I really want to see it in the dark, in its glory with the neon glow around the flat roofline. The place is so classic motel-looking and on my list of potential overnight stops. Not to mention, I have sudden visions of what Tucker and I could do inside one of the rooms.

Maybe his hand could actually cup my breast, pinch my nipple and relieve the pressure within the achy swell. Maybe his fingers could skate lower, between my thighs and quell the ache that's been building to volcanic proportions today. Maybe he could simply kiss me, fusing his mouth to mine, fueling the wattage of my desire.

Maybe I could wake up from my daydream and realize these things will never happen with him.

Tucker shakes his head as he often does at me, and we pull into the lot. "It's too early to stop for the night."

He's right and yet everything in me wants to give this place my dollars. *It's so cute.* Instead, I settle on another picture. Tucker has become quite the photographer and I don't know how he does it with the filters on my phone. He catches every expression, often narrowing in on my face. My smile is crooked. One eye droops a bit, but my eye color is bright in the sunshine. My complexion looks good. He's definitely playing with the filters.

We continue for the next twenty-five minutes turning left here, turning right there, as announced by the GPS until we enter downtown Joplin. The original route runs right through this town, and we find Mural Park, commemorating the old thoroughfare. Tucker indulges me once more with a picture before a partial car, embedded against the brick wall painted with a giant map of the journey to cross eight states over two-thousand miles.

"You mentioned your son likes art," Tucker says as I stare at the large design.

"He does. Penciling is his medium. He loves to draw, not paint."

"Do you have any examples?"

"I do actually. In my phone." I've taken pictures of Owen's sketches to share with my sisters. I'm proud of his talent. As Tucker holds the device, he helps himself to my photos and I scan the giant map one more time. We're a little less than halfway on the trail. We've covered quite a distance though, and I feel less aggravated about the sightseeing experiences today compared to yesterday. Tucker has settled into being a decent travel companion. Perhaps it's because he's driving.

"He's really good," Tucker states, holding out my phone for a second so I can see one of Owen's images. The detailed drawing isn't some coloring book sketch. Owen has edged the art up a bit, making the lines harsher, crisper, not soft and delicate. We've sold some of his prints—Owen's Originals—in our garden center gift store.

Tucker's brow pinches and I step closer to him, wondering what he's looking at next. Glancing over his arm, I notice he's stopped on an outline of me. Owen needed a portrait for his art class in high school and I sat for him. Saying I look seductive in the drawing sounds silly, especially since I'm his mother, but I was gazing at him over my shoulder for this sketch. A window in the background highlights my profile and Owen captured every detail, every shade, in the drawing. My lowered lids. My downward nose. My slightly upturned lips.

Tucker swipes the screen, and a second image appears of me staring out the window as if I'm longing to go outside. I spend a lot of time outdoors. I love the smell of wet soil, cut grass, and of course, fresh flowers. Maybe I was yearning to be freed from the confines of my house. The sketches are roughly five years old, shortly after my divorce from Adam.

"You're really beautiful, sunshine." His voice drops as he speaks, continuing to stare at the drawing captured on the screen.

"Thank you." My throat thickens and my voice cracks.

I'm not ever called beautiful as a compliment, and compliments in general make me slightly uncomfortable. Tucker sounds genuine enough in his statement, but I don't know how to accept it. I haven't felt beautiful in a long time and I'm not being self-deprecating. I'm being honest with myself at my age after living with a man who hadn't loved me for years. It's difficult to feel beautiful in such a situation.

As if Tucker knows this, he lifts his hand and brushes back hair loosened from my ponytail. His fingers linger around my ear and down the side of my neck as they did earlier today. *Was that only this morning?* When I was driving, I thought he might keep his hand on my skin, cup the back of my neck, or hold on to my shoulder, but he slowly released me then as he does now.

As we stand by the mural, a man with a guitar saunters over and begins singing the iconic "Get Your Kicks (on Route 66)." Tucker slips my phone into his pocket, grabs my hand, tugs me to him, and wraps his arm around my back. Swaying us left then right, he rocks to the music, and I laugh. I can't dance, and I struggle to keep up with his lead. My laughter only adds to my lack of rhythm, but Tucker doesn't give up. He presses me outward and pulls me back. We sway again before he twirls me, and I twist away from him. Snapping my arm, he tugs me back and I roll into his chest. In broad daylight, we dance in a parking lot to this street musician.

And I've never laughed so hard or felt so beautiful.

15

KANSAS – Still Day 2

Playlist: "Home" – Phillip Phillips

[Mae]

After Joplin, we exit Missouri and it's straight on to Galena, Kansas. The path through the sunflower state is the briefest, only fourteen miles and roughly thirty minutes. Being such a short distance, and the fact it's late in the day, Tucker asks if we can shoot for Oklahoma before we stop for the night.

When I agree, Cars on the Route is the next attraction on my list of must-sees. The white stucco structure with a bright red logo was a former Kan-O-Tex service station. The place has held many names, but its present name is a tribute to the Disney movie *Cars*, a favorite of my sons when they were younger. I'd be in denial if I said that animated film wasn't part of my inspiration to travel this old road through forgotten towns. Unfortunately, the location is closed but still a fun stop with more photo ops and I send a few images to my boys.

Neither Owen nor Wyatt responds, and I hope this means they are working hard at Mae's Flowers.

Only a few minutes down the road, we stop again at Eisler Bros. Old Riverton Store. This squatty building with red cedar siding is also on the National Registry of Landmarks and a quaint spot featuring a deli, souvenirs, and a variety of garden flowers and hanging pots. The sight of such items has my heart longing for my garden center, which is ten times bigger than this location. I promised Pam I wouldn't let guilt nibble at me, but it takes a bite at this roadside attraction.

Had it been selfish to travel alone? Should I have invited my sons?

I stare at a small collection of bright red geraniums warring with myself.

L.B. Dunbar

"You want a plant?" Tucker asks over my shoulder, curious about my staring at the terra cotta pots filled with the cheery reminder of home.

"Just a little homesick, I guess." I shrug because it sounds silly. This trip is something I wanted for me, but I suddenly miss my boys and my shop. To my surprise, Tucker runs a hand up my spine and squeezes the back of my neck.

"Maybe we should stop soon?" We already agreed to keep going, though.

"No, we can press on until Oklahoma." He needs to get to California. He's opened up a little bit more about his daughter's wedding. She's marrying someone he's only met twice.

"Don't you want to know more about the man dedicating his life to your daughter?"

"I trust my daughter's decision. She's grown into a smart woman with a good head on her shoulders. And a big heart. Plus, I've met him. There's no doubt when I look at him. He worships my Julia."

I remember once thinking I was a smart woman with a big heart. How foolish I'd felt once I'd learned how duped I'd been by Adam. Pam would tell me it wasn't my head I overruled but my gut. My instincts told me something wasn't right with my marriage, but I ignored the hint, or avoided the signs. I was so focused on the flower shop and my growing children, I dismissed what my heart suggested. My husband no longer loved me. Honestly, I no longer loved him either.

We'd been young and *so in love*, and everything happened quickly. College graduation. Marriage. Babies. And then the flower shop. That generous gift from his parents.

"I'm going to use the restroom," I tell Tucker, just needing a minute to collect myself.

"I'll do the same and meet you at the car."

Once I handle my business, I stand beside Louie waiting for Tucker. After he exits the store, he picks up a potted red geranium and walks up to me.

"Did you just steal that?"

"I'm a terrible thief if I did," he jokes. He cracks his throat like a police monitor and throws his voice. "Officer in hot pursuit of a potted plant poacher. Man wanted to give a beautiful woman some flowers."

I look at him as he hands me the pot.

"I don't want you to miss home." He drops the officer act and softens his voice.

Taking the pot from his hands, I lift the flower to my nose. Geraniums don't really have a fragrance other than earthy but clean, but I lower my lids to hide the sudden prickle of tears welling in my eyes.

"This was so sweet of you."

"They aren't exactly roses," he scoffs, but his gesture is more precious than an entire bouquet. "I hope they don't mean a bad omen, like death or despair." He grins extra wide after speaking.

Chuckling, I blink back the lurking tears and lift my face. "Actually, they mean hope. My son read *To Kill a Mockingbird* in high school, and he thought it was cool that a character named Mayella had a name similar to mine. I'm Mae Ellen. He told me how she planted red geraniums and he learned they were a symbol of hope and beauty in her unhappy life." How metaphoric I'd found his explanation. Maybe I surrounded myself in beautiful blooming plants to disguise the ugly unhappiness in my marriage.

"But actually, they are considered a protective plant in some cultures, according to legends." I peer up at him. "And that's probably more than you wanted to know about geraniums."

Reaching for my hair again, he scoops the loose locks behind my ear. "Whatever they mean, I just want to make you smile." His eyes avoid mine while he continues to wrap my hair over my ear.

With his words, my smile grows wider, and I giggle like a teenager. *What's happening to me?* And what's going on with him? He's been sweet throughout the day, and I can't dismiss the concept of a switch being flipped. Was his visit to that blues bar last night a turning point for him? He spoke rather passionately about music during our lunch. Whatever it is that has shifted his mindset, today's been a good day, and he has made me smile often.

L.B. Dunbar

I set the plant securely in the back seat, fastening a seat belt around it to keep the pot upright and smile once more at the gift. Tucker chuckles at my attention to the flower before we both climb back into the car.

There's one last place to visit in Kansas. We head for Brush Creek, where the Rainbow Curve Bridge goes over a marsh. Still a single lane road open to cars, we decide to park in a small lot and walk across it instead.

"Another bridge to cross." He arches one brow at me.

"Another bridge." Other than the physical ones, we've crossed several between the two of us and this white arched structure feels symbolic. A rainbow is a symbol of hope just like a red geranium.

After the brief walk—we agreed it felt good to stretch our legs—we continue on our drive, eventually taking a sharp left turning us due south until we connect with an alternate route labeled Highway 69. There are a thousand jokes waiting to be said here but I bite the inside of my cheek, fighting off naughty thoughts of Tucker, our bodies flipped and exploring one another. Mouth. Lips. Teeth. The struggle against my physical attraction to Tucker has grown triple-fold throughout the day, but I keep my flirtatious behavior in check.

Baxter Springs is the final destination suggested in Kansas, but we bypass the visitor center as it's closed.

"Fun fact. I think the name Radiator Springs in the movie *Cars* came from this town. The owner of Old Riverton Store was interviewed for the movie as well." Several locations we'd already hit and more to come are represented in the movie, and once again I think of Wyatt and Owen. How quickly they've grown. How close to being men they are. How much further they still need to blossom before becoming thriving adults.

"We need to find a place to stop for dinner before all these places close, and maybe we should find a hotel," Tucker eventually says.

"Motel," I remind him, emphasizing the *m*. We aren't near any major metropolis and although we've seen advertisements for commercial hotels ahead, I'd still like to find another mom-and-pop place. To my surprise, a quick internet search comes up with only chain hotels and limited availability.

"There's only one with two rooms."

"Book it," Tucker states, and I click the reservation. With the night's lodging settled, we park on Main Street and walk to a café. We decide on burgers, review our day, and chat a bit about his work. He already knows I own the flower shop and garden center, and I've explained its background. He finally offers more about his company.

"Impact was born from necessity. I have extensive history with marketing and media, and Mach had been working in the industry for years as well. We decided to combine our efforts and open our own office when I was thirty-five."

"And how old are you now?"

"I'll be fifty soonish." He cheekily grins, brushing off the exact date. "Anyway, we had a major client but took on several others, working with them on branding and social media influence specifically. It's a market that's boomed in the last decade."

"What drew you to marketing?" Everyone has a reason they were attracted to an industry, but Tucker hesitates as if contemplating his answer.

"Family business. I had experience in their marketing department first."

"But eventually, you wanted to break out on your own?" I ask, putting words to his past.

"Something like that." He drops the French fry he'd been holding in his hand and reaches for his glass of water. Drinking half of it in one hearty gulp, he sighs afterward. "We need to drink more water as we ride."

"If I drank more water, we'd be stopping even more frequently for bathroom breaks."

"I can't imagine us stopping any more than we already are," he mocks, sarcasm deep in his throat while his crooked smile lets me know he's joking.

Still, for a moment, I wonder if he's regretted our day when I've enjoyed it. "You didn't have fun today?" I hate that I'm holding my breath while I wait on his answer.

The corner of his mouth tips upward even further and he meets my gaze. "Yeah, I had fun."

L.B. Dunbar

If Saturday has been a good look on him, *fun* pushes him from handsome to stunning.

+ + +

When we arrive at the hotel, there's a problem.

"What do you mean you only have one room? I made the reservation for two."

"Yes, two people in one room," the clerk tells me.

"No. Two people. One in each room," I clarify. My potted geranium sits on the counter. Tucker dropped me at the door and said he'd bring in our bags once he parked. Glancing over my shoulder, I see him walking up behind me. After he paid for my room last night, I figured I'd cover his accommodation tonight although these rooms are much more than what he spent yesterday. With this mix up, it's half the predicted cost, but going to be double the trouble.

"What's wrong?" Tucker asks, stopping behind me.

"They only have one room," I say, huffing in frustration.

"You only reserved one room," the clerk clarifies again. "And it's the only room we have left."

Tucker stands so close behind me I feel his exhale against my neck. I cannot share a room with this man. His scent has been intoxicating. His change of attitude a wicked shot. I'm drunk on him today and need to sleep off a potential hangover.

"Tell me there are two beds." I'm practically begging the young clerk who isn't at fault for my inability to read a freaking reservation tab.

"It's a king."

Of course it is.

"Just give us the room," Tucker groans as my shoulders sag. His arm reaches around mine and a card is presented to the clerk.

"No, I got it tonight," I say, wielding my credit card before the hotel clerk. However, Tucker is quick to pluck the plastic from my fingers and tuck it into the front pocket of his jeans. There's no way I'm digging in there like he reached into my shirt earlier, so I guess I lose again.

Once we enter the room, we both stare at the single king-sized bed.

"I think I'll shower. Wash off the road," Tucker says, still studying the bed. Those silver eyes of his narrow, and if *he* thinks this is awkward, he has no idea how *I* feel. I can't imagine lying next to him in my heightened state of arousal. I'll never sleep.

"I'm going to step outside and call home."

Tucker peers at me, his brows pinching. "Don't go far, okay?" Outside is dark but the time is not extremely late. I need a minute to wrap my head around this sleeping arrangement and I want to check in with my boys. However, neither answers their phone when I call, and I return quicker than expected to the room. Uncertain what to do with myself, I sit on the edge of the bed fighting images of Tucker naked and wet in the shower. My imagination does nothing compared to the sight I get when the bathroom door opens and a rush of steam releases around the towel-clad man.

Beads of water still cascade down his bare chest, which hosts a smattering of hair near his pecs and a darker trail leading beneath the thin, white terry cloth hanging low on his hips. His abs are a washboard I want to scrub my undies against, but they won't come away clean. His short-cropped hair is darker when wet, making him look only slightly younger than he is but giving him an edgy appearance, dangerous even.

Yeah, dangerous for my libido which has been absent for years and decided to show up unannounced for a visit.

Scrubbing his hand over his hair, flicking water here and there, he dips his head and lowers his eyes. I notice the leather strap around his neck. A medallion of some sort lays against his chest.

"How are your boys?" he asks, but I swear he said breasts as mine tingle and ache, and I choke in response.

"What?" Then I realize what he said. "Oh, they didn't answer."

Tucker nods and a painfully awkward silence falls between us. His hand lowers to his chest and his fingers tug at the medallion. I can't look away from him. I'm trying. It's embarrassing, but I cannot force my eyes to move.

"You mentioned a bath last night. You can take one, if you want."

My lids finally close. I cannot sit in a tub, naked, and knowing all of *that* is outside the door. Standing in the shower will be difficult enough, and I immediately know what's going to happen to me. My body can't take all the stimulus of him dripping wet, in a low-slung towel, his hand dropping lower to rest on his hip. How is it possible to have that V-dip at his age? My mouth waters. I've never seen a man up close with this kind of body. I assumed men like him were touched up in images, placing their heads over younger bodies, but this is reality and Tucker is—

"Mae?"

"Yeah." I blink. "I mean. Yes. No. I don't need a bath. I'm not dirty. You're dirty. I mean, I'm going to shower." I stand quickly from the bed, tripping on feet that don't want to hold me up and stumble forward. Tucker reaches out for me but stops short and I'm grateful we don't connect because my entire body hums. I've never been so turned on without contact and I'm afraid I'll combust if he touches me.

"I'm. Shower. Yeah." I snort. I actually snort, and if I wasn't already mortified, that just killed me. I fumble through my suitcase, grabbing an assortment of I don't even know what and my shower bag. On shaking legs, I enter the bathroom and close the door a little harder than necessary. Within seconds the shower is on, and I strip off my clothes, finding his piled on the floor. I can't take anymore.

Stepping into the shower, the hot water doesn't even register on my over-sensitized skin. I slip fingers between my legs and find the nub thumping and throbbing in need. My body drips with desire and within seconds I'm coming so hard, my knees give. I fold to the bathtub floor, fingers still working my trigger spot. With my thighs spread, my hips thrust against my fingertips, chasing a second orgasm on the tail of the first.

"Oh God," I whimper, shocked at myself and unabashedly getting myself off despite my travel companion on the other side of a flimsy bathroom door.

It's all his fault. My hips rock and my fingers press, and another earth-shattering release steals my breath. Falling forward to one hand, I catch myself, closing my eyes as my body trembles and my chest heaves.

"What was that?" I whisper to myself, trying to focus on the porcelain underneath my palm. Shakily, I press my body upward and stand. Dipping my head back under the shower stream, I close my eyes once more and let the heat of the water calm my racing heart.

L.B. Dunbar

16

Playlist: "Simple Man" – Lynyrd Skynyrd

[Tucker]

Mae exits the bathroom in a halo of steam wearing a loose T-shirt. *Does that have a fraternity insignia on it?* And a pair of short, floral print pajama shorts.

"I forgot something." Her gaze sheepishly darts to me and away before she scrambles across the room for her suitcase. With something tucked into her fist, she returns to the bathroom and shuts the door once again. She wasn't wearing a bra, and for a second, I think that's what she forgot, but when she opens the door a second time, I can't visibly see anything, other than those lush breasts I traced with a fingertip earlier. Free from confines and perfectly outlined despite the oversized tee, their shape is exactly what I imagined as I took care of myself in the shower.

Clenching my dick in a tight fist, I only tugged three times before my fingers were covered in milky-white substance. I'm still semi-hard imagining Mae lapping up the mess. While the release left my body, I'm still in need of more.

Everything about Mae has had me on edge all day. Standing before that red rocker, I wanted to kiss her senseless, strip her of her bra and fondle those lush tits. Every fucking time she smiles, I want to reach for her and press my mouth to hers and capture the curve. And that laugh. That fucking cheery sound of delight I want to swallow whole and then make her repeat it over and over again. Maybe even feel it against my cock.

Wearing a pair of workout shorts, I've been sitting on the bed because it's the only place to sit. My mattress tonight might be the nasty rug and I'm hoping Mae will at least let me nab the spread off this thing. I move to stand to allow her the bed when her phone rings. She rushes across the room again, fumbling in her bag for it, and answers breathlessly.

"Hello." She pauses. "Hey baby." Her face lights up, and for a second, I wonder if she has a boyfriend she hasn't mentioned. Seems like his name would pop up in our conversations, but I've only caught her ex's name, Adam, and her two boys, Wyatt and Owen.

I settle back against the pillows I was propped up against on the bed for another second.

"I'm sorry. Did you check your bag?" Immediately, Mae's shoulders lower and her body sags forward. With a hand on the dresser opposite the bed, she holds herself upright and I watch her reflection in the mirror over the furniture.

"Well, how about your drawers? Maybe the top one where your socks should be."

Another pause.

"Okay, well…I don't know about blueberries. Look in the fridge. Second shelf, left corner. Or check the freezer. There might be frozen ones there that work."

After a breath, she speaks again. "Why are you at the house? You should be at your dad's."

As if Mae isn't already hunched forward, she lowers her elbows to the dresser and pinches at her forehead before meeting my eyes in the mirror. Immediately standing upright, she takes a step back and collapses on the edge of the mattress. Her eyes avoid mine in the mirror while I watch her in the reflection.

"Wyatt, I can't help you from here. Ask him." Her tone turns firm, going into mom-mode. From what I've surmised, she's a good mother. Good mothers miss their children as she did today. Good mothers talk about them like Mae does. Pride rings in her voice when she mentions Owen's drawings or Wyatt's achievements on the ice.

"Okay," she huffs, scrubbing at her forehead again. "Is Owen around? I tried to call him, too."

Another pause.

"Hey honey," she greets, and her smile is restored. She listens a while and then speaks. "So today we went to a few places that reminded me of the movie *Cars*. We saw a— Yeah, I'll hold."

L.B. Dunbar

Shaking her head, I see her eyes close through the mirror. "Okay, yeah." *Pause.* "No, it's fine. I'll call you tomorrow night."

Mae waits a beat, but even when she says, "Bye," the word is cut short. She clicks off the phone and holds it in her lap, staring down at the device.

Eventually, looking up, she meets my eyes in the reflection once more. She shrugs. "They're busy and they're teens."

I don't like her weak smile and I nod once in sympathy. "That's only code for they're assholes." Through the mirror, I grin back at her, and she softly chuckles before tossing the phone onto the dresser where it clatters against the geranium's clay pot.

As I've been sitting on the bed, I swing my feet to the floor and balance on the edge. "I can take the floor." There's a sliver of space between the bed and a wall with a window, and another strip between the foot of the bed and the dresser. Neither offers much space plus the floor looks rather uncomfortable.

"Look, we're both adults. We aren't married to others. We aren't in relationships." Mae pauses, waiting on me and I nod. I've been on random dates but nothing serious since Rochelle. "It doesn't need to mean anything. I can stay on my side of the bed."

"What are you saying?" I question, glancing at her over my shoulder.

"We can sleep together." Her face turns bright pink, and although I know what she means, I like the color on her skin. "I mean—"

I hold up a hand to stop her. "I know what you mean."

Mae offers a tender smile to accept the *sleeping* arrangement and I pat the bed behind me and wiggle my phone which I hold in my other hand. "I need to check on a few things." I quickly ease back against the pillows I propped against the fake headboard and stretch my legs, crossing my ankles.

Mae distracts me as she climbs up her side of the bed. My gaze focuses on her position, the kitten-like crawl and the curve of her ass in the air clad only in those shorty pajamas. I swallow the dryness in my mouth and try to pull my attention from her, but I can't.

She was too adorable in her flustered babble when I exited the bathroom. She's attracted to me on some physical level, and I'm attracted to her. My fingers had a mind of their own today, reaching out and touching her on occasion. I wanted to touch her more, stroke over that soft skin and confirm it's even softer in other places. I've only had a hint of the soft spots on her neck, her breasts, her belly.

"What could you possibly be checking on a Saturday night?" she pokes fun at me.

But I don't answer, watching as she pulls back the covers and kneels. Sweet Jesus, I want her kneeling before me. Thighs spread. Shorts rising. She has so much leg on display and the tee covers her bottoms, giving the impression she's wearing only the shirt. If Mae wore only a T-shirt to bed, there'd be a serious struggle to keep my hands to myself. Whether she believes it or not, I am a gentleman, but I'm at the end of the tempting rope that's Mae.

I remain where I'm seated as Mae slips under the sheets and lays on her back. "You don't talk much about your son."

The comment surprises me. I've told her more about Julia and the upcoming wedding, but she's right, I haven't mentioned Jude much.

"What should I say?"

Mae rolls her head on the pillow to look over at me. "You mentioned you don't see eye-to-eye with him. Is this a new development or a phase he didn't grow out of when he was finished being a teen?"

She's only asking because she has her own set of boys on the cusp of twenty and I weigh how much I want to share with her. I've only known her for two days, and while I didn't trust her with a cup of coffee forty-eight hours ago, there's something about her that says I can confide in her on a deeper level. Then again, we are only riding companions, and in a few days, I won't ever see her again. The thought instantly causes melancholy. Does she really need to know things about me? So much of my history isn't pretty.

I glance up at the red geranium sitting on the dresser, positioned as if placed with pride. Hope, she said earlier. The cheery flower symbolizes an emotion I haven't felt for a long time. The sensation of trust. The concept of anticipation. The desire for something. My eyes drift to Mae, catching her watching me with those big blue eyes. *Is she hope?*

Instantly, I decide whatever I say to her, she won't judge me.

"When my wife died, Jude discovered he wasn't my biological son."

Mae's eyes widen but she remains quiet.

"He was resentful. Not that I am his father, as I've been there since his birth, but angry that he hadn't known the truth."

Mae's continued silence opens the door for the rest of the story.

"My own father wasn't a good dad or even a decent man. He had multiple affairs on my mother, which led to several illegitimate children."

"So, you have siblings?" The question surprises me for some reason.

"Yes." How deep do I go into that history?

"And your parents died in a plane crash," Mae states for clarification. "How old were you?"

"Twenty-three." My entire life crashed that year. "Within months of their death, my grandfather discovered my father had gotten a young woman pregnant."

"How young?" Mae asks, her voice holding a hint of concern as it should.

"She was just nineteen."

"Oh God," Mae whispers.

"Yeah. Well, Grandfather couldn't let that mishap go. She was a family friend's daughter, and she went to him when my father died. Dad promised to take care of her. She didn't know what to do."

I remember the call I'd received from Grandfather. Rochelle and I had been friends our entire lives. I didn't understand at the time how she could have fallen for Dad's seduction. I even worried at first that he hadn't seduced her but simply taken what he wanted. She'd threatened to tell her parents about her condition and how it happened. Back then, I hadn't known what the big deal was. *Let her parents know the truth.* My father was scum.

There was more to the story, though.

"Grandfather asked me to come home and marry her."

"Where were you?" Mae asks, and I pick at the spread beside me.

"I was in California." The band was on its way. We'd had a few hits, although our second album wasn't selling like the first. We needed something that made us unique. Made us different. Although, I didn't want to sell out and become something I wasn't. I'd already tried that.

"And you went home, to Chicago."

I shrug, mimicking my new friend. "I married her." Simpler said than our marriage was in reality. I hadn't done it for money. I did it for Grandfather. Her father was a potential investor in Ashford's, and they needed the capital to continue to grow, to continue their worldwide expansion. My father had been key in acquisitions and development of properties. Upon his death, Grandfather panicked. His son, a chief business developer, was gone, and he'd impregnated the daughter of a major investor as well as a long-standing family friend.

Field Stevens would not have appreciated the infidelity his friend committed with his precious daughter. It was bad enough he thought I'd slept with his princess out of wedlock. He never put together the fact I was in California while she was in Chicago, but we stuck to the story that I'd slept with her in my grief around the time of my parents' funeral service. Her father was none the wiser when Jude was born too early to match up with the timing.

"And you gave up a dream to be a father."

"Something like that," I state, staring down at the black screen of my phone.

"What else could it be?"

There was so much more to the story. How I'd always admired my grandfather. He believed in me, and I trusted that faith. He thought I could be someone special in the music industry. When he asked me to come home, I misunderstood it as a temporary setback, not a permanent end.

"What was your dream?" Mae asks.

I close my eyes a second before opening to meet her eyes. She's only asking for the truth. She won't even recognize who I am if I share the details with her.

"I was in a band. We were on our way." I lift a hand, mocking myself as I wave it like the upward trajectory on a graph.

Mae perches on an elbow, facing me. "You were a rock star?"

"Something like that," I say again, scoffing as *star* might be a little bit of an exaggeration, but we were definitely rising, up-and-coming according to the charts. We had a decent mix, a distinct sound, but one that wasn't unique enough.

"That makes sense," Mae suddenly says, dipping her eyes to my naked chest and the medal I wear.

"What makes sense?"

"You have the whole rock star vibe going on here." She waves a hand up and down at my upper body and I chuckle. Mae isn't starstruck, but she's ogling me, and heat creeps over my skin. Her appraisal is a nice sensation. She isn't looking at me because she knew, she's looking at me because she didn't.

"So, you quit the band," she clarifies.

"I quit the band." I struggle to control the wobble in my voice.

Instantly, I remember saying the damning words to Lawson and Denton, both of whom stared at me in shock. In some dingy recording studio, when we could not have splurged for a nicer one, I spilled the news. Our second album wasn't selling. We'd agreed to merge with Lawson's sister and hire on a young drummer named Hank Paige. Everything was happening so fast, but we hadn't had a single practice together as the new group.

I quit.

They didn't need the details. It was too complicated to explain. In hindsight, I was only twenty-three. I recall the pressure in my chest and the lump in my throat like it was yesterday. Saying the words nearly broke me. I never expected music to leave me, but it did. I swore I'd never quit anything again. Not my marriage. Not fatherhood. Not future business endeavors.

"When did your wife die?" Mae asks, interrupting the memory.

"Three years ago."

Mae remains quiet another second, and I expect her next question to be, how?

Instead, she simply says, "I'm sorry that happened to you." She hesitates and her eyes roam down my body. If ever I thought Mae might hug me, this is the moment. I almost see her struggle. She wants to reach for me. Or maybe I just want her to pull me into her. Strangely, I want her comfort.

"There's still time to mend the relationship with your son," she says next, as if I haven't mentioned the band or the details of Jude's birth.

"Your boys will come around, too." Isn't that how this conversation started? Mae only wanted reassurance her boys will grow out of a phase, and I'd exposed more than she asked for. My father certainly hoped I'd grow out of the phase that he believed music was for me. His wish was granted, only he'd gone about destroying that dream in ways I'd never anticipated.

Mae waves a hand and pffts. "They're just assholes."

"Yeah." I weakly smile at her sympathizing grin.

Sons can be that way. I remember when I was one.

17

OKLAHOMA – DAY 3

Playlist: "Blown Away" – Carrie Underwood

[Tucker]

To my surprise, I felt a little lighter than I expected sharing what I shared with Mae. The topic was heavy but telling a stranger hadn't been as difficult as I thought. Maybe because Mae was still a stranger in so many ways, her opinion of my tale didn't matter. Then again, deep inside, I realize that I do care what Mae thinks of me.

While Mae promised she'd stay on her half of the bed, I wake with her body molded to my back and a hand on my ass—inside my shorts. Laying on my stomach, her cheek presses into my shoulder blade while one of her legs is hitched over one of mine. She shifts to rub her nose against my spine and absentmindedly presses a kiss to my back before settling into position again.

Softly, I chuckle, and she stiffens. The air stands still before Mae yanks her hand free of my shorts and pulls away from me, rolling onto her back. I lift my head, moving it on the pillow so I can face her. Remaining on my belly, I press the hard length of my dick into the mattress in hopes of keeping it from Mae's attention. He'll need his own special attention once I can slip into the bathroom.

"Good morning." I greet her.

"I was not hitting on you." Her declaration comes so fast the words rush together and panicked eyes meet mine before flicking back toward the ceiling.

On our first day together, I'd accused her of hitting on me, where she made it clear she wasn't. I hadn't wanted that kind of behavior because of my past, but I also wanted Mae to know *me*. I wanted her to like me. Not the former husband. Not the widower. Not the businessman.

Not even the failed rock star. Just me. And I was convinced she wouldn't once she learned more about me.

"I don't know why I did that." She says to the ceiling, refusing to look at me. "I'm used to sleeping alone. I only sleep on one side of the bed. I never move around."

I know what she means but I'm not complaining. I'm not even suggesting she was attempting something with me. Her body against mine felt nice, comforting and warm, safe and…hopeful. Subconsciously, I might have known she was there because I slept like a rock. After spilling my guts to her last night, I thought I'd fight the memories and wrestle the regrets, but I slipped blissfully into sleep after only momentary thoughts of the past.

I couldn't change what my father did.

I couldn't change what my grandfather had asked of me.

I couldn't change my decisions either.

"Don't worry about it." My eyes roam the topography of her body, noting the hills of her breasts and the curve of her hips. Next, I focus on her lips. Mae has lips begging to be kissed. She said last night sharing a bed doesn't need to mean anything and it doesn't. *It shouldn't.* But I can't shake the feeling inside me that we're crossing more than bridges, one slow step at a time.

Mae rolls to her side and scoots off the bed, still avoiding a glance at me. "I'm going to get dressed." The statement says everything. We need to keep moving. We shouldn't linger, especially in bed.

But her lips need to be kissed and I want to be the lucky bastard who kisses her.

While she heads for the bathroom, I shift to my back and scrub two hands down my face before reaching for my phone. Picking up the device before I even leave the sheets is a terrible habit. If I were home, I'd hit the gym and rid myself of the tension under my skin. I also need to ward off the raging hard-on I have. Mae had her hand on my ass, but her nearness alone brings on desire and raises my dick to full mast. Her scent lingers beside me, and I want to turn into her pillow, inhale her floral scent and whack off on these sheets.

Instead, I groan once more, toss down my phone and rise from bed.

+ + +

The hotel offers breakfast, but Mae and I decide to stop at a coffee shop for a quick cup and something light. We had enough food on bread yesterday—a sandwich, a burger—and I'm hoping I can convince her to pick up the pace on our journey and have a decent steak later when we arrive in Texas, today's destination.

"Look, it's one of those leave-a-book, take-a-book shelves." Mae points to the bookshelf as we wait for our coffee order. I nod with disinterest and Mae picks up a book. Doing a double take, I instantly recognize the title and the woman on the cover.

Mae runs her hand affectionately down the jacket of the hardcover. "I've read everything she wrote." Admiration fills her softened voice. "She really helped motivate me to take charge of my life and quit taking Adam's bullshit." Her palm rubs once more over the paper covering.

"So sad how she died." Her head pops up and there's a look in her eyes. One that is tender but puzzled. Her brows pinch. She drops her gaze back to the book, flipping it over. There's another image on the back plus a brief biography of the author including her path as a motivator, an influencer, a supporter of women, and her devotion to her family which included a husband and two loving children.

"Rochelle Ashe was an inspiration," Mae offers, speaking affectionately to the book.

"She was a liar." The harsh truth escapes before I can contain the words.

"Ashe," the barista hollers, calling out our order. "Ashe with an e."

I step forward to swipe our to-go cups from the counter and turn back toward Mae. She's still planted by the bookcase.

"She died in a plane..." Mae's voice falters and her head whips upward. Her eyes meet mine, confused, questioning, clicking together the puzzle pieces.

"We need to hit the road, sunshine." I fight to keep my voice steady. There's no flirt in my tone or hint of an answer to what she's wondering. Without looking back at Mae, I carry both our cups and a bakery bag out to the parking lot and Mae follows, the slap of her sandaled feet quick behind me. She's wearing another pair of jean shorts and a body-hugging T-shirt today. Her hair is down, but I expect her to tuck the pretty strands into a messy bun eventually. The air here is humid and warm.

"Tucker." Her tone questions me as we near the car. "Was she your wife?" Exasperation—or is it astonishment—rings from her interrogative while I place the to-go cups on the roof and hit the fob to unlock the car.

After setting the cups inside in the cup holder, I start patting my pockets. Back pockets. Front pockets. I brush past Mae who remains standing near the driver side of the car and pop the trunk. I open my laptop bag, frantically searching within the multiple pockets for my phone.

"Tucker," Mae's voice softens, and a hand comes to my wrist. "You can tell me."

I'm still leaning over the trunk, hands in my bag when I stop. I do not want to talk about this. "Why would you think such a thing?"

"Ash with an e?"

I could deny I was married to the famous influencer. I could pretend I've never heard of her, but I'm certain Mae must have known. Why wouldn't she? Jane knew I was married to Rochelle Ashe, who had taken my stage name as her own.

Placing my hands on the edge of the trunk opening, I exhale. "It's not like you didn't know, right? Jane told you. That's why you were hitting on me that first day."

"What?" Mae's mouth falls open. "No, I didn't know anything."

She'd given me the short list of what she did know about me, and widower was on it. She must have known the truth of who my wife was.

"Jane told you."

"She didn't." Something begs me to believe Mae, but my steamrolling thoughts overrule.

"Yes, Rochelle Ashe was my wife. She died in a plane crash and what people don't know is she was leaving me to run off with her boyfriend."

What they also don't know is that I'd caught onto her affair months earlier, and I'd asked her for a divorce weeks before that fateful plane trip. Before the plane when down with my still-wife and her lover on board.

"All those Liven Up Thursdays were bullshit. We fought constantly. *I love my husband more than anything*—" I throw my voice in a mocking feminine sound and toss my arms up into the air. "It was all for show. *Family is everything.* She was a terrible mother." I have no idea why I'm telling Mae any of this, but I can't seem to stop myself. "She didn't believe in equality for women, either. She believed in her own bottom line and the adrenaline rush she got when people loved on her."

Rochelle was an attention whore and she learned it well from her father. He was a charismatic man, but so was mine, and perhaps that's what attracted my eventual wife to sleep with my father before I married her. She became pregnant with dear old dad's child, who I claimed as my own. I was the father of my brother, technically, but I'd never thought of our situation that way. Jude was my son. *My son.*

"I'm so—"

"Don't." I snap, turning on her. "Don't say you're sorry." I reach for the trunk lid and slam it in place.

"I lost my phone," I bark as if that's the issue at hand instead of the revelation of one more secret to this woman. I don't know why I'm suddenly so angry. Maybe I just didn't want Mae to know this piece of my past. This drowning weight suffocating me along with so many other things.

I recall the look Mae was giving that damn book. The one where psychologists wrote the details and Rochelle claimed the information as her own philosophy. What started as simple blogging led to a movement, and I bought into the appeal. I believed in the power of Rochelle and the message we spread to others, only it all backfired on me.

"We can go back to the hotel."

"What?" I don't understand Mae's suggestion.

"For your phone. Maybe you left it in the room."

In the room, where I want to rewind, and pretend I never mentioned Jude's birth or my failure as a rock star. Then we'd never be here, where

Hauling Ashe

Mae learns about Rochelle. None of my thoughts make sense, and I'm not being fair, but I can't see further than hitting this highway and getting the fuck out of here.

Doubling back feels like a waste of time but we're only five minutes from the place. Without a word to Mae, I step to the driver's door, and she circles the back of the car. I start the ignition before she's even entered, and her seat belt is hardly on when I slam into reverse and turn back for the hotel.

The girl working the desk has to escort me back to the room, which hasn't been cleaned yet, and I search the dresser, the nightstand, and finally the rumpled sheets on the bed before finding the damn device.

Taking a final glance at the bed, I pause with visions of Mae pressed to my back, her hand on my ass. Her soft kiss to my skin. She'd done it all subconsciously. Not because it was me, but because I was a warm body, filling in for someone else, as I'd always been.

+++

When I return to the car, Mae holds her phone.

"Messaging all your friends to tell them what a fake your idol was?" I sneer.

Mae turns to me, horrified. "I would never do that to you." Her shrill voice says it all. She wouldn't. She's not like that and in only two days, I know better. I know her, and I instantly regret what I've suggested.

"And if you must know, Mr. *Ass*ford, I was texting my son who found time to chat with me while I waited for you."

Fuck. She's... This isn't on Mae. This is all me.

As she sets the GPS on her phone, I start the car, and we pull out onto Route 66. Within minutes it rains, and the weather feels fitting. The weight of the air outside the Prius is heavy and humid, but the temperature inside is cold and still. Mae and I don't speak. I owe her an apology, but I don't know what to say. She deserves to know more, but not yet. Not until I can settle my nerves and right my mood.

We detour to what's called Ribbon Road, a thirteen-mile segment of the original road remaining in Oklahoma. I want to curse this trip and

121

the history it continues to bring forth. I'm starting to think all these byways are scams and I just want to hit the highway and speed along, skipping every fucking mile of this memory lane. Damn the reminiscences of other people taking vacations and seeking destinations, as Mae calls it. What a fallacy.

Search within for inspiration. Be your own motivator.

Rochelle's conference voice rings through my head and I hate myself for how I'm acting toward Mae. More honestly, I hate Rochelle.

Keeping my thoughts to myself, we rumble down the gravel-covered road as it ripples under the hard rainfall.

Mae eventually opens her mouth, holding it agape like a child, allowing the vibration of the vehicle to force a rumbling, bopping sound from her throat.

Ah-ah-ah-ah-ah.

Unable to help myself, I laugh without humor. *Is she kidding me?*

Mae turns to me, mouth still wide, while the repetitive sound reverberates out of her. As if having a will of its own, my mouth mimics hers, popping open, and allowing the jiggling of the car over bumpy road produce the strangest music with Mae.

Suddenly, I feel better than I have in a long, long time.

18

Playlist: "Drive" – The Cars

[Mae]

Rochelle Ashe was his wife.

As a powerhouse in the industry of self-motivators, especially for women, her books inspired many. *It's Your Life* was about her struggle to be responsible for her own well-being. She proclaimed that she wanted to help others find their worth, as women, as mothers and wives, and business owners. I believed her. I drank all the Kool-Aid she passed out and I cheered on her success. I wanted the best for her and was even envious of the life she lived. Her world looked picture perfect.

Glancing over at Tucker, I realize I've had the same thoughts about him. He looks pulled together and packaged all pretty, but underneath that fine-lined skin and those silvery eyes is just a man, and I remind myself of that. He's been hurt as I have, as many people in marriages have been, and he suffered a double whammy with her infidelity and then her death.

Did he love her? He'd told me last night about his son and how he gave up his dream to return home and marry Rochelle at his grandfather's request. That's a big ask and I wonder if Tucker's grandfather appreciated the sacrifice his grandson had made.

Whether he loved Rochelle or not, he had another child with her, assuming Julia is biologically his, and he stuck out his marriage. Maybe sticking with it became easier if he loved her. He's obviously upset by her affair and her untimely death, and rightfully so in both respects. I recognize the pain of finding out your spouse cheated, since it happened to me, but then to lose his wife as he lost Rochelle—it's devastating.

Tucker's sour mood continues as the rain dampens the spirit of our trip, and I let him be. I don't know what to say. There's no comfort to offer in this situation.

L.B. Dunbar

+ + +

One thing I do not want to miss in our travels is something called the Blue Whale of Catoosa.

We veer off the highway to find the structure built of pipe and concrete on private property. Parking near the attraction, I'm once again giddy to see something from the original route.

"Did you know this was an anniversary gift from the husband to his wife?" I toss out the question as we exit Louie, even though I know Tucker didn't know about this gift.

The air is muggy and hot, and the pond where the whale structure perches gives off a pungent scent. "For their thirty-fourth wedding anniversary, he gave her this." I wave out a hand at the open-mouthed sperm whale replica.

"Fool," Tucker mutters but I'm not letting his mood ruin this moment.

"This is a grand gesture. It's so romantic." Large and slightly obnoxious, the whale makes a statement, especially when you learn the history. The man loved his wife.

Glancing over at Tucker, I realize small gestures can speak volumes as well, like giving a girl a red geranium because she misses home. The potted flower is buckled once more in the backseat. I'd consider the gift romantic, but based on Tucker's mood today, he's anything but interested in romance. Yesterday, he was only being nice, generous even, as he's been so far on this trip by paying for meals and our overnight stays.

Today is another story.

The rain begins again as we travel toward Tulsa, driving into the center to be greeted by a welcoming sign over the highway. At the Tulsa Expo Center, we see the Golden Driller, a seventy-two-foot statue that puts the Muffler Men to shame.

"I bet he has one big drill," I mutter, comparing the potential in his pants to the Gemini Giant's rocket. Tucker doesn't even crack a smile at my joke, and between the heavy rain and his sour mood, my enthusiasm dampens as well.

Eventually, we stop at a diner in Stroud and have lunch. The waitress recommends we stop at a nearby vineyard, and I ask her questions about the Great Dust bowl and *The Grapes of Wrath*, John Steinbeck's famous book about people moving west from this area. Tucker snorts like I'm ignorant, or maybe the pleasant waitstaff is, in his opinion. His assholishness from our first day together is returning. Still, I ask him to take us to the recommended winery, where I buy several bottles of local wine, one of which I plan to drink in its entirety tonight.

When I request that we stop for the third time along the route leading to Oklahoma City because I need the restroom, Tucker doesn't contain his irritation and I'm done.

"What is your problem?" I snap.

"This is stupid."

"What is stupid?" I ask wanting clarification.

"Us taking this road trip based on other people's journeys."

That's it. He can insult the Blue Whale. He can huff at a waitress. He can even hate me but I'm not putting up with his attitude anymore.

"Isn't that what you did? Took a journey down someone else's path for you?" I don't know why I say it like I do, but it hits me so hard. He gave up his dream, lived someone else's, and now that the truth is between us, he's taking it out on me. I don't mention his wife's name, but he must know who and what I reference. She became famous. He didn't.

While it's totally out of line for me to speak as I am, I'm pissed. "Are you upset you disrupted your life for her?"

He gave something up to gain something else. He became a father, a husband. They were a success as a couple and he's successful in his own right with Impact. This I know from Jane. My sister is financially well off.

"Hadn't you done the same thing? You said you followed your husband."

"It was called love. I made a sacrifice."

"And how'd that work out for you?" he snaps.

"How'd *that* work out for you?" I already know the answer. She was having an affair. It happens. It isn't right. It isn't easy to accept, but

125

L.B. Dunbar

it happens. If he loved her, that hurt. Even if he no longer loved her, the betrayal still stings. Then she died, and he mourns her death. No one wishes death on someone, no matter how betrayed they feel about that person.

But he's angry with *her*.

The car fills with heated breaths and we pull into a service station because this confrontation started from my need to use the bathroom. When we stop, I hastily open the door but then I turn toward him.

"Give me the keys."

"What?" His head snaps in my direction.

"Give me the damn key fob."

"Why?" His forehead furrows.

Because I don't trust you. I almost say the words but staring back at him with his arm draped over the steering wheel and his body positioned to face me, I realize I'd be lying. In only two-plus days, I trust him more than I ever trusted Adam, which makes no sense. I hardly know Tucker Ashford and Lord knows he's full of secrets.

Are they secrets, though? Or is it just his life, and these things are private? He didn't have to share with me about his son, his band, or his wife. Even though he accused Jane of telling me about him, she hadn't hinted at his son issues, his rock star history, or his marriage troubles. She once gave me a personalized, autographed copy of Rochelle's book and I didn't even question how she got it. She never revealed to me that one of the two men she works with was the husband of my idol.

Without thinking, I make a suggestion. "We're almost to Oklahoma City. Maybe we can find you a flight and you can fly the remainder of the way to California."

Tucker's mouth falls open. Color drains from his face and then his expression hardens. "Didn't you need the bathroom?"

I do need to pee, and badly, but I'm worked up and with his crappy attitude, I'm worried he's going to steal my car and leave me in the middle of Oklahoma.

"Mae, go."

I shift from the seat and slam the car door. My heart races and my bladder aches. Rushing to the restroom, I barely make it to the toilet. I'm

126

shaking from our altercation *and* the need to relieve myself. I should not have said what I said. I should not have worded my thoughts as I did. And I definitely should not have suggested a flight.

He did make sacrifices, too. He returned to Chicago because his grandfather asked. He married a woman because of obligation. He stood by her when she became a name.

And he can't take a plane ride because so many people in his life have died in them.

Returning to the car, I enter Louie full of regret. Tucker sits stone-still with his arms wrapped around the steering wheel. He doesn't peel out of the lot as I expected. He doesn't gun it for the expressway.

"I'm sorry," I say, although he's said some hurtful things as well.

Not addressing my apology, he says to the steering wheel, "Maybe I should just get in the backseat. I have work to do."

"It's Sunday." As if that explains anything. If Saturday looked good on him, Sunday looks lost. "You don't need to get in the back," I mutter.

"Yeah, but I should let you drive. It's your car. Your trip." He pops open the driver's door and I stare after him. Without exiting the front seat, I climb over the center console and settle into the driver's position. While it's only been one day, this space feels foreign. Louie is not even my car, but Tucker doesn't know that yet.

"He didn't mean anything, Louie," I say to the dashboard, giving the dark curve a rub like a favorite pet. Tucker opens the front passenger door, shoves back the seat to accommodate his longer legs and folds into the seat. Immediately taking out his phone, he faces the screen while I back out of the lot, and we return to the route.

Shortly, we near Oklahoma City. There's much to be seen here but I don't want to stop. Instead, I continue around the state capital and veer onto I-40 straight west to Texas.

Texalo is a city on the edge of Oklahoma before entering the Longhorn State and I don't want to miss the place. The heavy rain and the silence in the car for the last two hours sets the mood to enter this ghost town. The area is depressing. The effects of the major highway caused travelers to bypass this now-forgotten community and wiped this place out. Rundown buildings abound, one of which is even a historical landmark with nothing remarkable about it. The shell of a building covered in rust and surrounded by dried weeds hints at history long forgotten.

And isn't that the way of some things in the past? They are best left behind to rust and rot and disappear. Restoration is frivolous. There is no point in bringing up the could-haves and the should-haves. We make a decision, and we can't go backward. We can turn around, start again, but we can't ever change the original direction. The hint of the first path will always remain, worn with divots and ruts, whether visible or not. Maybe under weeds. Maybe turning to rot. The path is there, though, but the journey is done.

Even traveling the same route twice isn't quite the same. You can't ever duplicate that first pass. Something is markedly first because of its originality, creativity, or thrill. The first kiss. The first sexual experience. The first marriage. These are things that cannot be replicated. However new experiences on an old road can happen. A first kiss with a new person. A first sensual encounter with another human. A second chance in a different marriage. We can only look toward the future, despite our powers to glance in rearview mirror.

As for the history of this place, it's haunting. Someone knows the truth. Isn't that what ghosts do? They scare us with what they know and what they've seen. They are the revelations and regrets we hold deep within us. And we need to face those phantoms, that past, that history, before we can let them go. Before we can be set free to live our lives for now. And maybe love again.

I reach for Tucker, wrapping my hand around his wrist, hoping he'll feel in my touch how sorry I am. Sorry about his wife. Sorry about my husband. Sorry that people have to take shit in their marriages. Love is hard work, but that doesn't mean it should whittle a person down to nothing but shavings. Yet, it happens. Someone else can strip you to your bones and you'd still give them your femur. That's sacrifice. That's what love is.

When Tucker doesn't respond to my touch, I slip my hand from his warm skin.

Hauling Ashe

In less than a thousand yards, we cross into Texas, and the weight of hurt and heartache in this car is as heavy as the rain pelting our windshield less than half an hour ago. We've put in three days, and I need a break from Tucker and this front seat.

"Let's stop in Shamrock," I say, breaking the code of silence between us. Maybe the name alone will bring us some luck.

Tucker doesn't respond at first. His attention remains on his phone until finally he announces he found availability at a commercial hotel chain. He books us rooms for the night.

Two. Separate. Rooms.

19

Playlist: "Free Fallin'" – Tom Petty and the Heartbreakers

[Tucker]

What the fuck am I doing? Why am I blocking her out? This is all me and as soon as we head to separate hotel rooms, I hate myself all over again. Today has been fire under ice. The constant downpour has been a damper on everything including my mood, which already was a thunderstorm.

Everything from Mae's admiration of Rochelle to her discovery that Rochelle was my wife has been on my mind. When Rochelle passed, the divorce papers had been drawn up and were in my desk. She would be served upon her return from a trip to Montana, but the private plane went down, and all were lost. Pilot. Attendant. Rochelle. And Marty Haggen, her literary agent. They'd been together almost a year when I discovered their more intimate relationship. Rochelle told me she'd end it. We'd seek couples' therapy. Hell, we hosted couples' retreats on marriage and stoking desire. I hated how fake we were. Everything I'd left behind when I went to California, I had become. Pretending to be someone I wasn't.

With thoughts overwhelming and energy under my skin, I can't stay in the hotel room all night alone. I'd love a good gym, but this place doesn't have more than a treadmill and I need something that allows me to roam. I walk a main street and find an old bar. Motorcycles are parked outside the place, but inside is a mix of patrons. Families. Couples. Groups of friends.

I wander to the bar and order a Heineken, then immediately notice a piano tucked into the corner of what looks like a dance floor. The parquet floor isn't much more than a square, maybe nine by nine, near the end of the L-shaped bar counter. Maybe the area is a makeshift stage. I noticed a sign on the door boasting live music on occasion.

After handing me a beer bottle, I tip the male bartender and ask, "Mind if I sit at the piano?"

"Have at her," he mutters in a soft Southern drawl as he nods at the lone instrument.

Sitting on the wobbly bench, I take a deep pull of my beer. My attention falls to the keys—fifty-two white and thirty-six black. The perfect combination. Closing my eyes, I picture my hands moving over ebony and ivory, playing songs from memory, writing new ones. Lawson was a good songwriter, guitarist, and singer. Denton played guitar and sang back-up. I didn't consider myself much of a singer, but I could harmonize, and I was versatile. Guitar. Drums. Harmonica. But the piano was a focal point in the living room of my childhood home. No one forgets their first love. I was prodded to play the instrument to entertain guests at dinner parties my parents hosted. Being musically talented was acceptable when the skill benefitted Jonathon Ashford.

When I selected music I wanted to play, Dad disapproved.

"What is that fucking racket?"

When his father gave me my first harmonica, Dad wanted to toss the gift away.

"I'll only buy him another one," Grandfather threatened.

When I got my first guitar, I practiced when Dad wasn't home, which was often.

"That's lovely, baby. You could be a star one day," my mother cooed.

My fingers hesitate. Curled at the knuckles, they bend and quiver, eager to touch the eighty-eight keys that I walked away from years ago. I gave up the band, my friends, and California. I became a father and a husband, instead. So many times, I wonder why I did it, and deep down inside I know the answer. I was twenty-three at the time. I wasn't a child, but I wasn't adult enough to make good decisions. My parents had died. Grandfather called. Rochelle needed me.

Sacrifice, Mae called it. *Love*, she said.

There was a time I thought I loved Rochelle. We eventually had Julia. I worked in the marketing department of Ashford's. She stayed home and raised our children. I never faulted her for Jude's paternity. He was mine. He had my blood through my father. The Ashford line was intact, and Jude would inherit the company one day. Only, with a downturn in department store patronage, the company was sold minus one location shortly before Grandfather's death. His life's work was gone. Maybe that's what lead to his fatal heart attack.

I don't trust myself to touch these keys just as I don't trust myself with Mae. There's nothing I want more than to bury myself inside her and wipe away all the memories for a little bit. That wouldn't be fair to Mae, though. I've been unfair enough today.

The piano rests within eyesight of the long bar counter and the scattering of tables in the center of the place. Booths line the wall near the dance floor and curl around the L formation to the front door. Glancing up, I notice when Mae enters. She's wearing a dress and she wobbles, suggesting she has on heels of some type. Her hair is down but flattened a bit as it must be raining again. She walks to the bar, clutching at her crossbody bag, and takes a seat, hesitating a second to look around her. The bartender greets her, and she gives him that smile. The one I want only for me.

My fingers fall to the keys, and an ominous sound thuds into the bar. The overhead music drowns out the sharp clunk and Mae doesn't notice me in the corner tucked beside the counter. From this vantage point, I watch her as she orders a drink and casually sips from the straw, still glancing over her shoulders once or twice before turning back toward the television behind the bartender. Eventually, a man in a leather vest approaches her, and I'm close enough to hear their conversation.

"New around here?" The worst pick-up line ever.

"Just passing through," she offers.

"Aren't we all?"

"I'm hoping with a name like Shamrock, some luck with rub off on me."

Oh sunshine. I shake my head and watch as a devilish grin curls the biker's lips. I can almost predict what he'll say next.

"I'd like to do some rubbing on you, pretty lady."

"What?" Mae says, giving a nervous laugh and lifts her glass for another drink. Her lips close around the short straw, and I watch the biker watch her. He's picturing those lips wrapped around a body part of his, just as I want them wrapped around mine.

"Runnin' the route?" he asks.

"On a road trip," she offers and I'm shaking my head again. She's giving him too much information.

"On a bike?"

Mae lightly chuckles. "In a Prius."

The biker gives a hearty laugh in response. "You need to spread your wings and fly, baby. Back of a bike is the only way to enjoy this road." He pats his chest, and I see what he's doing. *He's* the road he wants Mae to ride. When he reaches out to brush her hair over her shoulder, that's my cue to intervene. No one's touching her but me.

I stand and grab my beer, and that's when Mae notices me. Her eyes fix on me, holding mine as I stalk around the bar and stand behind the biker.

"Babe, whatcha doing?" I ask.

Her brows rise and her eyes shift to the biker. He's leaning on the bar with his back to me and he turns his head, peering at me over his shoulder. He's bigger than I am, broader and wider, but Mae is not leaving with him.

"This your girl?" he asks, keeping his profile to me.

"Yes, she is." My eyes latch onto Mae's, and her brows hitch higher. I'm waiting for her to deny it, but she doesn't.

"Shouldn't be leaving such a pretty thing unattended," he warns.

"Went to play her a song when you stepped up." There's a warning in my voice. I'd never leave such a beautiful woman alone and yet I did, didn't I? I booked her a separate room and headed to my own because I'm angry at someone no longer alive and not worthy of my resentment.

"Didn't see your claim." His message is clear. He noticed Mae the second she walked in, and I wasn't with her.

"He's the one who owns the Prius," Mae interjects. Her eyes sparkle at the admission although it's not the truth.

Shifting to eye me better, the biker's gaze scans me up and down and he mutters, "Pussy car." I'd like to agree with him, but I don't in order to keep the ruse with Mae. I could add some snide comment about getting pussy in that car, but I don't say that either. I hold his gaze. Dark eyes narrow on mine. One punch and he'd take me out. My last bar fight was a long time ago, and even then, it was only the one time. But I'll take the hit for Mae if that's what comes of this encounter, because only over my dead body is she leaving with this man.

"Got it," the biker huffs, tipping up his chin and dismissing me. He glances over his shoulder at Mae. "Make sure he takes care of you, sweetheart."

Mae's gaze returns to me. "He does," she lies. The fib is like a stab to my chest. I've been an awful person today, and I should explain myself, but I can't. I don't know what happened.

Biker Dude pushes off the bar and stalks back to wherever he came from, and I pull up the stool beside Mae. My eyes roam the side of her body. The dress wraps around her, accentuating her curves. She's wearing thick wedges, and the strap on the shoes matches the color of her dress. She's overdressed and out of place in this small-town bar, but her appearance is also making her stand out. She's a ray of sunshine in this dark haven.

"Come here often?" I ask, and she chuckles.

"That was almost worse than his line," she says.

"But you were falling for his line, weren't you?"

"It's nice to be hit on." Her eyes lower to the counter and her fingers run along the side of her tall, thin glass before she looks up at me again. "I didn't see you when I came in. Were you playing the piano?"

"No. I used to play but I don't anymore."

"Why not?"

I glance over at the instrument. "I just don't, I guess. When I moved home, I tried but it felt like every note was a reminder of what I'd given up. What I quit. I hated being a quitter. I didn't own a piano. I had a harmonica and I'd steal out back to play it until I lost the instrument." I could have gone to Grandfather's home for a piano. I could have returned to my parents' condo on Lake Shore Drive, but I didn't want to go back.

"Harmonica?" She smiles.

"I'm full of a lot of hot air."

She chuckles.

We silently sit at the bar for a minute until I ask, "Would you have really left with him?"

Mae turns her head, peering over her shoulder in the direction of Biker Dude and friends. "I might have been in a little over my head with him." She weakly smiles back at me.

"But it was nice to be hit on," I comment, an edge to my voice.

She shrugs and I want to still those shoulders. "It's nice to feel wanted by someone, even if it is only a flirty pick-up line. I'm sure he didn't mean anything by talking to me."

"Mae," I groan. "You're beautiful. He meant all his innuendos about road trips on him."

"Road trips on him?" Her brows rise.

"Come on. I heard it a mile away. Riding the road on his bike. He wanted you to ride him."

Mae tips her head and shifts her eyes in his direction. "Really?"

I scoff. "You can't be that gullible." The word upsets her and those blue eyes cloud over. I've hurt her again.

"And how would you hit on a woman?"

"I wouldn't," I quickly retort.

Mae watches me and I don't like the way she's looking at me. "Is that why you're always telling me not to hit on you?" Her voice lowers, cautious and curious.

Swiping a hand over my head, I shift on the bar stool to face Mae. "Women used to hit on me all the time when I was with Rochelle. She'd be giving a conference about female empowerment, and her speeches made women bold as her words intended, but many took that boldness to a new level. Maybe they wanted to tempt the unobtainable. Maybe they wanted to push at my devotion to Rochelle. I have so many come-ons in my memory, I could write a book."

This makes Mae lightly chuckle. "What would they do?"

"What didn't they? Room keys. Napkin notes. Strong suggestions. I even had a woman slip me her underwear with her phone number on it."

"No." Mae laughs, horrified at the same time.

"Yes."

L.B. Dunbar

"Well, I'll make sure to keep my undies on." Her laughter continues and she arches a brow. "And you would have never done those things, hitting on woman in such a manner, when you were in your band?"

"I didn't need to. Women love a man in a band."

Mae smiles large but she goes quiet at this statement. Our eyes meet.

"I wouldn't know how to come on to a woman, Mae. I haven't had to do it in a long time."

She shifts in her seat and faces me. The stools are close, and I spread my thighs to allow her knees between my legs.

"Practice on me." She sits up straighter, flips her hair over her shoulder and braces her hands on the tops of her legs. She looks like she's ready to be schooled in the art of pick-up lines or preparing for battle, which might be the same thing.

"I'd start with an apology."

Her shoulders lower a bit. "That's a terrible opening line."

"It's honest. I'm sorry about earlier."

Mae stares at me a second, her gaze roving over my face, before she waves a hand dismissing me. "Water under the bridge, and we've crossed several of them." I chuckle at her remark, and then she says, "Now, try again."

Keeping my eyes on Mae, I search for the right comment to pique her interest. To hint that I'd be interested in her for a night.

"I'd say something like, you're a ray of sunshine beneath the clouds."

"That one sounds familiar," she says, pursing her lips and tilting her head.

"Then I'd add, I felt your warmth from across the room. You're the match to my soul and the spark to my heart. You light me up."

Mae slowly grins. "Okay. That's... wow, that's nice."

"How about my heart is an hourglass and yours is the sand, but I won't let you slip away."

Mae dramatically fans her face. "I'd say I might be interested in riding *your* bike." She bursts out laughing and I smile back at her. Our eyes lock and I want to reach for her. I'd waste no time if I were really hitting on her. I'd touch her, giving off the physical hints of how much I

136

want her. Fingers on her neck. Tucking back her hair. A kiss to the corner of her smile.

"If you really want to apologize, you don't need to hit on me, though." She clears her throat, and her tone turns less playful. "I want to hear you play the piano."

"Mae." Her name is a quiet plea. *Don't ask this of me.* Her eyes watch mine dart away from hers. I glance over at the piano in the corner. I can't. I can't do this, not even for her.

"It's okay. You don't have to do it. It's kind of a grand gesture." Mae pauses. "I wonder if that biker knows a tune."

"Oh, you play dirty."

"Dirt is my thing. How's that for innuendo?" She slowly smiles. "Besides, I thought we were only practicing your pick-up lines." There's a question in her voice. Was I hitting on her? Was I genuine or was this just pretend? My opening come-hither line was an I'm-sorry-statement. Playing the piano seems to be the only way to let Mae know I'm sincere. I meant it—all of it—pickup lines and apology.

A grand gesture. Mae mentioned such a thing earlier today as we stood by the giant blue whale attraction propped in a pond. I don't remember the details of the structure other than a husband built that whale for his wife, confirming his love for her. At the time, I scoffed. Who wants a silly cement whale as a gift? But I recall Mae saying something about the couple's children and grandchildren enjoying the thing for years. When a man loves a woman, he gives her what she wants. He proves himself with something as simple as a red geranium or as giant as a replica whale.

Or playing the piano because she asked.

Slipping from the stool, I turn from Mae and head to the piano once more. My body hums. My heart hammers. I jiggle my arms. I can do this. I can do it for her.

I slide onto the bench as my mind runs through tunes. I'm so out of practice this could be an epic fail. Like walking away from the band. Like giving up on a dream. I glance up at Mae. Her elbow is bent on the bar, her chin propped in her hand. She's giving me the dreamiest look and I imagine playing the piano for a woman like her back when I was

137

in my twenties. When I was young and didn't need to hit on women because they hit on me. Mae would have been the type of girl I should have come on to. She would have been the right woman for me.

A song comes to mind and I'm curious if I'll remember it correctly. Placing my fingers on the cool keys, I press down. The trill notes vibrate into the bar where overhead music and the chatter of patrons still rings higher than the sound. I ripple my fingers over the keys as a warmup, and a current of energy prickles up my arms. Adrenaline surges through me and my blood flows like rapid rivers. I feel alive like I haven't felt in a long time, and I repeat the rumbling down the length of the keys before settling in place.

Hitting the first note, the harmony comes back to me. Lawson and I wrote this song about not letting go of the woman of our dreams. I don't know if he ever found his. He'd been best friends with his sister, and the relationship was one I didn't understand. I thought she'd hold him back. I was wrong.

As the notes flow and the rhythm falls into line, I'm transported back in time while fully present where I sit—a dark bar in Texas trying to apologize to a woman I hardly know, and yet who knows more about me than anyone at this point. The melody leaves my fingertips and floats over the keys, stirring up a swirl of dust coating my memories. The song carries on and when I hit the last note, I'm almost melancholy to finish. Staring down at my fingers, bent over keys I haven't touched in over twenty-five years, something swells in my chest and my vision blurs.

Damn, that felt good.

I blink and look up, registering that a few people closest to the piano clap. Mae remains at the bar, a hand over her mouth. Her eyes wide.

"That was so beautiful," she says on a whisper when I return to my stool. "The song sounded so familiar, but I can't place it."

"It's old. It's called 'Sand' by Colt45." Our band name stumbles off my tongue, sticky and unfamiliar. I don't talk about them often. I say the name rarely.

"Oh my gosh, I loved that song when I was younger." Mae hums off key and I'm certain she has the lyrics wrong in her head as she does with most songs. Only, she opens her mouth, and the words fly out.

"I'm an hourglass. You're the sand. I won't let you slip away."
She's close but not quite. Still, she continues. "Fragile but strong, this can't be wrong. I'll hold you close. I won't let you slip away."

Her eyes widen as she looks at me. "You used song lyrics to hit on me?" She shrieks before laughing and slapping my shoulder. "That's cheating."

It might have been, if that song wasn't mine. Written almost thirty years ago, the lyrics are more appropriate than ever. I don't want to let Mae slip away.

L.B. Dunbar

20

TEXAS – DAY 4

Playlist: "Deep in the Heart of Texas" – Gene Autry

[Mae]

Shit. I drank too much. I hadn't been sloppy drunk or ready to vomit but those margaritas had been strong, and I downed them too fast. When we eventually walked back to the hotel, my limbs were heavy, and my body swayed. I might have been slurring my words. There's also a heavy weight at the base of my spine as I lay flat on my belly on a diagonal across my hotel bed. Opening my eyes, I glance down the side of my body to find Tucker next to me, his head on my lower back. One arm drapes over the backs of my thighs. He's scrunched up into a corner of the bed, holding onto me like a life preserver of sorts. I'm still wearing my dress from last night, minus my bra somehow. Everything else feels intact as I'm certain we didn't do anything, not even kiss.

What I'm slightly shaky about are the details of him being in my room. With the marching band in my head, I can't recall all that was said last night.

Reaching awkwardly for his head, I brush over his short hair and he startles. Lifting his head, he stares down at my covered backside. His hand coasts up the back of my thighs, and over my dress, before his head twists. He notices me gazing at him over my shoulder.

"Good morning," I croak, my throat dry. My tongue feels like I licked a cat.

"Hey." His greeting cracks and he shifts, flipping himself to his back in the sliver of space on the bed. "How are you feeling?" He rolls his head and rubs a hand down his chest. Last night, he wore a dress shirt, sleeves rolled to his elbows, and a pair of suit pants to the bar. Presently, he's still wearing his pants, minus his shirt and belt. His firm chest is on display. His leather strap necklace rests on his sternum. He was

140

overdressed for the small-town tavern, drawing attention to himself with his good looks. *Or was it the music?* He played the piano last night and I'd held my breath at his rendition of "Sand," a sultry ballad song about someone slipping away and someone else not wanting them to go.

"I definitely overindulged," I grumble, tipping to my side and placing a hand over my forehead. I'm an idiot, because riding in a car today with a hangover might be a nightmare, not to mention that even though I've slept, I don't feel rested. "How did you end up in here?"

I'm horrified that I might have coerced him into my room. *Did I hit on him?* He explained what happened in his past—all those women wanting him despite his faithfulness to his wife. He even explained how it wasn't me so much as a gut reaction when I asked for his number on the street that first morning.

"You're making up for having my suit cleaned with this trip." That made me laugh.

Did he open up more about Rochelle being unfaithful to him in the end? I'm certain he did. He told me he'd filed for divorce before she took that trip with her lover. His use of the word would be almost comical, except I don't know how else to describe a person one has an affair with. He or she is not a spouse. They are not the person one took vows with, made promises to, or hitched a life around.

"I was worried you'd get sick. After I walked you in here and you passed out on the bed, I went back to my room and grabbed my things. Brought them back here."

I sit upright and notice his bag in the corner of the room.

"I'm sorry you lost out on that money."

He rolls to his elbow and peers at me. "It was worth it." Those silvery eyes flicker with mischief and I see that man women would have hit on over the years.

Hesitantly, I lick my lips. "Did I hit on you?" I close my eyes.

"Sunshine, I'd like to play this up and say that you did, drawing out the torture, but you're looking a little green already and I don't have it in me to torment you today. We're good."

"Oh…good." *Thank God.* I don't want him to lump me in with those other women, even if he no longer has his wife. I don't want to be just

L.B. Dunbar

another woman hitting on a hot man slipping him my room key. I'm certain I would have been disappointed. He wouldn't have been here this morning...or even participated in a *last night*.

"Let's shower and get something to eat." The statement catches me off guard and he must sense my unease. "Unless you aren't hungry?"

Food isn't the issue, but the first directive implied we'd shower *together* which is ridiculous. Why would he shower with me? Why would he want to shampoo my hair and let me soap up his body and then allow our skin to slip and slide together? I need to clear my head of all sexual thoughts about this man when he's been nothing but sweet toward me.

He apologized for yesterday. I accepted his gesture. He played the piano.

"No. I'm hungry. You can shower first."

"Are you sure?" When I nod, he easily rolls in the opposite direction and slips a hand in his pants. I shouldn't take a peek, but I can't miss what he's trying to disguise behind the silky fabric. *It's only morning wood*, I tell myself. A phenomenon all men experience. I close my eyes again and slip lower on the bed, smoothing a hand down my wrinkled dress and wait for Tucker, trying not to picture him taking that bulge in hand, soaping himself all up and yet getting dirty in my shower.

+ + +

Shamrock is full of Route 66 nostalgia. A restored Magnolia gas station graces a street corner as the building sits on an angle next to an old hotel that had been converted to the Pioneer West Museum. The once popular Tower Plaza and U-Drop Inn Café with its iconic Conoco lettering on a tower was another inspiration in the animated movie *Cars*. Visually restored to its earlier glory, the location offers a modern-day charging station and I plug in the Prius when we arrive there for breakfast.

We move in slower motion this morning, or maybe that's just me with my dull hangover. I'm not as young as I used to be, and I don't even try to pretend I'm not hurting. Tucker found ibuprofen for me, and we seek greasy breakfast food to help soak up the alcohol still swimming in my stomach.

It won't take us long to travel through Texas and we agree to go as far as we can into New Mexico. As I-40 covers most of the iconic Route 66, following the original path closely, we stick to the expressway and pull off where we can for attractions.

We drive through McLean, which boasts that it is *the* heart of Texas.

We pass a Phillips 66 gas station, which looks more like a small house, and I jump out to have my photo taken hugging yet another historic gas pump.

On our way to Amarillo, the next major city along the route, my phone rings through the car's speakers. Because it's Monday morning, I'm assuming the call is one of the boys before they go to work. The caller ID on the dash reads Wyatt and I press accept.

"Good morning, sweetheart," I say more cheerful than I feel.

"Mae?" My ex-husband's voice fills the car.

"Shit," I mutter under my breath and feel Tucker's head turn in my direction. "Let me pull over and take this." I click on the hazard lights and slow to veer onto the shoulder. I'm driving this morning because Tucker admitted he needed to do a few things related to work. However, he's sitting in the front seat beside me instead of the back where Gemma the geranium is securely buckled. As I begin to merge onto the shoulder, a firm hand takes the steering wheel and forces the car to stay on the highway.

"What the heck?" I mumble, quickly glancing over at Tucker who shakes his head. We aren't pulling over for this, his wagging head says.

"Are you talking to yourself?" Adam snaps. I don't respond as I click off the hazards and accelerate. I'd rather not have a conversation with Tucker listening, or any conversation with Adam for that fact. "You stole my car."

"It's not your car," I argue back. "It's Wyatt's." My teenage son wasn't happy with the dad-mobile, as he called it, he received upon graduating from high school. Although the distance to Wyatt's college wasn't far, Adam didn't want to drive back and forth, moving Wyatt in, or bringing him home for visits, so he bought our son transportation. I'd always been curious where Adam got the money.

"And you stole from me," I remind him, sheepishly shifting my eyes to Tucker and back to the road. Tucker's head takes a sharp twist in my direction. "Now we're even," I lie.

"I should send the cops out after you," he threatens.

I'm immediately angry. I'm hungover. It's Monday morning and I don't need this old argument with him. "You wouldn't dare, or I'll have you in court for embezzlement."

Adam had been stealing funds from the landscaping business and garden center, alternating between the two to disguise what he was doing—having affairs with other women. I have the financial records to prove it, and in another foolish agreement with him, I decided not to press charges. He would owe me the money. *Stupid, stupid woman.* It's a miracle he kept up with child support, but as Owen turned eighteen before his senior year in high school, that ended. Adam and I are supposed to split college tuitions and the money I would earn from driving Tucker is going to cover my share of this year, at least for Owen, who will be a freshman.

The line goes silent for a second before Adam mutters, "Let's not do this."

"Yes, let's not." I pause. "You know what's sad, Adam? It's Monday and you just noticed I have this car." I'd called home on Thursday evening and somehow got Adam on the line after speaking with the boys. He hadn't even mentioned Wyatt's car then. My eldest son wanted a new truck, but it wasn't economical or practical. I own two for Mae's Flowers, one of which is a beater and Wyatt prefers to drive that around town. *It's chill,* he tells me which I think is code for some concept I probably don't want to know the meaning of.

"I was busy this weekend," Adam huffs.

I bet he was. He has a new girlfriend after the one he *didn't* leave me for got tired of waiting for him. Wyatt informed me on Saturday night how he and Owen went back to my house because their father said he had out-of-town plans for the weekend. At eighteen and twenty, they were old enough to be alone, but I thought it'd be good father-son bonding time to stay at their father's house for two weeks like they had each summer after the divorce. As my boys approached manhood, I was wrong once more about Adam.

"Adam, be a father. Step up for them."

"I don't need this from you," he mocks and beside me Tucker speaks up.

"Hang up," he demands, his tone sharp and commanding.

"What was that?" Adam asks.

"It's—" *No one? Nothing?* I don't want to deny Tucker sitting beside me, but I also don't need to explain myself to Adam. Quickly catching Tucker's eyes, he shakes his head again, warning me not to clarify.

"Mae?" Adam shrills through the line.

"I gotta go." I reach forward and press end on the call and the car falls into heavy silence. Tucker continues to stare at me, waiting on an explanation, and I shrug.

"He stole money from our joint businesses. His own, the landscaping side, was easier to disguise because I didn't have access to the books for that division. However, Adam had access to the accounts for the flower shop and garden center, and admittedly, I've never been good at the accounting. It's one reason I hired on Pam as my manager at first." Tucker knows Pam is my business partner. "She caught what she thought were errors. When we took everything to an accountant when separating the businesses in the divorce, I learned the truth. It'd been a little bit here and a little bit there. Nothing large enough to be noticed, but the dollars added up. I always wondered how he bought this car for our son, but I honestly don't think the money he took was to save up for Louie." I stroke a hand over the dashboard.

"Mae, you should have pressed charges."

"I'm a sucker for promises." My voice is bitter. *Fool me once, shame on you; fool me twice, shame on me.* Fool me three times? There isn't even a saying for that. It renders one speechless by the sheer stupidity.

"You still can."

"Actually, I don't think I can. It's been five years and there's some statute on the timing." I don't know the details, but after Adam was legally removed from any connection with the flower shop and garden center, I didn't care to follow through with my investigation. He had his business. I had mine. We had to grin and bear it with the community, putting up a false front that we were a united, professional team while we hated each other. Adam didn't always purchase his flowers from me for his landscaping jobs and that was his loss. I didn't have a say in how he did business. Many of my customers were do-it-yourselfers and for those who wanted additional help, I'd allow my staff to be hired on the side for a small service fee. We weren't exactly competing with Eden Landscaping, just beating Adam at his own game.

"I can have someone look into this for you," Tucker offers, and his concern is welcome but not necessary.

"My brother is a financial investor. He checked things out as well and offered the same thing. He knew a guy." I drop my voice to sound gangster-ish. "He also gave me some of the capital to buy Adam out and remove him from the business." Paying Adam made me sick, because he'd taken money from me, but funds needed to be exchanged in some manner, so the sale was on record that I purchased his share. "Garrett owns ten-percent just to have his name in our books. Pam owns a forty-percent, and I own the rest." Pam's husband was happy to invest whatever amount she needed as a wedding present when they'd married.

Tucker swipes a hand over his head. "What a fucking asshole."

"Yeah."

"And what a schmuck to call with your son's phone."

"He does that sometimes because I have him in my phone as Sperm Donor."

Tucker laughs before reminding me, "He wasn't worthy."

The statement warms me. "Right again, but I wouldn't trade my boys, so there is that." It's hard to fault Adam a thousand percent because he's the one who gave me Wyatt and Owen. At least, *his sperm* helped me conceive them.

"We developed Impact because of something similar." Tucker narrows his eyes toward the windshield as he speaks. "At first, Rochelle

146

and I had been partners while I worked in marketing for the family business. As she grew, we formed a corporation, and I became chief executive officer and head of marketing while she remained president. Ten years in, she was even bigger than we ever anticipated. Machlan and I formed Impact and made Rochelle a client. Some days I'm so grateful for the twist in my life."

It sounds like another story, but I'm still focused on how easily he's opening up to me.

"She was just such a—" The car jostles and a tire *thump-thumps*.

"Oh my God." My hands grip the steering wheel tighter, struggling to keep the car steady. I'm afraid to remove my hands from the wheel and Tucker hits the hazard lights. Cautiously, I take my foot off the accelerator, steer toward the shoulder on a lopsided car and slow until I feel comfortable tapping the brakes. One thing Granddad taught me was never slam the brakes or you'll spin out of control. Once I cut the engine, we both take a moment to exhale in relief. I shift my gaze to the rearview mirror; thankful another vehicle didn't run into us as we slowed.

"Are you okay?" Tucker's looking at me, but I can't seem to turn my head. My eyes remain on the road before us, grateful we're off to the side.

"I'm fine," I lie. Going seventy miles an hour when the tire punctured has my heart racing.

Tucker warns me to stay in the car before he pops out the passenger door, but I'm opening the driver one as well. The car rattles as a semi-tractor trailer truck speeds past us and Tucker and I meet at the trunk.

"What did you hit?" he asks, not accusing me, but curious. He glances down the highway for something.

"I have no idea." I don't see anything either. I *hadn't* seen a thing in the road, but the left back tire is shot.

Tucker reaches out for my arm and runs a hand down it. "Okay. I can fix this." He pops the trunk and starts removing our suitcases. The spare is in a hatch underneath them. With our luggage on the side of the road, he hikes the spare tire out of the well and I remove the jack. There's a funny-looking crossbar tool that looks like a giant X and while I know it's for removing the lug nuts, I twirl the metal tool in my hand.

147

L.B. Dunbar

"I should have been a baton twirler," I say over the roar of more vehicles whizzing down the highway. Tossing the lug wrench into the air once more, I overshoot, and the heavy metal tool flips out toward the asphalt and bounces away from us. I step forward onto the highway pavement.

"Mae!" Tucker hollers at the same time I hear the harsh horn of a semi-truck. Hands on my hips drag me backward and slam me awkwardly against the open trunk.

The heavy weight of a fast-moving tractor trailer whizzes past the car, shaking us in its wake. Tucker's hands cup my face before cupping my shoulders and slipping down my arms. Then I'm pulled into him, colliding with his firm chest as the tightest embrace circles me. Awkwardly, I lift my arms and curl my fingers into his T-shirt just above his lower back. His arms squeeze tighter before one hand coasts to the back of my head, fingers dipping into the base of my messy bun. The other hand palms my back, skimming downward to rest at the top of my backside, pinning me tightly against his chest. His heart races and matches the galloping of mine.

We don't speak.

Tucker continues to hold me, breathing heavily near my ear. The hand inside my hair slowly lowers to my nape before curving to the side, nearly circling my throat. The other hand slips under my tee, smoothing up and down my warm skin, soothing me as if I'd been hurt. However, this desperate embrace feels like it might be comforting him as well as me. I lift my own hands, scrubbing up his taut back and palming his shoulder blades, clutching at him. His wandering hand stops moving, pausing on the clasp of my bra. He breathes in. He breathes out and I follow his lead. Our chests heave together, against one another before his hands move once more. Fingertips skitter down my spine while his other fingers work their way back into my hair.

His face joins the movements. His cheek rubs against my jaw. The stubble that's been filling in over the course of the last few days is sharp but tickles. A shiver ripples up my spine, and he brushes his jaw against the side of my face before lowering for my neck. I twist my head to allow him better access to my skin and he continues to paint my neck, my jaw,

148

and my cheek with that scrubby scruff. A breath whispers over my ear as we remain plastered to one another, clinging to one another.

I've never been so turned on from a hug in my entire life.

"Mae," he whispers at my ear, continuing to move his cheek and stroke my back. There's so much said in my name, but I can't comprehend anything. Is he asking me something? Is he telling me something? Is he simply confirming I'm standing here before him?

I'm desperate for him to press me against the side of this car and kiss me like I've never been kissed before.

The thought causes me to place my hands on his shoulders, needing him to release me before I do something stupid like attempt to kiss *him*.

"Not yet," he hums at the soft push I give his upper arms. The hand in my hair slips lower once again and skims the side of my neck. His palm on my back moves to the edge of my waist and he rocks his hips forward. The long, hard shaft behind denim wedges against my lower belly.

"Mae," he whispers again, keeping his hips forward, his erection against me. His hand on my throat moves lower, my heart races in my chest and his forehead meets mine. I close my eyes and his nose swipes against the tip of mine.

"If it isn't coffee, it's a busy street," he mutters, rolling his head against my own. It takes me a minute to remember he tugged me off Adams Avenue when I was looking for my dropped phone and taxi horns blared.

Pulling back, he presses a kiss to the tip of my nose. The touch is so soft it's like a whisper of air. Next, he kisses my forehead, and another tractor trailer whips past us, laying on his horn. I flinch and Tucker tightens his hold once more.

"We need to get off the side of the road," he says, but his voice is quiet and deep. He's speaking to my lips.

I nod to agree with him, but I don't want him to let me go and he must feel the same because he draws me back against him. One more stroke of his palm up my spine. One more dip of his fingers into my loosened bun. His cheek moves against mine and then he's gone, stepping back, his hands slowly slipping free like he's releasing a ribbon.

He presses the bulge in his jeans against me one final time, not even hiding the fact he's hard. He extends his arms and takes a step back before he swipes a hand down his face. He's been drained of the tan coloring in his cheeks. I scared him as much as I frightened myself.

I open my mouth to apologize. I don't know what I was thinking other than trying to lighten the mood between Adam's call, Tucker's confession, and the flat tire. However, he turns, giving me his side, and checks the road. The lug wrench is in the second lane farthest from us and Tucker checks the coming traffic once more. Sensing he's clear enough, he races for the tool and returns to me.

"You stay here." He points at me with the wrench, and I accept his demand with a nod. I'm not arguing with him about another thing because he just saved me from being roadkill on Route 66.

21

Playlist: "Unchained Melody" – The Righteous Brothers

[Tucker]

Fuck. I'm shaking. The spare tire is in place. The old one tossed in the back and we're on the road to Amarillo again, but I can't stop the tremble in my hands. All I saw in my head was Mae being flattened on that road, much like the nightmares I have in my head of Rochelle and Marty during a plane crash. Much like my parents in the same manner.

Once I pulled Mae from the highway and the near miss of a semi-tractor trailer, I couldn't get her close enough to me. I wanted her under my skin, and I didn't want to let her go. Still, we needed to get off the edge of the highway and now we need a new tire. We find a tire shop with a few hours' wait in Amarillo, and we're directed to historic Sixth Street, a business district reminiscent of Route 66. I don't feel like shopping. I can't concentrate on anything, but Mae and I walk the blocks to stretch our legs and calm our hearts. At one point, I grab her hand because once again, I'm afraid to let her go.

We aren't looking at anything specifically, just walking hand in hand when Mae finally says to me, "Aren't you hot in those jeans? We should buy you some shorts."

I have shorts with me, but I'd been saving them for Napa. I also have workout shorts, but I wouldn't wear them traveling.

"It's not like there's an Ashford's around here," I blurt without thinking and she chuckles before she stops. Still holding her hand, I take a step forward and turn to face her.

"Wait." Her eyes meet mine as they so often have with questions. "Like the department store? Ashford's in downtown Chicago?" Mae's brows crease and she tips her head to the side, staring at me. "Your last name is Ashford."

"Yes." I state the obvious as Mae puts things together.

"Are you... Is that your family business?"

"It was."

Her hand slips from mine and I instantly miss it. Reaching out for her fingers, I link mine with hers, holding the tips more than her hand. I don't want this to change things.

"Sunshine," I plead.

"You're so full of surprises." Her brows sternly pinch, or maybe that crease is because she's confused. "How many more secrets do you have?" Her voice lowers, the tone hurt. I'm not holding out on her, it's just that I've already shared so much.

"That might be my last one." I'm so bare to her, raw even. The only thing left is telling her more about the band, but I'm not certain those details are necessary. I failed as a rock star.

Mae shakes her head. "So what? You're the heir or something."

"Jude is the heir. He's the CEO with forty-nine percent in the only store." The original flagship store is the only location that remains as the place where it all began. A buyout happened with another department store chain, converting most locations to their brand. Jude wasn't happy to see his inheritance chipped away and it's another grievance he wants to lay on me. However, the decision to sell came from his great-grandfather and the board of directors. Maybe Grandfather wanted Jude to start from scratch. Maybe he wanted Jude to rebuild. Or maybe he wanted Jude to stop acting like a spoiled brat. I was just like Jude as a kid.

"It's another reason I started Impact. I needed something that was mine. Not Rochelle's. Not my son's. Not the family's."

Despite all I'd done, Grandfather left that one store to Jude in his will. He liked to tell me I'd always been able to forge my own path, which was such bullshit. I'd given in to his, married a woman to save a business agreement and the family name. Grandfather didn't live to see the day when things began to sour with my wife or how much my son would come to despise me.

"What is love, son? We come from families that merge." My grandfather held such an antiquated philosophy, but twenty-seven years ago what could I do? Like Mae said about her sperm-donor husband, she

wouldn't trade her kids. I wouldn't give up Jude even though we disagree on almost everything.

"So, you are an Ashford, as in Ashford's department store. You were in a band. You were married to Rochelle Ashe, influencer phenom, and you now own your own media company specializing in influencer branding and social media marketing. Do I have that right?"

"Sounds about right," I say. Rather than sounding impressed, though, Mae looks upset. Her hand tugs free of mine again and she begins walking.

"Mae?" I follow her, my stride lengthening as her pace quickens.

"What the hell are you doing with me?" she barks, waving out her arms and turning on me. "You could afford a private jet. You could cross the country in your own fancy vehicle. You could have found another driver and paid them triple."

"Please don't make this about money and you know why I don't have a private jet."

Mae huffs and turns her back on me once more. Her sandals flap on the cement sidewalk and her ass sways as she stalks off. I race after her again, catching her arm and gently forcing her to stop.

"Mae. It's nothing."

"It's not nothing and it has nothing to do with money. Why are you keeping so much from me?"

Why would I open up? The words tingle the tip of my tongue, but I don't say them because I have already told her so much. She knows my secret about Jude. She knows the reason behind my grandfather's request. She knows I quit a band. She knows I wanted a divorce from Rochelle.

"I'm not. Mae, I've told you more than I've told any single other person ever. Even Mach. And I'm happy I'm on this trip with you."

"You are not," she scoffs.

"Don't say that." My voice turns harsher. My tone serious. I've enjoyed our time. It's been a rollercoaster ride, but I'm glad to be on this trip with her. I'm excited to share this experience with her. In fact, I might be happier than I've ever been. "I can't think of anyone else I'd rather cross the country with."

"Taking other people's journeys," she mocks of words I tossed at her only yesterday.

"No, Mae. Taking our journey. Making this ours. Yours and mine." I point between us. "We're making a new history here."

Mae turns her head, then lowers it. She shakes it side to side and blinks.

"Sunshine?" I reach for her chin and tip her face up. Her eyes close.

"Look at me, sweetheart." Her lids lift and liquid fills them.

"You can be kind of sweet sometimes," she says, so softly, so quietly, and once more I want to kiss her. I'd longed to put my mouth against hers and kiss her with everything I had as we stood on the side of the highway. Now we are standing on a sidewalk, and if my mouth presses hers, I don't think I can stop there. I want to brush my lips over every inch of her. I want to run my tongue over her skin. I want to savor her, devour her, and then I want to enter her, joining us as only two people can. I want to make history, as I said. Hers and mine, together.

"Let's get some lunch," I say instead before I kiss her along this route we're traveling. I'd press her up against a building just as easily as her car, but I want us to be alone when I do. I want to take my time with her because like that song I sang last night, she's grains of sand, and she'll slip through my heart if I don't hold on tighter.

+ + +

With the setback of a flat tire, we delay even longer when we experience The Big Texan, a touristy restaurant in Amarillo known for a seventy-two-ounce steak. A giant bull statue stands outside the place and Mae has her obligatory photo taken, commemorating one more stop along our travels. I can't tackle a seventy-two-ounce steak, but I'm ready to eat hardy. I'm starving as the adrenaline rush of nearly losing Mae settles down.

Eventually leaving Amarillo, I'm so protein full, I need a nap. Mae asks me to drive, and I wonder if she's still shaken from earlier. Outside Amarillo, we find Cadillac Ranch, an iconic stop on a frontage road. Ten Cadillacs dating from 1949 to 1963 stand half buried in a field with their tailfins upright, or what would have been tailfins if they hadn't been removed as souvenirs over the years. The draw to this location is the fact you *can* deface the vehicles, which have been here since 1974. Mae tells me all this as we near what is considered roadside art.

"Graffiti is encouraged, I don't have spray paint," she explains. "But I have a permanent marker."

Permanent ink will make such a small mark on these classic Cadillacs, but I follow Mae's lead. The stench is acidic with both animal droppings and aerosol, but we make our way to the first car and Mae hands me a marker. Wandering from car to car, she finds a small space on each one and signs her name adding a quote from a notebook she pulled from her bag.

Though she be but little she is fierce.

Nevertheless, she persisted.

The words are motivational, and while the first is classic Shakespeare and the second is modern women's movement, Mae also has a few song lyrics. One of them I recognize.

"I'll find you on the open road." *Wait for me* is the next line and Lawson Colt's voice echoes in my head.

"Why did you pick this one?" I ask Mae wondering if she had a crush on Lawson as many girls did when we were in our early twenties.

Mae shrugs as she does. "I like that song."

The idea strikes to write other lyrics.

My heart is an hourglass and yours the sand,

but I won't let you slip away.

Time stands still as I long for you,

but I won't let you slip away.

You're the song in my head.

You're the hope I hold for one day, one way.

And I won't let you slip away.

Stepping back, I stare at the lyrics, wondering what inspired me to write them. What had I been thinking at nineteen when the song came to me? Why had I forgotten it? Is it possible I wrote this song for this very moment, for this very woman? The thought seems absurd and a bit deep, yet I stare at the words before looking at Mae, smiling to herself as she

155

moves on to another Cadillac. I don't need to mark them all. I'll only mark this one that was the year of my birth, a time when cars were big and people took road trips, searching for something. Or maybe someone.

Mae comes back to me and stares at the words I've written. I step forward and sign my name, the once-familiar autograph returning. The scribble is almost illegible with a capital T and a swooping A.

"If you could leave your mark on the world, what would it be?" she asks, staring at the cars covered by decades of graffiti. Somehow, I don't think she means literally decorating old vehicles but something more monumental. Something long lasting.

"I'd want to write a song that everyone sings."

Mae smiles. "Music is the universal language. Not everyone needs to sing your song. If you only touch one heart, you've made your mark."

I turn to Mae, who is so good inside. She deserves my final secret and I nod at the car.

"I'm Tucker Ashe. I was in the band Colt45, and I wrote that song." I turn away from her, staring at the lyrics, now permanently printed on a classic Cadillac. "The one I played last night, called 'Sand,' I haven't played since I quit the band."

Mae looks up at me, staring with her mouth agape before she punches my arm. "Get out."

I turn my gaze back to her. "It's true. My stage name was Tucker Ashe. Ash with an e. Not very original and not inconspicuous enough to distinguish me from my family, but that's who I was when my father got a girl pregnant, and my parents died. When my grandfather called, I left my rock star dreams behind."

Mae continues to stare at me, eyes wide then brows pinching.

"That's my last secret, Mae. There aren't any more."

When she doesn't say anything, I tip up my chin. "I'll meet you by the car. Take your time here." If she wants to mark every one of them, if that makes her feel memorialized forever, she can have her time in the limelight. I had mine for the blink of an eye.

22

Playlist: "Kiss Me" – Sixpence None the Richer

[Mae]

I'm still stunned at what Tucker tells me is his last revelation. To prove himself, he pulls up the song from his phone when I return to Louie, and he points out his voice as the song plays. He harmonizes in the background and quietly sings over the lyrics.

"Holy shit," I blurt as I shift in the passenger seat to face him. We're still parked outside the Cadillac Ranch as the melody fills the car. I watch Tucker hold his phone like the device holds all his secrets and he moves his lips while harmonizing with the lead singer.

"I cannot believe you are a freaking rock star. You said you were in a band, not Colt45. That was more than just some band. You hit charts. You made headlines. You were on the cover of teen magazines."

Tucker chuckles. "It's not a big deal. Not anymore."

"Are you kidding me?" I shriek. "Here I'm running around writing quotes on old cars, and you've already made a mark on the world. Your song touched more than one heart. I'm certain of it. It touched mine." I poke my chest.

This is unbelievable. I might not have known his name. I might not remember his face, but I remember the song. Like he said, hearing music evokes a memory. In my head, I see myself when I was young, googly-eyed for love ballads and rock stars, and hopeful of meeting a man someday, falling in love with him because he'd been waiting for me.

"Wow." I sigh. I don't know what else to say. "You're going to tell me you're royalty or something next, aren't you?"

"No, Mae." He laughs again. "I'm just a man."

He's so much more than a man. He's complex and incomplete. There are still holes in his story, and I want the voids filled in. Thankfully, he gives them to me as we drive toward our last stop before leaving Texas.

L.B. Dunbar

"Everything seemed to be happening at once. We'd put out a second album, but it wasn't selling like the first. I wanted to chalk it up to beginner's luck on our first one and dismiss the second. It was only one album in a long list of what we had planned. Then, Lawson was pushing for his sister to merge with us, and my parents died. Kit had lost her husband and had a kid but was on the brink of making it big. Girl-lead bands were hot. Lawson didn't mind singing with his sister. They'd been raised singing in the church choir together, and Kit had a smokey, seductive sound despite that gospel training.

"Anyway, he wanted to join her. She had an agent while we were indie, which wasn't half as popular as it is today. We'd be Kit Carrigan and the Chrome Teardrops. Lawson and his cousin were onboard for the change. I wasn't happy. They hired some young guy to be a drummer and I felt pushed out. I played drums, but also the piano, guitar, and harmonica. But how many guitarists do you need? And her sound didn't call for a keyboard."

Tucker sighs. "Then my grandfather called, and I don't know…maybe I took it as my sign to leave. It was my escape from them, but I didn't go out on my own or join up with another band like I thought I might. I fell into fatherhood and the business world as I'd been destined. As I'd never hoped to be. And *they* went on to be famous."

Kit Carrigan was a rock goddess. The kind of woman every girl wanted to be as a teen—edgy, seductive, enticing. She had a smokey voice like Tucker said and a hot guy band behind her. I didn't know about this transition from Colt45 to Chrome Teardrops. Their sounds were distinctly different.

And I'm sorry for Tucker's loss. Sometimes things just aren't meant to be, but no one wants to hear that when such a big dream has gone goodbye.

"I'm sorry you felt pushed out or that you had to leave them, but you were still a star in your own right. You had your time and it's never too late to have it again."

Tucker snorts. "I *will not* be going back. Those guys didn't know what to say when I left, and I left. I mean, I walked out and never looked back, but they didn't either." There's an edge of regret along with bitterness mixed in his voice.

"You never know," I offer. "Maybe they missed you. Maybe they want to reconnect and don't know how. There's a second chance at everything." Then again, sometimes people come and then go from your life, but still serve a purpose in the time they shared with us.

"Yes, and sometimes a second chance isn't necessary."

I don't like the sound of that statement although I understand. The philosophy is the same as saying sometimes things just aren't meant to be.

+ + +

We stop before a sign that states we are at the midpoint between Chicago and Los Angeles and snap another picture. Tucker takes a selfie of both of us, journaling more and more how together we are on this trip. Not *together*-together, just sharing the experience. His hug from earlier is long gone, almost a memory like the road behind us. He hasn't held my hand since we got the car back with fresh tires—because I couldn't just replace one but had to balance the upgrade with a replacement of the other rear tire. I consider his earlier handholding as a sort of aftershock of my near demise on the road.

"Will we make it by Wednesday?" I ask, suddenly concerned for him. He needs to meet his daughter there, where they plan to drive from L.A. to Napa. Julia actually lives outside Pasadena, but his original car service was taking him to a location in downtown Los Angeles. "I can take you to Pasadena. Our route runs right through there."

I don't want to intrude, and I don't need to meet his daughter, but I can deliver him directly to her. He'd miss out on the final stop—Santa Monica and the Pacific Ocean—but I'm not certain he wants to complete the full journey. His destination is different than mine. All along, his expectations have not been the same as mine.

"What's next for you, Mae?" He rubs the leather bracelet on his wrist. "What will you do once you drop me off?"

L.B. Dunbar

I have some vague plans in my head but nothing concrete yet. "I'll just return to Michigan."

Tucker glances momentarily over at me. "I don't like you driving alone. What would you have done if you were alone when that flat tire happened?"

He sounds like Jane, and I shrug. "I would have figured something out. Called AAA probably." I can change a flat tire but practicing the skill in the driveway and dismantling a wheel on the side of a busy highway were two different things.

"And last night? That biker was hitting on you. That could have gone wrong fast, sunshine," he chides, but I like to think I could have handled myself there as well. The man was only being friendly, flirty even, but he wouldn't have wanted to take me for a ride on his bike or otherwise.

"Mae, it's like I can read your thoughts and you're wrong. You're too fucking beautiful for your own good."

I laugh at the vehemence in his compliment and brush it off. "Well, I appreciate your concern, but I'm a big girl. I take care of myself."

Tucker purses his lips, not liking my answer but letting the discussion drop.

We drive through another ghost town, this one on the edge of Texas before entering New Mexico. Evidence remains of what once was here, like the final town we saw in Oklahoma, and once again I consider the ghosts that haunt us through our lives.

Like Tucker and his band—his once friends who he left behind, and who equally left him to move on and become world famous rock stars. He's lost so much while gaining just as much. He doesn't see the balance, or perhaps it's difficult to understand the equation as he traded one thing for another and doesn't feel he had a choice. No one wants to be stripped of their dreams. Just like these old towns, the decision to put in a major expressway stripped them of dreams once held by business owners. They were everyday people who just wanted to leave their mark, and did, for a little while.

+ + +

160

Into New Mexico we go, and I'm excited. I don't know what to expect but I'm imagining a lot of Southwestern bright colors and Mexican-inspired buildings. However, the map leads in two directions, one an original route and the other an alternative. In order to stay on schedule for Tucker, I mention skipping the road to Santa Fe. The cut saves an hour and spares sightseeing extras including a trip along the High Road to Taos and the Turquoise Trail, both meanderings through deserts and mountains. I keep my disappointment contained as I promised to get Tucker to his daughter in a timely manner. I still don't see how Wednesday will work but we've covered considerable ground every day.

Most of the other attractions listed for Route 66 in New Mexico are hotels and pit stops, and as much as I hate to bypass them, even I'm growing weary of every rundown or restored gas station.

"I promise I'll bring you back to New Mexico someday. We can see the entire state," Tucker says. The suggestion is a pretty promise and I've had too many of them in my life, so I don't take to heart his words. Instead, I smile weakly, knowing after this road trip I might never see Tucker again and how awkward will that be because my sister works for him.

We decide Albuquerque will be our stop for the night. As a major city on the route, I sense Tucker is desperate for a high-end, commercial hotel and not a roadside motel. The concession is another I make because he's been a good sport at my constant calls to stop and he's really opening up to me.

When we pull up before a large building that screams expensive rooms and lots of luxury, I'm immediately worried about cost and even suggest he stay here alone.

"I can pick you up tomorrow," I tell him.

When he parks under the entrance canopy, awaiting valet parking, he turns to me. "Mae, we aren't staying in separate locations. We aren't even staying in separate rooms." He stares at me, waiting for me to challenge him. His silvery eyes are like ancient jewelry and warn me not to argue with him, confirming he wants us together.

"This will be my treat." He's hopping out the driver door before I can argue this last statement. He's already paid for every night's lodging, even losing out on a second room last night to share mine. Still, he's gone to check-in while I wait in the car, staring up at a building I'm certain I couldn't afford to enter let alone rent a room within. When Tucker returns to me, he's all business-like, opening my door and helping me out of Louie. He opens the back door for Gemma the geranium, handing me the plant and my large bag.

"The bellhop will bring up our luggage." The trunk is popped, and a man steps over to retrieve our suitcases, placing them on a cart. Tucker leads me inside with a hand on my lower back, and for just a moment, I see how the other side lives. He's in his element here while I'm sorely out of mine.

"We can order room service," he says, although I can't imagine eating since the steak at the Big Texan. We take an elevator to our floor, and our bags arrive shortly after us. Once Tucker tips the bellhop, the door closes, and the silence is almost deafening.

I stand near the end of a king-sized bed while a rectangular table serves as both desk and two-person table. There's an oversized dresser with a bar inside one cabinet and a refrigerator with snacks in the other. A flat-screen television hangs over the large furniture.

"Mae," Tucker hesitates, swiping his hands up and down his thighs. "We can do as little or as much as you want. It's your call, but after today, after earlier, I just want to hold you tonight."

"Don't you think you should kiss me before you decide how far you want to go with me?" I surprise myself with the bold question.

Tucker steps up to me, cupping my cheek with one hand. His thumb strokes over-heated skin. "I'm going to kiss you, Mae. But the rest is up to you. Your call for what we do. Or don't." His eyes search my face before dropping to my lips where his thumb strokes over the upper bow then curves along the lower.

"And if I want to go all the way?" I whisper, finding myself even bolder than I was a second ago.

"Then I say, thank fuck," he whispers before his mouth crashes into mine. The kiss isn't soft and tender, but one that claims me, marks me, warns me. I'm never going to be the same after tonight.

23

Playlist: "Come Away with Me" – Norah Jones

[Mae]

Our mouths meld together, exploring one another before his drops to my jaw, to the side of my throat, to that sensitive place close to my clavicle. When he nips me there, my knees give out, and an arm catches me around my back. His mouth returns to mine but his fingers tug at my T-shirt, lifting the material up and over. When our lips separate, his eyes drop to my breasts, heavy and full in a light blue bra. He absentmindedly tosses my shirt and flattens his palm on my chest. Watching the movement of his hand, he slowly drags it over my skin before cupping me, squeezing the achy swell. He seems fascinated and the thought is both strange and empowering.

"It's been a long time," I whisper.

"Since you've had sex?" His gaze leaps up to mine.

"Since I've been kissed." My voice cracks and his brows pinch but his lips return to mine, sweeter, softer, taking his time while his hand palms my breast and squeezes me hard over the silky material. Within seconds, he has my bra unclasped and I'm exposed to him, feeling more naked than ever.

"You're so beautiful."

I shrug.

"Mae, if I see you shrug again, I'm going to spank you."

My mouth falls open. "You wouldn't." I lightly laugh but those silver eyes lock on mine and I see he just might punish me. I don't know how I feel about the possibility although I understand it's pretty common in the new age of dating. I don't understand it. I don't *have to* understand it. My body reacts and I'm almost tempted to shrug again. But I don't. I don't want to stop the direction he's going, taking things slow as he kneads and massages, lowering to lift one large globe and latching onto it with his mouth, sucking at the swell before sweeping to the nipple and twirling his tongue around the hard nub. He does the same to the other breast, then returns to my mouth, kissing me hard and intensely.

I slip my hands under his shirt, sliding the soft cotton upward until he pulls back and tugs the collar from behind his neck, removing it in that way only men can, making the move sexier than any motion has a right to be. And I'm already turned on more than I've ever been in my life. My body hums. My skin tingles. I'm so wet, it's going to be embarrassing when he finally touches me.

When my breasts connect with the heat of his chest, I hum into his mouth which has returned to mine for another searing kiss. He's branded on me, forever inked, leaving his permanent mark with unspoken lyrics. I'm never going to be the same after this trip, this night, this man.

Next, he removes my shorts and underwear in one slick motion as he lowers to kiss my belly and nip at my sides, sucking at the fleshy parts that typically embarrass me. He abruptly stands and tugs down his jeans. He's still wearing that medallion on a strap and the leather band at his wrist, plus his dark blue boxer briefs, but evidence of his excitement is hardly contained. The outline of him is long and large, but I only get a quick look before his mouth is on mine again and he's lowering me to the bed. I sit first until he breaks free of my mouth and presses me back by my shoulder. He dips over me, kissing me hard once more before traveling down my body—chin then throat then chest.

"You're the route I plan to travel tonight," Tucker says into my skin as he moves to my belly. Pulling at flabby flesh once again with his lips, making me self-conscious while feeling worshipped at the same time.

"Route forty-three," I anxiously joke.

"Route Mae and me." His head moves lower. His mouth sucks at my hip. My hands cover my belly with its tire rut effects of having children. Without looking up, Tucker forces my hands off my stomach, holding them at my sides while his head dips between my thighs. My legs dangle off the bed and he's kneeling between my knees. I lift my head but fall back when the first lap hits me. He doesn't even start gently with the tip of his tongue but goes full force, using the flat of that strong muscle to swipe up me. The next shock is the tip, twirling at my clit, and my eyes roll back. I can't remember oral sex, but I'll never forget this moment.

My legs twitch and his tongue moves. A finger joins the band down there where I throb and I seep, and I want this man more than anything.

"Give me one of those orgasms that are all yours, sunshine."

I scoff because I plan to. He can take them all for all I care as long as he doesn't stop sliding his tongue through my slit. My knees lift and my hips rock and his hands clap over my thighs, holding me still. The tension builds and I mutter incomprehensive words of *right there* and *ohmygod*.

Tucker hums against me. Another lap. Another lick and I shatter. More than a crash, but a break of my body occurs. I'm tiny fragments of myself. My head lifts. My hands clutch behind my thighs. I want to pull Tucker inside me and live in this mess between my legs. I'm wrecked and panting when he drags back, pressing a kiss to my inner thigh before nipping at my flesh.

He stands tall before me and it's almost unfair how perfect his body is. Those abs. That smattering of chest hair. The trail leading into those briefs, which lower and expose him to me. His cock stands at attention, thick and ready.

He steps over to his bag and returns quickly with a few packets. Tossing one on the dresser, he opens the other, and I wonder if this means I'll get him more than once before I've even had him the first time. Once will never be enough, and if anyone ever called me selfish, this is the moment I might agree. I want him all to myself on repeat.

I scoot up the bed, and he follows me. When my head hits the pillows, he guides himself between my spread legs, swiping the tip of his dick up and down through the moisture at my center.

"Still good with this?" he asks.

I could comment that we've passed the point of no return, but I don't. Sarcasm has been stripped from my vocabulary as have all words. There is no going back. No U-turn. No turn around.

"You're so wet," he moans next.

"You did that." His mouth was heaven down there.

"And you loved it." He's teasing me, flirting with me.

My voice drops when I respond. "I do." I could love this man, which is a silly thought to have in the position we're in. *This is only sex.* This is only one night, or maybe the remainder of this road trip, but it won't ever be more than a moment in history. Tucker and me. I don't allow myself to digest that further because he is sliding into me.

"Mae." My name catches in his throat, and he swipes hair back from my face as he enters me slow and easy, taking his time to fill me. I'm stretched in a way I haven't been in half a dozen years and him inside me wipes away the only one before him. There's no doubt Tucker is going to teach me about my body tonight. He will replace all my memories of sex before this moment. And just like this road trip, I'll be able to say I traveled him well once.

He pauses inside me, brushing his fingers on the sides of my face. "Still good?"

So good. I nod and he moves. Rhythm I'm certain is automatic in a man who loves music takes over. He rocks his hips, and my body responds. His shifts one way, my body follows. He leans back, looks between us, and watches as he glides in and out of me. I risk a glance. We're really doing this. With lights low in some swanky hotel, I'm having sex with Tucker Ashford. *Ashe.* The name suits him because he's been born again and again from dust.

And he's reviving me.

My heart races and blood flows only to one place in my body.

"Tucker," I warn, questioning myself. The only time I've had a multiple orgasm was the other night in the shower. I've read about them, heard about them, but my body typically doesn't give me another turn. Maybe that has more to do with my past, and I instantly erase the thought. This is me. This is Tucker. And I'm going to come again.

"That's it, sunshine. Give me another one of those precious orgasms." I have no idea what he means, but the way he's bent his knees and my lower body balances against his thighs, he's rubbing me right where I need to set me off once more. My hands clamp on his face but he's not lowering to kiss me, instead concentrating on the way we move together.

"Get there," he demands and I'm on my way as he moves faster, rubs harder.

"Ohmygod," I cry out as I feel everything rushing, rippling, reaching only one spot and I burst. Colored rainbows of light sparkle around me. Tucker speeds up, slapping his hands under my backside and squeezing me hard as he pummels into me until he abruptly stills. Holding us pressed together, as close as we can be, he pulses inside me. His neck strains. His eyes close. He's the most beautiful man I've ever known.

When those silver eyes open again and fall on mine, he slowly smiles, giving me that grin where one side rides higher than the other. We don't look at one another long before he lowers to kiss me just as intensely as before. His kiss is a full body sensation, not just an experience of lips joining, and I treasure the feeling after what we just did.

"I'll be right back," he quietly says. After slipping free from me, he rushes to the bathroom but quickly returns with a washcloth. I need a minute and excuse myself for the bathroom. Returning, I find Tucker under the covers, his bare hip exposed, and I hesitate between grabbing pajamas and staying naked. I don't typically sleep in the nude, but Tucker is giving me a look that says *get in this bed* and I climb up beside him. When I slip my head to his chest, he rotates to his side and within minutes, we're wrapped together like some twisted knot. Legs entwined. Arms around each other. I nuzzle his neck and fall asleep in a position I'd never imagined sleeping in.

24

NEW MEXICO – DAY 5

Playlist: "Chasing Cars" – Snow Patrol

[Tucker]

In the morning, our upper bodies have drifted apart while we slept but our legs remain entangled and I'm hard as ever. I wake finding Mae already eyes wide open, staring up at the ceiling, and I wonder what she's thinking, what she's feeling.

Last night had been amazing.

Rochelle and I had an active sex life despite our troubled relationship. Being young when we married, we'd given in to the youthful ease of sleeping together. She was a spitfire and sometimes sex was the only thing to settle her. The connection reminded her I was there for her. I was the one present. She hadn't mourned my father and admitted the affair had been a mistake. A young woman taken in by the attention of someone older, someone experienced.

The lusty behavior led to Julia's birth, and I'd fallen into the path forged for me of fatherhood and working for the family company. Her father invested as Grandfather wanted. Rochelle was a stay-at-home mother as she wanted to be. Life moved forward. However, she grew restless, which led to blogging about her daily life, which turned into a college degree in modern women's study and a master's in psychology, all for a woman who originally only dreamed of staying home and raising kids. She crossed the line to working mother and balancing everything. I was her partner, her lover, her best friend. Or so she said to the world.

We were anything but behind closed doors.

Still, sex happened. How else can you profess Makeout Mondays or Liven-Up Thursdays unless you practice what you preach? And as much as we'd grown stagnant, we still tried to follow her rules. It hadn't helped. We were two separate entities sharing a home. When Julia

169

moved to California for college, the empty apartment was the end of everything. Rochelle's platform had shifted from young marriage to motherhood of older children. *When your kids become your best friends,* she'd profess. Julia had been close to her mother, but they weren't the same people, and my daughter hated the spotlight.

My eyes remain on Mae with these thoughts. She's more like my daughter in that manner. She doesn't need limelight. She didn't need fame or attention.

What does she need? Would I be enough for her? The question seems impossible to answer. I've never been first in another person's life. The thought feels like another unfulfilled dream.

"We should probably get moving," I say. We have miles to cover today. Yet, I don't want to leave this bed. Today is Tuesday and we still have the rest of this state plus all of Arizona and California to cross. I don't foresee making it to Julia by noon on Wednesday. I'm not even certain I'd make midnight, and suddenly I don't mind. We have wiggle room as Mae said when we started our journey.

But then what? I lose Mae. I don't like that thought.

"Yeah," Mae softly replies, rolling from the bed. But I'm on my knees on the mattress before I know what I'm doing, reaching out for her wrist and stopping her retreat.

"Wait." Kneeling as I am, I'm fully on display, cock stiff and pointing at her. It knows what it wants. Mae and I meet eyes. "We don't need to rush."

With our eyes still on one another, hers drop, scanning my body. Her perusing gaze is like a soft caress as she dusts over my chest where her fingers played with the coarse hair last night. She eyes my abs, and I suck in a breath, emphasizing them further for her inspection. Finally, her sight lands on my cock, hard and stiff and so ready for her, longing for her. Morning wood is a blessing and a curse, and right now I want her to use *ohmygod* on me in both manners.

"It isn't fair," she whispers and my brows pinch wondering what she means. "That body is a weapon. Maybe not of mass destruction but..." Her voice falters. Does she think I'll destroy her? She's already ruining me. I didn't know it could be like this. This yearning to be with someone has consumed me, especially since yesterday. Riding out the remainder of the day in the car with her was too much. I just wanted to pull into one of her roadside motels and book a room for the afternoon, bury myself inside her to keep her close and off the fucking roads.

My face heats at her assessment of me. I'm a vain man on a good day, but the appraisal from a woman like Mae is extra sweet. As I tug at her wrist, she lurches forward, catching herself on the mattress but I continue to gently pull her, forcing her back up on the bed. I fold to my back, hinting at what I want. Mae crawls over me and straddles my dick. She's already wet and so warm, cradling me in that soft spot on her. Her hands come to my chest and coast over the tight skin, solid muscle, and coarse hairs with a hint of white in them. I'm coming out of said skin as I want her again.

"Kiss me," I demand.

"I have morning breath." She giggles as she rubs forward and back over me.

"I don't give a shit." I jackknife upward and take what I want from her. Cupping her cheeks in both hands, I kiss her as I did yesterday. Mae kisses back, fierce and hungry, just as I'd hoped she would. She said it's been a long time and I can relate, and I've missed kissing like this. Guiding her down over me, I lean back, keeping her connected to me with this kiss. Her wetness coats me, and the heat of her folds against the length of my cock feels amazing. I want to slip into her bare but I'm practicing safe sex here.

Breaking free from her lips, I tip my head and reach for a condom I'd placed on the nightstand last night. Mae watches me as I roll it on. Her blue eyes are wide and bright, and hunger fills them once more. I want her mouth sucking me dry but right now, I want to be inside her more than anything. Once I'm covered, Mae tips up on her knees and I hold myself in position. The anticipation is too much and already I feel my lower back tightening. My balls hitch and suddenly I'm surrounded by Mae.

"Fuck," I ground out as she takes me deep, sliding to the hilt. She didn't waste any time, just dropped, and I'm inside, and damn, I want to stay here. I'm desert and she's sunshine, and she's going to scorch my heart.

Immediately, Mae moves, bopping up and down on my length. Her breasts jiggle. Her fingertips claw at my chest. I love watching her, but her eyes are closed.

"Look at me, sunshine." Her eyes pop open but too quickly, they close again. "Keep them open."

Mae opens once more, but she fights the battle. "It's hard to look," she whispers, and I wonder why. Did she always close her eyes during sex? I don't want to think about her with that dick ex, but I want an answer.

"Why?"

Mae keeps moving, slipping up and back on me but she answers. "It helps me fantasize."

Now, I can take that two ways. I'm not doing it for her, and she needs something playing out in her mind, or she's used to having sex that way, where she needs to pretend. Where she needs to visualize something else, hear something else, sense something other than what she's actually doing.

"Fuck that," I mutter. "Play out the fantasy on me."

Mae falters a bit, but I clap my hands onto her hips and rock her back and forth. In and out I slide, holding myself at bay until she gets what she wants from me.

"What do you need Mae? Keep your eyes open and tell me."

Her eyes widen and she continues to ride me. She shifts so her clit hits my pubic bone. Her pace hastens.

"Need dirty words, sweetheart?" I question. "Want me to tell you how much my cock loves your pussy?"

"Jesus," she mutters, and I've hit one target.

"That's it, sunshine. Fuck me hard." As she moves faster, I'm gritting my teeth. I need to come. She has no idea what she's doing to me, rocking my world as she is. She reaches for my hand and draws it between us. I know what she wants next, and my thumb finds that nub, driving her harder to the finish.

"Mae. I gotta come. I wanna come so deep inside you, but I want another one of those pretty orgasms. One where you drip all over me." *Make me yours, Mae.*

She asked about making a mark on the world, and I mentioned some damn song. But her—*this*—she's leaving a mark on me, and it's going to rest there indefinitely.

"Tucker," she whines, calling me by my formal name and riding out the syllables. Her eyes shift in color from sunshine blue to passionate indigo. Her sweet mouth hangs open as she mutters *ohmygod* and *so good* on repeat. Her breath hitches and then she's shattering. With her pussy closing around me, clenching, clutching, she pulls from me the release I've held back as long as I can. I jet inside her while she's squeezing me, and I swear it's only prolonging the pleasure. I'm never going to be the same after this woman, this road trip, and a fucking car named Louie.

Eventually, Mae collapses over me, and my arms fall to my sides. My heart races and my chest heaves. I just need a moment as silver dots speckle before my eyes.

Mae shifts but I catch her, lifting the heavy weight of my arms and wrapping them around her back to keep her in place over me. I just want to hold her as I told her last night. I just want to hold on a little bit longer to whatever it is this woman is doing to me.

25

ARIZONA – Still Day 5

Playlist: "Under New Mexico Skies" – Syd Masters

[Mae]

"If we bypass Los Lunas, it gives us an additional forty minutes," I suggest once we've grabbed a quick breakfast. We've been looking at the digital map. Tucker's getting anxious. He was supposed to meet his daughter by noon tomorrow but that's out. We have too much distance to travel.

"I told Julia I'd keep her posted on my travels, but she should go ahead without me."

He's driving once again, and I crane my neck so I can look at him. "What are you thinking?"

He scoffs. "I'm thinking anytime tomorrow isn't possible. We can't make it that fast and still see the sights."

I feel bad about yesterday and the lost time with the flat tire. While it wasn't my fault, we were hours off-course due to the tire change. I've already given up the original path through New Mexico, and figure one more small concession won't matter. New Mexico is a bust. We'll stick to I-40 most of the way until Arizona. I'll just have to return some day, and I say as much to Tucker.

"I'll make it up to you. We'll come back." I don't believe his promise to bring me to Santa Fe sometime in the future, but the thought is still sweet to hear. There isn't a future for us. We are only the here and now, and last night is already history—not one I'll soon forget, though. My clit still pulses, and I'm wet again. It's going to be a long uncomfortable day because I want him so much.

He's like spicy food you crave but shouldn't eat. You want the dish regardless and devour it anyway.

Hauling Ashe

Keeping to the interstate highway, we're bypassing the sights, which is just what the modern expressway did, and pinches of guilt sprinkle over me. I'm cheating my trip. Tucker told me how great Albuquerque is as a city and suggested we should explore it a bit, but this trip isn't about major locations. The forgotten small towns are my passion. Their livelihood and their mystique are the spots I want to visit even if they've been stripped of their magic. Once I reached the Southwest, I wanted to explore the natural wonders in this portion of the United States, but I'm only speeding by the beauty outside my window as we rush through the desert landscape.

I've hinted at seeing the Grand Canyon with no response from Tucker. The national treasure isn't located on Route 66, but it's so close, I don't want to miss it. I could suggest we don't need to stop, but I've been enjoying us doing everything together and the last thing I want to do is cut this trip in half or circle back without him. I don't want to reverse and fill in the holes by myself which is a million miles from how I felt when we started out four days ago. I've enjoyed sharing every experience with Tucker and the thought of a U-turn without him is depressing.

In addition, I argue with myself that I'm *not* doing what I've always done. I'm not letting something else, or in this case, *someone* else, dictate my schedule and sabotage my plan. This is my trip, but I've made a secondary pledge to Tucker to deliver him to his daughter. With all he's revealed to me, getting him to Julia feels like a new priority. While our timing is now off, I still intend to keep my side of the bargain, especially knowing why he doesn't fly.

Before leaving New Mexico, we pause in Gallup. I get another look at a Muffler Man, this one called the Cowboy Muffler Man, complete with cowboy hat and a gun. I mention to Tucker how I'd wanted to take a picnic on this trip. Classic, cold fried chicken was the perfect meal, and I should have stopped to pick some up at the various recommended restaurants back in the Midwest. We're too early for lunch when I mention this, so a break at Red Rock Park is out. Tucker suggests we stop somewhere in Arizona and have an authentic southwest dish instead. Again, I acquiesce.

175

We make another pitstop at a Native American shop, filled with knick-knacks and jewelry and I break down to buy my first souvenir—a silver cuff bracelet with turquoise stones. While not a traditional souvenir, I don't want the typical. I want something that will conjure a memory, a moment, and I assign the bracelet to last night and this morning. While New Mexico isn't getting a fair shake from me, this beautiful state gave me quite the generous memory. Glancing at the bracelet will always remind me of the past twelve hours.

I pass on a matching pair of earrings, which dangle like teardrops. They're pretty but I don't know when or where I'd wear them. My line of work doesn't call for fancy attire and I don't date, so there's that. Tucker offered to buy me the set, but I refused. Something like a bracelet and pair of earrings feels like a gift, and I don't feel right accepting the gesture.

When we return to the car, Tucker wears another leather braided band on his wrist with rough turquoise stones interwoven, and I'd like to say we match, but it's just too cheesy to consider.

+ + +

Crossing into Arizona, my breath is taken away immediately. The setting is gorgeous and bright, rich in red color just as I imagined it might be. We'll follow I-40, as my research into the trip shows most of Route 66 in Arizona is covered by the modern expressway. The landscape is beautiful, and it's the only sight I want to see right now.

Since Tucker has given up arriving in California tomorrow, he suggests a visit to the Petrified Forest National Park. We both agree we could use a walk to stretch our legs.

"But first, I need to get out of these jeans."

If I thought that was code for getting naked in the backseat, I'm wrong. He needs some shorts. However, Tucker has been more than affectionate today. He's held my hand or touched my thigh as he's driven. He's kissed me quick but often when we've stopped for breakfast, gas, and our mini-shopping trip. With his mention of stopping once more at the Tee Pee Trading Post in Lupton, Arizona, he lifts my hand and kisses my knuckles before scraping his teeth over them. It's more affection than I'd had my entire marriage.

Inside the trading post, I wander while he finds something to wear. If I expect him to suddenly look like a tourist, I'm wrong. He steps out of the dressing room in olive green walking shorts and a gray tee that says Arizona across it. He could be a spokesman for the state and their outdoor adventures, and once more I shake my head at his good looks.

"You know, being a marketing man, you should whip up something for Prius. Instead of this poor car having a bad rap as the dad-mobile, you could show them what the modern dad looks like."

Tucker chuckles. "And what's that?"

I wave a hand up and down before his body, focusing on the heavier scruff of silver and ink on his face, and the tightness of his body. He's one hot DILF and I'm happy to have done him. Prius would sell a ton of automobiles if they used his image for their campaigns. *Hot dads do it eco-friendly.* He cares about the environment and his body.

He laughs again as he spins to look at himself in the mirror. "Look alright?" he asks, smoothing a hand down those firm abs under body hugging cotton.

I hum in response, and he glances around before tugging me into the fitting room. With the curtain closed, I'm against the wall and he's kissing me senseless. His mouth ravishes mine before he moves to my jaw.

"You make these little sounds when you come. Just like that hum."

He might make me come kissing me like he is. Hungry lips and a twirling tongue make my knees go weak. Too soon, he finds the willpower to pull back; however, I remain slack against the wall a moment, trying to catch my breath.

His hand caresses my face, and he stares at me, smiling that crooked grin before taking my hand and exiting the small space. I wish I could read his mind and know what he's thinking when he looks at me. Can he see in my eyes how I feel about him? Only five days and I'm falling so fast there isn't a safety net that could catch me. And I'm going to need catching. I'm going to need something to cushion the crash when this man and I inevitably part.

26

Playlist: "Take It Easy" – Eagles

[Tucker]

Our next stop is Winslow and for the life of me I can't think of why that name sounds familiar. Mae has been wiggling in her seat and I'm wondering if she needs the bathroom. She cannot sit still as she reminds me for the third time we need to stop in this small town.

Pulling into the area, a giant Route 66 emblem covers the brick paved corner of Route 66 and North Kinsley Avenue. A statue of a man stands on the corner with a brick façade behind it that reads: Winslow, Arizona.

"Just park anywhere," Mae says, her voice rising with excitement. As we cross the street near the statue, I see a bright red truck with a flat bed and wooden gates on the side.

"Is that a flatbed Ford?" As soon as I say the words, the song hits me. "Take it Easy" by the Eagles is a famous song about a man on a road trip with worries on his mind. He's standing on a corner in Winslow, Arizona when he meets a woman who propositions him, wanting to know if love can save him.

"Here." Mae hands me a small brown bag, folded over at the top and I question her with a look before opening the package.

"Mae," I whisper, staring inside the bag.

A harmonica.

"A guitar is probably more appropriate for the corner, but I had no idea if you played. But you mentioned the harmonica and there was so much heart when you spoke about it. I just thought—"

My arms are around Mae and I'm crushing my lips to hers, kissing her despite other tourists on this corner. Pulling back before I take this moment to the level of indecent exposure, I rest my forehead against hers.

"This might be the nicest thing anyone's ever given me." I still have one arm around her as Mae beams up at me.

"I didn't know if there was a certain kind or whatever but—"

"It's perfect." I cut her off again. "But where did you find this?"

Mae sheepishly smiles and all she offers is, "Along the way." My own smile grows large enough my cheeks ache.

"Mae Ellen Fox, if you tell me you own a flatbed Ford I might have to marry you."

Her face pinkens, and I realize what I've said. I'm teasing her, of course, and she turns her head to glance at the truck parked on the corner, playing up the motif of the nostalgic song. She doesn't answer me but peers back at me with a tighter smile.

"You should play something," she says, her voice quiet.

"Right here?" I laugh.

"Standing on the corner, definitely." She slips from my arms, and I stare back at this incredible woman who bumped into me on a street corner in Chicago with coffee in her hand. Who would have known five days later, I'd be road tripping across the country, and she'd give me this gift? A gift I'm nervous to play as it's been so long.

"I don't know if I remember," I say, holding the instrument in my hand.

"I bet it's like that piano," Mae softly says. "You didn't forget. You're just out of practice."

There are so many things I'm out of practice at and could use a good teacher. Mae might be that mentor who restores my faith in things like hope and love and loyalty.

"Try it," she whispers, easing back another step as if I need the space to play such a small wind instrument.

With shaky hands, I lift the four inches of metal to my mouth and blow. The first shot is sharp, and I flinch at the crack of noise so close to my face. Mae chuckles nearby and I close my eyes, bringing the instrument to my lips once more. On the second try, I'm better.

The song flows outward a bit rough and a little scratchy but eventually, I'm at the refrain and it comes smoother. The melody is not meant to be played in entirety, but the chorus works, and Mae sings off key before belting out the final *crazy*. She breaks into her own rendition of an air guitar solo, and I add my sound to her silent mix. When I end, the tourists near us clap, and I laugh harder than I have in a long time.

A couple offers to take a picture of Mae and me, and then I ask them to take one of us by the flatbed truck because this girl really is going to save me.

When we leave Winslow, I know what I have to do. I've already told Julia it's going to be a day-by-day thing on when I can arrive, and I'd update her. I'll never make tomorrow at noon, and a selfish part of me is glad. Although I don't see Julia unless she comes to me, and we could use some father-daughter time, I need these additional hours with Mae. I need to do right by the woman driving me to my daughter. I just need to be in Napa by Friday afternoon.

"Let me check in with Mach." In the early afternoon, I'm two hours behind Chicago's time zone. I haven't conducted a stitch of business today. However, the call is a ruse. I search the internet instead. My heart races. I'm not certain I can do what I've planned for Mae, but I need to try something, as much for her as for me. It's time.

We decide to skip a meteor site but at the same exit is a strange-looking geodome building and Mae looks up the history of the building. Another inspiration for the movie *Cars*. Basically, Route 66 is running parallel to the original road or underneath where we currently drive, and my big-hearted driving companion obsesses over things we pass that are lost and forgotten on the side of the route.

"That's not art," she complains of a former diner and gas station covered in spray paint. "That's vandalism in comparison to the Cadillacs."

I don't disagree with her and let her ramble.

"And why aren't those two arrows moved to the casino on the opposite side of the highway?" Two giant metallic arrows—literally named Twin Arrows—stand parallel to one another as markers of someplace once important in time. "They could be a historic landmark and a point of interest." They've obviously captured *her* interest.

Hauling Ashe

Eventually, the landscape changes once more from dry, flat desert to a mountainous terrain of evergreens. Road markers tell us our elevation has increased.

"What is that?" Mae asks, as if she doesn't recognize a mountain off in the distance or the obvious snow at the top. We're nearing Flagstaff which can be forty degrees cooler than the southern portion of Arizona on any given day. My tour guide looks up the mountain—Humphrey's Peak—and reads me information about it. "It's breathtaking."

She's used the word to describe numerous things we've passed, and in my opinion, *she's* the attraction stealing my breath. I'm still not certain what she expected to happen on this trip of hers, but I know what's happening to me. I'm falling in love with her. In five days, I feel freer than I've felt in twenty-five years and it's damn refreshing.

When we near Williams, I exit the highway and Mae twists to look at me. She's been admiring the landscape shift from desert to mountain, lost in her own thoughts for a moment.

"Bathroom break?" she questions.

"Something like that." I sheepishly smile at her as I'm certain she read the sign that mentioned the Grand Canyon. Off the highway on a two-lane road leading north, Mae continues to stare out the window as the land is flat and empty.

"You know, it's sad to put it this way, but you could bury a dead body out here and no one would be the wiser."

I laugh at the assessment of the large, flat, open space. "Thinking of committing murder?"

"I've considered it," she teases. "I bumped into this guy on a sidewalk in Chicago and he was such a flirt. He hit on me."

"Did he now?" I smile, wondering where she's going with this.

"And then he conned me into giving him a ride across the country."

"Conned you, huh?"

"And I gave in, but man, I wanted to toss him in the trunk on occasion. I could have buried him out here and no one would miss him."

"You might not be wrong about the missing part." I'm not certain who would miss me if I were gone. The thought is morbid but I'm playing along.

181

"Eventually, though, I decided he wasn't so bad."

I reach for her hand, which I haven't been holding because of her internet searches in the last hour, and I pull her fingers up to my lips, kissing her there before scraping my teeth across her knuckles. I can't wait for another night with her and seeing this vacant land gives me another idea, but I need to get us through the first stop. I need to *live* through the next one.

"I'd miss you," Mae whispers with her hand at my lips.

I close my eyes for the briefest second while I drive, feeling the same way.

I'd miss you, too, sunshine.

+ + +

The closer we get to our destination the more nervous I grow. Mae has gone quiet as the signs advertise more and more about the Grand Canyon—tours, camping and helicopter trips—and I have no doubt she knows where we're headed. She was so disappointed when we had to skip Santa Fe and the drive to Los Lunas, but she put on a brave face. And I haven't missed her hints about the Grand Canyon. While the location is not on the route, the destination was a point of interest for old-school 66 travelers and we were too close to bypass such a national treasure.

"They say a helicopter ride is really the best way to *view* the Grand Canyon," she emphasizes. "To experience the canyon, you need to hike it, but I don't know how I'd do at camping in it."

"Ever been camping?" I ask.

"Only kind of vacation I ever had before this one."

The comment startles me. "You've never been in a hotel before?"

"Oh, I have. I've just never been anywhere on a vacation that warranted a hotel."

"Never?" I can't believe it. Surely, she's been somewhere other than her home state.

"Went everywhere in a camper or stayed in camping cabins. Been in an Airbnb but not a hotel for an extended stay."

I'm stunned. "This must have been a huge risk for you then. An adventure to stay in roadside motels and such." It's not really a question, just an observation. Mae is curious. She needs to travel. She needs to experience places and I feel guilty once more that we cut a few stops out of her trip. But I'm hoping our next excursion makes up for some of the loss, at least a little bit.

Mae shrugs even though she knows I hate it. It's her way to dismiss something serious.

"Life is full of risks, but I got tired of never taking any."

I swallow a lump in my throat and consider what I'm about to do. "This trip was really brave of you, Mae."

Her neck cranes so she faces my direction. "I thought it was stupid?"

She teases me but also questions me. I'd said it. Plus, her sister told her the trip wasn't smart or safe. I'll agree on the safety part. What would have happened to her if she'd been alone on the road with that flat tire? Or worse, been taken in by a biker in a bar? But unsafe and unsmart do not compare to the courage she has to risk this trip anyway.

"No, sunshine. I think you are very brave."

Softly she smiles, turning her head away from me and staring out at the scenery around us.

When we pull off the road leading to the Grand Canyon, Mae spins to me once more, a question in her expression. When she sees the helicopters in the near distance, her mouth falls open.

"What are you doing?"

"I want to be brave like you."

Her hand comes to my wrist as I pull into the parking lot. "Tucker, you do not need to do this."

"Why not?"

"Because I know how you feel about flying and I would never push you to do something that made you uncomfortable."

"You aren't pushing me." I pause. "Or rather, maybe I need a push, Mae. I can't be scared my entire life."

"But flying is a big deal."

"And it's the best way to view the Canyon."

"I was just saying—"

"And I'm just saying... we're going to see the Grand Canyon and we're going to do it the right way."

Mae glances toward the building and the row of helicopters on landing pads.

"It's not in the budget," she whispers. I admit, the expense isn't cheap, but I wouldn't have expected Mae to pay the amount even if she could splurge on the fee. Twisting back to me, her eyes search mine. "I don't want you to do this."

"Why?" We lock eyes a second. "Because of the money?" She wouldn't let me buy her the new silver bracelet she wears, and we've fought over every hotel expense and dinner bill. She's not paying for this, though. "It's my treat."

"It's too much." Her hard glare tells me she doesn't mean the money. She's worried about me and her tightening clutch on my wrist says as much.

"If you don't want to do it, we don't have to." I'll admit my heart is racing and I'm having second thoughts, but I won't chicken out unless she's adamant she wants to pass.

"Aren't you afraid?" she whispers.

"I am, Mae. I'm frightened out of my mind, but I want to do this. With you, I want to do this." I reach for her cheek and pull her to me, brushing my lips over hers. "Not going to lie. I'm going to be squeezing the crap out of your hand, but with you, I'll be safe." Everything in me says I'm speaking the truth.

I'm safe with Mae.

She softly chuckles. "You know I can't assure you of that, but this is almost too exciting to pass up." Her enthusiasm slowly climbs again.

"Then don't pass. Do this for me. Do this *with* me." I'm giving her this gift because she deserves it. She's already given me so much and that damn harmonica, now in my pocket, is the best gift I've ever received. But I also want her to do this with me even when I know I need to take this flight for myself. I need to brave my fear of flying, if only in a helicopter. I hate being afraid and she said it so perfectly. I'm *tired* of not taking the risk.

27

Playlist: "Bulger's Dream Olympic Fanfare" – performed by John
Williams and The Bands of HM Royal Marines
"The Star -Spangled Banner/National Anthem" – performed by
Whitney Houston

[Mae]

I'm stunned. By his insistence. By his gift. Tucker is nervous. The stiffness of his body hints at his unease, but as we walk along a mural inside the waiting area, I silently point out to him the chopper company's safety record. Only six deaths in seventy years. The odds seem in our favor. When our name is called, we're introduced to Troy, our pilot, and then led to the helipad. Instructions are given about the harness belt and safety regulations, then we're told to sit back and relax. I'm between Troy and Tucker as we sit in the front of the copter. The bubble glass windshield is perfect for viewing.

"Have your phones ready," Troy cheerfully suggests. I do hold the device in my hand, but with my other hand, I'm clutching Tucker's. Admittedly, I'm anxious as well. I've never flown in something like this, and I talk myself out of *what goes up must come down*, reminding myself of the safety record of the company. I also say a silent prayer of gratitude for this opportunity. I never in my wildest dreams imagined I'd be taking a helicopter ride over the Grand Canyon. And it's all possible because of Tucker. He's braving his fear for me.

I squeeze harder at his clenched fist which is white knuckling my fingers. "Doing okay?" I ask him despite the earmuff style headphones protecting us. It's also the mode of communication with the pilot and a soft audio-recording plays us the history of the forest beneath as we approach the canyon. Troy explains our flight pattern and I marvel at the steadiness of his control.

Tucker stiffly nods and keeps his eyes forward. Troy already explained where the airsick bags were located and emphasized using

L.B. Dunbar

them if we felt ill. "I've seen it before. I repeat, do not be afraid to use them." He laughed.

Eventually, music fills my ears and Troy warns, "This is the best view." The music reaches a crescendo of drums, and the helicopter pulls off the cliff and over the canyon. My heart drops, but it isn't fear. It's the grandeur and the beauty of this country, my country. The land looks untouched by time although erosion and climate change have had some effect on the canyon environment. This place is truly a wonder and it's hard to believe such a beautiful space exists when people live on top of one another in large cities. There is still so much area uninhabited on our planet.

And this right here is the pinnacle of my spiritual road trip.

I wanted something to wow me, overwhelm me, and it's right before me in the majestic, rich red and soft pink rock formations. Turning to Tucker, I check on him and realize he's also been a huge part of this soul-searching journey. I can no longer imagine taking this trip without him, and I'm grateful once more that I didn't have to. He's been beside me through it all and I'd never change this new piece of my history.

"Isn't it beautiful?" I say to him, yelling over the noise of rotating propellers. Tucker slowly turns his head to me, eyes wide and dry.

"So beautiful," he says, keeping his gaze on me for a moment. His hand is clenching mine so hard it's possible I might bruise from his hold, but his touch will be worth every purple mark.

"You're doing it," I tell him, smiling large. *He's flying.*

Slowly, his mouth crooks. The corner lifting only slightly. *Thank you*, he mouths to me or at least that's what I think he says.

I grin again and turn back to the view. As best I can, I try to take pictures one-handed. We've already established I'm not great at selfies, but it hasn't mattered. Even if I had both hands, phone cameras could never do justice to what's before us.

Eventually, I drag Tucker's hand to my lap and squeeze. "Keep it right here," I say to him, trying to slip my hand free for a steadier hold of my phone. Tucker nods but his eyes show panic and I wait for him to make the decision to release me. Cautiously, his fingers come free and quickly slip to my thigh, clutching my muscle there instead. I snap as many pictures as I can before we move forward, and I take Tucker's hand again.

The entire flight lasts forty-five minutes and we land effortlessly, like buttering a biscuit. Troy takes a picture of Tucker and me outside the helicopter and we thank him for the ride.

"So, what did you think?" I ask Tucker, who has been suspiciously quiet. I don't want to push but it's almost like I feel his thoughts rotating like the propeller of the copter. He's spinning in circles inside his head, and I'm worried the flight was too much.

"I think we need to check into a hotel."

Not the answer I was expecting, I watch him as we cross the parking lot for Louie. Tucker hands me the keys and I silently take them. He tells me the name of a place where he booked us a room for the night, and I remember passing the hotel on our way here.

He remains so quiet, I'm freaking out by the time we reach the lodge and check in. He's resorted to one-word answers with the clerk at the desk and I silently follow Tucker to the room. If he's having a panic attack, he isn't letting on. Maybe he's having a delayed reaction to the experience. He definitely held it together in the air. No sickness. No perspiration. No breathing issues. I really expected all those things from him, but he didn't react other than squeezing the blood flow out of my hand.

He opens the door to our room and allows me to enter first. I've hardly set Gemma down on the desk when the door slams shut, and I hear his suitcase drop behind me. I turn to face him, but I'm stopped by his hands at my hips and his mouth on my neck. We're both sweaty from an earlier hike at the Petrified Forest and the intensity of the helicopter ride, but Tucker does not seem to care. He's sucking at my skin and shoving my T-shirt upward.

"That was incredible," he mutters into my neck.

Holy shit! My entire body relaxes after that comment. My shoulders lower, releasing tension I didn't realize was pressing on me. Off comes my shirt, and next pops my bra. Allowing it to slip forward, Tucker's hands cup both breasts, massaging and squeezing. Pressing them together and pinching the already taut nipples, his mouth moves along

L.B. Dunbar

my shoulder and back to the side of my neck. He's devouring me and my skin ripples with goosebumps.

"Tucker." I lightly laugh his name as his eagerness turns to urgency.

"I need you, Mae." One hand lowers to my shorts and releases the button. Hastily pushing the material over my hips, he forces me out of them. I reach for the dresser to steady myself as I kick off my shoes and step out of my shorts. Tucker tugs off his T-shirt and spins me to face the dresser. Our eyes meet in the mirror. He lowers his gaze and reaches for my underwear, pushing it down my legs until the material drops to the floor. The distinct unzipping of his shorts fills the room, and he barely has his shorts and briefs to his hips before he's bending me forward and rubbing his hard length between my thighs.

"You're so ready for me, sunshine, and I need to be inside you. I need to feel you surrounding me."

I'm not certain where this sudden rush is coming from but I'm thinking it's the adrenaline surge from his flight experience. Instead of being in shock, he wants sex. He needs to feel this connection with me and I'm willing to give it to him. Shock will come next, along with a crash, but for now, his release is my goal.

"Take me," I demand, and he slams into me. He's long, and the sudden rush forces me forward, hips hitting the edge of the dresser as he fills me.

"Mae," he strains, jackhammering into me. There's nothing slow or gentle about the rapid rhythm he sets. The dresser bangs against the wall and I hold on as he surges into me on repeat from behind. Risking a glance toward the mirror, I see my breasts jiggle uncontrollably. My hands struggle for something to hold onto on the smooth surface. Tucker's eyes are lowered to watch himself enter me. Sensing my eyes on him, he looks up. His expression is intense.

"You fit me, Mae. How is it that this happened?" His question is full of disbelief. He almost sounds angry as his hips thrust and the gentle slap of us coming together echoes after his words.

I don't answer him. He's not looking for an answer. He's chasing something and I'm offering myself as an escape. When his fingers come forward to stroke over my clit, I'm not certain I can reach where he wants me to go as fast as he's moving.

"Just you," I mutter to him, attempting to brush his fingers away from me.

"No," he commands, pulling out and turning me to face the bed. He guides me forward until I have nowhere to go but bending toward the mattress. He guides both my knees to the edge of the bed and with my ass in the air, he slams into me again. I cry out as he holds my hips, tugging them toward him while he fills me to the hilt. There's something about this position that opens me more to him. I feel exposed and wild in equal parts and when his fingers dip back to that sensitive nub, I give in to the growing flutters in my belly.

"I will not go without you."

There's so much intensity in his statement. So many ways I could read into his words. For now, I only feel him and the command of his body to bring mine to the same place as his. We're heading for a cliff, cresting the edge, and with a final flick of my clit, he sends me tumbling over with a long, lone groan. He pulls out of me, laying his sticky length against my rear cheeks and jets off on my lower back. His fingers still work me, and I continue to cry out as the release pours from me. I'm dripping with desire and unable to stop myself. I've never experienced anything like this, and it's embarrassing while thrilling.

While still breathing heavily, I mutter a curse and press back as if I want to leave the bed. Tucker holds me in place. "You're okay," he says as if he's read my thoughts.

I almost can't think it. *Did I just wet myself?*

Tucker answers me before I ask. "You squirted."

"I what?" I shakily scoff, collapsing to the bed on my stomach.

"The intensity. It caused your body to react. It happens." Why don't I know anything about this sensation and why did that feel so incredible?

"Stay here," Tucker says to me. I can't move anyway. I'm certain my legs won't carry me. Tucker stumbles behind me and I assume he's heading for the bathroom. Then, it hits me he wasn't wearing a condom.

When he returns to the room, he mentions the same thing. "I pulled out."

I could argue with him that isn't the safest method. "I have an IUD." I don't know why I offer the information. I don't want to delve into his sexual history or provide mine. I appreciate the condoms he wore yesterday because I don't know who else he's been with since his wife's death.

"I'm always careful, Mae. I wouldn't have done that if I wasn't safe." The assurance is a small consolation to a bigger elephant in the room. What just happened? What came over him and why did I love it so much?

He sits next to me on the edge of the bed and swipes at my back. I remain on my belly as he speaks.

"That was so intense." While I'd like to think he means the sex, I believe he means the flight.

"You did good," I remind him. I don't want to point out the obvious—he survived.

"Thank you," he says softer, still stroking my lower back where he's cleared the mess. "I couldn't have done that without you."

"You could have," I say. "You were ready." He could have flown at any time, but he needed the right motivation. Perhaps seeing the Grand Canyon was inspiration enough. The experience cannot be replicated. The only way to see the immensity of the canyon is to fly over it.

Tucker slowly nods beside me. "I'm exhausted," he admits as everything comes to a crash.

The flight.

The sex.

He falls to his back, tossing the towel to the floor and turns his head to look at me. "Let's nap," he whispers, and he stretches out an arm to tuck me into his chest. He presses a kiss to my head and quickly falls asleep while I lay there listening to his heartbeat.

He's a survivor. He's going to be okay after we separate.

Me? I'm not so certain.

+ + +

We sleep for a good ninety minutes before rising and showering. We could have prolonged the intimacy by showering together, but Tucker suggests I go first. He wants to check in with Mach and Julia. He hasn't conducted any business that I know of today. His daughter is another story. I feel awful he won't make it by tomorrow, but he assures me once I exit the bathroom that it's fine. As long as he gets to her by Friday, he's not concerned. He's told me more about his relationship with his daughter, explaining how proud he is that she followed her own path and became a baker instead of an internet celebrity. He admits there's still time for her to do anything she wants in life, and right now it's making cupcakes.

In what seems like typical father of the bride fashion, he knows nothing about the wedding ceremony, other than the cost. A vineyard resort has been rented out. He's met his future son-in-law only twice and has the typical concerns for their future. How will they support themselves? Will his future son-in-law always deserve his daughter? He admits Julia has a large inheritance and with the strong head on her shoulders, he hopes she'll keep that financial gain in perspective. He doesn't have any hint that her husband is after her for the money.

"Rochelle died before they were engaged but Chopper seems committed to Julia's heart more than anything." The sentiment is sweet. I don't question the name Chopper. Tucker informed me it's a nickname for Charles Henry.

Once we've showered, Tucker suggests dinner. The sky is shifting in color, and the time is late. We eat at a diner near the lodge. When we finish, Tucker drives, pulling out of the lot, turning south instead of north.

"Where are you going?" He's headed in the wrong direction.

"I have somewhere I want to show you." Quietly, we drive down the highway leading away from the Grand Canyon area. I watch the sky as if I can see the earth rotating and the day shift to night. As the overhead succumbs to darkness, Tucker leads us down a dirt path and cuts the lights. We stop in the middle of the desert where I joked you could bury a body.

191

L.B. Dunbar

"Let's get out," he says, already opening his door and rounding the car for mine. He pulls a blanket I had on the floor in the backseat out as well and drapes it over the hood of the car. After helping me climb up, I lean back on the windshield and look upward.

"Wow," I whisper when he climbs up next to me. He places both hands behind his head, eyes aimed at the sky. We're quiet for a moment, observing stars popping here and there, coming into view as the sky darkens. The moon is off in the distance, and a soft glow hovers around the nighttime jewel.

"Was I too rough earlier?" he quietly asks as if he's afraid to break the silence around us.

"No." I softly chuckle. "I liked it." Rolling my head, I see the corner of his mouth curl.

"I've liked everything we've done together, sunshine." He gives me a quick glance but then turns back to look at the heavens.

"Me too," I whisper back to him. Waiting a minute, I finally ask what I've been holding in since we landed. "Was today difficult?"

"Not as difficult as I thought. I was freaking out if you couldn't tell." I could and I couldn't. "My heart raced and for a second before we took off, I almost asked to be let out."

Oh boy.

"But then I remembered what you said. I didn't want to be afraid. What was the worst that could have happened to me?" He turned to look at me. "We would have died together."

With sadness in his voice, something more lingers. I'd like to believe if death by helicopter is how my demise is intended, there wasn't anything I could have done about it. I could avoid so many things and still die from a slip in my own bathtub. Being cautious and being ridiculous are too different concepts. It wasn't like I planned to never bathe because there was a risk in my own shower.

"I don't want to die yet," I say for some reason.

"A man isn't dead unless he's forgotten," Tucker whispers.

I'll never forget you.

"We aren't going to die, Mae," he adds. "We have a lot of life still to live." That certainly sounds positive but sitting under the stars feels

192

ominous. We are only small specks in the universe around us. We don't matter in the grand scheme of things, but we matter in the little ways. We matter to our families, and our friends, our businesses even, but most importantly, we matter to each other. In this moment, on the hood of a car, we matter here, on this day, in the time we shared in a helicopter ride and a hotel room.

We continue to watch the moon rise and the sky fill with more stars. I only recognize a few constellations, but my knowledge is enough. I don't need to know them all. I don't need to know everything that will happen in my life. Whatever is planned next for me will just happen. I will control what I can, accept what I cannot. The most important thing is I don't waste a minute of right now.

Shifting, I settle into Tucker's chest, and he lowers one arm to wrap around my back. He kisses my head as he'd done earlier.

"This is better than any drive-in," he says, reminding me of my excitement to experience one and my shock that he hadn't ever been. He is right in some ways. Who needs a movie projected on a screen when nature has so much to show us? And in the soundtrack of the night, I hear the dialogue of the universe telling me to treasure life…and never forget this road trip.

28

Playlist: "Born to be Wild" – Steppenwolf

[Tucker]

God, her pussy is sweet. Mae drips against my tongue as I spread her out on the hood of the car. Eventually, our stargazing turned to a heated make-out session, and I need her again. She's given so much to me but giving me her body is the ultimate gift.

She told me when we started this trip her orgasms are all real and all hers. There's no doubt in my mind about the realness of them. The evidence is on my lips. As for being all hers? I want to claim every one of them. I never want her to experience one alone unless I'm watching. Selfishly, I want them all.

Mae cries out in the night, a howl at the moon, as she gives herself over to me and comes on my tongue. When she finishes, I slip her lower on the hood and loosen my jeans.

"Here?" she questions.

"What better way to experience a drive-in?" She chuckles until my tip hits her wet center. Her legs wrap around my hips, and I slide into her without hesitation. She's wet perfection, and since I know about the protection in her, I'm bare again. I want to feel her warmth surrounding me, and my eyes roll back at the heat as I'm seated within her.

"Tucker," she strains, looking around me, and I turn my head only enough to notice headlights aimed in our direction.

"Shit." I pull out of Mae and reach for her hand, tugging her upright. She slides off the hood, struggling with her shorts wrapped around one ankle and I grab the blanket. We race for the car doors. Once inside, I can't judge the distance of those lights but notice them bounce on the rough terrain ahead and sense the vehicle coming in our direction. I don't hesitate. Starting the car, I hit reverse without the lights on. Turning around as best I can on the trail, I do a three-point and gun it down the gravel path. Pebbles kick up behind us and I speed in the direction of the main road.

"Oh my God," Mae shrieks, glancing over her shoulder. She has slipped up her shorts, but they remain undone at her waist. She only has on one sandal. "Do you think they saw us?"

I'd like to think they were too far away, but I don't know where they came from.

"I don't know." I'm out of breath and my heart is racing. We could have been on private property for all I know, and I wouldn't have cared if I got to finish what I started with Mae. I have a serious case of blue balls and a semi-hard dick weeping in my pants. "I need to turn on the lights."

The illumination will give us away, but I can't see without them even though my eyes have adjusted to the dark and the moon offers only a dim glow. With a click, the beams go on and I swear whoever is behind us is gaining on us. The reflection of light in the rearview mirror blinds me. As we near the main road, I should slow down, but I want us on something paved and stable. Thankfully, there's no car coming in the direction I intend to turn, and we pop onto the highway running toward the Grand Canyon. Mae jostles beside me as her Louie isn't equipped for a car chase. As we head north, the vehicle behind us, which I can see is a truck from the height of its headlights, follows us. Our lodge is nearby, but I don't want to lead them there; however, we need to get off this road.

I bypass our place and holler at Mae. "Hang on."

Cutting the lights again, despite being on the highway, I slow only enough to make a sharp turn into another hotel parking lot and circle around to the back of the building. There I pull into one of the farthest parking spaces between two other vehicles and cut the engine. Mae breathes heavily beside me. Twisting in her seat, she's been watching out the back window. I tip my head and then roll it on the headrest to glance out my window.

"Did they follow us?"

"I think they're gone." Her voice chokes around a breathy laugh. "Maybe *we* scared them."

I start to laugh, really laugh. Maybe our situation was nothing, but I did have my cock buried in her and she was in a compromising position on the hood. The other vehicle's appearance was so out of nowhere and exactly how this entire trip has been. I couldn't have predicted where we've been and the adventures we've had. Nor the ones I still want to take with Mae in the future.

"You owe me a sandal," Mae says, breaking into my thoughts, and I laugh even harder while she joins me. The sensation of deep laughter feels good after my first flight and the fast fuck in our hotel room.

"I'll buy you a closetful." I reach for her, cupping the back of her neck and tugging her toward me to kiss her like I can't get enough of her. I'll give her an entire wardrobe if she wishes. In only days, she's become everything to me.

Mae makes me feel. For the first time in a long time, I'm alive, renewed, revived. She sees who I was, and who I am, and accepts that I'm a combination of the past and present. She makes me want to dream again, to hope in what lies ahead. I want to ignore expectations—ones imposed upon me in the past and unwarranted ones I've placed on myself for the future. Mae gives me the permission to be free to be that person who loves music. I am allowed to explore my history and open the pathway for a return to a long-suppressed passion. Every mile we complete, my path becomes clearer, and I want Mae on the remaining road trip of my life.

And I tell her this with my lips on hers as we kiss like reckless teens until I need to take her back to our hotel room where I can show her better what she means to me.

29

CALIFORNIA – DAY 6

Playlist: "Arizona" – Josh Kerr

[Tucker]

It's Wednesday and we are three hours away from California.

Julia was understanding when I told her on Monday I wasn't going to make it, but I'd be at the vineyard on Friday if I had to hitchhike my way there. I hadn't asked Mae to take me to Napa. The deal was as far as Los Angeles. She continues to avoid discussing her plans after she drops me off, and I'm beginning to grow anxious about what is next for her.

Would she want to see me again?

I want to see her. I don't want us to part ways like this trip never happened. But I'm not convinced we can continue what we have during this trip once we return to our respective homes. Our lives are very different. She is a small-town girl; I'm a city man. We each own a business and have obligations. And the one thing I swore I'd never do again was give up my life for a woman.

Still, my current journey is following Mae's path and it leads us on a brief jaunt off I-40 to return to Route 66 near Seligman through Peach Springs to Kingman, where gift shops and restaurants call to travelers. The buildings are worn from the desert heat and sun. After a stop for breakfast and a picture before a famous east-west chart in Kingman, we continue onward.

The drive toward Oatman, another ghost town on the edge of two states, is narrow and curvy and rising in elevation. Once we arrive in the old mining town, Mae squeals with delight.

"They really do have wild burros wandering the street." She explained how once the miners exited the area, they turned their burros loose to go rogue. "Oh, I wish I could take one home," she coos.

197

L.B. Dunbar

I just shake my head. She's adorable.

From Oatman to Needles, California, it's a thirty-minute drive and while I can say I made it to California by Wednesday, I'm nowhere near my final destination. Our drive through the Mojave Desert is filled with gorgeous landscape once again and my driving companion marvels at the beauty of our country. Mae is so in awe of everything she sees.

"For a woman who loves plants, you seem to love the rocks and dirt just as much," I joke.

"Give me rocks and fields, or something like that Jane Austen once said, and I'll be content." Mae weakly smiles to herself as she stares out the window.

I've held her hand as much as I could until the switchbacks along the road needed my attention when we exited Arizona. With us officially in California, Mae grows quieter. We continue to pass rundown buildings and former hotels, but she isn't asking to stop for photos. Her head stays turned to the side, watching the landscape go by out her window, but I'm wondering what is on her mind.

Absentmindedly, I stroke my fingertip up and down her inner thigh. She's wearing a short dress today made of light material and giving off a 1960s prairie vibe. She had another pair of sandals in her bag, but I'm still committed to replacing the shoe she lost. I chuckle to myself with thoughts of last night. I really wanted to fuck her on the hood, underneath the stars, but we made up for the loss when we returned to the lodge. The endorphin rush of being with Mae isn't subsiding. It's growing every second we're together.

As we drive down a particularly empty stretch of road, my fingers wander up her thigh, forcing her dress to lift and Mae eventually glances down at what I'm doing on her leg. Her head pops up and she looks at me, but I only catch her out the corner of my eye. My fingers slip higher, and Mae spreads her legs.

Sweet Jesus. I can feel the heat coming from her and my fingers brush over the wet strip of her underwear.

"Mae," I groan, frustrated with myself that she's ready for me. I can't get a good angle at her with my hand while I'm driving, but I try, cupping her and rubbing at the sensitive spot covered in cotton.

198

Eventually, Mae pushes my hand away from her and slips her own between her legs.

"What are you doing?" I stammer, fighting to keep my eyes forward. "Are you trying to cause an accident?"

I can't watch the road and watch her, but somehow, I think that's what she wants. She wants to taunt me from the seat beside me.

"Don't tease me," I groan, choking when Mae's fingers slip between her thighs and her head tilts back. With the heat index outside this car, within minutes of pulling over and shutting off the engine we'd be drenched in sweat. The idea of stopping to fuck her in the backseat is too dangerous to risk. Not to mention, the backseat is too small.

"Mae?" I groan, peering to the side again, watching her fingers move over her center as her dress rises up to her hips. I don't know what she's thinking but I don't want her to stop. This scene will be one more in my memory box of this trip and Mae.

Her smile. Her touch. Her scent.

As Mae's fingers rub faster and her legs spread wider, my cock hardens, and I loosen my shorts by popping the button.

"I want to taste you, Mae. I want my tongue on that sweet pussy."

Her back arches and she groans, fingers slipping inside her.

"That's it. Let me hear you have an orgasm. Give me another real one, sunshine."

Her mouth curves, knowing what I reference.

"Even though you're doing this to yourself, you like teasing me, don't you? But you're letting me have this one like all the others. Like when my mouth is on you, or when my dick is inside you."

"Tucker," she cries out as her head tips forward. She comes undone in the passenger seat.

With my attention forward, I reach for her, dipping my fingers between her legs and touching that ripe wetness. Pulling my fingers free, I slip them in my mouth, sucking at her essence. Mae opens her eyes and I sense her watching me. She quickly unbuckles, kneels on the passenger seat, and then reaches for my zipper.

L.B. Dunbar

"Mae, whatcha doing?" I struggle to keep my foot steady on the accelerator and I'm grateful not another car is near us, but we still don't need to veer off into the desert landscape or stop beside the road.

Within seconds, Mae has freed my cock from my shorts and boxer briefs, curling her fingers around the hard shaft and tugging at the stiff length.

"Fuck that feels good."

Mae swipes her hair over one shoulder and lowers her head, her tongue coming forward to lap at my tip, seeping with need for her.

"Mae. *Fuck*. Mae." I can't form a sentence as her mouth opens and she tries to take me deep, despite my shorts in the way and the steering wheel beside her head.

And then, I see it. A police car up ahead.

"Sunshine," I warn, placing a hand on her shoulder. "Mae stop! There's a cop."

She releases me. Her head popping up just as we pass him. I'd checked my speed, but I had no idea how fast I was going or if I was staying in the lines as I approached him. Sure enough, he pulls out behind me. After a quick glance in the rearview mirror, I then shift my gaze to Mae.

"Where did that come from?" I anxiously chuckle, trying to catch Mae's eyes but she faces forward.

"Welcome to California, Mr. Ashford. Our estimated time of arrival at your destination is five hours."

"Mae," I chide. I reach for her, cupping the back of her neck as I did last night in this same position, only Mae tugs back and I don't like it. She's retreating from me before we even reach the end of the road.

Then it hits me. *I* need to be somewhere, but Mae doesn't. She could drop me off in Pasadena as she suggested and carry on in her travels. Only, I've already told Julia I won't arrive today, and she should leave without me. My daughter has a gaggle of women looking out for her, supporting her, and they can get her to the resort by this evening.

I just need to be there in time to walk my daughter down the aisle.

Which isn't exactly true, but I'm struggling with Mae pulling away from me.

200

"Don't do this." My eyes shift right, catching her settling her clothing and then tucking her hair up into a messy bun.

"Do what?" Mae questions, still fixing her hair.

"Say goodbye before it's time."

Mae rolls her lips and nods slowly, keeping her gaze trained on the windshield. A siren fires up behind us and we both look toward the back window. Within minutes we're lying about Mae dropping her phone and my swerving as she searched for it.

And the farce feels too real, like she hadn't done what she just did, and I feel Mae slip away from me a little more.

30

Playlist: "California Dreaming" – The Mamas & the Papas

[Mae]

We travel through the Mojave Desert. Louie is not meant for off roading, so we admire the landscape as we pass rich, sandy soil and a variety of cacti. As much as I hate to admit it, I can't take the dry heat, so a side trip to explore is skipped. We should have stopped for lunch near Ludlow, but I'm not hungry and we stick to snacks, prolonging our drive until Barstow. The sky overhead is vast and a solid bright blue, and another moment of feeling small and irrelevant overwhelms me. The world is so much bigger than me.

We've passed a few more ghost towns, and while I nostalgically marveled at them in the beginning of our trip, the depression of these ruined towns and forgotten byways is hitting me.

Don't say goodbye yet.

Will Tucker forget me? Will this trip be another memory he wants to disappear? He dismisses his band life like it happened a million years ago. He acts like he's forgotten how to play an instrument, which clearly isn't the case. He doesn't want to talk about Rochelle, or their life together, and it's one more omission from his past.

Will he erase me next?

At Barstow, I-40 ends, and we bypass I-15 to stick to the original route. Tucker doesn't seem in any hurry to reach his final stop, although we get closer by the mile. He told me he told his daughter to go ahead without him. We haven't discussed how he's getting to Napa. We haven't talked about what I'm doing next. We're avoiding the obvious. We'll be reaching his original destination soon and then we part ways.

When we stop at Elmer's Bottle Tree Garden, I try to muster the emotion I had at the red rocking chair back in Missouri. These old glass bottles are being repurposed into art and it's another example of taking something no longer useful—empty soda and beer bottles—and making something beautiful with them. Of course, the glass is not all clear soda and brown beer containers, but an array of colorful greens and blues. The designs give me an idea for a garden art project. Pam designed programs at Mae's Flowers where we offer a garden project class once a month. Snapping a few pictures, I send them to her as a suggestion of something we could offer in the future.

"I should have collected more things along the way," I say for no reason. I'm not a collector by nature. I'm more the type that if something no longer has a use, I let it go. I don't like clutter. But I still should have purchased more souvenirs or tokens to remind me of where I've been. Absentmindedly, I reach for the silver cuff bracelet I bought back in New Mexico.

"You'll have all the memories," Tucker says beside me. We've grown quieter since my little side-seat show. I don't know what came over me. He was stroking my leg and I was imagining us last night on the hood of the car. While we didn't get to make love properly under the stars, I wanted him to take me under all this sunshine. The heat here is a serious deterrent, though. Still, I couldn't shut down my body. I've *never* acted the way I behaved. Touching myself. Climbing over him. Desperate to give him road head. The behavior was so unlike me, like so many things have been on this trip.

"Memories can fade."

"That's rather pessimistic of you," he huffs, but he's the master of letting memories slip away. He's going to forget everything. He's going to forget me.

I shrug but he grips my shoulders, squeezing at the tops of my arms.

"Stop it," he demands.

Stop what? I want to snap. Stop thinking about us ending? Stop thinking about him? Stop my heart from feeling? I can't turn it off like a switch. I'm not wired that way.

"I'm not doing anything." I sound like a petulant child.

"That's exactly it. You're acting weird. We have hours to go, and I don't know where your enthusiasm went." His silvery eyes search mine and I'm tempted to shrug once again but I can't with his hands on my shoulders.

Funny how days ago, *it was days to go*. Now, we are down to hours. "I'm just getting weary of the car." We've been confined for six days on what was intended to be a fourteen-day trip. I didn't exactly volunteer to shorten my plans, but I still did it, if not begrudgingly at first. Originally, I'd been wanting to slow the pace, take my time. With Tucker's need to get to California, everything has been a rush, including this relationship we've developed.

"Do you want to stop visiting attractions? Or take a break?" Tucker's voice lowers, his hands slipping down my arms and circling my wrists. This touch is the first he's given me since the car sex-show. He hasn't kissed me since this morning. I don't know why any of it bothers me or why I'm even thinking of such a thing.

"No, we should just keep going. We're almost to the end." *We need to finish this trip.*

Tucker's hands slip away. Staring down at me, he stands taller and slides his hands into his pockets. He's wearing the shorts he bought only yesterday with another tight-fitting T-shirt. This one is white and his leather strap, normally tucked inside his shirt, hangs outside the collar today. He told me the medal is St. Benedict. Tucker admitted he wasn't particularly religious, but the medallion belonged to his grandfather. The memento was intended to remind him there are things he can change and things he can't, and he needs to accept the difference.

"Mae." Tucker says my name, pausing as if he's about to say more. His head turns to the left, and he squints in the sunshine. Slowly, he shakes his head once and turns back to me. "You're right. Maybe we should just keep moving."

He spins and stalks toward the car while I take my time, giving the glass bottle art one more glance. I take another mental photograph hoping the memories won't fade but shine as brightly as these containers reflecting under the sun.

Near Victorville, we're back on the interstate, which covers the original route, and we weave our way south to San Bernardino. The landscape changes once more and we let the road trip soundtrack be our tour guide. We could cheat and cut off San Bernardino but route 66 does lead in that direction before taking a sharp turn west and heading straight on to the ocean.

I don't want to cheat, and I say as much to Tucker. "Let's just keep to the route as best we can."

We near a Wigwam Motel, similar to one we passed in Arizona, and notice a giant orange stand that looks old and authentic. Next, we see a sign for the original McDonald's.

"That is not the original," Tucker defensively argues. "I'm a Chicago man, and it started near there." He goes on to give me the history of Ray Croc, and how the original hamburger stand was in a suburb of the big city. McDonald's headquarters is actually outside Chicago as well. It's more information than I ever thought I'd learn about the world-famous fast-food franchise and might be one of the first times our entire trip that Tucker is full of random facts. His enthusiasm for their history, along with the reality of this thought combine, and I start to chuckle, breaking some of the tension I've held since morning.

When I smile at Tucker, he smiles back.

"There she finally is," he whispers, reaching out to cup the back of my neck while he drives. He squeezes and keeps his hand on my skin as long as he can before he needs both hands on the wheel again.

"I met Lawson Colt in a small dive bar outside L.A.," Tucker says, surprising me. "I was newly eighteen, full of piss, and ready to live my life. I didn't want to be under the confines of Ashford's. I didn't want to go to business school. I wanted to play music. My dad was so angry."

Tucker pauses and I hold my breath. He hasn't shared any of this with me before.

"Lawson's cousin was also in the band. His name is Denton Chance, and he understood my anger. His father had been some small-town mayor and he didn't want his son playing music either. Fortunately for Denton, he was at least the athlete his father wanted."

"Denton Chance?" I question. "My sister in-law is named Dolores Chance. Her brother's name is Denton."

Tucker's head turns sharply toward me. His voice is full amazement. "Get out."

L.B. Dunbar

"I'm serious. She's from a small town in Georgia named Blue Ridge."

Tucker's mouth falls open and his eyes shift to briefly glance at me. "No fucking way," he mutters under his breath. Vaguely I remember that Denton was once in a band, and I don't know why I never put it together. Tucker and Denton had been in Colt45 *together*.

"Mae, this is unbelievable."

"Yep. Denton went back to their small town and gave his sister his car to drive to California. She fell in love with her brother's neighbor, if you can follow that, who was Garrett, *my* brother. Now they're married and live in Blue Ridge. He started a vineyard there." Because we came from a small river town, and our grandfather worked in a local factory, our Granddad's dream had always been to own some land. Garrett wanted to fulfill that dream for him.

"Anyway." I wave a hand. "Continue with your story."

Tucker clears his throat. "So, I'm eighteen and playing in a bar. I don't know anyone out here and these two guys come in. Roughly the same age as me. They say they like my sound and my talent and want to know if I'll play with them. Lawson could sing. Denton played guitar. I could play whatever they needed. Piano. Drums. Guitar."

"Don't forget harmonica. You're really musically talented," I interject, noting the number of instruments he has mastered. He brushes off the compliment and continues.

"Colt45 was a name Lawson loved. He thought it sounded badass, old-school metal rock, but we'd have a twist on it." Tucker bitterly chuckles. "Then we couldn't get a break. That second album. His sister showing up. Her husband's death. My parents' death. Rochelle. Everything piled up." He sighs and swipes a hand over his hair. "Maybe I gave up too easily."

I smile weakly at him. "Or maybe it wasn't your full journey. That isn't always easy to hear, especially as you started out on that path. But you weren't meant to end on it, or you would have. I believe in that. Everything happens for a reason, and we don't always get to understand those reasons." I softly chuckle. "If only we did, it'd be so much easier to accept some things or avoid situations completely." Like a husband

206

who cheats in your marriage or steals money from your business. Like falling out of love with the person who swore commitment to you. Or like meeting a man on a road trip and falling in love with him.

"Yeah, probably," Tucker says, his head tipped to his fist while his elbow balances on the door. I reach for his arm, wrapping my hand around his wrist near the original leather band he wears and the new one he purchased. "We almost match," I say, as my left wrist nears his right and I tinker with the new strap on him.

"I bought it, so I'd always remember." He glances at me and takes my hand, lifting it to his lips and lingering as he kisses the back. "You're not going to be easy to walk away from, sunshine."

And everything in me wants to tell him not to do it.

But I don't.

L.B. Dunbar

31

Playlist: "California Soul" – Marlena Shaw

[Tucker]

Something in my chest—my heart or my soul—thrived in California and I'd left that piece of me behind. The emptiness inside me was deepest every time I'd returned to the area. This time was different. The vacancy behind my ribs wasn't there. The space, once full of air, feels fuller, peaceful, almost content. Maybe what I needed was coming back here to find what I'd lost. Turning to look at Mae, I wonder if I'd ever lost anything. I had my heart the entire time. I just needed the right person to remind me. Remind me of the harmony of attraction. Remind me of the powerful rhythm of love.

As we near Pasadena, memories return like harsh waves against beach boulders. One after another crashes through my mind. I'd been to California since first leaving. Rochelle held a conference or two here, and Julia eventually moved into the state. But I didn't visit often. I could count the total number of times on one hand. With Mae beside me, I ponder what she'd think. Maybe all I got was my fifteen minutes of fame. No more, no less. Moving forward with the guys wasn't meant to be. Being a part of Colt45 was a blip on their radar but maybe being with them was a blip on mine.

Eventually, Lawson Colt got all the accolades for talent, and there was no doubt he was talented. In my heart, I knew I was better. I had more skill than just the guitar and a voice, but then again, our skills were simply different. Again, no more, no less.

When we near South Pasadena, I suggest a stop I hadn't paid enough attention to when I visited Julia once. *An ice cream treat in celebration*, I tell Mae. Fair Oakes Pharmacy and Soda Fountain is an original Route 66 attraction, and Mae agrees to the destination. Upon entering, she finally smiles one of those genuine grins I've missed throughout today.

"Ice cream could spoil our dinner." She gives me her best mom voice, but she's too cute to pull off stern and reprimanding in her excitement to be among the music and memorabilia here.

We haven't made plans for dinner actually, but it will be part of the conversation we have once we reach the pier. *What next?* The question is the first thing on my list to discuss. I want to see her again. I don't want this to be the end, as she hinted earlier. I meant what I said, she's going to be hard to walk away from, so I don't want to walk away. This time, in this place, I'm making my own choices, and I choose Mae.

"I only want to spoil you," I say and Mae blushes.

Her sweet rosy cheeks warm me, and I rub a hand up her back before leading her to the counter to order ice cream. Mae has dreams of grandeur about what life must have been like on this iconic road. The travels. The stops. The dates along the way. Couples sharing experiences, she called it, explaining drive-ins and diners. Sitting here eating ice cream at an old counter with bright red stools and lots of chrome around us, I envision what she meant. This is a classic date, and I can't recall ever going on one like it. Just a guy and his girl, sharing an ice cream sundae.

I've eaten so poorly on this trip I've probably gained ten pounds, and I'll take every ounce of them, if I get to keep this woman. Watching Mae savor the chocolate ice cream at one end of the sundae, I take another mental photo of her. She mentioned how she should have collected things along the way when we stopped at the folk-art bottle garden, but I've been collecting. The memories. The snapshots. The pieces of my heart that she's put back together.

Leaning forward, she shows me a picture she took of our sundae.

"Ice cream with my guy. That should be your caption," I tell her. Like the selfie pro Mae has become on this trip, she plans to post the photo like a true foodie. Her personal social media chronicles our adventures, but we made an airdrop folder for images, and there are ten times as many in the file.

Mae snorts at my suggestion and I wonder what would be so wrong about saying I'm hers. We started this trip with rules and crossed every boundary, but maybe she isn't interested in something long-term. Maybe she's just been melancholy that her trip is nearing the finish line, not that

209

we are at the end of the road for us. Like going to summer camp where the time will pass, and people will go their separate ways when summer is over.

This isn't some damn band camp, though.

When we finish our ice cream, our journey will be delayed further by the lateness of the day and Los Angeles traffic.

"My daughter's cupcake shop is around Pasadena somewhere," I say as we idle along with the other cars on the overcrowded highway that feels like a parking lot.

"Should we have stopped?" Mae asks.

"Could you eat a cupcake on top of that ice cream?"

"There's always room for a cupcake," she teases, restored to sweetness after our sugary treat.

I laugh. "There are actually two locations now. Because Cupcakes is owned by her future mother-in-law. Julia's inheritance covered the investment to open a second location." I pause, recollecting Rochelle's upset that Julia enjoyed baking instead of public speaking.

"You're returning women to the kitchen," Rochelle barked.

"I'm learning how to run my own business," Julia argued back.

My sweet girl had slowly learned how to hold her own with her mother.

"I'll make certain to find the place after the wedding." After the wedding, when I come back to the area and what? How am I getting home from here? A secondary car service was booked for my return to Chicago leaving on Monday. Knowing the track record of the transportation company coming west, I should confirm my eastward plans. However, I'm still hoping I can convince Mae to share a ride back to Chicago. We can take the highway I drove to get here all those years ago and I can show her all the places I discovered along the way. I'll be the tour guide this time.

"How are you getting home?" she asks, and I don't know whether I'm relieved or nervous to discuss this topic.

"I was hoping to convince this incredibly annoying driver with a car named Louie to return me to Chicago."

Mae's brows lift. Surprise is written across her face. "Really?"

"Absolutely." I pause. "Look, I didn't really want to have this discussion in traffic, but I don't want you to go back across the country alone." I want to be your man, going with you.

"Oh," she says, her voice faltering.

"What's *oh*? I can't read *oh*, sunshine."

She shakes her head. "It's nothing. You know I planned this trip alone in the first place."

I arch a brow and side-eye her. "And how'd that work out for you?"

She fights a slow smile. "This annoying man weaseled his way into a ride, and I've been stuck with him for six days."

I laugh as I inch forward in the mess of cars. "That bad, huh?"

She shrugs, and for the first time, I take that action from her. "It hasn't been awful." A smile fills her voice.

"Maybe I can make it up to you." Wiggling my brows, Mae lightly laughs at me.

"What did you have in mind, Mr. Ashford?" A full wattage smile brightens her face.

"You'll see."

+ + +

When we arrive at Santa Monica Pier, the area is crowded as I'd expect for the end of a summer day. We finally find a place to park and walk to the famous pier stretching into the Pacific Ocean. Just like in Chicago, the starting point for Route 66, the Santa Monica area has had several official ending points. Mae warns me she read it can be a bit anti-climactic, so she's focused on the pier as her formal finish line. To our surprise, an unofficial sign stands on the entrance of the pier.

Route 66. End of the Trail.

Mae actually hugs the post and I take several pictures, plus selfies of us, before bringing her in for a tight hug.

"You did it, sunshine. You drove Route 66." The feat is quite the accomplishment, and while I technically drove a portion of it, *we* did it together.

"How do you feel?" I ask next.

211

Is she inspired? Is she restored? Does she have vision and purpose as she thought she would? Laughing at these ideals like I first did when she told me about them no longer feels appropriate. I've had my own epiphanies on this adventure, including reminders of what I've lost, but also what I've gained. Holding Mae tighter, she's the gift I've received on this trip. Her smile. Her laugh. Her touch. Even her orgasms. But I want her heart.

"I don't know," she says, her voice bewildered. "Maybe it hasn't hit me that it's over yet." Her eyes leap up to mine and the trepidation I saw earlier today returns.

"Well, it isn't over yet. We need to celebrate. A ride on the Ferris Wheel. Or a trip round the carousel. Then dinner and the sunset."

Mae stares up at me. Her mouth falls open and then snaps shut.

"Not getting rid of me yet, sunshine," I warn, attempting to keep my voice light. *Don't say this is the end.* "What were your plans for tonight?"

"I told you my brother has a place here. I was going to stay in his condo for a few days." The few days is news to me, but good news all the same.

"Come with me to Julia's wedding," I blurt.

"What?" Her forehead furrows.

"Come with me. Meet my kids. Be my date for the wedding this weekend." We can work out later how we will fill every weekend after that.

"You just want a ride to Napa," she jests lacking humor, her shoulders falling within my embrace.

"I do." I admit. "But I'm also not ready to say goodbye. Spend the day with me tomorrow. We can do anything you want. We can go to the observatory or tour Hollywood. We can lounge at the beach. Anything that doesn't involve riding in a damn car." And allows me to touch her all day, freely, continually. I rub both hands up her back and press her tighter against me.

"Let me stay the night with you and spend the days with me," I plead. I'm almost begging, and I'm not opposed to getting down on my knees if I need to. I'm not ready to give her up.

With a slow jostle of her head, Mae grins and that's my answer. I'm so relieved I kiss her with everything I can against the post that marks the end.

Only, I want this to be a new beginning.

32

Playlist: "Wildest Dreams" – Taylor Swift

[Mae]

We eat a late dinner at an overpriced seafood place near the pier. Then we return to the beach, lay out the blanket from Louie, and watch the sunset. All around us I notice people stopping to pay homage to the glory of the sun dipping toward the ocean. It's a beautiful night.

Tucker and I remain quiet, each lost within our private thoughts. My head is fuzzy with wine and things I don't want to think about. Tucker lies back on the blanket, a hand behind his head while the other hand absentmindedly rubs at the base of my spine as I sit upright beside him.

We're at the end of a long journey and it's been a long day, but it doesn't feel like the end as much as it did this morning. Maybe I've accepted our fate is to part or maybe it's that he asked for more time. Tomorrow. The wedding. How long will we prolong our goodbye?

As the sun lowers and darkness falls over us like a heavy blanket, Tucker sits upright. Bumping me in the shoulder, I glance over at him. His face is close and his smile crooked. The creases around his eyes accentuated.

"Kiss me." His eyes hold mine and I smile. "Kiss me like you'll miss me, Mae."

Twisting, I clamp my hands on his scruffy jaw and devour his mouth. I pour everything into that kiss because I *will* miss him. I will miss this trip and his presence. I will miss his mouth and his crooked smile. His laugh and the teasing shake of his head when I've gotten excited over the simplest sight along the way. I'll miss the sweetness of a potted geranium and the chivalry of diner dinners.

I kiss him with a road map of memories that will never leave me and yet reflecting on them will never do the recollections justice.

The reality of Tucker is what I want. His touch. His presence in my life. Just him.

My wishes scatter, though, when he tips me backward, positioning his body partially over mine, and we make out on a public beach as the sun sets on our adventure.

+ + +

"This is some place," Tucker states as we enter Garrett's condo along the beach, north of Santa Monica. My brother has lived in California since he left home after college, but I haven't been to this specific location.

"Garrett's rich." There's no reason to sugarcoat his financial status. He owns an investment company. He's like *Shark Tank*, the television program where investors agree to take on new products or put capital into existing companies to help them level up. Garrett is always investing in things to either grow them or dump them until the next investment comes along. "Denton Chance lived across the hall for years."

Tucker stares at me as we stand on either side of the large kitchen island that separates the modernized kitchen from a sitting area. A large sliding glass door and balcony are beside the living room portion. The view will be breathtaking in the morning when we can see the ocean.

Eventually, Tucker shakes his head. "I still can't believe how small the world is." He lightly chuckles referencing my connection to his former band member. "And your brother left here for Blue Ridge to build a winery."

"He left for Dolores. He made a sacrifice." *It's called love.* I don't need to repeat my words from when Tucker and I argued. However, I feel the need to defend my brother's actions. He gave up this place in order to fill his heart. And he didn't leave it. He still owns the condo, renting it out on occasion, keeping it available at other times.

"I didn't mean anything by that," Tucker defends in return and my shoulders fall.

"I know. I'm sorry." I'm tired. It's been a rollercoaster of a day and a long one at that. I'm also on edge from our make-out session, which I

L.B. Dunbar

wish had turned into more. Despite our sexy antics over the past few days, though, I'm not really into exhibitionism.

Tucker rounds the counter and cups my face. "You're giving me tomorrow." He isn't asking but a question still lingers.

"Tomorrow," I whisper.

"Let's just take it easy all day. Stay in bed or hang at the beach."

I nod to agree with him. We need a day of nothing. No maps to follow. No sights to see. Just us.

"Why don't you take a shower? I'll go after you. We need some sleep." He's right. I know he's right and yet I'm afraid to sleep. I'm afraid to lose precious minutes with him, but I acquiesce.

Eventually, I'm grateful for the precious, solitary moments in the shower. Wash. Rinse. Repeat. Condition. Shave. I use the time to allow the warm water to wash my worries down the drain. At least for a little while.

As I pull down the sheets of the bed in Garrett's guest room, Tucker takes a shower. I'm wearing a fresh T-shirt I found in my brother's dresser. Tucker finds me lounging against a stack of pillows against the headboard. He's wearing only a towel around his waist as he peers down at me.

"How tired are you?"

"I found a drawer of sex toys," I blurt, my face heating at the discovery I don't think I was meant to see in my brother's nightstand. I have no intention of using or borrowing those things, but I can't seem to keep this secret. Tucker drops the towel at his waist and narrows his eyes at me.

"I have a sex toy for you." His voice is completely serious, but I break into giggles. I'm exhausted, but the sight of him is awakening parts of me that won't rest without his touch. There's a collection of candles on the stand next to my side of the bed and Tucker lights them, then he turns off the lamp and crawls over me. Within seconds, the tee I'm wearing along with my underwear are removed and we lay beside one another as we did on the beach. Only Tucker's hands roam, coasting along the length of my arm and the curve of my hip. He travels back up my stomach and over a breast.

His hand curls around my neck and he kisses me deeply before slipping his lips to my jaw and along the column of my throat. He's taking his time, marking me, outlining me with his mouth. Tonight will be about making more memories as Tucker goes slow, and sweet, and softly down my body. He sucks at my breasts and licks the nipples. He kisses my belly and nips my thighs. He trails all the way down to one ankle and back up the other leg before he focuses on my center, ready and dripping with need.

"You have the sweetest pussy," he says before his tongue flattens to swipe over sensitive folds. Then the tip of his tongue narrows in on my clit and two fingers take their time to dip in and out of me. Every moment is measured and paced, and the languid delay is both torture and tease. The anticipation is building like a lazy wave.

"Give this to me," he says at my center. "Give me everything."

He has no idea what he's asking and how much I want to give him my all. My heart, my soul, my *everything* as he says, but he only means my orgasm which comes on a slow crest and lasts long like an idle tide. When I can't take anymore, he presses a kiss just above my pubic bone and returns to my mouth for another deep kiss. Gently, I press at his shoulders, forcing him to roll over.

With him on his back, I take my time as he did. With his thick shaft in my hand, my mouth graces every inch of his skin over his chest and along his waist. While I kiss him everywhere, my fingers stroke his stiff length, gently tugging and teasing as he'd done to me. He groans and hisses, and I recognize he needs more. My tongue brushes the tip of him before I open wide and drag him deep. This is so much better than the roadside head I attempted to give him only this morning. I lap and I lick until he begs me to stop. Hollowing my cheeks, I suck hard until I'm suddenly pulled off him.

"Enough," he growls, flipping me to lie flat on the bed. He crawls over me once more and easily slips into me without preamble. He didn't need to warn me. I wasn't going to reject him. My legs spread and hook over the backs of his. His hips rock, moving his dick deliciously in and out of me. My hands rub up his back. His fingers massage my breast. We aren't in a rush as we continue to touch and explore until our bodies can't hold off anymore.

"Sunshine," he strains, signaling his patience is at an end and with his finger at my clit I tip easily over the edge again, giving him the orgasm he asked for. Instantly, he stills his hips but pulses inside me and I have a new definition of making love. *I love him.*

Tucker doesn't immediately pull out but lingers over me, kissing my nose and my eyelids before the soft brush of his lips meets mine. Then he holds me, and I clutch at him, afraid to let go too soon of one more memory.

33

Unplanned DAY 7

Playlist: "You Matter to Me" – Jason Mraz and Sara Bareilles

[Tucker]

We sleep in and Mae makes us breakfast with eggs that look freshly purchased and bacon left in the freezer. It feels good to eat something home cooked and linger on her brother's balcony with our coffee. Garrett's place is swanky, and the kind of condo I'd hoped to own one day, had I stayed in California. The place has a perfect view of the Pacific Ocean. In Chicago, my condo has a view of Lake Michigan, and while I am reminded of home being here, this isn't the same. Thinking of home reminds me I want to discuss a few things with Mae.

"Come with me tomorrow," I say again, implying my daughter's wedding. I'm asking for one more day. Actually three, as I want her attendance for the entire weekend. I'm only putting off the inevitable, but I'm also hoping I can convince her to give us more time. Like a person who has room for a cupcake even after an ice cream sundae, I'm not full of Mae. I crave more.

"I can't," Mae immediately states to my invitation.

"You can," I argue.

"No."

"Yes." We fight often like this. Two simple words with opposite meanings and yet Mae and I have come to so many agreements along this trip.

"I don't have anything to wear," Mae points out.

"You're beautiful. It doesn't matter what you wear."

She waves a dismissing hand at me. "You're the father of the bride. You'll be in a tux."

"It's a suit, actually." Stating the details isn't helping my case but Julia's wedding is rather casual despite being at a winery rented in its entirety for her celebration. Her fiancé isn't a fancy guy, she'd told me, and they'd opted for light gray suits for the men in varying styles.

"Well, it matters to me what I wear, and I don't have anything."

"*Well*," I exaggerate. "You matter to me, and I want you there."

Mae blinks at me from across the small table on the balcony.

"I can take you shopping for something if that's what will convince you to attend this wedding with me."

She breaks the hold my eyes have on her and peers out toward the ocean.

Somehow, I've said the wrong thing. While I watch her, I recall her telling me about her brother and his wife. He was almost fifty and had never been married when he met Dolores, Denton's sister. I'd asked Mae yesterday for more about their relationship. If he owned a business here, how did it work for him to be in Georgia? The question felt silly after all that happened back in 2020. The world learned to work remotely from anywhere during a major pandemic.

Could I work somewhere other than Chicago and still give my all to Impact?

"I'll drive you to Napa, though," Mae states, interrupting my thought. I don't miss how she isn't agreeing to accept my invitation to the wedding, but this is a small step in getting her closer to attending. "But it's going to cost you extra," she teases, turning back to me.

"I'm good for the money."

Mae will receive payment for driving me. I want to see her well compensated for her time and the gas, but the concept leaves a bitter taste in my mouth. *This wasn't only a business arrangement.*

My response has Mae tipping up her head once and glancing back out at the view. I've said the wrong thing again.

With our conversation already open about driving, I decide to keep pressing. "How are you getting home?"

Mae laughs almost bitterly. "The road is my goddess. She'll lead me where I need to go."

That's not the answer I want to hear. I don't like her traveling alone. And I want to be with her.

"Come to the wedding," I ask again. "We can drive back to Chicago together."

Mae's head lowers, and her fingers fiddle with the hem of her T-shirt. The one she wore last night before I stripped her naked and made love to her.

"It's too much," she whispers. "It's too important of an event for me to barge in and meet your family. This should be family time," she emphasizes.

Join my family. Mae is sad with hers. Her divorce. The behavior of her teenage sons. The separation from her sisters. She can be part of my family. We can be one together.

I have no idea where these thoughts come from, but I've been thinking so much about the band and how I might have let them down when I left. They were my family for a short while and they'd been important to me. How had I let those relationships slip away when I once cared so much for those guys?

I had all the answers, but the bottom line rested with me. I hadn't looked back any more than they looked forward at me.

I won't do the same thing with Mae.

"Mach will be there," I try to assure her.

"I don't know Mach." She doesn't. She knows of him, from what her sister tells her, and from what I've learned, that includes Jane having a major conflicting crush on my business partner.

"Let me introduce you to Jude and Julia." I'm nearly begging, and I reach for her hand across the small space separating us. I want to take us wherever the road leads, and hopefully that's meeting children and figuring out how to be together somehow.

"I'll think about it." Her quiet response isn't a no but it's also not a yes. It's like her dismissive shrugs. It's a way to end this conversation and I concede for the moment. But I'm going to convince her.

Something tells me I need her to be there with me.

+ + +

221

L.B. Dunbar

Mae and I cuddle on the couch after a long afternoon of sunshine and a delivered dinner. We found a bottle of wine in her brother's extensive collection and popped the cork, hoping it wasn't something he was saving for a special occasion. Mae also found a series of classic movie DVDs and put one on. With our bodies spooning, I'm eager for her within minutes.

I don't want to waste a second we have together talking about things heavy and hard, but I need to know why Mae is pulling back from me. Even held within my arms, I feel her slipping away.

"What would it take to keep you forever?" I whisper at her ear.

"Trust." She doesn't even hesitate in her answer.

The directness stiffens my spine. "And you don't trust me?"

Her head tilts, and she looks at me over her shoulder. "I trust you." Her brows pinch, surprised that I'd ask such a thing. "I trust you with my body."

My mouth falls open, ready to ask her what part she doesn't trust me with, but I think I know.

Her heart is fragile as is mine.

Tickling my fingers up her arm, I mutter at her neck again. "Then give me your body." If she isn't listening to my words, maybe she'll feel my emotions in our joining. I want us to be together for more than a few days on a highway.

My hand moves to her loose pajama shorts, and I remove her underwear along with them. Next, I press at my own shorts, quickly freeing myself as well. My heavy dick falls against her ass, and I rock forward. Mae presses back. While laying on our sides, I wedge my leg between hers, spreading them so she hikes her thigh over my hip. My fingers easily find Mae wet and ready, and I stroke her a few minutes before slipping into her. Keeping my fingertips on her clit, I set a steady pace until our skin slaps and the scent of us coming together fills the room. Mae's clutching the cushion and I'm clutching her hip, and together we dance.

Eventually, I pull out and Mae whimpers at my absence. I guide her forward to the floor, keeping her face to it. Once we wedge ourselves between the low table and the couch, I hitch Mae's ass in the air. She's on her knees, elbows bent, and I slide back into her. Stroking a hand up her spine and back down, I bring my thumb between her crack.

With just the slightest of pressure, I tease her here. Mae whines with a low moan of tension and curiosity. Her body's natural reaction is clenching to hold me out while she's open to letting me in.

"What will it take for you to trust me with more?" I ask, still playing at that pucker as my hips rock and my dick dips deep within her.

"Are we really discussing this now?" She scoffs then groans as I tap the spot within her to set her off. My upper body straightens as I surge forward with a hand on her hip and one on her ass.

"I want everything from you, sunshine." I thrust forward again. "Come to the wedding with me."

There's so much more in my invitation. *Be mine, Mae.*

"No," she groans again but her body reacts. The hand on her hip slides forward and I pluck at her clit while I tease her back hole. Mae breaks with a sob, and a jumble of words. "So good. So big. *Ohmygod.*"

"The wedding, Mae. Be my date," I demand.

"Tucker," she hollers, still coming over me. The intensity of her tips me over the edge and I slam into her, holding her at the hips to keep me to the hilt. I spring like a faucet and tilt my head back as the release escapes me. Spots of silver dance before my eyes and I blink to focus.

"Be mine," I whisper as I collapse over her. We're tucked between furniture which isn't the most romantic location but my desperation to be inside her overcame me.

I want her body and her heart. Her soul and her thoughts.

I don't need her past. I want to be her future.

L.B. Dunbar

34

Playlist: "Blackbird" – The Beatles

[Mae]

I couldn't believe I agreed to drive him to Napa. I don't know why I am prolonging things, but when we can't make it to the bedroom, pausing in the kitchen before he has me against the island counter, kissing me like I'm the air he needs to breathe, I accept that leaving this man will take willpower I'm not certain I have.

I'm a contradiction. One moment I'm clutching at him, hoping he won't walk away from me. The next minute, I'm pushing him away out of fear he'll too easily leave me behind. I'll be nothing more than a glance in his rearview mirror.

How long do we do this dance before the song ends?

Staying would only prolong the inevitable.

He doesn't need to introduce his children—at his daughter's wedding no less—to some strange woman who gave him a ride across the country. I'd like to think there could be another time, a better time, for such introductions. But all I have in my head is how Tucker lives in one place and I live in another, and we both own a business and have adult children, or in my case, nearly adult.

We'll say goodbye eventually and dragging out that end date does nothing but widen the gap his absence will leave in me.

Declining the invitation to his daughter's wedding feels like the only control I have left over this situation. I need to protect my heart, but it becomes extremely difficult to follow reason and emotion when he hitches my body up on the countertop, spreads my legs wide and settles his face between my thighs. He should have been a singer. His tongue is insane and my body hums for him with each pass over my sensitive folds.

"You're my road goddess, Mae. Don't leave me alone on the journey of life."

Sweet Mother, my eyes prickle at the tenderness in his tone, the plea wrapped in the passion. His tongue laps. His lips kiss. He's delicate while demanding as he encourages the storm raging inside me. The tension is unparalleled. I hardly recognize my own body. The things I've done with this man. The things I've offered him. None of it makes sense yet I don't want to question any of it. I just want to enjoy him in the few hours I have left. I just want to *feel* in the minutes that remain.

"Tucker," I curse his name as I come to the edge once again. How is it possible to have so many orgasms in so few days? I've never been like this—desperate, ravenous, unquenchable. The open road has been an aphrodisiac, but we are no longer driving. This is the final rest stop only I don't want to rest.

I don't want this feeling to stop.

Within seconds, my body breaks again, crashing like the ocean on the beach outside this condo. Tucker is quick to pull away and pummel his shaft greedily into me. My eyes roll back. My orgasm wasn't finished and his entrance into me prolongs the sensation of rolling waves and foaming waters. I'm a mess between my thighs. He does this to me. He makes me wild for him.

"Your body is my road map, sunshine." His hands coast up my belly and cup both my breasts, squeezing them together as he rocks into me. "I'll never be lost again."

The tears threatening to fill my eyes blur my vision. Why is he being so sweet? Why is he doing this to me? Can't he see I'm struggling enough as it is?

My legs dangle off the countertop. His hands grip my hips. I'm a ragdoll to his ministrations and then he stills. Only his cock jolts deep within me. My head rolls to the side as his leans back. He's as seated as he can be. Then he collapses over me, catching himself on his forearms beside my shoulders. Leaning forward, he kisses me, long and slow. He takes his time until we separate. Our eyes lock and everything is said between his steely grays and my light blue ones.

Stay.

I can't.

Don't leave.

L.B. Dunbar

I must.

Did I trust him?

Fear lives deep inside me. I need to believe he wants more than an additional ride and a date to his daughter's wedding. Otherwise, a major pothole will remain where my heart used to be. Each day will be one more day driving the wedge wider and wider. But with his body blanketing mine, and his eyes searching my face, I am almost willing to risk a crack in my surface.

Hesitantly, he pulls back and holds out a hand to help me sit upright. I need a shower, and he reads my thoughts, leading me to the primary bathroom where we take our time to soap and shampoo one another. No words pass between us. This moment is for memorizing one another. Inhaling the scent of our combined shampoo and body wash. Imprinting the feel of our flesh and the shape of our bodies. Internalizing the taste of tongue and lips and skin.

The moment is almost too much until he has me pinned against the sliding glass door to the balcony within minutes of exiting the bathroom. My shower-warm body presses into the air-conditioned cool panes and my sensitive breasts peak against the windows. With the lights off behind us, no one can see what he's doing to me. I'm certain this is something no one else wants to witness, and yet all my inhibitions are gone. I'm naked and spread, plastered to the window while his hands explore my back, my hips and my ass. His mouth sucks at my neck.

"Keep your hands up." I'd laugh at the directive if my body had a will of its own, which it doesn't. I'm completely at his command. He slips a hand between my legs, toys with my clit and I respond like I haven't been touched there repeatedly in the past few hours.

"You want me," he says. "Let the rest of you have me."

My head taps the glass before me, and I roll my forehead back and forth. He has no idea what he's saying, what he's asking.

He doesn't rush but strings me along, flicking at the sensitive nub, drawing me closer and closer to the proverbial edge. Once I'm almost there, as if he can read my body, he slips inside me from behind again. His fingers remain on my clit while his thickness glides in and out, the tempo slow and measured. He wraps one arm around my waist and bends

226

his knees to accommodate the height difference between us. He keeps the pace of steady taps while he plucks the trigger spot on me. The heat of his chest, the chill of the glass, the touch of his fingers, and the drag of his cock drive me into sensation overload. Then I'm coming again, spilling over him and down my thighs. My cheek presses on the window and my breath fogs the pane as I moan in a way I've never sounded before. Pleasure and pain. Passion and penance. My skin squeaks against the window until he stills, jetting off inside me once more.

My eyes close as we remain against the window, chests heaving, breaths heavy.

I'll never be the same and everything I said to Jane when she convinced me to drive Tucker across the country was wrong.

I would end up needing him. I just don't know how to keep him.

+ + +

Daylight comes too soon. We've miscalculated the distance to Napa Valley from the Santa Monica area, and it will take us seven hours straight up I-5 instead of six. I drive while Tucker rides beside me working on his computer once the time zones align. In so many ways, our position reminds me of when we started on this journey a week ago to the day, only he was sitting in the backseat, stewing over my annoying need to stop every so many miles.

"Sunshine?" He breaks into my aimless thoughts. The soundtrack of our trip has fallen in rhythm with the wheels on the road, and I'm numb to the sound.

"Huh?"

"Want to stop and grab breakfast? Maybe more coffee?" We hadn't eaten anything this morning because it was early. Gas station coffee had been our only option.

"No, we should keep going." My voice is hollow. My mind empty for the moment.

"Mae, we should talk."

I don't like the sound of that. *What is there to say?*

227

L.B. Dunbar

"Let's not." I swallow around a sudden lump in my throat. "You work."

His laptop is open, but he hasn't been typing. He's been looking out the window more time than not. Sneaking a peek at him, I turn my head back to the windshield just in time to see something large and low coming at the front of the car.

"What the—" Something collides with the front of Louie. "Oh my God. *Oh my God.*" With shaky hands, I reach for the hazards.

"What happened?" Tucker asks as I continue to shriek.

"I think I just hit a bird." My voice ripples with panic and my body shivers. I steer the car to the side of the road, and for a moment, I'm reminded of pulling over for our flat tire. Was that only a few days ago? How different Tucker and I are now, compared to hundreds of miles and three states away?

Once stopped, we both exit the car at the same time and round to the front. Sure enough, a giant blackbird is wedged into the front grill. I bend at the waist, clutching my kneecaps and closing my eyes. I feel sick. Not like I'm going to vomit, just gut-curdling sick.

I killed a bird!

"This is a bad sign," I mutter to the gravel under my feet.

"What? It's a bird. A dead bird, not a sign."

"Did you know that a dead bird is a sign…of death."

Tucker softly chuckles. "Well, yes. He's dead."

I stand to face him, hands on my hips. "Oh my God," I whimper again, before risking another glance at the poor thing, flattened against the silver grate.

"Mae—"

"No," I say, stealing his words. This is a sign of the end, just as Tucker and I will be. We are over.

"Sunshine." Tucker steps up to me, cupping my shoulders before tugging me to his chest. We've hardly touched this morning. I'd considered the absence a reaction to all our affection being used up yesterday. His lips press to my forehead. "A dead bird can also be a sign of rejuvenation."

"How?" I mock. "He's dead." My forehead presses into his sternum.

"Well, he could rise up from the ashes."

I pull my head back and look at him. *Ashe.*

"He could be a symbol of being born again," he adds.

Taking another peek around Tucker's arm, I'm certain that poor thing isn't rising up from anything. "We should bury him."

"What?" Tucker glances down at me.

"We need to return him to the earth."

Tucker stares at me, his arms slipping from my back. "Oh yes, let me grab the shovel and coffin out of the trunk."

"Tucker!" I shriek. "I cannot keep driving with a dead bird stuck to the grill."

He hangs his head. "Do we have a plastic bag or something? I'm not risking some bird disease by touching a wild animal."

I'm instantly relieved he's offering to remove the blackbird because I don't think I can touch the poor thing without freaking out. Searching the backseat, I find plastic grocery bags left over from snack purchases and double them together. After holding out the bags, which Tucker begrudgingly takes, I stand to the side of the car while Tucker rounds to the front. With both his hands inside the wrappings, he leans forward, extending his arms as far as he can without getting too close to the wedged bird.

To our surprise, the thing flaps and squawks, one wing spreading as Tucker tries to contain him. He unintentionally drops the bird, which is larger than it appeared against the grill. Within seconds, the bird attempts flight but doesn't get too far, before dropping into the grasses on the side of the road.

"Should we try to catch him? Find a vet or something?"

Tucker glares at me as he rolls the plastic bags into each other. "I need some serious hand sanitizer, and no, we need to let nature take its course here. He'll mend on his own or become one with the universe as all wild things do."

Glancing up at him, I fight a sudden smile. "That was very a hakuna-matata of you."

L.B. Dunbar

"Ha-na what?" He looks over at me with the plastic rolled into a tight ball.

"*The Lion King.*" When he continues to stare at me, I shake my head. "Never mind. We have a winery to find." I could use a good glass of wine or an entire bottle, but that isn't the mission. Moving forward, I need to get Tucker to his daughter as I promised.

For some reason, I take another glance toward the bird, or at least in the direction of where it disappeared.

Was it a sign? Does it mean a new beginning…or the end?

35

DAY 8

Playlist: "Say Something" – A Great Big World, Christina Aguilera

[Tucker]

"Dad? Where have you been?"

My daughter rushes me, quick to contain me in her arms when we finally arrive at The Vineyard Inn. How do I explain the wild week I just had trying to get here for her wedding?

"You're three days late," she admonishes me as we embrace outside the quaint winery resort. The entire place has been rented for this intimate occasion. The owners were happy to accommodate us and Julia's desire for a fairytale wedding.

I've made it here in time for the rehearsal dinner tonight but not the prior days' activities of wine tasting and vineyard tours. The additional festivities did not exactly seem to fit my future son-in-law.

Still, as I stand here, I'm conscious of the woman behind me, leaning against the car we just spent an entire week trapped inside together. I should introduce her to my daughter, but I'm frozen in time when Julia pulls back and stares up at me with her mother's eyes.

Her gaze, so like Rochelle's, haunts me in an unsettling way.

"It took a little longer to get here than I thought," I admit. My meaning is multi-faceted. It took more time to cross the country than I expected, but it also took years to arrive at the decisions I've made in the past seven days.

"Are you okay?" my daughter questions, still clutching my upper arms like she's afraid to let me go.

"I'm fine." The statement feels true for the first time in years. I really am better than I've ever been. I hadn't known how bad off I was, and I owe it all to the ray of sunshine behind me.

"I wish your mother could be here." The statement holds truth, but it's equally false. Rochelle loved our daughter more than most things, but not quite as much as her business plans and her social media following. For Julia's sake, Rochelle should be here because no woman should celebrate her wedding day without her mother. As my daughter has kept me up to date on everything, I understand that Chopper's stepmother, Lily, along with a contingent of other women—Edie, Midge, Ivy, and Ester—have been tremendously helpful in the planning of this weekend. I haven't met any of them but cataloged their names.

On the other hand, it's a relief Rochelle isn't here as it's been a struggle over the last few years to reconcile what she did and how things ended. Her death was unfortunate. Her betrayal, however, was the unparalleled grief I didn't think I'd recover from. Only the past week has proven I am healed. I am better. I am whole. I no longer want to give my thoughts to Rochelle.

I turn to glance over my shoulder, relieved Mae is still here.

"How much does he owe you?" Julia asks, breaking out of my hold and approaching the beautiful creature waiting next to the vehicle. A fucking Prius. I might have thought the car atrocious when we took off from Chicago seven days ago, but in time, Louie has grown on me. I bite my cheek to stifle the chuckle at the nickname this crazy, adorable woman gave our transportation.

"Oh, he…already paid in full." Her eyes meet mine, and I swallow around a sudden lump in my throat. She hasn't been paid yet.

"Julia, this is Mae Fox."

Julia extends a hand, ever the proper and polite woman she was raised to be, although not as assertive as her mother. "Nice to meet you. Thank you for driving my dad across the country." She chuckles softly. "I hope he wasn't too much trouble."

Mae's eyes meet mine again after she shakes Julia's hand. "He was tons of trouble." The gleam in those blue eyes hint at the issues I caused, and I want to remind her how much of a pain in the ass she was at times as well. Instead, I fight the smile at the memory of the type of trouble we caused together.

"Are you staying for the wedding?" Julia asks, and my mouth falls open ready to answer on Mae's behalf when she answers instead.

"No," she states as I interject, "Yes."

Julia's gaze swivels from Mae to me and back to my reluctant driver. "Are you staying at the resort?"

"No," Mae says again while I command, "Yes."

Again, Julia glances between us. Her mouth opens and then shuts. "How will you get home if Mae doesn't stay?"

The question is legitimate. I'd already cancelled the car service despite not having assurance Mae would return me—us—to Chicago.

"I'm afraid I was a one-way ticket," Mae says. I step forward, ready to argue with her, but Julia's unexpected hand on my arm stops me.

"I'm just glad you're finally here. I was getting worried." The softness in my daughter's voice reminds me that she has already suffered a great loss, and I hate that I've caused her additional concern, especially as this weekend should be a highlight in her life. Hopefully, she'll find the happily ever after I didn't have.

"I should..." Mae hitches both her thumbs, one pointing more aggressively at her car covered in dust and splattered with bugs. Bird feathers are still caught in the grill at the front. I fight the smile caused by memories from our trip. Sadness also fills me. I don't want her to go.

"Stay," I whisper, breaking from Julia's hold.

Mae's eyes shift from me to Julia behind me. "I don't think that's a good idea," she mutters.

I know her concerns, but my hands clutch at her shoulders. Our eyes lock, and I soak in the warmth of her looking at me, while reluctance laces those bright eyes.

"Dad?" Julia's tender voice is like an ice bath, reminding me why I'm here.

"Congratulations," Mae states to my daughter, slowly slipping her arms from my grasp. "You're very pretty, and you'll make a beautiful bride."

Glancing back at my daughter, I note her red hair and pale skin is nothing like her mother's, and yet every feature is somehow one-hundred percent Rochelle. After Rochelle died, I boxed up all her photos, sending what I thought Julia might like to her and storing the rest. Mission number one upon my return home will be to get rid of those images.

Mae makes her way around the car.

"Where will you stay?" I question. We fought almost every night we stopped for lodging, and I paid the bill. As she opens the driver door, I call out her name, "Mae."

"I'll find some place nearby for the night." Her voice drops, and I circle the car.

"Don't do this." My own voice lowers as I near her open door, positioned like a shield between us. Cognizant that my daughter is watching me interact with this stranger to her, I struggle with what my heart wants most.

"Mae," I warn again. She can be so stubborn.

"Enjoy your wedding and congratulations," she says glancing over the car, addressing my daughter before slipping into the driver's seat and tugging the door closed. Firing up Louie, the engine purrs to life, and I want to throw myself against the hood to stop her from leaving me.

Instead, I step back, and Louie glugs forward.

"Dad, who was that?" Julia asks, stepping up to me as I watch Mae pull away.

"She was..." My cross-country driver? My new friend? My whole heart?

"Dad?" I blink at Julia's voice. Turning to face her, I fight the sudden ache in my chest and the desire to lash out, calling Mae a mistake.

"She's nobody," I lie, wrapping an arm around my beautiful girl, who has grown into a confident woman. "Now, where is that future son-in-law of mine?"

The term is strange on my tongue, although I'm hoping in time, I might get to know a little better the man who has captured my daughter's heart.

"He's inside with a few of the others." Julia hesitates. "Daddy, I have a surprise for you."

I'm not certain I can handle any more surprises after the week I've had. Mae was the surprise of a lifetime. Peering once more at the now-vacant spot on the drive before the entrance, I exhale.

"What's the surprise, Jellybean?"

She smiles at the endearment. "You'll see." Her anxious smile does nothing to reassure me, but she slips her arm around my waist and leads me forward. Everything in me fights the pull to take one more glance over my shoulder. I release one final hope into the universe, wishing on geraniums and rainbow-arched bridges, that Mae might change her mind. She might come back to me, but as we cross into The Vineyard Inn lobby, I accept that Mae is gone.

And my heart just drove off in a vehicle named Louie.

36

Playlist: "Look Away" – Eli Lieb, Steve Grand

[Mae]

The moment I saw the beautiful, young redhead pacing outside the entrance, I knew who she was and who she was waiting on…and I couldn't stay. I don't know why I couldn't say yes, but I couldn't intrude on this special occasion when Tucker needed to be reunited with his children. He hadn't seen Julia in almost a year. Her wedding is precious time they should spend together. Tucker also needs to regroup with his son who sent a scathing text yesterday when he learned his father wasn't in Napa already as planned.

Be mine, he'd said last night. Doesn't he know I already am his? In heart and mind, body and soul, I belong to him. He'll always have pieces of me as I'll have slices of him, but I don't see how we'll work.

I should have left him yesterday in L.A. and continued on my way, but I'm weak. I couldn't be the one to go. He needed to walk away from me, and the winery was the perfect place to make our separation happen.

I'm reminded of how I'd clung to Adam. I didn't give up on our marriage even though he had. I'd stuck with him during promises and pretty words, and I'd been a fool. I told myself I'd never do it again, and yet I was. I was hanging onto hints of a future when things said might have only been sweet words in the heat of passion.

You're a road goddess, Mae. Don't leave me alone on this journey of life.

There's a long winding drive leading up to the winery, but I can't see through the tears clouding my eyes. I brake where I am and give into the ache in my chest. The sobs rattle out the open window and my body rocks back and forth. I grip the steering wheel in an effort not to turn around and to hold myself still. I've told myself I can take eight minutes to cry, one for each day we were together, and then I need to quit. I need to stop crying over things I can't have, like a man who isn't mine.

"Mae?" I turn my head toward the feminine voice softly calling my name. "Mae, is it really you?"

I'm puzzled to find Mati Harrington, now Mati Chance, standing beside the car. With her lion-red hair pulled into a ponytail, and dressed in workout clothing, my sister-in-law's sister-in-law stares at me.

"Mati? What are you doing here?" My voice cracks and I'm painfully aware that tears are running down my face.

"I'm wondering the same about you, but I'm more *concerned* about you. Are you alright?"

Staring back at Mati, I'm immediately ready to state my standard answer but fight the phrase I too often say. *I'm fine.*

I am not fine. I am anything but fine.

"No," I whisper as the tears fall harder and I grip the steering wheel tighter. "No, Mati. I'm not." I glance up at her, for some reason willing her to let me explain everything that's happened. I need to tell someone. I need someone to hear the entire story just to confirm it happened. I fell in love with a man on a road trip and I don't know how I'll survive the wreck in my heart.

"Why don't you park, and we can talk, okay?" Mati hesitates and I slowly nod. I set Louie into drive and pull into the back of the lot beside a large winery truck. Mati helps herself to the passenger seat and I shift to face her. She lifts her phone.

"Give me one second to tell Denton where I am. Then I'm all ears." She sends her text and then for the next I don't know how long I tell Mati everything. The spirit trip idea. The coffee accident. The con of my sister who talked me into taking a man across the country. The stops. The fights. The connection.

Mati's expression shifts throughout my expounding. She smiles softly. Her bark-brown eyes open wide. Her forehead furrows, and then she gives me a sheepish grin.

"You know, Denton and I were supposed to take a road trip once upon a time and he left me behind." I vaguely remember hearing this story at Dolores and Garrett's wedding. "We didn't get to take that trip for almost thirty years."

"That's a long time to wait."

L.B. Dunbar

Mati chuckles. "In many ways, I didn't wait. I lived my life but when the opportunity arose to reunite with Denton, I took the chance. We can't always understand the paths we're led on in life, Mae. Sometimes the road leads in directions we thought were right, and they were for a while, like having the children you have. You wouldn't trade them, correct? But at some point, we need to turn back. U-turn on the road. Whether it's to make amends with family or find an old love; reconnect with forgotten friends or stick it out with a new one." Her voice lowers. "Some roads are endless."

"And some are dead ends."

Mati laughs once again. "I don't think this one is, though." She reaches for my wrist. "The man is Tucker Ashford, right? He's the father of the bride."

I nod. "Are you here for the wedding?" I hadn't known Mati would be here. I didn't know anyone invited to this celebration and it was another reason not to attend. The spotlight didn't need to be on the father-of-the-bride's new...lover? Driver? Friend?

"It's a funny story, actually," Mati begins, and I listen as she explains the plan the bride and groom have in store for four long-lost friends.

"And Tucker has no idea?" I ask.

"From what we learned when we arrived yesterday, I don't think so."

"Oh my God, this is amazing and terrifying. He could hate this." I stare out the windshield a second, collecting my thoughts.

"He could."

"Or he could love it." I've seen how his eyes glow when he plays music. How he's so lost in his head and the music is all he feels. He's missed it. Without ever saying as much, I can sense how much he has missed playing instruments, and how deep down he has missed his old friends.

"That could be true, too," Mati teases, squeezing my wrist. "But either way, I bet he'd love for you to be here with him. He'll need you, Mae." *Didn't Jane say something similar?* "Because I bet there will be

238

all kinds of questions, and issues and emotions he can't tackle on top of his daughter getting married."

"Why would Julia do this? Why would she plan something like this during her wedding?"

Mati shrugs as I often do. "I don't know, other than she wanted to do something special for him."

Well, special is certainly one way to put it and suddenly, I know what I need to do. I start the ignition on Louie and put him in reverse.

37

Playlist: "What Hurts the Most" – Rascal Flats

Tucker

I follow Julia's lead into The Vineyard Inn. The resort is attached to a family-owned winery, once run by an older couple who came to America as young immigrants and settled into their homeland's heritage—making wine. Julia loves the romantic tale of the two, who died within twenty-four hours of each other. When the wife fell sick, the husband came to tell her goodbye. She passed within the hour. He died peacefully the next day. Now the place is run by their granddaughter, who is also the local doctor, and married to a former MMA fighter. They have three small children.

My daughter loves the romance of this place, although I've been told it had a reputation in the past for clandestine affairs. Rock stars would hide out here. Movie producers would lure young actresses to this place for illicit trysts. And there were years when a group of Hollywood women celebrating their divorces arrived as a sort of support group, called the First Wives Club. The new owners sought to rid themselves of that stereotype, as they themselves were married and in love. They didn't wish to promote adultery on their premises.

And my daughter was about to have a fairytale wedding in a beautiful vineyard while my heart took off down the drive. Entering the lobby, I stop when I see Jude coming toward us. I hear voices chattering off in the distance and a huge sense of loss hits me.

"Wait," I say too loud. Holding up a hand, I stop my son's quick approach. "I forgot something." I begin to pat my pockets. I need to call Mae. I need to beg her to come back. I need to find out where she's staying. Only I can't find my phone. *Dammit.*

"Dad, what's wrong?" Julia asks.

"You look like you lost your phone," Jude adds, as I'm anxiously patting my pockets while I spin in a circle. Then I reach for my bag and frantically search the inside.

Fuck it. I turn for the door as if I can catch Mae, as if she hadn't driven away. I watched her go. Still, I rush back out under the portico, and stare down the drive leading out to the main road.

Nothing. She's really gone. I hang my head and stare at my feet, covered in flip-flops I didn't expect to wear other than in my room. I'm not really dressed as father of the bride in my casual shorts and a T-shirt Mae gave me from her brother's condo. Fox Investments, it says across the back. I'll be looking into his company when I return home.

"Dad?" Julia calls out once more from behind me. "What are you doing?"

I turn my daughter who looks nothing like her mother and my son who looks everything like my father, and stare at them together. So many thoughts race through my head—all I've done for both of them. I love them more than anything, but I recall what Mae said on our trip. Now was her time. Her kids were grown. Her marriage over. Her business a success. She could live a little and that's what the road trip was to her. I should tell them about Mae. I should explain everything and how differently I feel having met her. How I don't want to let her go, but it doesn't appear I have a choice. She's gone.

"I think I left my phone in the car," I say instead.

"We can call the service. Maybe she can bring it back to you."

Bring my heart back? I shake my head and consider how Mae isn't a transportation company. She is a beautiful woman who went out of her way to get me here as fast as we could go without sacrificing her entire trip. Sacrifice, she said. That's what love is. I glance up at my children once more and remind myself I made the right decisions. All those years ago, I did what I felt I had to do. I went home.

If I lost my phone, I'll need to ask Mach to contact Jane who can get ahold of Mae. Will she come back? Or is she too far away? Not enough time has passed for her to travel a great distance. I could still catch her. With renewed hope, I step toward the lobby once more. "I need to find Mach."

241

L.B. Dunbar

From our check-in last night, he made his flight and arrived yesterday evening. He must be around here somewhere. I head for the lobby and Julia follows me.

"Why is he acting like a psycho?" Jude mutters behind me but I ignore him. I don't need his attitude right now.

"I need to find Mach," I repeat.

"He looks different," Jude keeps mumbling more to Julia than to me. "Tan even. Did you take a vacation before you got here?"

"It's called relaxed," I snap, suddenly feeling anything but; however, the last few days I've been more at ease than I've been in years. In the moment, I'm as tense as I've always been.

"Dad, I have a surprise for you. People I'd like you to meet." I pause at Julia's hesitant tone. I should finally meet Chopper's father. His name is Brutus, and he owns a restoration auto-garage where Chopper works. While their last name is familiar sounding, it was too much of a long shot that they'd be related to a man I used to know, and I never inquired. I hated when people asked me about being affiliated with Ashford's, even though I was one.

"In a few minutes, honey. I need to talk to Mach."

"You've had all week to talk to Mach, and you are two days late," Jude interjects. "You need to be present for Julia."

I spin to face my son and bite my tongue. "I am here for Julia. I just need a minute."

"It's fine," my daughter says, turning from her brother to me. "It can wait a few more minutes. We'll find Mach first." She hesitates as she looks back at Jude.

"You've already been waiting. This is bullshit. He can go now and find Mach later." I'm not surprised at my son's tone, but I am surprised he'd brush off Mach. He has an affinity for him. He is his uncle after all, and we share a strange bond between the three of us.

"It's okay," Julia says, patting her brother's chest while giving me a second cautious glance. Taking a deep breath, I exhale.

"No, it's fine. You're right. Show me your surprise, Jellybean, and I'll find Mach in a few minutes." I figure the sooner I get this over with, the faster I can get to Mach. Then, I'll politely excuse myself and get

242

Mach on the task of stopping Mae from driving too far away. Julia leads me into a small wine bar with a scattering of tables. I hear the bellowing laugh of a man where a few tables are pushed together and then see the face of someone I haven't seen in almost thirty years. A few heads turn at the table as well and I stare directly into my past.

Seated there are Lawson Colt, Denton Chance, and Hank Paige...my old band.

+ + +

I just stand there and stare, uncertain how to address them or what to say to them or why they are even present.

"Lawson?" I question first. With hair slicked back and down his neck, he looks every bit like himself only grayer, fuller but more solid than fat. He stands and holds out a large hand.

"Long time, Ashe," he states, his Southern drawl apparent. "And I go by Tommy Carrigan now. Just me being me."

I blink as we clasp hands and shake. He pulls me into a hug and the unfamiliarity of him has me stiffening when I don't mean to. He releases me and steps back allowing me a look at the next man.

"Tucker," Denton Chance says formal and tight. He holds out a hand as well and we shake, more businesslike. He looks as he did when we were eighteen with his model-worthy cut cheeks and bright eyes. He's also more solid or has he just filled out from the lanky stage of teenagers? His hair is lightened as well. We've all aged.

Finally, Hank Paige stands. He looks almost exactly the same with a solid frame and a powerful smile. He is slightly younger than us and I remember considering him a kid when I was all of twenty-two at our first meeting. "Don't know if you remember me?" he states, holding out his hand next. Our time together was short in the transition from Colt45 to Chrome Teardrops. I hadn't played with the shifting band when Hank had been a new hire.

"What are you all doing here?" The vineyard is rented for the sole purpose of the wedding. Everyone present is supposed to be from the guest list, which is relatively small. The intimate collection mainly

L.B. Dunbar

includes Chopper's family, which is bigger than ours, and the couple's friends.

The men look at one another as they clearly know something I don't. "Well, Chopper is my nephew," Hank explains first. "Julia is going to be part of my family."

I hear what he's saying, but I'm struggling to comprehend. All this time, my daughter has been around him. He's the man I never inquired about and here he is. It's all surreal.

"Hank and I reconnected a few years ago," Lawson—*Tommy*—adds, clapping Hank on the shoulder and squeezing him. "Our wives are good friends."

"You're married?" Of course, they'd be married. It's been twenty-something years. Still, the dots are difficult to connect as Tommy was a self-proclaimed bachelor and Hank was in love with Tommy's sister, Kit Carrigan. *Their* lead singer.

The memory of Kit hits hard. She died too young of breast cancer. I remember it making the news. Rochelle had been a fan of her female-empowerment movement to never marry. The father of her child had an overdose when Kit was practically a child herself.

"Got married four years ago last New Year's," Tommy proudly states.

"It will be four years this August for me." Hank clarifies. He nods at a man standing off to the side. He's not as bulky as Hank and his hair is solid white but he isn't much older than us. I instantly see the resemblance to Chopper who has been standing nearby as well.

"Brut." He offers. "Brut Paige, father of the groom." He smiles and I introduce myself in the same manner as father of the bride.

"Groom," says his son, patting his chest while smiling at me with a goofy grin and pride in his voice. The idea he's getting married, and to my daughter, practically makes his tattoos glow. He steps forward, greets me, and tugs me into a hug.

"Don't be upset," he whispers next. "She did it with love."

In the moment, I both appreciate his words of support and his attempt to relieve tension, but I'm also still confused. Chopper releases me and steps over to Julia, circling his arms around her from the back.

They're cute together and I'd focus on them more if I could wrap my head around these other men being present.

"I think Dad is a little stunned," Julia says, her voice high and tense.

Stunned does even begin to describe how I'm feeling. "I still don't understand."

"Brut is Hank's older brother. And I know you didn't play in their band officially, but you did play with Tommy and Denton," Julia clarifies my own history to me. "And as they're friends—Brut, Hank, and Tommy—we spend a lot of time with them. Denton and Mati live in Blue Ridge, but I thought it'd be nice to reunite you all. For my wedding."

Blue Ridge. The town is so familiar, but I suddenly can't place it.

Julia licks her lips nervously. "And play something."

"What?" I snap. This is unbelievable.

"We're getting the band back together," Hank chuckles and slaps me once on the shoulder blade.

Only, I shrug away from him. Fingers pressed to my forehead, I scrub at the onset of a headache. It's all too much. Mae leaving. The band present. Julia's wedding. I just need a minute and I need to find Mach. Suddenly, my best friend is the perfect excuse.

"Can you excuse me a minute? I need to find my business partner, who is around here somewhere." I scan the small selection of tables as if I'll find the man, as if I'm willing him to appear.

"Sit. Have a drink," Tommy suggests, waving at his table. I'd love nothing more, but I need to find Mach. I need…Mae. Like I'm taking that first flight once more. I know I can do this as long as I have Mae by my side. I need her sunshine. My hand slips into my pocket and I find the harmonica she gave me, and while I'd like to pull strength from the gift, it isn't enough. I need her here with me.

As if the universe is both working for and against me, Mach enters the small wine bar. After quick introductions, I pull him aside, explaining my urgency to find Mae.

"We'll just order you a new phone. It can be here in a day, and we'll transfer everything."

I don't care about contacts and social media apps. All my photos are on that phone. Then I remember Mae and I airdropped a folder together. But still, I need access to *her*.

"It's not about the fucking phone," I say, my voice rising, and I glance over my shoulder to see my old band and new in-laws staring at me. Turning back to Mach, I tell the truth. "I need Mae."

Mach eyes me before a slow smile curls his tight lips. "Interesting."

"Mach," I groan.

"Okay, okay." He reaches for his phone and sends a text to Jane. I wait, staring down at the device in his hand. He shakes his head. "She likes to play this game when she's pissed at me and not answer right away." He chuckles to himself, and I wonder what kind of game he plays with her. I'm reminded that Mae suggested Jane has a crush on Mach. Does he feel the same way about Jane? *Whatever.* I don't have time for this kind of office scandal.

"Tell her it's about Mae."

"I did. Chill." He laughs again at my frustration, and I swipe a hand down my face.

I glance once more at my daughter waiting patiently with her fiancé and his family. His family's friends who happened to be my former band.

Play something, Julia said. She cannot be serious. While my children know I was once in a band, they also know I don't like to talk about those days. We eventually had a piano in our home but neither child played well, and I ached when I listened to them. My fingers itched to touch the instrument, but the reminder was too painful.

I scrub at my head again.

"Relax. Maybe you need a drink." Mach is the second one to offer the suggestion. What I need is some air. It's all too much too fast.

"Yeah, just...I need..." I don't even finish, just point toward the hallway and head toward the exit of the small lounge. In my rush to put space between myself and my thoughts, I turn the corner too quickly and slam into someone. Wine splatters across my chest and I reach out to right the person, clutching at feminine shoulders to stop her from falling back at the impact. The glass drops to the floor and shatters as our eyes connect, and I inhale, taking my first real breath in the last hour. Relief washes over me as wine seeps through my T-shirt.

"Sunshine."

38

Playlist: "Good As You" – Kane Brown

[Mae]

Wine soaks my shirt and I glance down at the glass I dropped. The shattering made quite the noise. Strong hands cup my shoulders, pressing me back while holding me steady. We collided hard into one another, but I look up once I hear my nickname said in breathless relief.

"Tucker," I whisper.

"You came back." His voice cracks. His eyes are wild, and he places one hand on my cheek.

"I didn't get very far," I admit, still embarrassed that Mati found me sobbing in my car on the driveway. She'd been out for a run she told me, keeping up with her personal conditioning as a women's volleyball coach at the college level. She is a little thing for a volleyball player, but she has intense drive and passion for the sport.

"I need you," he says.

On those words, his mouth crushes mine and I'm clutching at him. Wet, wine-covered shirts plaster us together, but I don't care. It's only been an hour or so, but I missed him. I couldn't drive away after telling Mati everything and hearing what was next for him. Hearing him say he needs me, I was exactly where I should be—in his arms. With one securely at my back, the other tightens around my shoulder. His fingers dig into my hair. We kiss like we don't have an audience, which we must, because clapping occurs around us.

Slowly, Tucker pulls away, and I tuck my head into his chest. He waves out at the people surrounding us, but the person I'm most worried about is the female voice softly questioning, "Dad?"

"So, I brought back your phone," I state a little too loudly, as I step back from him, and awkwardly search through my cross-body bag which also bears the burden of our collision. Wine seeps into it. I pull forward the device and Tucker chuckles before wrapping his arm around me and tugging me into him again.

With his chin on my head, he says to his daughter, "This is Mae. She's more than my driver."

"We noticed," a rough voice says at the beautiful redhead's side, and I instantly see the resemblance to Tucker.

Despite what I know of Jude's parentage, I imagine he's exactly as Tucker looked at twenty-seven. Even down to the edge on his face, reminding me of when I first met Tucker and he was a tight cannon on the verge of exploding.

"Jude," Tucker sharply addresses his son. "This is Mae Fox. She's my—" He pauses unable to explain who I am to him, and I should pull out of his arms again. Instead, I reach a hand toward Tucker's son.

"*She's* happy to meet you," I mock. Jude stares at me before accepting my handshake.

Tucker releases his strong hold, and he glances at me. "We're a mess." He chuckles and I laugh as well. We certainly are, in more ways than just wine on our clothes and the tear stains around my puffy eyes.

"This is Mati, by the way." I wave at where she stands beside me. Her husband stands at her side. Tucker glances between them. "Remember I told you Mati is married to Dolores's brother. Dolores is Denton's sister. They all live in the same small town together."

Tucker laughs harder. "I can't keep up." He shakes his head.

"Why don't you two go clean up and meet us back here in a little bit?" A man with a smooth, rich Southern drawl states. "We'll be waiting on our girls to get back from the spa."

"Oh my gosh, that's where I should be," Julia says, glancing up at a nice-looking, younger man with tattoos covering his arms. She tips up on her toes to kiss him quick and eases away, but he catches her by the elbow and pulls her back to him. He gives her another kiss, a little longer, a little deeper, before releasing her and she giggles. Then she turns and walks in the opposite direction of our audience.

"If you'd all get out of the way, we can clean this up." A hard masculine voice comes from behind me, and I turn to find another man with heavy tattoos and thick arms crossed over his chest, arching a

L.B. Dunbar

teasing brow at our collection of people. I'd forgotten about the broken glass, and I lower to pick up the pieces.

"I'm sorry about this."

"Mae," Tucker groans at the same time the tattoo man crouches and catches my wrist.

"I got it, beautiful. Go take care of yourself and him." He nods in the direction of Tucker, and I stand again, noticing the deep stain of wine on Tucker's T-shirt. Mati had poured me the glass from a sampling bottle on the front counter. The gift welcomes people as they check in. I hadn't taken a sip before colliding with Tucker.

"I don't have a room," I state, and Tucker groans my name.

"Where are your bags, sunshine?" he asks.

"In Louie."

Tucker laughs again, light-hearted but too high for him, and tucks me back under his arm. "Be back in a bit," he says over his shoulder as he leads me to the parking lot for my things.

+ + +

Once we enter Tucker's room, we've hardly settled our bags when he's on me. Fingers in my hair. Tongue in my mouth.

"We should talk," I mutter against his lips.

"Talk with me inside you."

Okay then. My shirt is peeled off and his comes next. Then Tucker lowers his mouth to my neck, licking at the sticky wine mess on my skin.

"I could pour an entire bottle on you and drink you up," he says into the crook of my neck and shoulder.

"Please don't." I laugh at the thought and then a small thrill runs up my center, imagining him trailing wine down my body and chasing the spill to lap at each drop.

I'm in the headspace now and I make quick work of his shorts, where the waistband is soaked with wine as well. Off go our shorts and underwear before I'm falling back to the bed, Tucker coming down with me. He wastes no time touching me, dragging the head of his cock

250

through folds already seeping for him. When he slips inside me, we both groan in relief at the connection, and he pauses when he's buried deep.

"Are you sore from last night?" We'd made love three times, desperate to hold onto every last minute. The only thing aching on me is my heart but for now it races. I shake my head.

"You feel good," I whisper.

"You make me better." The statement doesn't exactly match what I've said but I don't question him when he begins to move and our hips dance in a pattern I've learned with this man. With a hand at my hip and his other behind my neck, we're quick to roll with one another until he's begging me to get there, and my fingers find my clit. I crash over him, crying out his name, until he stills and pours into me. He collapses over me, wrapping his arms around my back and rolling to his side but keeping us connected.

"I'm so happy you returned," Tucker says.

"I knew you'd miss your phone," I tease.

"I missed *you*, sunshine. I already missed you." His voice softens while the words run deep and he kisses me once more, keeping me close for a little longer.

Eventually, we slip apart, and he lays on his back telling me all that happened. Then I tell him what I learned from Mati in the car. I'm on my belly, pressed up on my elbows while his fingers lazily toy with my hair.

"It's all so surreal," he says glancing up at the ceiling. "The guys are here, and Julia wants me to play something at the wedding. It's too much."

"Maybe she knows you've been missing something important inside you. Or maybe she knows you need this to finally heal."

"Heal from what?" Tucker asks, his question sharp.

"A lost dream. Or the betrayal of Rochelle."

"She died," he says, his brows pinching.

"She had an affair."

"Julia doesn't know that."

"Are you sure?" This wasn't something I'd expect father and daughter to discuss, especially in the early days of Rochelle's death. Tucker wanted to protect his daughter from all things negative surrounding Rochelle. Maybe he'd held back but a mother might not have. Rochelle might have told her daughter what she planned to do. How she was leaving her father, for whatever reason she might have given. Mothers and daughters share things. Fathers only try to protect their little girls. At least, that's what I'm told. I never had a father who made me feel safe like Tucker wants to do for Julia.

He looks away from me again and I reach for the medallion at his chest, fingering it against the strap. He covers my hand, flattens my palm against his skin, keeping his over mine.

"Sunshine." He swallows. "I need you to stay the weekend with me."

When his eyes meet mine, I've never seen such raw honesty or such desperate desire. I couldn't pull myself away again if I tried and I slip up to kiss him, assuring him I won't leave him behind again. We'll figure out the future somehow. For now, it's only another three days. I can give the time to him. We have wiggle room.

39

Playlist: "Harvest Moon" – Neil Young

[Tucker]

Mae squeezes my hand as I lead her to the wedding rehearsal. Of course, she has to let me go so I can practice walking Julia to the magical vine arbor designed for the service. The early evening wedding will be outside, and the reception will include a wine tasting hour next to a river on the edge of the property, followed by dinner in a new ballroom constructed inside an old barn no longer used for preparing wine. Miniature tea lights dangle from the ceiling, decorating the old worn structure in a shabby-chic country vibe.

Rochelle would have hated it, but Julia beams as I walk her down the outdoor aisle and practice the pass off to Chopper. My heart crashes and shatters and comes back together as this is the natural progression of things. A man wants his daughter to find a good person who loves her and respects her, and I'm confident Chopper does. He's a dreamer like her, but he's also solid and she deserves that.

Once the rehearsal finishes, the party takes over the small bar again, sharing a meal with only immediate family at our table. Mae and I have met Lily, Brut's wife, and their two children under four. I can't imagine starting over near fifty, but I quickly learn how Lily and Brut are reunited lovers.

"She's the one that got away," Brut teases, pulling his wife close to him and pressing a kiss to the short honey-blond hair at her temple. "Got her pregnant so I didn't lose her again."

He's teasing. I've learned the complicated backstory to their relationship. Brut raised Chopper as a single father his son's entire life. Lily and Brut's renewed relationship leaves me with questions. Could I start over so late in life? Could I commit to someone like Brut and Lily are committed to one another? Rochelle and I had been in our own worlds for so long, the adjustment to her passing wasn't what one might expect. The idea of her being gone was more upsetting than her absence. We hadn't been together for a while.

I reach out for Mae's hand under the table and squeeze. Getting her pregnant to keep her won't be happening, but I'm trying to figure out how to make things work between us.

Hank also sits in the room with his wife, her three teenaged sons, and their daughter, also under age four. So much has changed, as it should, but I'm still struggling to wrap my head around all the connections and the fact that the men from my former life are present.

Tommy and Edie, and Denton and Mati join us shortly after we finish eating, since the evening activities include all those present at the resort. Julia and Chopper have a small, tight circle of friends, ranging in ages, so it's an eclectic group. Jude remains sullen and on the edge of the crowd. He loves his little sister. He's protective of her, but he doesn't like this scene and too soon he's absent.

"We should practice something," Tommy eventually says, sauntering up to me. He holds a whiskey in his hand while Hank's hands are suspiciously empty.

"Need something?" I say to the former drummer, nodding at his empty fist.

"I abused the privilege, so I'm good."

Wow. I'm proud of him for getting clean. Being a rock star can be hard on the body, and sex, drugs, and rock and roll are no joke. Alcohol is its own demon and I'm glad he's tackled it.

"So...practice?" Tommy says, his Southern drawl thick. "It's been a while."

"We just played together last October," Denton interjects. My brows pinch. *They've already gotten back together?* Then why do they want me? I quickly remind myself this reunion isn't their wish but that of my daughter.

"I was obviously thrown off when I saw you guys, and I didn't have anything to do with this plan. So, I understand if this isn't really your gig. You don't need to do this." With the four of us huddled together, Brut joins us on the tail end of what I've said.

"Julia wants it," her soon-to-be father-in-law reminds me.

"You know, I never thought you liked me, so if you still don't want to play with me, after all this time, just say it," Hank says, his voice deep as his eyes narrow at me.

"Not like you? Are we kids in a schoolyard again?" Tommy scoffs, chuckling to keep the sudden tension low.

"Hank, you promised no bullshit," Brut adds.

"It's not bullshit. We have some unresolved shit and maybe we should resolve it before tomorrow," Hank states, glaring at me.

"There's nothing unresolved," I point out.

"The hell there isn't," Denton interjects next. "You quit. We were just getting our feet wet with Kit and you bailed."

"I—" I was twenty-three. More than a kid but not really an adult. I had a grandfather I loved who'd made a request to save the family name and I honored it, while I owed my father nothing. How do I explain this to them? Do I even need to?

"Haven't you done anything you regret?" I retort to Denton.

His eyes cross the room where I see his wife looking up as if she senses him watching her and she softly smiles at him. Yeah, I remember his tale about leaving behind his true love. Took him twenty-seven years to find her again.

"We don't need to do *this*," Tommy says, pointing a finger in the space between us. "Rehash the past. We've all had our issues over the years."

"You aren't going to do this," Brut adds next. "For Julia and Chopper, you're going to play your damn instruments and make nice. She wants this and Chopper wants her happy."

I like my daughter's future father-in-law. He's a good man.

"My leaving had nothing to do with you, Hank," I say to him, giving him a firm look. "Nothing. It was all family bullshit."

"Know about that," Denton mutters beside me, which reminds me that he and I connected the best when we were younger. We both had shit fathers and came from backgrounds in the public eye. Whether his was small town and mine wasn't didn't matter. We understood each other then.

255

"We've all had family bullshit and made decisions accordingly." Tommy claps Hank on the shoulder and a private look occurs between them. I don't understand what it means, and I don't need to know. There's no sense in turning back the clock. We can't change the past.

"For Julia and Chopper then," I say, holding up my glass of wine.

"For Julia and Chopper." A crystalline chime rings out as Brut taps his glass to mine. The others follow suit while Hank holds up a fist on the edge of our collective glasses. We drink.

"Now, what the fuck are we going to play tomorrow?" Tommy says with a deep laugh and the tension breaks. A new anxiety hits. I have no idea what song my daughter wants to hear.

+ + +

I'm definitely feeling the buzz of good wine and renewed memories. The guys and I shared stories from the past for hours, skipping over the drama of me leaving, and the tumultuous relationship Hank and Kit eventually had. We talked about gigs and old names in the business, and in some ways, it was like I never left. In others, it was a reminder of all that I'd missed. Then I'd look up at Julia smiling at Chopper and him kissing her nose, and I knew I'd do it all again as I'd done it.

Mae's also tipsy. She easily got along with all the wives—Edie, Midge, Lily, and Mati. Mati especially wanted dirt on Garrett to take home and tease him about. From the sound of things, Mati and Denton are close with Dolores and Garrett back in Blue Ridge.

I'm still stunned that all these old connections have made new ones with my daughter, and the past few years they've circled her, included her, and now she'll be family with them. Was I not paying enough attention? How did I miss these people in her life? I can't recall Julia ever mentioning Tommy or Hank, but then again, I didn't know Tommy as anyone but Lawson.

Eventually, Mae and I stumble into my room, and I kiss her neck. "Still want to pour that wine over your body," I mutter into her skin.

She purrs and we knock into the side of the bed. Mae's wearing the dress she wore on our last day of road trip travel. She washed all her things at her brother's place, and she had nothing to worry about as she fit right in with the casual affair tonight.

"Have fun with your friends?" she mutters to my mouth, struggling with the buttons on my shirt.

I did have fun in a strange sort of way, but I don't want to discuss them.

"I want to have fun with you," I say to her, slipping my hand to the hem of her dress and skimming her outer thigh underneath it. The room is cozy, and the lamp on the bedside table is on, but I can see the moon through the uncovered window. It reminds me of the night we were on the hood of Louie.

"I didn't get to fuck you under the moon," I say, and Mae pauses.

"So, what did you have in mind?" Her hand coasts inside my shirt which she finally has open.

"Slip off your underwear."

Mae stares at me a second, before doing a slow tease of removing her panties without me seeing anything. She dramatically drops them on the bed, and I reach for her hand. After grabbing the half empty bottle of wine we started drinking earlier while we got ready for dinner, I lead us outside. The space around the main building is low lit. There are gardens and the wedding area, but off to the side of one barn-like structure, we find an outdoor swing. An honest-to-goodness wooden swing hanging from a large tree.

"Is this private property?" Mae whispers as if anyone can hear us.

"Guess we'll find out." The moonlight highlights a section just outside the tree line and I pull Mae against me. We kiss standing upright, swaying under the lunar light a second before I pull her toward the swing. I take a sip of wine straight from the bottle and set it on the ground, then lower myself to the wooden platform. I removed my belt in the room, so I loosen my pants and pat my lap. "Straddle me."

We chuckle as Mae tries to slip her legs over mine between the rope holding the swing. Eventually, we're tangled together.

"Spider cradled," she says. "It's how we're sitting on this swing." Her legs dangle behind me. With my feet on the ground, I use them for leverage to push against her. Her hands hold onto the rope chain. Gently

L.B. Dunbar

rocking, I nudge my stiff length at her center. My fingers fist in the back of her dress and tug it upward. The scent of her sex wafts around me.

"Take me out," I mutter to her neck, returning my hands to the rope.

Mae strokes me through the opening near my zipper. Pressing on the ground, I rock us back and forth again, not fully swinging, but subtly swaying. Finding the tip wet, Mae uses what I seep to moisten me. I continue sucking at the column of her throat while we gently move.

"Tucker," she whimpers.

"That's it, sunshine. Put me inside you." I still the swing so she can lead me to her entrance. Then I release my feet and slide into her as the swing rocks. Mae cries out at the intrusion and wraps her arms around my neck.

"Did that hurt?" I mumble against her skin.

"Do it again," she whispers, and I lean back to meet her eyes.

I repeat the process, stilling my feet and Mae slips back to release me. Then she settles at my tip, and I drop my hold and rock into her again. With her arms around my neck, she tips back her head.

Her eyes drift closed. "This is incredible."

I bite her neck and pull back once more. It's such a rush to fill her like this but I can't take much more. The need to really move, to capture the necessary friction, has my body humming. I swing into her again before curling my arm around her lower back and keeping her pinned to me. Using only my feet to press the swing back and forth, I hold her on my lap, allowing the gentle motion to aid us in coming together. Soon enough, her fingers dip to her clit and she V-s them in a way my cock feels her fingers, adding a second piece of tension as I glide in and out of her. We clutch at each other, the risk of slipping off the swing enough to heighten the need to hang on.

"Gonna…gotta…ohmygod—"

Mae breaks, and I follow as her channel clenches around me. I go off inside her, draining myself in her heat. Within seconds, she rocks back and forth with my length deep inside her.

"Another one," I choke, recognizing the signs that she could go again.

"I…it's never…I'm going…" Her stammer is adorable but what's sweet is how she comes undone a second time. Dropping her head to my shoulder with her arms wrapped around me, she squirms and squeezes until she's replete. I slide both my hands up her back and cup her shoulders, like a human backpack on her.

"Thanks for coming back, Mae," I whisper to her.

"Thanks for road tripping with me," she says before kissing me under the moonlight.

40

Playlist: "Yours" - Ella Henderson

[Mae]

The wedding is beautiful. Julia beams. Chopper stands in awe and Tucker appears as the proud father he is. It's a perfectly sun-filled early evening and the vineyard feels like it's in extra bloom just for this occasion. The rows of grapevines remind me of my hometown and the multiple wineries in the area. Homesickness hits, but not as hard as it did the day Tucker bought me Gemma the geranium, which sits in our room.

I smile to myself when we pass the swing in a train of golf carts leading us to a special wine tasting hour by a river on the edge of the property. Under white tent canopies, we stand around and savor various wines along with appetizers. The river looks refreshing for such a warm day, and for some reason, I imagine couples making love here in celebration of marriages.

When we return to the main winery, and enter the new ballroom inside an older structure, once again I think of home. The inside reminds me of a hometown favorite called Red Barn Table, owned by a good friend. We've had numerous celebrations there over the six years it's been open.

I've been in contact with my boys, learning on Thursday when Tucker and I spent the day in Santa Monica that Adam was spending the weekend away from them again. I didn't like the sound of that but didn't have a say from here. I'd asked Pam to send me proof of life photos to prove the boys had eaten, slept, and possibly showered. In the heat and dirt of working with plants all day, I assumed that they had. My thoughts briefly drift to home, but I dismiss them and enjoy the wonderful dinner eventually served. To my surprise, I've been added to the main table, where Julia and Chopper chose to sit with Lily, Brut, and Tucker. They didn't want a sweetheart table where they would be the center of attention.

"Another new suit," I tease Tucker, reaching for his lapel as we sit for dinner. I'm wearing the dress I wore the night he played the piano for me. The first night he fell back in love with the instrument once so vital to his life.

"Keep the coffee away from this one," he jests back before slipping his arm around my shoulder and leaning in to kiss my temple. I glance up to find Julia watching us. A slow smile curls her lips.

"You should talk, Mr. Wine Accident."

"How did you meet again?" Lily Paige asks, lightly chuckling.

We've already explained the circumstances. His transportation company canceled, and my sister works for his firm. I was coming to California anyway.

"She was looking for a sign," Tucker says, and I laugh.

"I was looking *up* for an actual sign that marks the beginning of Route 66."

"And then she bumps into me, spilling coffee all over my new suit."

"It wasn't everywhere," I clarify, as most of it ended up on me.

"I was so pissed. The transportation company had just canceled on me for this trip." Tucker smiles at me. "I think it was a sign my life was about to change."

I stare back at him, dumbstruck.

"And when I spun around, my tongue froze. A ray of sunshine was beaming at me, like the heavens opened and said *pay attention here.*"

I softly laugh. "That's dramatic."

"That sounds romantic," Lily sighs.

"I suppose it is if you like wearing coffee more than designer suits," I say, slightly uncomfortable with all eyes on Tucker and me.

"I'd let her spill coffee on everything I own as long as she looks at me like she did that day."

Lily turns to Brut, and they share a secret smile, and I risk another glance at Julia who swipes under her eye. Chopper rubs a hand up her back and leans in to kiss her neck, and I turn back to Tucker to find him still looking at me.

"You are my sign, sunshine," he says softer, only to me.

"A sign for what?" Instantly, I recall our discussion about that poor bird that flew into the car grill.

"A sign of everything I knew was missing but didn't think would ever happen for me." With his hand on the back of my neck, he pulls me to him, kissing me softly and quickly before releasing me. My face heats. Today is his daughter's wedding but I feel like the blushing bride on the eve of a life-changing moment.

+ + +

As the night wears on, Tucker and the guys get closer to their big reunion performance. They had a practice earlier this morning, but Tucker is nervous, and I have an idea. Excusing myself, I head back to the room, remembering what he'd placed on the dresser. When I return to the barn, I'm almost to the entrance when I'm stopped outside by Jude.

"You shouldn't be here," he says without greeting.

He's been eyeing me on occasion throughout the day, but I've ignored him, brushing off his behavior as a spoiled twenty-seven-year-old. I haven't missed the sneers he's given his father before shifting into tight smiles on behalf of his sister. He doesn't seem to comprehend all Tucker did for him, but that's the way of children. They never appreciate the sacrifices of parents until they are parents themselves. In his case, Jude's entitlement might never allow him to see the light.

"Excuse me?" I say.

"He loved her, you know. That's why he was upset. He didn't want her to run off with someone else. He wanted their marriage to work." His statement is in complete opposition to what Tucker told me, but I don't share that with his son.

"What happened in your parents' marriage is between them." Children aren't necessarily privy to all that goes on behind their parents' door. My own boys weren't blind to how their father and I didn't always get along, but they also didn't pay enough attention to notice how truly unhappy I was with their dad.

"But it wasn't. They were a very social, visible couple, and he loved her. She loved him, too."

If she did, I don't understand why she'd have an affair, but I don't mention that either. Adam told me how much he loved me, yet he still slept with multiple other women. The lies people tell don't always make sense.

"Again, that's between them." I don't need to remind this young man that either way, his mother is deceased, and his father is free to conduct himself in any manner he wishes. It didn't mean his heart felt any more or less for his once-wife.

"He'd had an affair first." The words hit me straight in the chest, but I don't want to believe him. I *don't* believe him, but a niggling of doubt settles in. Could Tucker have done that? If he was unhappy? If they had been so estranged like he said?

"He couldn't fight the ghost of my father."

A sick gleam forms in Jude's eyes and I wonder if he understands that his biological patronage came from a sperm, in a man who no longer lives, who shouldn't have been with a near-child like his mother. His *dad* was the man inside the barn. The one he isn't defending but attacking with his words. Tucker is the man who raised him, took care of him and his precious mother, and Jude should be grateful. Tucker could have turned his back. He could have told his grandfather to go to hell. He could have been so many other things than this spoiled child's *dad*.

"I don't think that's true." There's no way Tucker felt unequal to his father and I'm confident in my defense of Tucker on this matter.

"She loved him more."

I scoff. At nineteen, did his mother recognize that a man twice her age with a wife wasn't in love with her? He'd used her young body for his own purposes and got her pregnant. Working with the assumption Tucker told me everything, as I believe he has, Jude has some nerve assuming *I* know the truth of his birth. Perhaps this was a test, to see how open Tucker has been with me. Either way, it's a cruel joke for Jude to speak so openly about something Tucker tried to protect. He did what he did to prevent this very thing from happening—damaging the family name with their history.

He has no idea what he's talking about regarding his parents, but now isn't the time to set him straight.

"I don't think we should be discussing this." I step left, but Jude blocks me, and the clang of instruments floats out to us. The music fades out and I recognize it's only a sound check. "Don't do this."

I hate to beg or plead with this man-child, but I need to get to Tucker. I don't care about his son. I care about the man inside about to take a giant risk to his ego and his past.

"Go home."

"Excuse me?" He has some nerve.

"You'll never measure up to her. And he'll never love a...*chauffeur*." Jude blocks me further, arms crossed and shoulders back. Tipping his head, his gaze roams up my body and he sniffs with disgust.

This trip had certainly become much more than just me hauling Tucker to California. It had become something larger. I draw a long breath, ready to put this misinformed, spoiled twenty-seven-year-old in his place when my phone rings in my hand. Assuming it's Tucker wondering where I am, I answer it without thought.

"Hello."

Owen's voice cracks through the phone. "Mom. It's Wy- Wyatt...it's bad."

Spinning away from Jude, I take a few steps to the side of the barn. "What happened?"

"He was at work. And the table collapsed. Mom, you need to come home." His breath falters through each choppy statement.

"Okay. Okay," I gasp. My hand covers my mouth and fear fills my gut. "Where the hell is your dad?"

"Not here," Owen's voice cracks again. *Is he crying?* Shit. *Shit.*

"Where's Pam?" To be honest, she'd do a better job of shepherding my boys through this situation than their father would.

"She's with Wyatt in the ambulance." He sniffled.

Ambulance? My stomach cramps around the growing knot in it. "I'm in Napa but let me get to an airport. I'll take the first flight out."

"Come right to the hospital, okay Mom?" The panic in his voice along with the sudden sob reminds me of when he was a little boy. He's struggling with his emotions, afraid to let his fear show, but unable to control being a sensitive boy.

264

"Okay. I'll let you know my flight information as soon as I know it." Hanging up I take only a second to process what's happened. My children need me.

Spinning back toward the open barn door, Jude is no longer in sight, but I find Brut at the edge of the entrance.

"Mae, where have you been?" A second later, he's holding both my shoulders. "Are you okay?"

"I'm not," I admit and quickly tell him there's an emergency at home. "I need to go, but I can't tell Tucker. He needs to be focused on Julia. Please, Brut. He can't know until later, after he plays for her."

Brut glances over his shoulder at the men gathered on the low stage. Laughter surrounds them. Tucker needs to be here for his daughter, but more importantly, he needs to do this for himself. He needs to prove to himself that music is still inside him, yearning desperately to come out. It's an absent part of him he no longer needs to deny. Julia asked him for this gift, because she knows…somehow, she knows he's been missing this part of himself.

And I need to get to my sons.

"Can you give this to Tucker? He'll need it before he plays." I hold up the harmonica I saw him slip from his shorts and set on the dresser. Maybe he wanted it with him today. Maybe he didn't. But the sentimental gift might bring him luck tonight. He played beautifully on the street corner in Winslow. He can do it again.

"You should just tell him. He'll understand," Brut encourages me, but I see he's torn. Brut's admiration for his now daughter-in-law has been apparent all weekend. He doesn't want to hurt her, and I'll never forgive myself if Tucker follows me instead of playing for Julia.

"You can tell him later. For me," I say.

Brut's brows pinch. "I don't like this."

"Brut, I need to get to my boys."

His shoulders fall. He's been a single father most of his life. He knows the position I'm in. My children need me, and I have to go.

"How will you get home?"

I explain how I'll Uber to the airport. I can leave Louie for Tucker, or better yet, I'd always planned to sell the car when I got to California.

265

Flying home was on the original itinerary. The spirit trip was one-way. "My ex-husband bought it with borrowed money." I choke around the lie. "And my son doesn't want it. I might need the money for his medical expenses anyway."

"We could have it shipped to you," Brut begins but I'm already shaking my head. The expense is one I can't afford, nor do I want. "Okay, I run a restoration garage. I can unload it for you. Leave the keys at the front desk and text me when you get to the airport." Brut lifts his phone and takes my number, adding it to his contacts and texting me his. "Are you sure about this?"

I'm not. I should talk to Tucker. But not now, as I need to get home.

"I've got to go. It was a beautiful wedding." I press up on my toes to kiss Brut's cheek and race back to the room, gathering my things like a runaway bride and escaping the resort before doubt settles in.

41

Playlist: "In My Life" – The Beatles

[Tucker]

My palms sweat. My heart races, and Mae is nowhere to be seen. She excused herself before we started our sound check, saying she'd be right back. Only a few minutes ago, I noticed her by the barn door entrance, lingering in the doorway with Brut. From this distance it was hard to tell what they were talking about, but Brut held her shoulders at one point. I didn't like it. Although I know he's a happily married man, I don't like the sight of someone else touching her. Mae is mine.

As Denton strums a guitar and Hank raps out a few beats on the drums, I stare at the keys under my fingers. Tommy taps at the microphone, and I glance up, seeking Mae. Brut walks with determination toward the stage.

"Mae asked me to give you this." He hands over my harmonica and I'm stumped.

"What? Where is she?"

Brut holds his head still. "She went to your room." The struggle on his face hints there's something he isn't saying.

"Should I check on her?" I shift to stand.

But Brut holds up a hand. "She doesn't want you to miss this moment." Brut stares at me, keeping his eyes on mine but I can't read what he isn't saying. The guys are waiting behind me and despite sensing something is off, I accept what he says. Still, my chest pinches at her absence. Mae would want to hear what we have planned. My road trip lover with her giant playlist of songs will appreciate our set.

"Everybody having a good time?" Tommy bellows, gripping the mic. "We want to thank Julia and Chopper for including us in their special day and giving us this opportunity to reunite. We can't promise we'll be great." He pauses to chuckle. "But these old guys still have talent, and I wouldn't want to be on any stage with anyone else."

"Hey," a voice calls out in the crowd, and I recognize Gage Everly, the lead singer of Collision, the band Tommy now manages.

"You'll get your turn tonight, kid," Tommy jokes of his charge, who is also his nephew by marriage and not a kid at over thirty. Julia volunteers at his wife's music therapy school. My daughter has such a generous heart.

"We thought we'd start out with a Beatles classic in honor of the lovely bride and per Chopper's request." Tommy pauses. "Here's 'Julia.'"

As we begin the song, Chopper leads my daughter onto the dance floor, and they curl into one another. The love between them fills the room and I wish Mae was here to witness this moment. Still, I fall inside the song and let the music wash over me, a baptism of sorts to be on this small stage with these guys again. Maybe the sensation is more rising up from the ashes, as I've felt less than whole for so long, and this moment seems to be restoring the fire inside me.

We continue on, playing a song request from Julia for Chopper. Tommy still has a growly tone when he sings but admits he can't hit the high notes he once did. His rendition of "Patience" is more Chris Cornell than Axel Rose. I'm not certain I understand the depth of this song in connection to the newlyweds, but Julia and Chopper began dating shortly after Rochelle's death, and Julia has hinted that Chopper has the patience and willpower of a saint.

Eventually, we play "Wait for Me," our signature single as Colt45 and I desperately want Mae to hear the words. The ones she wrote on the edge of a Cadillac in Amarillo, Texas. As we fade off on that one, we nod at one another with sheepish smiles. It's been a long time.

"We have one more song to sing, although we didn't practice it. We're hoping this guy still has his memory of it," Tommy teases as he points at me. "He should. He wrote it. This is 'Sand'."

My eyes leap to Tommy and then out at the crowd where my daughter's mouth falls open. I scan the guests once more wishing for Mae to appear so I can sing this song for her. Instead, I sing it for myself, closing my eyes and visualizing the notes.

I'm an hourglass and you're the sand,

but I won't let you slip away.

Fragile but strong, this can't be wrong.

I'll hold you close.

I won't let you slip away.

As we finish the sultry sound with Tommy's voice doing it justice just like he did nearly thirty years ago, I immediately know what I need to say to Mae. I need her to know I'm in love with her.

I hit the final key and stand. We take goofy bows as the guests applaud for us, and then I hop from the stage. We'll be taking a little break and then Gage Everly promised to sing a song he wrote just for Julia and Chopper as their wedding gift.

"Dad, that was incredible," Julia says, rushing to me once I'm on the dance floor. "You never mentioned writing a song, only being part of the band."

I softly smile at her, reaching out for her face. "Wasn't worth mentioning," I say brushing off the accomplishment, although it was our *second* famous hit. Back when hitting charts and ranking were important to us. Then finances and fame got in the way, and Tommy wanted more. He deserved more, as did the rest of them, and they joined with Kit and skyrocketed to the top, earning money and accolades.

"We have our dance coming up," Julia reminds me, teasing me, as I'd struggled to pick a song for our father-daughter moment.

"I won't miss it, Jellybean," I assure her. "I just need to find Mae."

Julia smiles. "I really like her, Dad. She's good for you." My daughter's approval gives me the extra boost I need to tell Mae how I feel tonight. I don't want one more day to pass without her knowing I love her.

"I'm going to look for Mae but save that dance for me." I lean forward and kiss Julia's cheek then head for the barn entrance.

As I near the exit, I find Jude lingering. "Hey, have you seen Mae?" I ask him.

Despite Brut's telling me Mae went to our room, I'm unsettled by her disappearance. She missed our little concert.

Jude grips my arm to stop me from continuing forward toward the inn. "I sent her away."

L.B. Dunbar

"You mean you sent her to the room." My brows pinch, puzzled by the edge in Jude's tone.

"I mean, I told her to get lost," Jude clarifies. "I told her to leave."

"You what?" My body tenses as I face my son. A man who is a mirror image of me and my own father—*our* father. His attitude suggests he's even more like the old man than I've considered.

"You don't need that kind of woman, Dad."

"And just *what kind of woman* do you think Mae is?" I snap, not really concerned about my son's opinion but curious all the same. I'm certain he hurt Mae's feelings somehow.

"Someone after your money, after the attention, after the fame."

"You have no idea what you're talking about." Jude grew up in his mother's limelight like Julia. A puppet in her performance as perfect mother and ideal wife. He bought into her act as she spoiled him, but Julia was her favorite. Julia didn't conform, which drove Rochelle to desire more connection with our daughter.

As for Mae, I don't believe my Prius-driving, stop-at-kitschy-locations, experience-the-road, and save-the-bird lover is after anything other than...my heart?

"Mach told me how you paid her to drive you here."

"I—" I did do that. But she could take all my money as far as I'm concerned. The only commodity I want is her heart in return for mine.

"And now she's gone, as she should be. She took your money and ran."

I don't believe him. That can't be true. "You don't know what you're saying." Mae would never do that. She hasn't been paid yet and she wouldn't leave me behind. She wouldn't leave me *again*.

I reach for the harmonica in my pants' pocket. She offered her gift to me, through Brut, as silent support. That was my Mae. Considerate. Loving. Dedicated.

"You don't need that kind of trash."

"You watch your fucking mouth." With fists clenched, I step up to my son. I've never touched my child in a physical manner but I'm on the verge of punching Jude, who's an adult with a sour attitude.

"You don't need someone like her."

270

"You have no idea what I need, kid," I mock.

Jude is jaded. He lost out on his inheritance. He's scrambling with a department store under an antiquated name. He's resentful of the firm I built with Mach instead of returning to Ashford's, and he's pissed at his paternity without realizing it never mattered. It shouldn't matter. I *am* his dad, although not his father.

"You'll throw everything away just like you did with Ashford's," he warns me as if he's so wise. "She won't be good for you."

There's so much to tackle here. "Are we having this argument again? Ashford's was never going to be mine. It's yours now. You do with it what you will. As for Mae, who are you to decide whether she's good for me or not? It's not your call. It's my choice, and I choose Mae. She's better than anything I've experienced. And I'm not throwing anything away."

"You're willing to sacrifice everything for some car driver you paid to bring you across the country?"

Sacrifice? I glance back at the guys huddled near the stage. Julia and Chopper are still standing with their arms around one another on the dance floor. My attention returns to Jude, and my gaze roams up his body. The one I didn't create but that shares so much of my DNA.

"I know all about sacrifice, Jude. I've done it multiple times, but one time in particular stands out to me." I narrow my eyes at him. "And it was love." I pointedly stare at him, long and hard. I'm not certain my son will ever comprehend the depth of what I gave up for him, what I did for him, and that's on him now. He's an adult. I won't coddle him. I won't cave for him.

I'm also not about to lay some convoluted blame on him for decisions I made, even if I felt at the time, they weren't my choices. Maybe Jude will understand one day when he's a parent, if he ever gets to that point in his life. He'd have to be open to love and accept the meaning of family—love *and* sacrifice. I'm not certain he'll ever get there.

As for Mae, I'm not giving up anything. Mae is love and I'll be going after her.

+ + +

Before I make it out the door, a call for the father-daughter dance rings out, and I return to the dance floor to take my daughter in my arms. Gage Everly sings a slow country song about wishes for my child and the happiness I hope she finds in life.

"I'm so happy you're here, Daddy. Thank you for everything."

"Anything for you, baby girl," I tell her, squeezing her hand in mine. "I wish your mom was here." It isn't a lie. Julia should have had her mother present, although the influence of Lily and company has been everything I could hope for in strong, kind women to befriend my daughter. Lily's touch is everywhere in the details, and so is that of Ester Banks, an older co-worker at Because Cupcakes. They both took Julia under their wings in the industry and in life, and I'm grateful to them.

"It's okay, Dad. You don't have to miss her."

I still, shocked at the statement. "Why would you say such a thing?"

Julia shrugs in my arms, reminding me of Mae. "I know things. I just want you to be happy. I don't think I can recall you smiling as much as I've seen you smile with Mae. It's a reason I wanted to reunite you with the band."

I stare at my daughter.

"Mom loved you. She did, despite what she did." A heavy pause falls between us, and I'm reminded of what Mae suggested. Julia might have known of her mother's affair. "But she always said a piece of you was missing. A piece she couldn't fill and kept you separate from her."

"Jellybean—"

"Let me finish, please." We both wait a beat, and she continues. "Maybe being with your old friends will bring the music back to you. Maybe that's the piece you held back. You never played the piano in the house. You'd stare at it like it would hurt you to touch it, but I think that look was really longing. You'd given up so much for us. For Jude. For Mom. Even me."

"I didn't give anything up," I defend, swallowing around the thickness in my throat.

"You walked away from them,"—she nods in the direction of my former band members—"and the timing adds up to Jude's birth. I'm so sorry you didn't go back. Whatever happened, I'm sorry you didn't return to your dream."

I'm reminded of what Mae said. It took a ray of sunshine and a cross-country trip to learn that dreams don't change, but sometimes the paths do. We're led down one road but it's not the road we're meant to finish our journey on.

"I've been fortunate to have other dreams instead," I say, staring down at my little girl who is now a beautiful woman.

"I want you to have all the happiness in the world like I have with Chopper."

"I do, too, Jellybean." And I will, once I find Mae.

When the dance ends, I press another kiss to Julia's cheek. "I love you, baby girl." I cup her face and rub my nose against hers as I did when she was just a child and then I step back, accepting that she's a woman, with a husband. One day she'll have a child of her own, and she'll understand all the more how the roadmap changes and detours happen, and sometimes, the path never circles back.

+ + +

I finally get a chance to escape and check on Mae once Chopper dances with Lily during the mother-son dance. The dance is a token of his love for his stepmother, who has only been his stepmother for a few years. He had a friendship with Lily prior to Brut finding her again and the story is quite the tale.

A hand catches my sleeve as I'm attempting to step away again. "Hey, I need to tell you something." Brut stills me.

"Brut, I really need to check on Mae." Frustration sets in as it's been more than half an hour since she disappeared.

"That's what this is about."

Instantly the hackles on my neck rise. "What about her?"

"She left."

L.B. Dunbar

"As in went to our room?" I clarify, tipping my head and lowering my voice with a calm I don't feel.

"No, she left. Her son had an accident, and she went home."

"What happened to him? Will he be okay?" Concern for her child races through my head.

"She didn't have all the details, just that it was bad and he's at the hospital. She went to the airport. I got a text from her that she found a late-night flight. She'll be boarding soon."

She went to the airport? "Why the fuck didn't you tell me earlier?" Mae needs me. She's been here for me, and now she needs me, right?

"Because she knew tonight was important. Julia needed you to sing with the guys. Maybe you needed it too." He pauses and arches a brow. "The harmonica?"

It's a question I can't answer now. "I need to get to Mae."

"She's gone. On an airplane." Brut gives me a sympathetic look. They all know I rode across the country because I have a fear of flying. The guys even remember how I freaked out after my parents died and we needed to catch a flight to make a gig. I practically needed to be tranquilized to get on that plane. I drank so much I'm surprised the airline let me board, but back then security wasn't half as strict as it is now.

"What about Louie?" That damn Prius. My chest aches with fond memories of that car.

"She wants me to sell it."

"What?!" I bellow. "Why you?" But I quickly remember Brut owns a classic car repair shop. "Why sell it?"

"She said she might need the money for her son."

I'm still puzzled why Mae didn't just come and tell me she was leaving.

"She left the keys at the front desk for me, and her plane takes off any second," Brut adds.

I'm caught between anxiety for Mae's child and my own emotions. My heart beats in sympathy for Mae and I hope her boy is okay, *but she actually left.* There's no reverse here, no U-turn. She's really gone this time. I still can't wrap my head around her leaving without a word to me.

Did she believe whatever Jude said to her? I'm not buying it. Mae is stronger than spiteful words from an arrogant man. Hell, I'm proof of her strength. She handled me across two-thousand miles and seven days.

Then again, a simple goodbye wouldn't have been enough. There are so many more words to be said between us.

42

THE NEXT DAY

Playlist: "Scars" – James Bay

[Mae]

"Wyatt, stop fidgeting," I warn my son as he sits on the hospital bed, his leg lifted in traction.

While Wyatt's broken leg is certainly upsetting, it wasn't quite life threatening like Owen led me to believe. Unfortunately, I had not been able to reach Pam while I raced to the airport. She had extensive medical training from her previous work as an EMT, and a simple phone call with her would have explained his condition. She had been with Wyatt when he was taken by ambulance to the hospital. In a second attempt to reach Pam, she'd been in the surgical unit when I called.

I hadn't bothered to reach out to Adam.

It wasn't until after I boarded the plane that a text came through with minimal details. We use wooden pallets on cinder blocks to hold up the plants, like bookshelves. Wyatt went to lift the corner of one pallet where the cinder blocks were precariously leaning due to excessive rain. His foot slipped in the loose gravel under the pallet. The cinder blocks tumbled over, and he lost his grip. He was nearly in the splits when the pallet came down on his upper thigh. The pressure of pounds of plants, along with the angle of the fallen pallet, chopped at his bone. I wouldn't have expected Wyatt to be so brittle, but an accident is an accident and a break a break.

"We need to get you out of this bed and back on the ice. You're missing valuable training time," my son's father says from the other side of Wyatt's hospital bed.

The insensitivity of my ex-husband should not astonish me, but it does. I shake my head at him.

"What?" he drones. "I'm just saying—"

"Adam, stop talking."

He shakes his head at me.

"Where were you?" I ask.

"I was out." As if that explains his absence. It's late Sunday and he's finally shown up.

I've been at the hospital for hours. I made an overnight flight to Chicago and caught a second flight to my small-town airport in the morning. Jacob Vincentia, Pam's husband, was kind enough to meet me at Cherry Capitol in Traverse City and drive me to the hospital. I haven't slept. I'm still wearing the dress from the wedding although I dug flip-flops out of my suitcase to replace the wedges I'd had on.

I'd give anything to have Tucker here with me. When I arrived at the local airport this morning, I sent him a text. With the time difference, I expected he'd still be sleeping. My hope was he had an amazing night with his old friends and his daughter's new family. He needed to reconnect with those people. I also hoped he'd let me explain myself and then want to reconnect with me. The reminder that I've left him once more is a struggle. But he needed to stay behind for his daughter. I needed to be here for my son.

"You should have been here," I say.

"Oh yeah, and where were you?" His gaze roams my dress.

I don't want to fight with Adam, but his explanation isn't good enough. I left my boys to be with their dad for two weeks. Two weeks out of fifty-two, and this is what happens.

"I'm not doing this with you," I mutter, turning back to our son, hating that he's a witness to another fight between his parents. He looks like hell although the pain is subdued by meds. He has a long recovery ahead of him and hockey may not be in his future. In a snap, his dreams might be shattered, and I'm reminded of Tucker again. How he had plans and hopes, and his path was cut short. We can never predict where we will go. We can't assume the final destination exists. We can only make the best of every trip.

Briefly, I wonder if that's what Tucker did with me. I can't seem to shake his son's words. Does Tucker think he was a means to an end? Does he believe that he paid for a service? What about the *extra* between us? Our connection felt so real. I want to refuse negative thoughts of him taking advantage of me, but standing across from my ex-husband, old doubts return. I hate that Adam has that power over me.

"You look different." My ex-husband's eyes shift to me once more.

"I am different," I say, defensively. Dammit, Adam should have no power over me. That was the point of my spirit trip. To find myself. To restore myself. To rev my engine. I almost chuckle at the notion. Tucker definitely started the ignition and accelerated all my sexual energy. He took me on the best ride of my life.

"What's different?" Adam asks, eyeing me as if he can visibly see on the outside the changes that have occurred within.

"*I'm* different," I say again.

I can't go back to being complacent about Adam's lack as a father or the fact he had two affairs and we ended in divorce. I also can't define myself by Adam's actions. I've learned better. I've had better, and it was in Tucker Ashford. *Ashe.* He made me feel alive. He also made me feel special. And even if it was a lie—and I haven't accepted that it was—it was real to me. *Our* road trip changed everything.

"You said that," Adam comments. He tips up his chin, eyes still leering at me. "We should grab a drink sometime."

He can't be serious. I stare back at my ex-husband. I don't need to explain myself to him. I couldn't, even as I accept I shouldn't. He'd never understand this feeling inside me. This new energy burning within. Despite Adam, I've learned I can love again. I love Tucker and I desperately want to tell him.

"Never gonna happen, Adam. Save that line for someone else."

"When can I go home?" Wyatt groans on the bed between Adam and me.

"Soon, baby," I say swiping at his hair. He needs a shower, but he'll only be allowed baths for a bit. He's a big kid and I could use Adam's help maneuvering my son, but like everything else surrounding my ex-husband, I'll need to fend for myself. I can do this. I'll figure it out as I always do.

"You're coddling him," Adams says.

"I'm comforting him, Adam. There's a difference."

"Stop fighting," Wyatt groans and I'm chagrined by my child. We shouldn't be literally arguing over him like this. Our son needs either a united front between his parents or two separate camps under a cease fire, not Adam and I at war.

"Where's the Prius?" Adam suddenly asks.

"I sold it."

"You what?" His voice cracks as it rises.

"Yay Mom," Wyatt mutters in his drugged-up state.

"You'll give me the money back," Adam demands.

"I'm giving the money to Wyatt." Louie was his car, and he wanted a truck. He can buy what he wants with the funds. While I told Brut I might need the cash for medical expenses, I don't. As for the money from Tucker, Jane still has it. I'm not accepting payment for the pleasure I took in my time with Tucker.

"You can't sell it without my consent."

"Wyatt's an adult and he owns the car. I can do it with his."

"I approve," Wyatt murmurs, a dopey grin on his face. I smile down at him, and he winks at me. "Hey Dad?"

"Yeah, son?"

"Can you get out? You're killing my buzz."

I stifle a laugh while Wyatt gives his father a goofy grin. However, something in his expression must tell his father he's serious. He wants him to leave.

"I'll visit when your mother isn't here," Adam huffs and pats Wyatt's good leg.

"Or don't," Wyatt mutters as Adam leaves. I'm shocked by Wyatt's behavior toward his father.

"Wow, you must really be high to kick out Dad," I tease.

"He's a buzzkill and he's wrong." Wyatt rolls his head on the pillow. "You look good, Mom. I like the dress and I'm sorry I ruined your trip."

I smile at the compliment. "You didn't ruin anything, honey. You know I'll always be here for you."

"You always are, which is why Owen and I wanted you to take the trip. You deserved it."

"I did," I admit. I deserved the time off, but now I'm back. Devoted mother once more.

"Did you have fun?" he asks, his lids lowering, his grin drooping.

"It was the best trip I've ever had," I tell him.

"Yeah?" He gushes. "So is this one."

He giggles and I get it. But I'd argue love is a much better high than the one he's on.

+ + +

When I don't hear from Tucker for three full days, I try not to panic. I hold off on calling Jane to see if Tucker returned to Chicago. He'd asked me to drive him, and I wasn't there to do it. Brut sold Louie and sent me the money electronically. I was a little surprised how fast the sale happened, but he told me he had an eager buyer.

Who wouldn't love Louie? I was heartsick at the loss of him for the memories the car held but I'd never be able to enter that car again because of those memories. Louie wouldn't be the same without Tucker.

Late on Tuesday, I'm at Mae's Flowers trying to catch up on some things. Although my vacation was supposed to be two full weeks on the road, I'm home early and it seems as if that's a blessing. Summer really isn't the time for me to take off.

"There's a package for you," Pam hollers at me as I cross the gift shop and head for the stairs leading to our office. *We have a corner office,* we joke, which includes two desks at ninety-degree angles, each looking out a window over the garden yard. When I enter the small space, a box sits on my desk with a cup of coffee next to it.

"That's strange," I say to no one. I didn't have a to-go cup of coffee earlier. When I reach for the cup to move it aside, I notice that it's hot and the heat-protecting slip around it reads, Sunshine, in marker print. My heart races at the name and I set the cup aside. Next, I open the box, which isn't sealed or even labeled with a mailing address.

Inside the cardboard, I find a note in crisp handwriting. *A road trip of moments.*

Underneath the note is a miniature red-rocking chair, like an ornament. Missouri is written on a tag attached to it. Next is a magnet of a bridge. Kansas is imprinted under the rainbow arch. A bottle of wine is also inside the box from the winery in Oklahoma. A medallion on a short string wraps around the neck. It's St. Christopher, the patron saint of travelers. Texas is tagged on the medal.

A small jewelry box contains the turquoise earrings to match the silver cuff I bought, and I smile as I touch the bracelet on my wrist. Turns out the color matches the dress I wore to the wedding. The earrings would have been a nice accessory.

A flat package at the bottom is a model kit of wood pieces to build a replica of the helicopter we took over the Grand Canyon.

A small hourglass with a grain of sand is next, stamped with California on the bottom of it. A note is attached.

My heart is an hourglass; yours is the sand. I will not let you slip away from me again. Not this time.

My vision blurs. The last item in the box is a picture of me standing before that hotdog-holding Muffler Man. The image where I assumed Tucker must have played with the filter because I'm smiling, and my eyes look bright. Flipping over the printed picture, an inscription is on the back.

Illinois – but I'd like to be your gift from that state.

On that, I collapse to my desk chair and cover my face, crying into my hands.

"Don't cry, sunshine." The strong masculine voice has me spinning in my seat. I blink through tear-filled eyes and try to focus on the man leaning against the open door.

"Tucker," I whisper.

"Hey, Mae. You forgot something in California." He pats his chest.

I weakly chuckle but tears still fall. "You didn't respond to my text." My voice cracks. I thought maybe he didn't want to hear my explanation after all, about my son, about the money.

"Would you believe I lost my phone somewhere at the winery?"

"Actually, I would." I laugh a little harder since he has a habit of leaving it behind, especially if his thoughts are elsewhere.

Tucker turns his head, chewing at his lip a second. His arms are crossed and he's casually leaning against the door jamb.

"I'm so sorry I left like that. I didn't know what else to do. Owen called and said Wyatt was in an accident. I couldn't get ahold of Pam, and I didn't want to ruin your moment with Julia." The words tumble out in a hiccupping mess. My eyes lift, locking on his as I remember what his son said to me. *A chauffeur.* "And I didn't take the money."

"I wouldn't have held it against you if you had. But Jane told me you refused to accept it."

"I didn't want it. It didn't feel right after—"

"After what?" Those silvery eyes dance as he pushes away from the door jamb and straightens, staring back at me.

"After I fell in love with you."

Tucker smiles, slow and crooked, as he steps into my office. "I'm sorry for what my son said to you. He had no right—"

"He was only protecting you."

"Well, I don't need protection." His eyebrows lift and the twelve-year-old inside me giggles. "You know what I mean," he teases.

"I do," I say. "But I don't want you to ever think I did what we did for some ulterior motive. I—"

"Mae," he stops me, dropping to a squat before me where I remain seated. "I love you, too."

Another tear trickles down my face, relief washing over me.

"Does that make you sad?"

I shake my head, unable to find the words to express my happiness at first. Then another deluge of hiccupping statements fumbles from my mouth. "I've just missed you so much and I was scared you misunderstood why I left. Then I was afraid you won't want to see me again. That the trip was just over, and I hadn't had the chance to tell you what I wanted to say."

"And what did you want to say to me, sunshine?" His voice lowers as his thumbs swipe the tears on my cheek.

"I wanted to thank you. Thank you for letting me drive you. Or you riding with me. Or however you want to look at sharing this trip. I found so many parts of me I didn't even know were missing and you helped me discover them. You are the only souvenir I want from this journey."

"Sunshine," he whispers, leaning forward to land on his knees and brushing at my face with both hands. "It was an honor to travel with you. You helped *me*."

"I'm sorry again I left so abruptly," I mutter.

"No apology needed. I understand why you did it, but Mae, you can't leave me like that again." He cups my face, forcing me to look directly at him. "You took my heart when you left."

He pauses while my heart hammers. Then he continues. "*We* aren't leaving us behind. This is our time. Mine and yours. And we're living it together, sunshine. We're loving it together because I love you. I want to be with you. Today, tomorrow, forever. The future is our highway, Mae. You are the road I want to travel. Take the ride with me."

"Absolutely, Mr. Ashford." I laugh swiping at my liquid-filled eyes. Slowly, deliberately, I smile, and his crooked grin matches mine. He pulls something from his back pocket and holds it up between us.

"It's a sign." He twirls a blackbird feather between his fingers. "A sign to set the past free and only look toward the future."

I nod, agreeing with him.

"You know what else is a sign? You have a flatbed Ford out there, Mae. Do you know what that means?"

I shake my head this time.

"I'm going to marry you someday." I recall him saying such a thing on the corner in Winslow. Assuming he was only teasing me, I didn't have the heart to admit then I did own a flatbed truck.

"But first, I'd like to take you on a date. I found fried chicken. How about a picnic?"

I burst out in both laughter and another sob. "Think it's okay to eat a fried bird?" I don't wait for his answer, cupping his face in my hands, I bring him to me, mashing our lips together. Through the salty liquid on my lips and his eager kiss, my heart calms and the sobs subside.

When we pull apart, resting our foreheads together, Tucker speaks. "How about that picnic? I have Louie outside."

"What?" I press back from him.

"Yeah, this annoyingly beautiful woman left him in California. I mean, who could forget a bright blue Prius sedan? I had to drive him all by myself and it took me fucking forever without my navigator." Tucker slowly stands, holding out at hand for me. "She left Gemma behind, too."

My geranium. I couldn't bring a live plant on the plane. "I left her to brighten your day. And so maybe you wouldn't forget me."

"Mae." He sighs when I stand before him. His arms circle around my back, tugging me to him. "Only *you* brighten my day, sunshine. And I'd buy you a whole field of geraniums, but I see you already own quite a few. How about a tour of Mae's Flowers? Then that chicken dinner and a tour of your bedroom?"

I like his way of thinking, but... "I have two teenage boys at home."

"Then it's time for me to meet them," he says. "I noticed a local motel. I could book a room."

"Oh, you don't want to stay in a motel..." My voice drifts as I see he's teasing me once more. He doesn't like motels. He's a resort kind of man.

"You're right. I don't want a motel. I want to be with you, but I respect that your boys are home."

"I can still make room for you," I say.

"That's exactly what I want to hear." He tugs me to him, slipping his hand around my neck and kissing me once more.

"Let's skip the tour of the garden center. I know the perfect spot for that picnic dinner. We can even take the flatbed," I offer.

"I have a blanket in the car," he suggests. The same blanket we spread on the hood in Arizona and I'm hoping it will get more use than just for picnicking. We both have the same thought and the corner of his mouth tips up as it does when he's grinning at me. Then we kiss again as reunited lovers do because lovers we are.

Epilogue

3 MONTHS LATER

Playlist: "Bless the Broken Road" – Rascal Flats

[Mae]

Tucker stayed with me for a week after coming all the way to Michigan. He'd been the one to purchase Louie, and I tried to return the money. Instead, Tucker traded in the car and got Wyatt a used truck. I paid off the difference with some of the money from the original sale. Of course, Tucker met my boys and helped out quite a bit with Wyatt in that first week adjusting to home and bedrest. His bigger body was too much for me to maneuver and Tucker took the lead, which was more than I ever expected. As he stepped up, I saw the man who made the decision to leave a band and dedicate his life to a family instead.

We talked a lot about Rochelle and Adam, and all the things we didn't want to happen to us in this new relationship. For now, we agreed to let the future take the wheel and see where the journey would lead.

We both owned businesses, but Tucker admitted his job was easier to work remotely from. Eventually, he spent more of his time at my place. He used Garrett, my brother, and his relationship with Dolores as his guide.

"Love shouldn't feel like a sacrifice, Mae. I'm not giving anything up except my heart if I don't stay with you."

When he returned to Chicago for business, I'd often take the days off to go with him.

We loved the mini-road trips, sometimes taking out time to explore US-31, the coastal drive down the west side of the state of Michigan. The shorter drives were always a reminder of that first trip. Where an annoying, unwanted passenger in Louie became the thing I needed most to heal my soul and make whole my heart. I'm not one of those women who will say a man did this for me. The *experience* did it. The adventure

285

of traveling alongside Tucker, through some sticky situations and some simply fun ones, restored me. Sharing our time, our history and our hurts mended both of us, renewing our spirits and perhaps our dreams. Especially the one that includes a future of love as an endless highway.

By autumn, both my boys went to college, although Wyatt no longer had hockey and was considering quitting school all together. I didn't like the sound of that, and once again, it was Tucker who spoke to him about dreams shifting and paths changing. Wyatt didn't like that his hockey future was over, but he was sticking with college in the end.

With the boys gone, Tucker and I didn't need to be sneaking around the house, and we shared my room every night together. He also bought a piano and a guitar, and evenings were a serenade of new songs.

"I went on a road trip with this awful woman," he sings one night. "And she had the most irritating playlist." His fingers ripple down the keys of the piano. "She gave me a harmonica. Is there anything that rhymes with harmonica?"

He makes a face that strains his neck and I laugh.

"She must have really loved you," I joke back, sitting beside him on the piano bench. "Giving you a harmonica and all."

"Oh, she gave me her all." His fingers dance over ebony and ivory once more. "She gave me her luscious body. Her beautiful heart. And her loving soul. And I fucking love her as well." He winks as he looks over at me.

"Yeah, she loves you, too."

He abruptly stops and shifts on the piano bench. "Come show me how much."

I slip over his lap as he pushes the wooden seat away from the instrument. Our mouths come together, and we kiss, long and sweet, like a new melody. We are a playlist. One that includes every love song. We'll be using it as the soundtrack of this continual road trip called life.

Epilogue 2

1

Playlist: "Road Less Traveled" – Lauren Alaina

[Jane]

"Mr. Wright, you have a delivery," I announce through my boss's open office door. He hates it when I call him Mr. Wright. I hate how ridiculously handsome he is.

With artfully sculptured hair in a perfect palette of chrome and ink, the same combination lines his firm jaw. His mouth wears a permanent smirk that could either tease you into submission or cut you to the quick. Despite his typical attire of business suits or starched dress shirts and crisp ties, there's an occasional hint of color on the skin of his hidden arms. The same arms which often bulge underneath the stiffness of his professional wear.

And I hate how attracted I am to him.

"Have Rebecca sign for it." Mr. Wright—*Machlan* Wright—mentions his assistant without even glancing up at me. He never looks directly at me, and I suppose it's for the best. If he did, my tongue might freeze under the glare of those earthy-brown eyes. Another part of me never ices over when he looks in my general direction, though. That area is all heat and pulsing thumps of unrequited desire for a man I equally loath and lust.

"She's at lunch," I remind him.

He peers at his watch. Flicking out his arm, he bends his elbow just right to turn his wrist and sexily gaze at the oversized silver band like a practiced male model. He works excessively hard, and it isn't surprising he doesn't realize it's lunch time for the rest of Chicago.

"Just have it brought up."

This is not my responsibility. I'm one of the top account executives at Impact, a media marketing company, and I've been working my ass

L.B. Dunbar

off under this man for eight years in hopes of becoming a full partner one day.

However, I seem to never say no to my infuriating boss.

"Sure," I mutter, although I'm anything but happy. From the moment Machlan and his partner, Tucker Ashford, hired me, I set out to prove my worth. Marketing is not a stagnant field, especially with the boom of social media. For a woman with no life outside of work, I've easily adapted to the changes over the past two decades. At the ripe age of forty-five, I've been in the business for a long time. I would have eventually retired from my previous employer if it hadn't been for a huge snafu that I swear will never happen again.

My pride and my heart cannot take another Ripley Edgar incident.

When I call down to reception on the ground floor of our Michigan Avenue building, the security man Pete, informs me the item is too large for the elevator.

"Is it a freaking elephant?" I laugh into the phone. Pete and I have good rapport. That tends to happen when you're the first one in the building or one of the last to leave at night.

"Nope, but close. Mr. Wright needs to come down to sign for it."

Curiosity has the best of me and knowing Mach—as the rest of the office calls him—won't take a break long enough to accept his own package, I decide to ride down the thirty-four floors to see for myself what's too big for an elevator.

Mach, pronounced like the industrial truck with a hard *k*, fits the man who is a little smug and a lot tough.

"Hey Pete." I give a little wave as my heels click against the pristine white tiles in the all-glass lobby. I love this building. I love this city. Chicago is a heartbeat and a far cry from the small town where I was raised in southern Missouri.

"Hey, beautiful." The portly, older man smiles at me while tipping his head toward the revolving door. "His *Mach*-esty's item is out there."

I grin at the nickname I often use to describe my boss—along with His Royal Pain in my Hiney-ness; and sometimes just He-Who-Shall-Not-Be-Named, otherwise known as Volde-*Mach*.

288

Hauling Ashe

Over the years, there's been all kinds of special deliveries for Mach. Bottles of alcohol with seductive messages. Once, a dozen balloons intended to be popped, revealing sexual suggestions inside. My favorite was the woman dressed like an elf who turned out to be a stripper. She already had carnal knowledge of Mach from a Christmas event he hardly remembered attending.

I strongly dislike how easily women flock to him, making me one of his many sheep. *Darn his charisma.* Then again, giving myself away to the shepherd is never going to happen again. I'd been the route of a lost lamb found and then tossed aside by a man who really could have had a bigger staff.

I learned my lesson. Beware of the wolf in sheep's clothing. Keep my lust to myself.

My tumultuously attraction to Mach is more volatile than puppy-love. I waver between deep displeasure with my boss's work ethic, which ironically matches mine, making me work too hard, too often without appreciation, and an overabundance of sexual attraction including fantasies of him taking me on his desk, showing me his gratitude for my tenacity. Most days, I want him to work me harder in ways that have nothing to do with client needs and market assessments.

Glancing through the immaculately clean glass, I don't see a package the size of an elevator lift. "What am I missing, Pete?" I crane my neck.

"That." Pete points and my gaze lands on something one would rarely see on the busy city streets of a major metropolis.

"That?" The item certainly is too large for an elevator. Not that it should be brought up to our offices. *That* belongs on the road but not traffic-packed pavement. *That* screams dirt, dust, and sweat; sunshine filtering through trees on back roads; and feet on a front dash with windows rolled down.

Staring at the delivery for Mach, I can't help but consider the contrast between it and the man upstairs, sitting behind a glass-surface desk in a corner office overlooking Lake Michigan. Between the black leather couch in his space and the sharp business suits he wears not one

L.B. Dunbar

speck of his persona coordinates with the item atop a flatbed Ford on the avenue waiting for his signature.

"That," Pete confirms with a large grin.

And I laugh.

READ what *that* is in: Merging Wright

+ + +

Thank you for reading *Hauling Ashe*.

Up next in Road Trips and Romance is *Merging Wright* – Jane and Mach's story.

You can meet the whole gang of sexy silver foxes, especially Chopper's father, Brut Paige in his story *Restored Dreams*.

Or read about Mae's older brother, Garrett Fox and his love, Dolores in *Wine&Dine*.

Even Mae's best friend Pam Vincentia has a story (where you can first meet Mae) in *Fight From The Heart*.

And finally, stay up to date on all things L.B. Dunbar with my once-a-month newsletter: Love Notes.

+ + +

Thank you for taking the time to read this book. Please consider writing a review on major sales channels where ebooks and paperbooks are sold.

More by L.B. Dunbar

Road Trips and Romance
Three sisters. Three road trips. Second chances of love.
Hauling Ashe
Merging Wright
Rhode Trip

Lakeside Cottage
Four friends. Four summers. Shenanigans and love happen at the lake.
Living at 40
Loving at 40
Learning at 40
Letting Go at 40

The Silver Foxes of Blue Ridge
More sexy silver foxes in the mountain community of Blue Ridge.
Silver Brewer
Silver Player
Silver Mayor
Silver Biker

Sexy Silver Foxes
When sexy silver foxes meet the feisty vixens of their dreams.
After Care
Midlife Crisis
Restored Dreams
Second Chance
Wine&Dine

Collision novellas
A spin-off from After Care – the younger set/rock stars
Collide
Caught

Smartypants Romance (an imprint of Penny Reid)
Tales of the Winters sisters set in Green Valley.

L.B. Dunbar

Love in Due Time
Love in Deed
Love in a Pickle (2021)

The World of True North (an imprint of Sarina Bowen)
Welcome to Vermont! And the Busy Bean Café.
Cowboy
Studfinder

Rom-com standalone for the over 40
The Sex Education of M.E.

The Heart Collection
Small town, big hearts - stories of family and love.
Speak from the Heart
Read with your Heart
Look with your Heart
Fight from the Heart
View with your Heart

A Heart Collection Spin-off
The Heart Remembers

COMPLETE PLAYLIST

"Unwritten" - Natasha Bedingfield
"Julia" - The Beatles
"You Don't Own Me" – Lesley Gore
"Sweet Home Chicago" written by Robert Johnson (1936)
"Life is a Highway" – Tom Cochrane
"Soul Man" - Sam and Dave
"Think" - Aretha Franklin
"The Piano Man" - Billy Joel
"When He Sees Me" (from *Waitress the Musical*) - Sara Barielles
"St. Louis Blues" - Louis Armstrong
"St. Louis Song" - Erin Bode
"The Thrill is Gone" – B.B. King
"Cars" – Gary Numan
"Let the Good Times Roll" – The Cars
"Route 66" – Chuck Berry
"Home" – Phillip Phillips
"Simple Man" – Leonard Skynard
"Blown Away" – Carrie Underwood
"Drive" – The Cars
"Free Fallin'" – Tom Petty and the Heartbreakers
"Deep in the Heart of Texas" – Gene Autry
"Unchained Melody" – The Righteous Brothers
"Kiss Me" – Sixpence None The Richer
"Come Away with Me" – Norah Jones
"Chasing Cars" – Snow Patrol
"Under New Mexico Skies" – Syd Masters
"Take It Easy" – Eagles
"Bulger's Dream Olympic Fanfare" – John Williams and The Bands of HM Royal Marines
followed by "The Star -Spangled Banner/National Anthem" – performed by Whitney Houston
"Born To Be Wild" – Steppenwolf

L.B. Dunbar

"Arizona" – Josh Kerr
"California Dreaming" – The Mamas & the Papas
"California Soul" – Marlena Shaw
"Wildest Dreams" – Taylor Swift
"You Matter to Me" – Jason Mraz and Sara Bareilles
"Blackbird" – The Beatles
"Say Something" – A Great Big World, Christina Aguilera
"Look Away" – Eli Lieb, Steve Grand
"What Hurts the Most" – Rascal Flats
"Good As You" – Kane Brown
"Harvest Moon" – Neil Young
"Yours" - Ella Henderson
"Patience" – Guns 'N Roses/Chris Cornell version
"In My Life" – The Beatles
"Scars" – James Bay
"Bless the Broken Road" – sung by Rascal Flats

MORE THAN YOU WANTED TO KNOW

In March 2020, the world stopped moving. People didn't travel or even leave their homes with mandated lockdowns and stay-in-place orders around the globe.

In March 2021, my daughter got married despite the restrictions, and Mr. Dunbar and I took a trip to Arizona, which brought to fruition this long-awaited story. A story I'd been wanting to write but didn't have all the pieces. A road trip involving discovery of oneself as well as a romance was no small feat to travel. I hadn't been all the places I wanted to write about...*or had I?*

In doing research, I learned I'd been up and down Route 66 in bits and pieces over the past few years, and so, so close to some major attractions I hadn't known existed. The history was lost...on me. In looking up various stops or locations I thought might have meaning to Tucker and Mae, I incorporated where I had been with places I wished I'd seen.

The great American road trip seems like a lost mode of travel and discovery. For me, as a kid, the open road was the only way we took vacations. My father was averse to flying and why stay in hotels when you have a camper? The sound of semi-tractor trailers whizzing over pavement holds found memories for me of long roads, idle hours, and needing to pee just when the pull-off for a restroom has passed. (Ask my dad about his frustration with that one).

Route 66 fascinates me. The ideas of a family vacation or the possibility of a honeymoon destination. The pitstops, the once-trendy spots, and the nostalgia of a time long gone with large cars, soda pop in a bottle, and music off a radio. Ah, the music! And of course, a quiet, uncongested road under blues skies along flat fields, dry deserts, and a hint of mountains in the distance. Stop looking at your screens, people, and look out the window. The scenery is breathtaking.

One day, I hope to travel Route 66 from start to finish. For now, I've been several places mentioned in this work in Illinois, over parts of the route in Missouri and Oklahoma, and a good portion of I-40 in

Arizona. I've even flown over the Grand Canyon in a helicopter. As for the final destination, I've been to Los Angeles and the Santa Monica pier. All errors in locations in between these places falls on me.

If you'd ever like to take Tucker and Mae's journey, I've included my sources for time and distance plus various attractions within each state. While not conclusive in the least, these are the places used to bring Tucker and Mae closer to one another. Maybe a road trip with your significant other, family, or friends, will bring you closer together as well. Take pictures. Talk often. Sing off-key. Make a mark.

Welcome back to the road. Happy traveling.

SOURCES

Maps per state, including estimation of time and distance.
http://route66roadtrip.com

LOCATIONS:
ILLINOIS
Route 66 Begin Sign
78-98 E Adams St, Chicago, IL 60603

Lou Mitchell's, Chicago, IL
http://www.loumitchells.com/

Gemini Giant, The Launching Pad, Wilmington, IL – Gemini Giant
https://geminigiant.com/

Illinois Route 66 Hall of Fame & Museum, Pontiac, IL
https://www.visitpontiac.org/2192/Route-66-Museum

Bunyon's – Tall Paul, Atlanta, IL
https://www.roadsideamerica.com/story/4064

World's Largest Covered Wagon, Lincoln, IL
1750 5th St, Lincoln, IL 62656
https://www.enjoyillinois.com/explore/listing/worlds-largest-covered-wagon

Cozy Dog Drive-In, Springfield, IL
https://www.cozydogdrivein.com/

Old Chain of Rocks Bridge, Madison, IL to St. Louis, MO
https://www.nps.gov/nr/travel/route66/chain_of_rocks_bridge_illinois_missouri.html

L.B. Dunbar
MISSOURI
The Gateway Arch – St. Louis, MO
https://www.gatewayarch.com/

Strings inspiration -- Hammerstone's, St. Louis, MO
https://hammerstones.net/

Meramec Caverns
https://www.americascave.com/

Fanning Route 66 Outpost
Route 66 Red Rocker – Fanning, MO
https://www.roadsideamerica.com/story/17781

Devil's Elbow Bridge, MO
Big Piney River, Missouri, Devil's Elbow, MO
At time of first writing was open. At time of publication possibly closed.

Wagon Wheel Motel
https://www.wagonwheel66cuba.com/

Munger Moss Motel, Lebanon, MO
https://mungermoss.com/

Classic Rock Coffee House, Springfield, MO
https://classicrockcoffee.com/

Route 66 Drive-In, Carthage, MO
http://66drivein.com/

Boots Court Motel, Carthage, MO
http://bootsmotel.homestead.com/index.html

Route 66 Mural Park, Joplin, MO
https://www.visitjoplinmo.com/business/route-66-mural-park

KANSAS
Cars on the Route, Galena, KS
https://www.travelks.com/listing/cars-on-the-route/16025/

Eisler Bros. (Old Riverton Store), Riverton, KS
http://www.eislerbros.com/

Brush Creek Rainbow Bridge, Baxter Springs, KS
https://www.roadsideamerica.com/tip/26271

OKLAHOMA
Ribbon Road, Miami, OK
https://www.theroute-66.com/ribbon-road-us66.html

Blue Whale of Catoosa - Catoosa, OK
https://www.roadsideamerica.com/story/14307

Stableridge Winery – Stroud, OK
https://www.stableridgewinery.com/

Texalo, Oklahoma
https://www.theroute-66.com/texola.html

TEXAS
Pioneer West Museum, Shamrock, TX
Magnolia Service Station, Shamrock, TX
Tower Plaza and U-Drop Inn, Shamrock, TX
https://www.shamrocktexas.net/

U.S. Route 66 – Sixth Street Historic District, Amarillo, TX
https://www.nps.gov/nr/Travel/route66/6th_street_historic_district_am
arillo.html

L.B. Dunbar
The Big Texan, Amarillo, TX
https://www.bigtexan.com/

Cadillac Ranch, Amarillo, TX
https://www.roadsideamerica.com/story/2220

NEW MEXICO
High Road to Taos, Santa Fe, NM – (Tucker and Mae did not visit)
https://www.newmexico.org/places-to-visit/scenic-byways/high-road-to-taos/

Turquoise Trail, Santa Fe, NM – (Tucker and Mae did not visit)
https://www.turquoisetrail.org/

Albuquerque, NM
https://www.visitalbuquerque.org/

Cowboy Muffler Man, Gallup, NM
https://www.waymarking.com/waymarks/WMXTRF_Historic_Route_66_Cowboy_Muffler_Man_Gallup_New_Mexico

Red Rock Park, Gallup, NM
https://www.gallupnm.gov/207/Red-Rock-Park

ARIZONA
Tee Pee Trading Company, Lupton, AZ
https://www.roadsideamerica.com/tip/2857

Petrified Wood Forest, Holbrook, AZ
https://www.visitarizona.com/places/parks-monuments/petrified-forest-national-park/

Painted Desert - Arizona

https://www.visitarizona.com/places/parks-monuments/the-painted-desert/

Standing on the Corner – Winslow, AZ
https://standinonthecorner.org/

Meteor Crater – Winslow, AZ
https://meteorcrater.com/

Twin Arrows Trading Post ruins – Cocino County, AZ
https://www.theroute-66.com/twin-arrows.html

The Grand Canyon
https://www.nps.gov/grca/index.htm

Seligman, AZ to Kingman, AZ
https://www.visitarizona.com/places/cities/seligman/
https://www.gokingman.com/heart-of-66

Oatman burros – Oatman, AZ
https://www.visitarizona.com/places/cities/oatman/

CALIFORNIA
Mojave Desert
https://www.nps.gov/moja/index.htm

Elmer's Bottle Tree Ranch, Oro Grande, CA
http://thebottletreeranch.com/

Wigwam Motel
https://www.wigwammotel.com/

Fair Oakes Pharmacy and Soda Fountain, South Pasadena, CA
https://fairoakspharmacy.net/

L.B. Dunbar

End of the Trail sign, Santa Monica, CA
https://www.santamonica.gov/

Santa Monica Pier, Santa Monica, CA
https://www.santamonicapier.org/

About the Author

Love Notes

www.lbdunbar.com

L.B. Dunbar has an over-active imagination. To her benefit, such creativity has led to over thirty romance novels, including those offering a second chance at love over 40. Her signature works include the #sexysilverfoxes collection of mature males and feisty vixens ready for romance in their prime years. She's also written stories of small-town romance (Heart Collection), rock star mayhem (The Legendary Rock Stars Series), and a twist on intrigue and redemption (Redemption Island Duet). She's had several alter egos including elda lore, a writer of romantic magical realism through mythological retellings (Modern Descendants). In another life, she wanted to be an anthropologist and journalist. Instead, she was a middle school language arts teacher. The greatest story in her life is with the one and only, and their four grown children. Learn more about L.B. Dunbar by joining her reader group on Facebook (Loving L.B.) or subscribing to her newsletter (Love Notes).

+ + +

Connect with L.B. Dunbar

CPSIA information can be obtained
at www.ICGtesting.com
Printed in the USA
LVHW050830020222
709967LV00008B/651

9 781956 337068